Praise for *Bubbles Unbound*

'Meet Bubbles Yablonsky, beautician, reporter-sleuth and blazing star of Strohmeyer's entertaining, establishment-bashing debut as a mystery writer'

Publishers Weekly

'A sexy, irrepressible heroine, riotous supporting characters, continual action, ubiquitous humor and even a makeup tip or two make [*Bubbles Unbound*] a highly recommended series debut'

Library Journal

'Sarah Strohmeyer's sparkling debut is a breezy and funny mystery with a heroine who dresses like a Barbie doll and kicks ass like a Marine. Bubbles is a wonderful creation'

Sparkle Hayter

Bubbles Unbound

Sarah Strohmeyer

headline

First published in Great Britain in 2001 by
HEADLINE BOOK PUBLISHING

First published in Great Britain in paperback in 2002 by
HEADLINE BOOK PUBLISHING

10 9 8 7 6 5 4 3 2 1

ISBN 0 7472 6728 6

Typeset by Avon Dataset Ltd, Bidford-on-Avon, Warks

Printed and bound in Great Britain by
Clays Ltd, St Ives plc

HEADLINE BOOK PUBLISHING
A division of Hodder Headline
338 Euston Road
London NW1 3BH

www.headline.co.uk
www.hodderheadline.com

For Lisa Sweterlitsch,
the original Bubbles Yablonsky

Acknowledgments

I WAS BLESSED WITH the joyful generosity of many wonderful friends, family members and, as hard as it is to believe, newspaper cronies during the writing of *Bubbles Unbound*. Above all, I wish to thank my mother, Nancy Jordan, who corrected my errors, steered my direction and always cheered me on. This book could not have happened without her.

Nor could it have been written without the encouragement of Janet Evanovich on whose New Hampshire kitchen table Bubbles was born. She has been an invaluable role model.

I am indebted to the many professionals in the beauty business who offered their assistance and beauty tips. Elaine Urban, owner of Elaine's Hair World on West Goepp Street in Bethlehem, Pennsylvania, graciously welcomed me into her salon. Tamsen Vanderlas, owner of Acme Hair; Sheryl Bellavance, manager of O'Brien's; and Sally Miller of Sylvia's A Gallery of Style – all Montpelier, Vermont, hair salons – were extremely helpful. Jane's Hair Dye was inspired by my lemon-headed nephew, Fernando Strohmeyer. Thank you to all the many people who helped me with the beauty treatments.

In addition, I was fortunate to hook up with a great agent, Heather Schroder at ICM, and a truly thoughtful and delicate editor, Ellen Edwards. Thank you, Brian Tart, for giving me a chance.

I owe a great debt to my husband, Charlie, who endured the beauty treatments and sacrificed work on his addition for my edification. Also, hugs to Anna and Sam. Let's hope this works out, guys. Thank you Lisa, Patty, Kim, Geoff, Medora and you naughty Middlesex girls for listening.

Finally, a big smooch to all my friends from Bethlehem, Pennsylvania, whom I knew back in the days of big hair and big steel, and who are always in my heart.

Chapter 1

FOR MOST OF MY adult life, people in this town have passed me over as just another dumb blonde fascinated by sex, soap operas and gossip. My name, Bubbles Yablonsky, doesn't help matters any. Nor does the fact that my profession is hairdressing, my body resembles a Barbie doll's and my fashion weaknesses are hot pants and tube tops.

Okay. So, I might not *appear* to be the brightest bulb in the vanity, but I know something even the police don't know. I know what really happened to Laura Buchman. Or, at least I think I do.

Like I told my boss and best friend, Sandy, seventeen-year-old cheerleaders as lively as Laura don't off themselves, not here in Lehigh, Pennsylvania. Lehigh is a no-nonsense, gritty steel town on the Jersey border. Here we treat our cheerleaders with a reverence customarily reserved for minor saints. Here the most important accessories a girl can wear are a homecoming crown on her head and a pom-pom in her hand. A cheerleader from Lehigh would be crazy to give that up.

1

And Laura was not crazy. Foolish, maybe. Naive. Girlish. Even reckless. But not crazy. I know because I did her hair the day of the so-called suicide. That was ten years ago.

Sandy's House of Beauty, my place of employment, hasn't changed much since then. It is still a circa 1960, pink-walled hair salon located on the South Side, four blocks from the maroon Lehigh Steel blast furnaces and right next door to Uncle Manny's Bar and Grille. This way the men can grab a beer and watch a game at Manny's while their wives get a comb and set at Sandy's. Many a Lehigh marriage has been saved by this arrangement.

It's a pretty tight community of Poles, Slovaks, Germans and Italians on the South Side. Frowning babushkas keep their tidy homes spotless, right down to the sidewalk cracks they scrub with toothbrushes. Every porch has a red geranium for color and a green plastic welcome mat for wiping feet. Every door is decorated with cardboard hearts, leprechauns or ghosts, depending on the nearest upcoming minor holiday. Every kitchen is filled with the spicy aroma of sausage and sauerkraut for dinner, which is served promptly at five. Every woman over forty gets her hair done at the House of Beauty.

We do a big blue-hair business at our salon, which is why the conversation stopped when Laura arrived as a walk-in that Friday morning in September looking as cute as could be. She was wearing a bright white

2

cheerleader's sweater on which was embossed a big brown *F*. I assumed *F* stood for Freedom High School, known in our part of town as the 'rich kids' school. Her wavy hair curled into a natural flip at her neck, and her overall demeanor was perky, perky, perky. Standing still she was exhausting.

Her hair, though, was a mess. Roots so dark they screamed for immediate emergency highlights – pronto.

'Can you take me?' she asked, holding out a golden strand.

'Honey,' I replied, steering her toward my chair, 'it'd be a violation of the stylists' code of ethics not to.' I launched into a major discussion of treatment options.

'Actually, I'm not looking for more highlights. I want to go black,' she said, appraising herself in the mirror. 'Jet black.'

'Black?'

'Black like death.'

'Freedom cheerleaders go black like death, then?' In Lehigh, we often turn statements into questions by ending them with *then* or *say*. Keeps the conversation going.

'They do when they're singing backup.'

I warned Laura that once she went black, there was no turning back. She'd either have to keep it black or grow it out.

'Do it!' she said eagerly. I snapped a plastic apron around her shoulders, mixed the dye (Mediterranean

Night) with peroxide and began squirting it over Laura's scalp, setting the timer for thirty minutes.

In the meantime, I handed Laura a Diet A-Treat Cola. She kicked off her sneakers and relaxed, began to open up. I tend to have this effect on clients, especially women. They trust me with their most personal secrets, most of which center around how much they despise their in-laws or other clients at the salon. When they talk, I keep my mouth shut and my ears open. You'll get no judgment from Bubbles Yablonsky.

Laura spent most of the wait raving about a garage band called Riders on the Storm and the to-die-for lead singer who sounded to me like he was overdue for a turpentine scrub and rabies shots. Laura said she had a major crush on him and that, on the following night, he was going to play down at The Mill, an old hippie hangout by the park once renowned for regular drug busts. He asked her to do vocals. Hence the radical hairdo and her efforts to drop five pounds by Saturday.

I rinsed out the dye with warm water. On her forehead Mediterranean Night left a thin line of black that I removed by rubbing it with cigarette ashes, an old hairdressing trick.

'Your parents must like him, say?' I asked, knowing full well the answer to that one.

'Uhm, it's just my dad and me, and he's totally out of it because he's never home,' she said as I massaged shampoo behind her ears. 'If he knew half the stuff

4

that went on under his roof when he was out of town, he'd flip.'

Ding! Off went my internal maternal warning bell. I conditioned and rinsed her. Then I sat her up and wrapped a green towel around her head. 'Like what kind of stuff?'

Laura hesitated. Could she confide in me?

'Like all the parties,' she said finally, 'and friends of friends I hardly know who *do it* in his bed.'

Laura didn't explain further, and I didn't press. How many times have I regretted *that*?

'She was slumming it, coming here to the House of Beauty, you know,' observed Sandy as we watched Laura step into her shiny, apple-red Honda Accord. A gift from Daddy, no doubt. Kids on the South Side don't drive red Accords. The only red vehicles they drive are rusted.

'Probably she didn't want her regular beautician to get wind of her skipping school and singing backup down at The Mill,' said I, the sudden voice of reason.

'Hmmm, I wonder. If you ask me, what that girl needs is a mother.'

The next day Laura was dead. Her lifeless body was found behind her house on a chaise longue in the pouring rain.

It was all over the TV news, complete with special reports on the intense peer pressure facing today's cheerleaders and shots of friends gathered on the Buchmans' front lawn, hugging and crying. As Sandy rightly assumed, Laura Buchman was from the privileged side of town, near Camelhump. She lived in a modern, cedar-sided house amidst crushed stone, trimmed hedges and an in-ground swimming pool.

None of the news reports mentioned her budding career as a groupie, the Buchman central party house or the scummy boyfriend rock singer. The coroner was mum about the cause of death, except to say preliminary examinations pointed to suicide. Already rumors were flying around town that Laura had killed herself with drug-laced Slim Fast, a freshly blended pitcher of which was discovered in her refrigerator.

'So, that's why she didn't care about turning black,' Sandy said. 'She knew all along she wouldn't need a color correction.' Sandy, who had obviously missed her calling as a nurse, handed me a cup of water to calm me down. She even looked like a nurse, from her neatly permed, short brown hair to her blue polyester uniform and sensible-soled Florsheims.

'She didn't kill herself,' I said, staring at the water.

'Oh? And how do you know?'

'A girl doesn't commit suicide right before singing backup for a guy she worships. At seventeen you *live* for that.'

I could not understand why the police weren't more suspicious, too. It made me angry. 'My question, Sandy, is why somebody doesn't care enough about this girl to at least look into the *possibility* that she was murdered?'

Sandy held up her hands in surrender. 'Don't yell at me, Bubbles. Yell at the police. You know how they think. They think murders just don't happen on that side of town.'

That seemed like a stupid policy to me, so I put a call in to the cops about Laura's last hair appointment. An overworked dispatcher took down the essentials and promised a response. I didn't hold out much hope, though. Lehigh's finest is essentially an oxymoron, and as I predicted, the men in blue never stopped by.

For the rest of the day I obsessed about Laura's death. Twice I left clients too long under the dryers so that their scalps turned the color of boiled lobster. Once I nearly nicked off part of an ear.

'You better go home early,' Sandy said, picking up a pair of scissors I'd dropped for the fifth time that day. 'Go get Dan the Man, that lame husband of yours, to wait on you for once.'

Dan the Man was not one of Sandy's favorite acquaintances. Sandy's low opinion of Dan stemmed from her fairly accurate observation that he treated me like soap scum. I put Dan through law school by shampooing days at the House of Beauty and waitressing nights at the Tally Ho Tavern after our daughter, Jane, was born. Jane's infancy was a blur of diapers and cream rinse, talcum and beer, thanks to him.

And what did I get in return? Bupkis. No champagne, no roses, not even a 'Thank you, Bubbles, for working two jobs so I could get a degree' note.

I pointed out to Sandy that Dan was busting his butt at work these days, trying to make enough money to move us to the suburbs. Two years earlier we'd bought my childhood home, a brick row house on West Goepp, from my mother, who was itching to live with her buddies at the brand-new high-rise apartments on the east side of town. The house became nothing more than a cramp in Dan's style. He wanted wide green lawns, a media room and landscaping. Our yard the size of a postage stamp was not cutting it for him.

So, I took Sandy's advice and went home early.

I trudged up the steps of my cement front porch, let myself in with the key and zeroed in on a black brassiere hanging from a living room lamp.

'What're you doing home?' accused a pantsless Dan the Man, his Jolly Roger hoisted high and waving in the breeze. He jumped up from the couch and grabbed the brassiere to shield his private parts, as though I'd never seen them before.

'Who's she?' asked a strange, nearly naked woman splayed on *my* couch, wearing *my* terry-cloth bathrobe.

'Come back in fifteen minutes, Bubbles,' Dan instructed, glancing at a brand-new Rolex. 'We're just finishing up.'

And I was finished with my thoughtless, ungrateful pig of a husband. Sandy was right. Dan treated me like dirt. It took no time at all for my high-heeled pumps to deliver a swift kick to Dan's jewels – and I don't mean the Rolex. As for the home wrecker? I popped her collagen-filled red lips with a neat right hook.

Dan was so incensed by my reaction, he packed up and left that night for good. Dummy that I am, it hadn't occurred to me that Dan's plans to get out of West Goepp Street never included me and Jane in the first place.

'You gotta take action,' Sandy advised that night as we gathered around my kitchen table for a private pity party of Newport Lights and Bartles & Jaymes. 'You're too good a person to have to suck this up, Bubbles. You have to get back at Dan. You gotta make him pay.'

'I gotta get more education, like Dan did.'

'You gotta be someone Jane can look up to.'

'I gotta find out who killed Laura Buchman.'

Sandy tapped an ash. 'It's a tall order. How're you going to do it?'

But I was barely listening. My mind was running over the day, from Laura's supposed suicide to Dan's infidelity. And from the recesses of my supposedly vapid brain bubbled up the absurd notion that the two events were somehow connected.

I later discovered that my hunches about Laura's murder were correct and that, yes, indeed, there was a connection between her and my ex-husband. Unfortunately for me, though, a group of Lehigh's most powerful elite was determined to keep the circumstances of her death a secret – even if that meant permanently silencing those who uncovered the truth.

And Bubbles Yablonsky was no exception.

✽ ✽ ✽

Over the next ten years, Laura Buchman's visit and death became a distant, albeit haunting, memory. Between the divorce and raising Jane, I had other recreations. Like inventing schemes to wreak revenge on Dan, none of which worked very well.

Then providence tossed me a bone when Dan made the foolish mistake of asking the court if he could stop paying me the whopping $150 a month in alimony.

Now, $150 a month doesn't sound like much to pay an ex-wife who put you through law school, especially if you are a promising lawyer such as Dan. But money wasn't the issue; getting me out of his life was. To understand why, it helps to understand Lehigh.

Lehigh is a town of haves and have-nots. The haves are steel excecutives and their families who inhabit well-groomed developments north of the river. The men play golf at the Greenbriar Country Club where the women, who tend to be genetically adept at growing perennials, play tennis three days a week. Once a year the company flies the whole family to a beachfront resort in North Carolina for the annual executive physical or to South America on the pretense of checking out copper mines. Full-time maids are not un-common.

I, on the other hand, am a poster girl for the have-nots. We live south of the river in brick row houses. Most men in our class work in the dirty, dangerous steel mills where blast furnaces and coke ovens radiate suffocating heat. On the weekends we shoot pool, go bowling and drink Rolling Rock. Each summer we hit the boardwalk at Wildwood, New Jersey, and eat fried dough with powdered sugar on the beach. It's pretty simple. What the haves have, we, the have-nots, don't.

Dan desperately wanted to be a have. He was so desperate that despite his love of cabbage rolls and the World Wrestling Federation, he decided to try and pass himself off as a WASP after our divorce. He went full Biff – bow ties, Brooks Brothers suits, preppy nickname. Even dyed his hair a yachting, sandy blond.

To his credit, Dan made tremendous inroads into this world by marrying Wendy Hauckman. While Wendy was no Princess Diana, she was the heiress of the Hauckman's Cheeseball empire. In marrying Wendy, Dan set himself up with bucks, beer nuts and bright orange cheese doodles for life. Every man's dream.

However, Dan still worked for a slip-and-fall law firm that advertised on the cardboard insert of yellow pages that they don't get paid until you get paid. Most of Wendy's country club friends were appalled, frankly, that Dan's clientele relied on bail bondsmen to spare them temporary incarceration.

Dan determined that what he needed was a corporate legal job. What he needed was to sever any ties to his working-class past, including me, a Polish-German-American embarrassment who barely squeaked through beauty school at Northampton County Vo-Tech.

At the alimony hearing, the judge agreed with Dan about the $150 a month. However, the judge ruled that, seeing as how I had put Dan through law school, it was only fair that he should pay for my continuing education. Dan coughed back a smile like a naughty boy caught stealing a cookie. He'd read my high school transcript.

I walked up to him after court and tapped him on the shoulder. 'I don't know what's come over me, Skippy. I suddenly got a burning desire for knowledge.'

'I'll alert Harvard,' he replied, clicking shut his gray calfskin briefcase. 'And you got it wrong as usual. It's Chip, not Skip.'

The very next day I showed up at the doorstep of the local community college, which is run out of an abandoned Two Guys Department Store. I was interested to read in the community college brochure that there'd been a small hike in tuition recently, to five hundred dollars per course.

I took almost every course the community college had to offer. Accounting. Business. Chrysler Dealer Apprenticeship. Entrepreneurship. Funeral Service Provider. Medical Transcriber. Plastics. Welding. Animal Cosmetology.

You name it, I studied it – and failed it. Bombed. Flunked. The big goose egg. Six years of community college down the tubes. I'm a hard worker and I try. I'm just not very strong in the academic department, especially when all I had to lose was Dan's money, eighteen thousand dollars of which I'd managed to misplace.

'Give it up, Bubbles,' advised my weary guidance counselor with the office in Aisle 5, Sheets and Towels. 'Stick to hairdressing.'

I was about to take her advice and call it quits when my life took a sudden turn for the worse. All our clients started getting their weekly comb and sets at Cuts for Less in the brand-new Lehigh Valley Mall. My tips dropped off dramatically, and I was strapped for cash.

There was no way I could be disloyal to Sandy and work at Cuts for Less. And there was no way I could stay with the House of Beauty and survive. My savings account contained just enough money to pay a minor repair bill on my Camaro, my Visa 'tin' card had hit its three-thousand-dollar max and I wasn't sleeping very well.

To make matters worse, Jane was beginning to notice our precarious financial status. 'Everything in this house is generic,' she observed one night at dinner. 'We have generic toilet paper. Generic soda. Generic coffee. Even generic mac and cheese. How much does that cost? Thirty-nine cents?'

I winced. 'Actually, it's a quarter with an in-store double coupon at the Shop Rite.'

'Aww, Mom,' she clucked sympathetically, 'I didn't mean to bum you out. I know you kill yourself to make ends meet. You can't help it if you're always down on your luck.'

I nearly broke a plate. Geesh! I didn't want my daughter to think of me as always down on my luck, especially since her dad was dining on Black Angus steak and Perrier these days. Jane was completely unaware that Dan's new fortune was not his own. All she knew was that his fifteen-room suburban palace and Eddie Bauer SUV made her life with me look desolate.

I got the impression she was wondering what was wrong with her lazy, loafing mother. What kind of loser lives in the same run-down house she grew up in, buys generic hot dogs and flunks every course at the community college?

Don't get me wrong. Jane isn't a bad kid. She's a great kid. Sure, she owes her hair color to the magic of Kool-Aid, which she washes into her hair nightly. Other than that you can't find a nicer or funnier sixteen-year-old. Or smarter. Member of the Liberty High School Math Team, president of the debating club.

And that was another thing. College. How was I going to pay for Jane's college? This is why I needed a new career. It was either that or give up altogether, go on welfare and beg for scholarships.

'No Yablonsky's going to go on welfare, and that's final,' pronounced my mother, LuLu, when I picked her up to take her to my house for Sunday chicken. 'What? You think your grandfather fled Gdánsk and escaped the Soviets just sose we could move to America and live off the state like Commies? I should slap you upside the head for that talk.'

There was no getting around LuLu Yablonsky. She might have the stature of a circus midget and the figure of a pickle barrel. She might brew dandelion beer in the bathtub and play the boombas past dawn, but she was four feet, five inches of pure power. If LuLu said no, then no it was.

So, I headed back to the department store community college, this time with solemn promises that I would pass my courses, whatever courses were left to take. My guidance counselor heaved a sigh and suggested journalism.

'Journalism?' I asked. 'What's journalism?'

'Perhaps we ought to forget it.' She put the forms back in the drawer.

I grabbed her wrist. 'Please. Give me a chance.'

'Okay, but we're at the end of the line, Bubbles. Flunk this and the only course left is taxidermy.'

Stuffed squirrels? Ugh. Journalism, whatever it was, was sounding better and better.

Well, I eventually found out what journalism was, and I'm pleased to say I was a natural. Because when you combine all that asking, snooping, investigating, not to mention the who, what, where, when and why stuff that reporting requires, it comes down to one word.

Gossip.

And gossip is how a neighborhood hairdresser like me earns her bread and butter. After years and years in the beauty biz, my sympathetic ear was superbly tuned for human tragedy.

Take the time our journalism class took a field trip to the Northampton County Courthouse to watch a trial. I missed the trial because I ended up in the courthouse bathroom comforting a sobbing woman. It took me almost an hour of commiserating and an entire roll of Charmin to calm her down.

When she finally got hold of herself she confessed that she was racked with guilt because her boyfriend had been charged with murdering her good-for-nothing, abusive husband when it had been she who'd shot the SOB all along. By the end of the day, she agreed to turn herself in and provide me with an interview. An exclusive interview, I might add.

'Have to hand it to you, Yablonsky,' said my journalism professor, Mr. Salvo. 'You got the knack.'

I beamed with pride. I mean, Mr. Salvo was more than just a journalism professor. He was also night editor of the *News-Times*, the Lehigh Valley's largest newspaper. Night editor for twenty years and looked it, too. Thin white skin and tiny eyes like a mole.

Unfortunately, while Mr. Salvo had the authority to assign me freelance articles, he couldn't hire reporters full time down at the paper. Only the editor-in-chief, Dix Notch, could do that, Mr. Salvo said, and Notch ordinarily required two years experience at a smaller newspaper before he'd look at a résumé. (Like I even had a résumé, ha!)

'I can't wait two years, Mr. Salvo,' I whined. 'I need another job now! A good job. A career.'

Mr. Salvo poured himself a cup of coffee from his Thermos. 'Why the rush?'

I explained about my cash situation and the House of Beauty. How I wanted to make Jane proud of her mother so she wouldn't think of me as some down-on-her-luck sad sack, how I wanted to send her to college and maybe even move off West Goepp Street.

Mr. Salvo stroked his nearly hairless chin and pondered this. 'What you need, Yablonsky, is a big break. A story so gripping Notch will waive the two-year requirement and hire you on the spot. You know, since the *News-Times* got bought by Garnet Corporation we pay better than most newspapers our size.'

'How much better?'

'Starting reporter like yourself? I'd say thirty-five thousand dollars plus stock options, full benefits including dental and two weeks vacation.'

I imagined how Jane would react if she heard that I was a staff writer for the *News-Times* with stock options, two weeks vacation and dental. 'Mr. Salvo, how do I get a big break?'

'If I knew that, Yablonsky,' he said, patting my shoulder, 'I wouldn't be teaching at a community college run out of some bankrupt department store, now would I?'

I continued to slog away down at the House of Beauty, picking up meager tips here and there. I finished Mr. Salvo's course with a 4.0 and accepted as many freelance assignments as I could from him. I wrote about spelling bees and historical society meetings, mistreatment of racing greyhounds and how to avoid Lyme disease. Blood shortages and storm damage. Strawberry picking and Fourth of July reunions of immigrant families.

But as I stepped over squished strawberries and petted anorexic – and often flatulent – greyhounds, I couldn't help wondering if this was all just a waste of effort. What made me think that I, Bubbles Yablonsky, hairdresser, would ever come across a story important enough to be the big break?

I had no idea at the time that Laura Buchman's death was the key to the biggest story to hit Lehigh in a decade. Or that I – and I alone – had heard the most significant clue to her murder. It took me an unexpected telephone call, one mutilated body and a series of misadventures to realize that.

Mr. Salvo calls this my big break, but I prefer to think of it as Laura Buchman reaching out to me from the grave. Like I said, women tell their hairdressers the deepest, darkest secrets.

Chapter 2

'IT'S FOR YOU, BUBBLES,' Sandy announced, pushing the mute button on the portable phone. 'Some nutcase. Sounds frantic.'

A frantic nutcase sounded a lot better right now than finishing the perm on Mrs. Sinkler. Mrs. Sinkler was on a serious fishing expedition to find out who my mother was dating at the senior center. It's a competitive game, being a widow. Even Mama's been known to cruise by funerals, looking to pick up fresh meat. If LuLu had someone on the hook, Mrs. Sinkler wanted to know who it was and what bait she used.

'Did I mention that your mother's bought a bikini?' Mrs. Sinkler called after me as I skipped over to get the phone. 'Do you think it might be Carl Johnson? He's not bad, even if he's got only one eye.'

I shuddered at the thought of Mama making it with a one-eyed geezer and punched the mute button. 'Bubbles Yablonsky.'

'Bubbles! We got an emergency.' It was Mr. Salvo and Sandy was right. He sounded more hyper than an

19

overbred poodle at the vet. 'I got a jumper and no staff. Can you cover?'

'Excuse me?'

He took a deep breath. 'Got a guy ten blocks from your hair salon on the Fahy Bridge about to jump. Came across the scanner a few minutes ago. Being a Friday evening, I've got no reporters to send. They're either out on assignment, on vacation or taking an early weekend at the shore.'

I couldn't blame them. It was the first week in August and, although late in the day, still a muggy eighty-nine degrees. I'd be at the shore, too, if I could afford it. The Lehigh Valley is no place to swelter in the dog days of summer.

'What do you want me to do, Mr. Salvo?'

Mrs. Sinkler was beginning to take out the pink-papered rollers herself.

'Just the basics, but be alert. I heard the cops talking. It's a father of three. Schoolteacher. Lots of human interest. Page one definitely if he jumps.'

Mr. Salvo made it sound like more a hope than a possibility. I scanned the day planner on which Sandy had scrawled down appointments in various colors of ink. After Mrs. Sinkler, Susan Saladunas came in at six-thirty. Late because she runs a fish market with her husband and Friday is their busiest day. Sandy would take her. I was free to knock off after Mrs. Sinkler.

Out of the corner of my eye I caught Sandy waving

her hands. 'Go!' she mouthed. 'This could be the big break.'

Anyway, Mrs. Sinkler was down to the last paper. 'I'll do it,' I said.

'Great. A friend of mine from New York is staying with me for the weekend and happens to be an AP photographer. I managed to talk him into shooting this as a favor. You can meet him at the opposite side of the bridge by the city center since they got this side—'

'Uh, Mr. Salvo?' I interrupted. 'I got a bit of a problem. No car.'

'In the shop?'

I didn't want to admit that the Camaro was parked in my neighbor's garage with a glove compartment full of bright yellow parking tickets. I'd forgotten about them until I received a kindly letter in the mail reminding me that if I didn't pay $145 to the City of Lehigh I'd be put on the boot list. That sum seemed a little unfair, so I threw away the letter and occasionally hid my car on private property. I've racked up so many tickets, the meter maids carry around pictures of my license plate in their wallets.

'It's just out of commission.'

'Okay, I'll have Stiletto pick you up.'

'Who?'

'The photographer and, uhm, that's another thing, Yablonsky. About Stiletto. He's kind of . . .'

I began rummaging around the desk drawer for a

good pen and a decent tablet. 'Kind of what? Gruff? Mean? Crude?'

'Wow. I can tell you got a good impression of men. No, it's more like ... You ever hear of the story of Ulysses and the sirens on the rocks?'

I rolled my eyes. Nerdy bookworms. Not what I need when I'm trying to take care of a client and get my sorry carcass over to a bridge jumper. 'Sounds vaguely familiar.'

'Well, that's what it's like for women with Stiletto. At least, from what I've observed.'

Mrs. Sinkler had removed all the rollers and was sitting with a bright pink cloud of papers in her lap. Her toe was tapping on the footrest expectantly.

'Can we get to the point, Mr. Salvo? My client . . .'

'Just bind yourself to the mast, Yablonsky, when you're around Stiletto. Okay? Keep yourself bound no matter what.'

I muttered a quick good-bye and hung up the phone. If anyone needed a trip to the shore, it was Mr. Salvo. Obviously the heat had cooked his brain.

'You going out on a story, Bubbles?' Mrs. Sinkler asked as I combed out her dyed ash-blond curls. What woman is born a natural ash blonde? No woman. Especially not sixty-two-year-old women like Mrs. Sinkler. I filled her in about the jumper, grateful, at least, that we had moved the conversation off Mama's erratic behavior.

'Maybe you'll see Mickey. He's working today from

three to midnight.' When Mrs. Sinkler wasn't analyzing the sexual affairs of her peers, she was boasting about her police officer son, Mickey.

I threw the comb in a drawer and shut it with my hip. 'It's amazing that you've memorized his work schedule like that.'

'Oh, I haven't. He calls me every morning at eight on the spot and lets me know where he'll be. Calls me before bedtime, too, unless it's late.'

Sandy flashed me a knowing look. Mama's boy.

'Hey, Bubbles,' Sandy said. 'I got a dress hanging in the back if you want to wear it.'

Why would I want to do that? I thought. I checked the reflection of myself spraying Mrs. Sinkler's hair with a heavy coat of Final Net. My golden blond hair was piled on my head under a bright pink chiffon kerchief, which coordinated nicely with the magenta halter top and black spandex hot pants. What was the problem?

'You think I oughta change?'

Before Sandy could answer, we heard the crunch of gravel on the street and three long honks. Sandy pried open the Venetian blinds with two fingers and peeked outside.

'Is someone coming to pick you up?'

I removed the plastic cape from around Mrs. Sinkler's neck and brushed her off. 'Yeah, the photographer. Is that him?'

'They say anything about him being Mel Gibson's twin brother?'

I gulped. Mrs. Sinkler hopped out of the chair like a bunny and flew to the window, yanking up the blinds.

'Holy Mary, Mother of God,' she whispered, crossing herself. 'To be twenty-two again.'

Honk. Honk. Honk.

I opened the bottom drawer of my vanity and re-moved my purse, putting a tablet and pen inside. 'He might be goodlooking, but he sure is rude,' I said, yanking open the door. 'Whatever happened to the days when men picked girls up at the door?'

Sandy grabbed me by the arm. 'Remember, Bubbles. Remember how you are when it comes to sex,' she warned. 'Keep your knees locked.'

I shook her hand off. 'Geez, Sandy, I'm not nineteen.'

Boy, the respect I get. Sure, I was careless about sex when I was a teenager – letting Dan knock me up at age seventeen being a case in point. How I ever allowed myself to get pinned to a Lehigh University fraternity floor by a dorky freshman with two beer cans strapped to either side of his head is a mystery I'll never solve. At least I got Jane in the deal. Besides, that was a long time ago. I was in high school then. Now I'm thirty-four, more mature. Sophisticated. I know what I want and I'm willing to hold out for it. I am woman, hear me . . .

The door to the House of Beauty slammed behind me and I stopped still. A tanned man who appeared to be in his mid-thirties sat in the driver's side of a black Jeep, top down, with white New York State license plates. His brown hair was longish, but not too long, and his tanned face was creased in all the right places, like he just finished a tough day in the sun rounding up cattle on a ranch. I couldn't tell what color his eyes were because they were masked by a pair of very dark, very expensive RayBans.

Sandy's warning to keep my knees locked suddenly seemed inadequate. What I needed was a dead bolt. Preferably one without a key.

Enough about the face. The body, or what I could see of it, was what really caught my attention. Specifically, biceps that strained his gray T-shirt and a broad pair of shoulders that begged for a massage.

Either he had worked very hard on perfecting this image, in which case I would have to slap him around a bit, or he came by it naturally, thereby requiring me to jump him on the spot. Both ways were trouble.

'You Yablinko?' he asked.

'Yablonsky,' I corrected.

'Goddamn! It's hot,' he said, turning the key and starting up the Jeep. 'Let's get going. I need some breeze.'

I was about to give him a lecture on the importance of etiquette, like ringing a doorbell, opening a car door, et cetera, et cetera, but thought better of it. Why waste my energy on that now? This guy was a project. A long-term project, I could tell. Months, if not years.

As soon as I was in the car, Stiletto stepped on the gas and we headed up Fourth Street. A canvas camera bag, frayed at the edges, lay on the floor, crowding my feet. I gently kicked it aside.

'Watch that!' He pointed to the bag. 'There's eleven thousand dollars' worth of equipment in there. Uh, what'd you say your name is?'

'Bubbles,' I said.

Stiletto held his hand up to his right ear. 'What? I'm kinda hard of hearing after the shelling in Bosnia.'

I leaned toward his ear and shouted. 'Bubbles. Bubbles Yablonsky.'

'Jesus Christ, woman! I'm not stone-deaf.' He gave his head a violent shake. 'My name's Steve Stiletto. Like the knife.'

'Or like the heel,' I said, adding quickly, 'You were in Bosnia?'

'Yeah, three years. For the Associated Press.' He shifted into third and we took the corner on two wheels, headed in the wrong direction.

'Mr. Salvo said they blocked off that end of the bridge, so we should go over the Hill to Hill Bridge and approach from the city center side,' I yelled, out of sensitivity for that auditory problem of his.

Stiletto ignored me and kept on going.

'Didn't you hear me?' I screamed.

'I heard you. This is a shortcut.'

I thought of those New York license plates. 'Listen, I've lived in this town my whole life,' I said, 'and I know my way around the South Side.'

'Wooowee. You steel-town girls think you're so tough,

26

don't you? Know it all. Seen it all. Done it all. By the way, you always dress that way on the job?'

I quickly assessed my hot pants. 'You got a complaint?'

Stiletto grinned and did one of those furtive, up-and-down glances men pull when they're trying to evaluate a woman's breasts. 'Not exactly a complaint,' he said. 'More like a curiosity.'

Aha! Stiletto was one of those men who thought I dressed this way for men. Well, if that was the case, then he was sadly mistaken. I dressed this way for me. It's a medical fact that my body won't accept cotton or wool, or drab colors for that matter. They make me itchy and depressed. I don't feel comfortable in anything that's not tight or stretchy or short. And if Stiletto – or any other man – doesn't like it, then he can jolly well keep his mind on baseball.

'You better treat me with respect,' I warned. 'We hairdressers own four-hundred-dollar scissors that can cut off a person's lips.'

'Ouch,' he said.

We zoomed down Fourth Street past a line of aluminum-sided white houses, the Elks Club Local 549, a pool hall, St. Sylvester's Church and rectory, Our Lady of Redemption, a pizza parlor and two red lights. Stiletto took a sharp right and then a left onto Third Street, which was lined on one side by Lehigh Steel hidden behind mammoth black iron gates. He went one block and turned into a steel employees' parking lot, shifting the Jeep into neutral and pulling up the brake.

'What're you doing?' I asked as he hopped out and talked to a guard in a little booth. The guard nodded and Stiletto shook his hand. Then Stiletto got back in the Jeep and we zipped across a parking lot filled with American-made cars. We headed toward the back of a warehouse.

'Are you crazy? Do you have any idea where you're going? I mean, you're not even from around here.'

'I'm from around here, all right,' he said as we drove down a narrow road that ran between a line of rust-red warehouses and the railroad track, which paralleled the Lehigh River. 'I grew up in this town.'

I studied him again. I'd never seen Steve Stiletto in my life, and I knew practically everyone in Lehigh.

'Where'd you go to high school?' I must admit I'm not as familiar with people who went to Freedom High School, being a downtown Liberty High girl myself.

'Moravian Academy, then Andover, Exeter. Got kicked out of there, finally, thank God. Took me long enough.'

I'd never heard of Andover and Exeter. 'Those in Allentown?'

Stiletto leaned over and patted my knee. 'You're cute, Bubbles.'

I frowned.

We left the line of warehouses and loading docks and arrived at the point where the railroad tracks disappear under the Philip J. Fahy Bridge. Even from this vantage point, we could see that the bridge above us had been evacuated except for several white police cruisers, ambulances and flashing blue lights.

The wind was picking up and black clouds were gathering in the sky. There'd been a thunderstorm every evening since this heat wave began. You'd expect the rain to cool things off, but it only made the humidity worse and sleeping sticky.

Stiletto pulled the Jeep next to the railroad tracks and killed the engine. He leaned under me and yanked out the camera bag.

'Let's go,' he said, getting out. I followed him and brought the strap of my purse over my head so that it crossed my body. I had the feeling that whatever Stiletto had in mind, it was going to require sneaking, climbing and sweating.

'What I suggest,' he said, zipping open the camera bag, 'is that we take the footbridge to Jefferson Park and the stairs up to the bridge. The cops will never let us get close to the jumper otherwise.'

Jefferson Park is a small island in the middle of the Lehigh River. Back in the 1950s when people were clean and wholesome, city officials decided to put a tennis court on the island and steps up to the bridge. It was a nice idea until drug dealers coopted it for their business twenty years later. To cut down on crime, the island's been closed to the public since the Reagan administration.

'Can you manage in those heels?' Stiletto asked.

I examined my feet, on which were strapped a pair of high-heeled black plastic sandals. 'I could cross the Sahara in these heels.'

'Not like you weren't warned.'

Stiletto led the way, taking long strides over the railroad tracks and down the gravel bank to the Lehigh River. From there we walked across a crumbling cement footbridge to the park, which was inconveniently barricaded by a six-foot-high chain-link fence. The grass was overgrown, and the netless red clay tennis courts were covered with weeds, broken brown glass and faded soda cans. Stiletto strolled along the side of the fence until he came to a hole some juvenile delinquent had cut for no good reason. I tripped after him, my heels sinking into the ground along the way.

We crossed the tennis courts and stood at the foot of metal stairs leading to the Fahy. With the traffic detoured, it was eerily silent. The bridge loomed huge and high, supported by massive steel beams around which fluttered a few gray pigeons.

'My best shot's probably going to be right there,' he said, pointing to a beam that ran crosswise, from the top of the stairs underneath the bridge. 'If I can crawl to the end of that beam, I'll probably be right below the action. Which is a lot better than shooting a picture of some cops standing around waiting for a guy to jump.'

'Where are all the other reporters?'

Stiletto screwed a lens onto the camera. 'Unless they did what we're going to do, they're killing time at the police barricades at the end of the bridge. Not my style, honeybunch.'

I glanced at him, at the beam and then at him again. 'What do you mean, what *we're* going to do?' I did not fancy the idea of hanging my derriere one hundred feet over water.

'You should climb the stairs and try your luck on the bridge. The cops won't let you get within twenty feet of the guy, but if you keep your mouth shut, they might let you stay. Seeing as you're braless.' Stiletto pushed down his Ray-Bans and winked at me.

I folded my arms across my chest. 'Maybe the cops have a point,' I offered. 'You know, with it being a prospective suicide and . . .'

But Stiletto was already stealthily climbing to the top. Even in this nerve-racking situation, I couldn't help noticing how nicely his perfectly worn jeans stretched across his trim behind and outlined the muscles of his thighs. Thank you, God, I whispered, for giving me such charming co-workers.

Now, the question was whether I was going to be half as courageous as Stiletto. I needed a big break, and I was never going to get it if I stuck to greyhounds and spelling bees. I slipped off my high-heeled sandals, stuck them in my purse and grabbed the stair railings. Those heels never would have made it over the steel mesh.

In no time, Stiletto was at the beam. He turned, gave me a wave and tucked his head. I saw him put down one hand and then a knee and crawl into the shadows under the bridge. His camera hung from a strap around his neck. I had to turn away. Him dangling like that over the water made my palms sweat.

I got to the top of the stairs and glanced down. Below me the trash-strewn tennis courts were the size of coasters. Above me I could hear a scanner squawking from a police cruiser right near where I was standing.

I took a deep breath. There was no thrill for me in the prospect of arriving, unannounced and unwelcome, at some high-tension suicide scene patrolled by cops and firemen. Stiletto was pushing me too hard. He might be used to Bosnia and creeping behind enemy lines, but I was new to this hard-news reporting shtick. Why couldn't I wait for word at the police barricades like all the other reporters? Why did I have to stick my neck out like this?

It crossed my mind to defy Stiletto, climb down the stairs and do what was right and proper. Then I thought of the thirty-five-thousand-dollar salary and the big break and what Jane would say if I told her that I had enough guts to crash a police scene in order to get a story. She'd be floored.

I closed my eyes and popped my head over the top of the stairs.

'Stop right there!' a voice barked. 'Don't take another step.'

I opened my eyes and nearly fell backward to my death. Staring me in the face was Mickey Sinkler and the black barrel of a police pistol.

'Oh, for heaven's sake, put that gun away, Mickey!' I scolded. 'I just finished a perm on your mother five minutes ago. What would she say if she could see you pointing a gun at me?'

Mickey Sinkler stared at me like I was Godzilla in drag, which was ridiculous since Mickey and I had gone through William Penn Elementary together. Back in first grade he used to entertain the girls by snorting green Jell-O up his nose in the cafeteria. Now he was a police detective with five kids. I'd heard it all from his mother. He hadn't changed much in the interim. Still had the stringbean body and the satellite dishes for ears.

'Bubbles?' Mickey squinted, putting the gun back in his hip holster. 'Bubbles Yablonsky? What in Sam Crow are you doing here?'

I squeezed around the bridge railing and stepped behind the cruiser, safely hidden from the other cops. I leaned down and slipped my sandals back on. Mickey's jaw hung open; since he was a congenital mouth breather, that was to be expected.

'I'm doing a story for the *News-Times*,' I whispered.

Mickey shook his head. 'You got to be kidding. Aren't you still a hairdresser down at Sandy's place?'

'We prefer the term stylist. Anyway, I've been free-lancing for months. Don't you read the paper?'

'Sure, the sports section. So, where's Lawless? He usually covers these things.'

Lawless was the *News-Times* veteran cop reporter. From what I understood, the cops loved him like one of their own, although in the newsroom he had the reputation for being chronically lazy.

I peered around the hood of the cruiser, trying to get a better view of the jumper, who was standing at the edge of the bridge opposite us. 'Beats me where Lawless is,' I said. 'Who's the jumper?'

Mickey, apparently sufficiently recovered from the shock of seeing me, mere hairdresser, at a police scene, said, 'You're not going to believe it. Remember Mr. Dudko from eleventh-grade physics? It's him.'

'No way! Mr. D?' I stuck my neck out for a closer look. I couldn't make out much. A squat man with a balding head wearing a short-sleeved baby blue polyester dress shirt. When he turned briefly, I spotted the outline of a pocket protector in his upper left-hand pocket. That was Mr. Dudko, all right.

A woman with gray hair in a bun, thick horn-rim glasses and a long brown skirt was earnestly talking to him over the edge of the bridge railing.

'Who's the frump?' I asked.

'A psychologist,' Mickey answered, scratching one of his oversize ears. 'Not having much luck, though. I think Dudko is really gonna do it. The school board told him today they were buying out his contract 'cause his students' test scores were the pits. He's been crying about his thirty-year career wasted, or some such crap.'

That was hogwash. Sure, I didn't learn anything in Mr. Dudko's class, either. Nobody did. That didn't make him a bad teacher. Physics is just a bad subject. Irrelevant to everyday life.

What Mr. Dudko needed was an Oprah-style pep talk. A shot of good old-fashioned self-esteem. 'Hey, Mr. D!' I shouted, waving my hand. 'Over here.'

'Cripes, Bubbles!' Mickey said under his breath. 'You'll get hauled out.'

Mr. D turned in my direction. The late afternoon sun glinted off his trademark steel-frame glasses.

'Who's she?' the psychologist demanded loudly.

I cupped my hands to my mouth. 'It's me. Bubbles Yablonsky.'

Two cops in dark blue uniforms started walking up the bridge to get me, their faces set in deep scowls.

'Don't you remember? Bubbles the gum chewer.'

Mickey grabbed me by the elbow and led me around the cruiser. I thought for sure Mr. D would remember me. Every day at the door to his physics class he'd hold out his palm and ask me to deposit the Juicy Fruit. We kind of had a bond, albeit a wet, sticky bond.

I must have been mistaken because Mr. Dudko took up a conversation with the psychologist instead.

Now I was being led down the bridge by Mickey and the two cops. Well, I'd taken a chance. At least I'd tried.

'Stop!' It was the psychologist. 'He wants to talk to her.'

My heart did a little quickstep. The cops mumbled something and turned me around. I *click, click, clicked* in my high-heeled black sandals back up the bridge.

When I got to where Mr. Dudko was standing I was blown away. The late afternoon sun lit up the Lehigh River below us and turned the steel factories on the left bank a coppery red. To the right, the storm clouds billowed black and threatening. Directly ahead, the old Hill to Hill Bridge with its salt-and-peppershaker towers connected the South Side to the historic section of Lehigh.

I'd never stood at the edge of the Fahy Bridge on a summer evening before a storm. The city should run tour buses.

'Wow,' I exclaimed. 'The view up here is terrific.'

'Oh, for Pete's sake,' said the psychologist.

'Come over here, Bubbles,' said Mr. Dudko in a shaky voice.

I tiptoed closer.

He looked like the same old Mr. D. His comb-over was a little grayer and, seeing as he was preparing to off himself, it made sense that the sweat stains in his armpits were a little larger. All in all, the same old Captain Physics from high school. Passed me with a D minus, God bless him.

'I mean closer, come on.' Mr. Dudko waved me nearer. 'Stand next to me.'

'Careful,' the psychologist whispered. She brushed a strand of gray hair away from her face. 'He's experiencing an episodic depression compounded by anxiety disorder and sublimated acrophobia.'

'Huh?'

'He wants to kill himself, but he's also afraid of heights.'

I wasn't a fan of heights, either. Stepladders give me chills. Yet, I thought of all those reporters back at the barricades wishing they were standing in my place right now. Talk about exclusive, whoo boy. Mr. Salvo was going to freak when he heard about me at the edge of the bridge, one-on-one with the jumper.

The cop in charge said it would be okay for me to join Mr. Dudko as long as I had a harness on. I handed my purse to the psychologist and a fireman had me step into what I can best describe as a big blue vinyl diaper. He threaded a nylon rope around my waist and over my shoulders. It was incredibly itchy and confining.

'Gotcha nice and secure,' the fireman said.

The psychologist gave me one last piece of advice: 'Whatever you do, try not to erode his deteriorating male-centered ego process.'

'Don't worry,' I said, lifting my leg over the railing. 'I've had lots of experience with deteriorating male-centered egos.'

I stood side to side with Mr. D on about three feet of a cement ledge. I hoped I wouldn't wee in my shorts. My palms began to tingle and, suddenly, I wished I was back at the barricades with all the other reporters, big break or no big break.

'Look down, Bubbles,' Mr. Dudko ordered, pointing a quivering hand toward the river.

'No thanks.' I kept my eyes straight ahead, like a good little acrophobic soldier. There was quite a wind, and I put a hand on the railing behind me to keep steady.

'Come on. I'll jump if you don't.'

Not fair, I thought. I took a deep breath and looked down. Below us the water rippled in tiny waves, and I could hear it lashing against the banks. I tried not to think about what might happen if I sneezed or if Mr. D accidentally tripped me.

'Let me guess, Bubbles, you're what, maybe one hundred fifteen pounds?'

'Not bad, Mr. D, one twenty-two to be exact. Remember, I'm pretty tall.'

Mr. Dudko nodded. 'Okay. One hundred twenty-two. And I'm, regretfully, one hundred seventy. Remember, I'm short.'

He smiled weakly at me.

'So,' he continued, 'let's say we were to fall at the same time . . .'

I put my hand to my chest. 'Oh, please, Mr. D, I got a teenage daughter at home and—'

He put his hand on my shoulder. 'Calm down, Yablonsky. This isn't an experiment, this is theory. Anyway, let's say we were to fall at the exact same time. Bubbles, who would hit the water first?'

I pondered this. Was it a trick question? 'Why, you would, Mr. D. You're fatter.'

'That's it!' he yelled, pinching his nose and bending his knees.

'No wait!' I begged. 'Give me another one.'

He lifted his fingers from his nose. 'Okay. This is a tougher question. But if a former student like *you* can answer it, I'll know I wasn't a total failure as a teacher, right?'

'Right, Mr. D.'

'Now, we just learned that heavy or light things fall at the same speed, correct, Bubbles?'

Is that what we learned? I shrugged. 'I guess so.'

'So, at what rate do they fall?'

'You want numbers?' I hate numbers.

'There's only one number,' he said, narrowing his eyes. 'And it's a constant.'

The psychologist whispered something behind me.

'I heard that,' Mr. Dudko accused. 'No cheating or the test is over.'

Let me tell you, I've never thought so hard. I ran over all the numbers I knew. Bake a cake at 350 degrees. Normal temperature is 98.6. My Lotto numbers: 12-11-5-25-3-16. The last is my daughter Jane's age. Double that and . . .

It came like a flash. 'Is it thirty-two feet per second?'

Mr. Dudko's jaw dropped open. 'Almost right, per . . .'

'Second!' I screamed. 'It's thirty-two feet per second per second. I can't believe I knew that.'

The psychologist let out a 'Whew!' behind me.

39

Mr. Dudko did a kind of two-step and grabbed me by the shoulders. His upper lip was lined with beads of sweat.

'Yablonsky,' he said gruffly, staring into my eyes so intently I saw my face in the reflection of his glasses, 'I remember the year you were in my class. You'd file your nails or gaze out the window while I tried in vain to teach you morons Newton's theory of gravity or the curve of a trajectory. And when you and the rest of your classmates consistently flunked those tests, I thought, Give it up, Dudko, you've got no talent. You're just a dud of an educator.'

Tears were beginning to well under his glasses and roll down his face. 'Well, today, I almost did give it up. For good. But today, I was shown that even you, Bubbles Yablonsky, airhead of the first order, managed to learn something in my class. Today you saved my life.'

I decided now was not the time to tell Mr. D that, actually, I learned this coefficient at the Two Guys community college. Semester number sixteen: Physics for Physician's Assistants.

He took a hand off my shoulder and wiped away the tears. The breeze from the approaching storm was picking up, blowing his comb-over to the wrong side of his head. It hung down in one greasy strip. When was he going to agree to get back on the bridge and go home?

'I'm so grateful, I could kiss you.' Mr. D pursed his lips and aimed for my face.

For a moment I forgot where I was – on a three-foot ledge one hundred feet over the Lehigh River. So when Mr. Dudko said that, the thought of being kissed by my *physics teacher* so grossed me out that . . . I kind of gave him a teeny, tiny push.

'Aaaghh!' he yelled, eyes wide open, mouth like an *O*, face a mask of panic. He teetered back a little, then forward.

I put my arms out and grabbed him. 'Don't . . .' I screamed as he fell backward. For a minute there I had him. He held on to me so tightly that I worried he would rip my arms out of their sockets. Then, out of nowhere, came a tremendous gust of wind, and before we knew what happened, Mr. D was over the edge.

Taking me with him.

Chapter 3

WE'RE GONNA DIE!' CRIED Mr. Dudko.

That was not what I wanted to hear.

At that moment, there was nothing between my black plastic-covered toes and the rippling Lehigh a hundred-and-something feet below. Mr. D was wrapped around me like those miniature koala bears we used to snap onto our pencils in school. I felt his fingers dig painfully into my flesh and his bad, bad breath on my face. I prayed deeply for the strength of vinyl and the nylon around my middle. I prayed that Mr. D wouldn't yank off my halter top and expose me to the entire town.

I felt a tug and looked up. A line of firemen had the other end of the rope in their hands.

'You'll be okay,' one called out as Mr. D and I were lifted. 'Have you on the bridge in a jiffy.'

'Awwrgh,' Mr. D moaned.

'I'm so sorry, Mr. Dudko,' I apologized as another gust from the storm sent us slightly swinging. 'I'm so very, very, very sorry. I never meant—'

'Shut up, Yablonsky.' Mr. D's glasses had slid down his sweaty nose. He pushed them against my shoulder to keep them up. 'This is all your fault.'

All my fault? I wanted to point out that I wasn't the one who had the bright idea of jumping off the Philip J. Fahy bridge in the first place. Then, with another whiff of breeze, the pink kerchief flew off my head. I watched sadly as it drifted into the air and fell slowly to the river.

Click. Click. Click. What was that noise?

I turned and spied Stiletto perched on the beam underneath the bridge, shooting away with his Nikon. He smiled and gave me a thumbs-up.

I was shocked. He did not even lend a hand. Not a look of alarm. Not a voice of concern. And I expected this person to ring a doorbell?

With one big yank Mr. Dudko and I were back on the ledge in less than a minute, although to me it seemed like an eternity. As soon as we were on the bridge, relief swept over me in waves, and I wondered if I had piddled, ever so slightly, in my shorts. Still, I hadn't felt so grateful to be alive on terra firma since a nasty plane ride I once took to Scranton.

The firemen practically had to use a crowbar to pry Mr. Dudko's arms from my body. Once he was detached, paramedics threw a blue blanket around him and hustled him off to an ambulance. He scrambled in and they shut the door.

The psychologist handed back my purse. 'If you hadn't gotten Dudko's question right,' she said, 'it might have been a very different outcome for him. Isn't the subconscious a remarkable phenomenon?'

I rubbed my red, raw midriff where the harness had nearly cut through my skin. Forget my subconscious, how about my belly? I sat down on the curb and took a blanket from a paramedic, who then handed me a Dixie cup of water. My legs felt like rubber and my spine like spaghetti. I wanted to go home and collapse into bed.

I downed the cup of water and noticed two cops in crisp blue uniforms standing in front of me. Between them stood a dumpy bearded man in khakis wearing a tweed jacket and holding a reporter's notebook. He appeared disturbingly cool. If I had to guess, I'd say that while I had been hanging in the breeze praying for the durability of man-made fibers, he had been relaxing in the air-conditioned comfort of a Crown Victoria police cruiser discussing the Phillies' latest slump.

'Is this our pretty heroine?' he asked, moving to a crouch by my side.

I brushed away a strand of hair. 'I wouldn't say heroine exactly, although the pretty's okay.'

The cops chuckled and rocked on their heels. The man in tweed smiled up at them broadly and extended his hand to me. 'I'm Bob Lawless of the *News-Times*, and I'm going to put you on the front page of tomorrow's newspaper, little lady. What do you think about that?'

I crunched the Dixie cup in my hand and tossed it in the gutter. 'I think that sucks.'

One of the cops went, 'Ahem.'

'Is there some sort of problem here?' Lawless asked, opening the cover of his notebook and clicking his pen.

'Yes, there's some sort of problem. I'm writing the story, not you.'

Lawless scratched his head and pretended to be confused. I decided to spare him the dramatic effort by cutting to the quick. I explained who I was, what I was doing here and how Mr. Salvo had assigned me the story. When I was done, Lawless's smile had straightened to a set line. He disputed my version of events and claimed that Mr. Salvo reached him at the courthouse, where Lawless had been waiting for a jury verdict, and assigned him the attempted suicide.

'Anyway,' he concluded, 'you are now part of the story. In fact, I hate to be the bearer of bad news, but you might even *be* the story, particularly if you face criminal charges.'

My throat tightened. 'What do you mean, *criminal* charges?'

Lawless stood up. 'Aiding or causing a suicide or attempted suicide is a second-degree felony under Pennsylvania law and, from what I understand, you actually pushed this poor man shortly before he was going to be rescued.'

I jumped up and balled my fists. 'Why, that's the most stupid, idiotic . . . I was the one who saved him. If it hadn't been for me, he would have—'

'Don't shoot the messenger,' Lawless interrupted,

writing my response down in his notebook. 'How do you spell your name again?'

My mouth clamped shut. This is what I got for trying to improve myself, for trying to set myself up as a role model for Jane. What kind of role model mother lives in the Northampton County Prison?

Lawless didn't get to ask me another question because the two cops intervened. I spoke with them for nearly a half hour, explaining as best I could how the push had been a knee-jerk reaction to the horror of being kissed by Dudko. I was just sad they were both men; a woman would have understood.

By the time we were finished, the bridge had been reopened and the entire sky was dark with thunderclouds. The trees along Third Street at the foot of the bridge were blowing so hard, their leaves were turned inside out. Neither the cops nor Lawless offered me a ride. They just stepped into the cruiser and drove away.

I trudged in the whipping wind to the end of the bridge at the intersection of Third Street and found Stiletto waiting for me in the Jeep, grinning from ear to ear.

'Hey there, Wonder Woman, looking for a ride?' he called out cheerfully. Big droplets of rain were beginning to fall. The Jeep remained uncovered and that seemed fine by him.

'Aren't you going to put the top on?'

'Don't have one. C'mon. Get in.' He leaned over and

opened the passenger side door. Well, at least that was a start in the manners department.

I got in and immediately covered my eyes as Stiletto pulled a U-turn in the middle of Third, missing an oncoming dump truck by inches. What is it with guys who drive like that? Is turning around the block too boring, or do they just like getting tickets – or getting killed?

'You sure showed me, hanging off the bridge like that,' Stiletto said as we passed an oblivious Lehigh patrol car. 'And here I figured you were some dainty girly girl who was afraid of ruining her manicure.'

'Lot of good it did me.' I explained about Lawless, the cops and my future as a convicted felon.

'Bull!' Stiletto said. 'They're not going to charge some poor hairdresser doing a good Samaritan. As for the story, yeah, I talked to Salvo on my cell phone a few minutes ago and he told me the situation was dicey and I should give the film to Lawless.' Stiletto shrugged. 'So what? There'll be more page-one stories, especially if you're willing to pull exciting stunts like that one back there.'

Stiletto's words were encouraging, but between you, me and the lamppost, I didn't believe they were worth beans. Excitement is not my middle name. Lorraine is.

The rain was falling steadily when we pulled up to the House of Beauty. My hair was one big mat of wet straw, my halter top was clinging to each valley and summit and I was damned uncomfortable. This rain, heat and polyester could only lead to yeast infections. Plus, the shades to the beauty shop were drawn and Sandy was nowhere in sight. The dashboard clock said seven-thirty. Sandy had gone home without me.

'Where to now?' Stiletto asked.

I gave him directions back to West Goepp. Stiletto pulled another U-turn and headed off.

Whereas the rain was melting me into an old hag, it had magically transformed Stiletto into Mr. Universe. The wetness accented the muscles in his jaw, and I could trace his pectorals through his damp T-shirt. My mind flashed to Mel Gibson's stormy luncheon scene in *The Year of Living Dangerously* and stopped. Don't go there, Bubbles, I told myself, remembering Mr. Salvo's admonition. Keep yourself bound.

We were about to cross the Hill to Hill Bridge when a sharp bolt of lightning flashed in the sky. Stiletto turned the wheel and drove down an access road that is popular among Liberty High School students because it ends under the bridge, where they can make the transition from teenager to adult in relative privacy. Stiletto stopped the Jeep. It was nice to be out of the rain.

'Look over there,' he said, pointing through the gray, rainy mist to the Fahy Bridge down the river. 'That's where you were hanging only an hour ago.'

It was pretty cool to think that I was so far up, so far above the water, helping a man about to commit suicide. I'd like to stress right here, not helping him *to* commit suicide. God, how do I get myself in these situations?

'You know,' Stiletto began, leaning back and putting his arms behind his head. 'I've worked with some big names in journalism. Christiane Amanpour. Arthur Kent.'

Arthur Kent. I thought back to the TV news coverage of the Persian Gulf War, Arthur in his leather bomber jacket, ducking his head at incoming missiles. 'Scud Stud,' I whispered.

'Scud Stud, my ass. Anyway, none of them would have risked their lives like you did, Bubbles. You blew me away today.'

'I did?' I twirled a strand of hair around my index finger. 'I blew you away?'

Stiletto smiled at my obvious fishing for more compliments. 'Absolutely. I'll admit, I had my reservations when I saw you today in those high heels. I figured you wouldn't make it halfway up the stairs to the bridge before you ran to join those wimps in the press pool at the police barricades.'

'Are you kidding? Me?' Why bother confessing now that those were my exact thoughts halfway up the stairs to the bridge?

'But when I heard you yell, "Mr. D! Over here!" I almost flipped off the beam below. Right then I knew you were no average reporter.'

'Reporter,' I whispered. 'I don't think anyone's ever called me that before. Hairdresser, mother, wife, ex-wife. Maybe stringer or correspondent. But no one's ever called me a reporter.'

Stiletto brought his hands down and turned to me. 'That's what you are, aren't you?'

'That's what I want to be. I still have a long way to go.'

'Not that long. I haven't read your articles, but then again, I don't have to. I've seen you in action and that's enough. You got the hunger, Bubbles. You're gonna go places.'

While the rain fell in sheets, then drizzle and then drips, Stiletto and I contemplated life and careers. I spared him the details about Dan. Instead, I chatted about dreams for my future, including why I wanted a big break and how I was really sick of writing about blood drives.

'I don't know if that big break will ever come,' I said.

'Big breaks usually come when you least expect them – and when you least want them.'

Stiletto's big break came in Zimbabwe, where he was working as a Peace Corps volunteer. A civil war broke out, and equipped with a Nikon that a friend (read *girl*friend) had given him, he shot pictures that got him a job with the Associated Press. After that it was Somalia, Bosnia and even Chechnya. Stiletto said those experiences taught him that there really was good and evil in the world and that good was worth fighting for.

When I asked him how he could bear living in camps without showers and toilets, Stiletto asked me how I could stand living in a steel town where everyone is gray and grumpy.

'I don't recall having any other choice,' I said, opening my purse and fishing for a brush. 'Anyway, Lehigh's my home.'

The clouds were breaking up, night was falling and it was obviously time to go. Stiletto turned the key in the ignition. 'That's the difference between you and me. I never had a home. Not a real one.' The engine whined and complained. 'It hates the dampness,' he said, tapping the gas. Finally the engine turned over and we drove up the access road.

I began brushing my hair. 'I thought Lehigh was your home. I thought you were from here.'

He shook his head. 'Not really. I got bounced around so much as a kid from boarding school to boarding school; I never learned to stay in one place as an adult. I'm not a put-down-roots kind of guy.'

I smiled to myself knowingly. Oh, yes, I've heard this line before. Don't think I'm going to marry you, babe, because I can't settle down. Got to hit the open road. Be a free man. Psychologists call it *fear of commitment*. Sandy calls it *playing cowboy*. And now that the Lone Ranger had dictated the ground rules, I bet his next move would be to try to lasso me into bed.

'Damn, I'm soaked,' he said, laying his arm along the back of my seat. 'My stuff's at Salvo's apartment, right up here on Fountain Hill. You mind if we stop off and get me some dry clothes?' Then he added softly, 'I got a bottle of chardonnay in the refrigerator. Why don't you come in and have a glass while I change?'

Did I call that one or what?

Now friends familiar with my lust for Mel Gibson and my lackluster sex life might assume that I would have jumped at Stiletto's offer. I'd recently sworn off the only men Lehigh had to offer – sweat-suited couch potatoes and Aerosmith wanna-bes. No more 'Cat Scratch Fever' karaoke for me, thank you very much. After Dan the Man, a couple of used-car salesmen and one Radio Shack clerk, I promised myself that the next guy in my bed would be someone worthwhile, someone who could take me around the world and light up my life with romance.

Stiletto might very well be that man. If so, I was going to play it smart for once. And that meant holding out. Besides, I didn't want Stiletto to get the impression that we steel-town girls were waiting around on a Friday night to entertain sophisticated New Yorkers like him. I had my pride. So I lied.

'I have a date,' I said.

'Oh,' he said, quickly hanging a left on the Hill to Hill and completely forgetting about those wet clothes.

We crossed the Hill to Hill Bridge and got on the Spur Route. I spotted Stiletto's car phone blinking a green light and asked if I could use it. I'd never used a cell phone before and this seemed like a good time to practice.

I dialed home. Nothing happened.

'This thing's broken,' I said.

'Did you press Send?' Stiletto asked in a patronizing way.

'Of course, I pressed Send.' I pressed SEND. Stiletto winked at me.

Jane answered the phone on the first ring.

'Where have you been?' she screamed. 'Do you know what's happened?'

That didn't sound very good. 'What?'

'The senior center called and said Grandma got in some sort of riot there.'

'Riot?' Mrs. Sinkler was right. Mama had been acting strange lately and not only because she wanted to impress old one-eyed Carl Johnson.

'Yeah, like a food fight or something. Tapioca and Jell-O everywhere. Anyway, the man from the center said Grandma and Genevieve kinda hijacked the senior shuttle. He wanted to know if Grandma drove it to our house.'

I closed my eyes. LuLu and her best friend Genevieve on the lam could lead to only one destination – the Westgate Mall.

I told Jane I'd head straight over to Westgate to find Mama and hung up.

Stiletto picked up the cell phone, pressed END and gave me a look. 'So let me get this straight,' he said. 'I'm supposed to drive you to the Westgate Mall so you can search for your mother who hijacked a shuttle bus?'

I stared at him in amazement. 'How did you hear all that?' I was too polite to point out that I thought he was deaf from all that shelling in Bosnia.

'A technique I learned from an acquaintance in the CIA. Oh, well.' He swung the wheel to the right, causing us to cross two lanes of traffic and barely make the exit. 'Gotta say, you're not exactly boring.'

Stiletto headed down Schoenersville Road and pulled up to the chained entrance of Saw Mill Park.

'What're you doing?' I asked as he got out of the Jeep and yanked the chain from its post. So much for that deterrent.

He hopped back in the car and drove over the chain. 'Taking a shortcut.'

'Another shortcut?' I looked around. It was spooky down here in the park. It had rained hard after a hot day and now, at night, layers of mist were rising from the ground, rapidly enveloping the Jeep in fog. The air smelled dank and earthy.

This shortcut did not seem wise to me. 'But the park's closed at night,' I said, suddenly noticing how dark it had become.

'Not for us.'

He stepped on the gas and rocketed ahead. Much faster than the maximum allowed park speed of fifteen miles per hour. The park road was unlit and, with all the trees, foliage and fog surrounding it, pretty dense. When I drive it, I'm on the watch for squirrels and other innocent animals that might run into my path. Not Stiletto. We must have been doing forty.

'Isn't this trespassing?' I inquired. 'Journalists aren't supposed to do that, right? Ethics and all.'

Stiletto flashed me a look and turned the wheel, narrowly missing a tree. 'You forget where I've been . . .'

'Yeah, yeah, I know,' I said. 'Sarajevo. Racing between bombs. Hanging over bridges. Shooting—'

Suddenly a stone wall sprang up in front of us, and I let out a tiny yelp. Stiletto yanked the wheel to the right and braked. 'Shit,' he said, obviously shaken. 'I nearly got you killed. This fog is so thick I can't see a foot in front of me.'

He removed a handkerchief from his back pocket and wiped the windshield. While he did that, I felt the fog settle on me like a blanket. My skin was damp with dew. Stiletto started up the Jeep and, this time, proceeded slowly, almost at a creep.

Baboomboomp.

The front left tire went up and down. Stiletto immediately slammed on the brakes again and the Jeep stopped on the dime.

'Now what?' Stiletto said, getting out. He leaned into my side of the car, opened the glove compartment and pulled out a flashlight.

'It felt like an animal,' I said, following him. 'I hope it wasn't a dog or a cat or something . . .'

Stiletto was as pale as a ghost, staring at the road in shock. I followed the beam of his light to what lay on the pavement between his front and rear tire and nearly passed out.

Chapter 4

IT WAS NOT A dog or a cat. It was a man lying straight across the road. And from the looks of it, a car had run him over, right through the middle. Blood was spread across his chest and groin. His hands and wrists were crisscrossed with blue veins. And, worst of all, his body from the shoulders up was under Stiletto's Jeep.

'I didn't hit him,' Stiletto said, shining the flashlight from head to toe. 'This guy was already dead.'

The only dead person I've seen was my father's mother, Nana Yablonsky, and she didn't look like this. She looked like she was on her way to a Labor Day sale at Wannamaker's, smiling satisfactorily in the white satin-lined coffin wearing coral lipstick and a floral dress. After the wake we gorged on borscht, stuffed cabbage and chocolate cake. In this case, I was trying my best not to throw up on the spot.

Stiletto ran his hands through the guy's pockets, looking for identification. I knelt down and, as much as it unnerved me to do so, picked up the man's wrist. It was cold and clammy. Stiletto was right. This guy was not alive when the Jeep ran over him.

'You mean someone hit him and left him here?' I asked, delicately placing the wrist back down. 'How could a person do that?'

'The world is full of jerks,' Stiletto said, standing up and reaching into the Jeep for the cell phone. 'No ID on him either.'

I peered down the road. It might have been a combination of my imagination and the fog, but in the near distance I saw a large shape and a soft glow.

'What's that?' I asked, pointing.

Stiletto put down the phone. He pulled out his camera bag from the back of the Jeep and, still carrying the flashlight, proceeded to tread slowly forward. I got up and walked right by his side. No one's going to leave me next to a dead body in a creepy park. No siree, Bob.

We arrived at a mammoth Range Rover parked slightly off the road on the grass. The soft glow I'd seen turned out to be the car's interior light, and there appeared to be someone inside. I hung back while Stiletto opened the Range Rover and peeked in. He was silent for what seemed like minutes.

Finally, I asked, 'Who is it?'

'Well, Yablinko,' he said, closing the door. 'Remember when I said there'd be more big stories? Why don't you lean in here and take a look.'

'I don't know,' I said, hesitating. One dead body a night is my personal limit.

'Go on. She won't bite.'

She? I leaned in the driver's-side window and was surprised to find a thin woman dressed in black and obviously unconscious splayed across the front seat. She was probably in her late twenties with, in my professional opinion, an excellently executed foil job. I also couldn't help noticing the neat French manicure and diamond-encrusted fingers, five of which were wrapped around a bottle of expensive vodka.

'Her name is Meredith Metzger, and she could buy and sell this whole town,' Stiletto said crisply. 'She goes by the name Merry.'

I studied Stiletto's face as he shined the flashlight around the car's interior. It projected pain, amusement and sadness. 'Okay,' I said. 'There's a connection between you two. What is it?'

Stiletto coughed and said, 'We fooled around in the pool cabana of the Greenbriar Country Club once.'

Stiletto handed me the flashlight and began rummaging around his camera bag.

'You're unbelievable,' I said, wondering at the pure *cojónes* it would take to have sex in a country club pool cabana. (Although I have to admit, I was slightly uncertain as to what, exactly, a pool cabana was.) 'Not only don't you have any journalistic ethics, you've got no moral ethics either.'

He snapped a lens onto a camera. '*Au contraire*. I thought it was very chivalrous of me to decline her rather passionate advances. She obviously was interested in going, shall we say, farther than would have been appropriate to go in a pool cabana.'

'So, why didn't you go *farther*?'

'Who knows? A rare flash of good judgment hit me, I guess. Anyway, I was glad we stopped when we did, especially when I found out who she later married.'

I swung the flashlight into the Range Rover and zoomed in on a huge diamond-and-sapphire ring on her left hand. 'Who did she later marry?'

'I'm sure you've heard of him.' Stiletto took a few warm-up shots. 'Former chairman of Lehigh Steel. Henry Metzger. Multimillionaire, benefactor and right bastard.'

I clicked off the flashlight so it wouldn't screw up Stiletto's photos. 'How do you know him?'

'Who in Lehigh doesn't know him?'

That was true. When I was six, molten steel was poured on my father in the ingot mold at Lehigh Steel, turning him into an instant human trophy. To this day my mother claims the accident was Henry Metzger's fault because he was too cheap to install ladles with sensors. Henry Metzger was practically a swearword in our house.

Stiletto took shots of the Range Rover license plate. 'Would you look at that?'

I came around to the back of the car. A flash went off, and I saw what had caught Stiletto's interest. I shined light on the tires. Bloody flesh stuck in the Range Rover's deep treads. Stiletto got up close and took more shots.

'That's so disgusting,' I said.

'That's not disgusting. That's proof.' Stiletto circled the car and was now inside the Range Rover, shooting pictures of the woman.

'Hey, Merry,' he was cooing, trying to rouse her. 'It's me. Steve Stiletto.'

I heard her mumble, 'Steve, help me,' but nothing more. I decided to walk back to the Jeep.

'So are we gonna call the cops, or what?' I asked, reaching for the cell phone.

'Not we. You,' Stiletto said, walking up to me.

I stared down at the phone. Stiletto was opening the back of his camera and removing the film.

'Why aren't *we* gonna call?' I said. 'How come it's *me*? You were just about to call the police before I saw the Range Rover.'

'Because if Henry Metzger's involved, I don't want to stick around.'

'Why not? What's he to you?'

Stiletto closed the camera and put it back in his bag. 'He's nothing to me, and that's the way it's going to stay. If he's involved in this, he'll make me talk to his lawyers and insurance agents and any number of drones who slave for him. I came back to Lehigh to run one errand, and I can't wait to scram. Twenty-four hours in this godforsaken depressing steel town is about all I can take.'

For some reason I felt hurt by that comment. 'Pardon me for living,' I said testily, leaning against the rear of the Jeep. 'And what's so important to bring you to Purgatory?'

'It's my mother's birthday tomorrow,' he replied, his voice dropping. 'I return every year to put flowers on her grave.'

Whack! I gave myself a mental kick. Good going, Miss Yablonsky. Open mouth, insert foot. 'Oh, I'm really sor—'

Stiletto held up his hand. 'Don't say it. It's been a long day.' He placed the roll of film in a black plastic canister and tossed it to me.

'Give this to Salvo,' he instructed. 'Writing an article that the wife of the most powerful man in Lehigh committed a drunken-driving, fatal hit and run is going to require proof. You'll need this.'

I clutched the canister. 'Do you mean to tell me that you're going to drive off and leave me alone in this park with a dead guy and a drunken debutante?'

Stiletto opened the Jeep's door and got in. 'As soon as I'm gone, you can call the cops. They'll be here in no time.' He picked up my purse from the floor and handed it to me. I threw it and the film canister on the ground.

Then I grabbed him by the arm. 'Hold on. You're not going anywhere. You're not leaving me with a mutilated dead body.'

'If you can hang from a bridge, you can hang around a corpse for ten minutes, Bubbles. Christiane Amanpour would.'

'Screw Christiane whatever-her-face. She gets paid big bucks to do that. Besides, I don't look forward to being grilled by Metzger's lawyers and henchmen either, you know.'

'Yeah, but you live here. It's no big deal for you.' Stiletto put the key in the ignition. 'Monday morning I've got a seven-thirty flight out of JFK for Mexico City that I can't miss.'

'You know what your problem is?' I said, wagging a finger in his direction. 'Your problem is you're chicken. Oh, sure, you might run off to Bosnia this and Chechnya that, but sometimes it takes a lot more guts to stay put in one place and face the demons. You're acting like a coward.'

Stiletto opened his mouth to reply and then obviously thought better of it. 'Where'd you get that line of mush, from a Journey album?'

'No. I made it up.' Although Stiletto might have been correct. 'Anyway, what does it matter? I'm right, aren't I? I got your number, Steve Stiletto.'

Stiletto turned the key. The engine whined and complained again. I remembered it hated the dampness. After mumbling a variety of colorful expletives, he tried it again and again. *Rrrrr.* No luck. The engine was flooded.

He grabbed that darn fraying camera bag and hopped out. 'The cops aren't going to be any too pleased that I left the scene. Tell them I'll call them when I get to New York.'

I put my hands on my hips. 'Leaving the scene of an accident is big trouble, Stiletto. I know. My ex-husband's a lawyer, and his clients do it all the time.'

But Stiletto just ignored me, per usual. 'See you around, Yablinko,' he said, turning into the woods. 'Good luck with your new career. Keep hanging off those bridges—'

'Wait!' I sprinted up to him, grabbed the back of his neck, pulled his lips toward mine and kissed him hard.

For a few seconds after I let him go he was speechless. I picked up my purse, the film and the cell phone and stepped back.

'What was that for?' he asked.

'For posterity,' I said. I didn't even know what *posterity* meant, it just sounded good. Secretly, I'd kissed Stiletto out of mere curiosity, and it was worth it. The kiss felt warm and real. Parts of me stirred that hadn't stirred in years.

'You know, it would have been fun,' he said, grinning.

'What would have been fun?' I stared at a drop of sweat running along his jawline.

'To hike with you over the Himalayas. To lie under a mango tree and watch a sunrise over the Taj Mahal. Yeah, it would have been fun.'

He gave me a wave and stepped into the underbrush.

Timing is everything, I thought. That's why I've got nothing.

I looked down at the car phone in my left hand and the film canister in my right. I decided to deposit the canister in my cleavage. Then I took the flashlight and walked up the road in the direction of the Range Rover, carefully stepping around the corpse without looking at it.

I found a rock and sat on it, softly singing all the verses I knew to 'Candy's Room.' A few frogs were croaking on the banks of the gurgling Monocacy Creek behind me, and the crickets were now in full force. The leaves were dripping from the rain, and mosquitoes – at least, I hoped they were mosquitoes – were biting my arms and ankles. Thick woods aren't my thing. I'm more a down-at-the-shore kind of girl. Not many snakes and centipedes down at the shore.

There was a rustle behind me in the bushes, and I took that as my cue to dial 9-1-1. The dispatcher promised someone would be right over. I pressed END and dialed Mr. Salvo at the *News-Times*.

Mr. Salvo wasn't in, so I left a message on his answering machine about the accident, Merry Metzger, the film and how his buddy Stiletto had abandoned me. A dose of guilt never hurt anyone, right? I promised to show up at the newspaper to write a story about it as soon as I was done with the cops. I pressed END and felt awfully, dreadfully alone.

There was another rustle in the bushes by the creek bank. My heart started beating faster. Maybe Stiletto was playing a joke. Maybe he hadn't intended to leave. Maybe Superman was dashing out of his phone booth right now.

Then I got the bright idea to walk down to the front gate and greet the cops. It wouldn't be leaving the scene of an accident, not if I was being hospitable. I didn't care. I couldn't take being that close to the dead body anymore. It was creeping me out.

I hadn't noticed that the flashlight was getting dimmer and dimmer. When I picked it up, it went out completely. Dead batteries.

Clutching the car phone, I began walking. At first normally, but once I was past the corpse, faster.

My heels went *click, click, click* on the blacktop. I was halfway to the gate when the *click, click, click* was joined by a *pound, pound, pound* from behind me. It might have been the blood in my ears, but I wasn't about to turn around and check. I picked up my step and ran.

The last thing I remember is frantically dialing 9-1-1 on that stupid cell phone and trying to figure out which button to push.

Later the cops would say that I tripped on my sandals. Or maybe a crack in the road.

All I know is that I fell down and hit my head on something hard. I slipped into a deep, dark nothingness, leaving all my fears and worries far behind me.

When I came to, the cops were arriving. My purse was beside me, but the film canister and cell phone were gone.

For that matter, so were Merry Metzger and the Range Rover.

Chapter 5

STILETTO WAS RIGHT. THE cops were mighty peeved to find that he had escaped their clutches. They began cursing and kicking the Jeep's tires and throwing a ferocious fit in general. Assuring them that he would call the police station as soon as he was back in New York had no effect. For some reason, they hated that guy.

Stiletto might argue that Lehigh's finest were biased against him because he was a pushy news photographer who was of the opinion that he had more important duties than answering a bunch of boring questions from some podunk police.

But I think the cops wanted to bust him because the left rear wheel of his Jeep was over the dead guy's hand. I mean, it's hard to ignore a piece of evidence like that.

'The only evident skid marks are behind the Jeep's wheels,' observed one detective, a big, muscular guy named Frye in a navy blue blazer. 'I'd say your friend Steve Stiletto is in significant trouble.'

A crew of technicians was measuring skid marks and taking photographs of the scene.

'I told you, Stiletto didn't hit him,' I explained, yet again. 'Stiletto made *those* skid marks when he was trying to avoid the stone wall.'

'Uh-huh,' said Frye.

It was that type of interview.

Nor was Frye any more receptive back at police headquarters when I described the Range Rover, the bloody flesh in its tire treads, and Merry Metzger's obvious intoxication.

'We checked,' Frye said in a monotone. 'The DMV shows no registration of a Range Rover to either Henry or Meredith Metzger. They buy strictly American, as should we all.'

Frye must have had a tour of duty in the U.S. Marines. His poker face was chiseled and he sported a crew cut. Plus he had the same bowlegged strut that many in the military adopt, as though his testicles had grown so big his thighs had to move over to make room.

'Did you talk to Merry herself?' I inquired of Frye. 'Did you call the Metzgers?'

'I believe that's police business,' Frye said. 'What's yours, Mrs. Yablonsky?'

'I'm a hairstylist. And it's Miss, not Mrs.' Frye was one of those men who couldn't see women as individuals, only as adjuncts to the males in their lives.

Frye took down a few notes. 'Hairdressing. That's a nice job for a woman. Must come in handy. Let me ask you a question, Miss Yablonsky. How well do you know Steve Stiletto?'

I fixed him with a level stare. 'What do you mean?'

'I mean, do you know who he is? Where he comes from? His criminal background?'

'Criminal background? He's a photojournalist for the Associated Press, he told me.'

'Uh-huh,' said Frye.

I wrapped a finger around a strand of hair and twirled it. 'What do *you* know about Steve Stiletto?'

Frye smiled. 'Only that he left the scene of a fatal accident.'

I was mighty grateful when Mickey Sinkler offered to drive me home in his cruiser at the end of his shift. Having never had so much as a speeding ticket – note, I did not say parking ticket – I am not used to cops. And today I'd been interviewed by them twice. Frye took his sweet old time with me and now it was past 10:00 P.M.

'That Frye didn't believe a thing I said back there,' I complained to Mickey as I nervously fiddled with the scanner buttons on the cruiser console. 'I told him and told him about Merry Metzger until I was blue in the face, and he brushed it right off.'

Mickey gently moved my fingers away from the buttons. 'Don't worry, he believed you, Bubbles. That's Frye's interviewing technique, is all.'

'Really?'

'Sure. It's old-fashioned, but effective.'

Only ten-thirty on a Friday night, and already Lehigh was closed down for business. The stores on Main Street were shut and the faux gas lamps on the sidewalk (part of Lehigh's 'historical renovations') illuminated empty benches and vacant corners. About the only structure lit up was the old white Moravian Church.

My stomach gurgled. I'd forgotten how starved I was. I had eaten nothing more than a Pop-Tart and a handful of Goldfish the entire day. All that swinging over the side of the Philip J. Fahy Bridge had built up quite an appetite.

In addition, my head was beginning to throb from the fall in the park. Mickey offered to drive me to the emergency room, but I didn't want to go. I wanted to go to the *News-Times* and write up my big break.

'So,' I began, moving into interview mode, 'do you think the police will investigate my Merry Metzger story?'

Mickey nodded. 'Absolutely. Hey, you're the only witness who stuck around.'

I shook my head. 'I don't know, Mickey. Do you know who she's married to? I thought Lehigh cops never dared to touch people like that.'

I recalled for him Dan's complaint that when steel executives were pulled over for DUI, they got a free ride home in a police cruiser and a cup of coffee. But when his low-life clients were busted for drunken driving, they got put in the slammer.

'Those were the old days, Bubbles,' Mickey said. 'The Lehigh Police Department's changed. We're not as

70

intimidated by steel now. You may not like Frye, but at least he's professional. He'll follow up your statement. He'll definitely investigate Merry Metzger's involvement in this.' He patted my shoulder. 'Of course, it would have been nice if you'd thought to write down the license plate number of the Range Rover, Bubbles.'

'Oh, that. I figured I didn't need to because Stiletto took all those pictures of the license plate.' I slapped my hand over my mouth. Oops. I didn't really want the police to know about that film.

Mickey slowed the car to a stop at the light. 'I didn't hear about any photographs, Bubbles,' he said, his big ears red from the street-lamp light on the corner. 'What happened to the film you say Stiletto took?'

I had to think fast. I figured the film canister popped out of my cleavage when I fell and was now somewhere in the long grass, along with the cell phone, down at the park. I didn't want the cops finding it before I did. Those photos would be locked up in evidence and out of commission if that happened.

'Stiletto has it with him – I think.' Curious. Was that a misdemeanor or a felony I had just committed by lying to the police?

The light turned green, and Mickey took a left onto West Goepp Street, clutching the steering wheel like an old lady. 'If you do know where that film is, that might be considered withholding evidence, Bubbles,' he said cautiously. 'You might want to call up Frye and amend your statement.'

I said, 'Okay,' out loud to Mickey. I said, No way, to myself.

Mickey pulled the cruiser up to the curb in front of my house. Jane threw open the screen door as soon as we parked.

'Wow, is that Jane?' Mickey asked, peering across me through the window. 'Has she ever grown. She should meet my Michael Jr. We should all get together.'

Lord, do I hate it when married men come on to me. 'Listen. Mickey,' I said, reaching for the door handle, 'you're a great guy, but you're also married. . . .'

'Not me!' He pointed to his chest. 'I'm not married. Not anymore.'

'What about your five kids?'

'Four at home,' he said. 'The middle one's in juvie detention. Complicated situation. Had a lot of difficulty after Sue left and the divorce, you know. The youngest, too. Four years old and still not potty trained. Can you believe it? Do you know how hard it is to find diapers for a forty-pound kid?'

My empty stomach churned. Five kids. One a juvenile delinquent. One old enough to read and still in diapers. Not what you'd call the perfect setting for a romantic situation.

'You find Grandma?' Jane ran down the front walk, flung herself against the cruiser and scanned the backseat. 'Where was she? At the mall?'

'What's this?' Mickey asked. 'You missing your mother?'

'Tell you about it some other time,' I explained, opening the door. 'I'm sure I'll see you around.'

Mickey tipped his hat in a manner that was painfully awkward. 'I'm counting on it.'

I waited until Mickey had turned the corner before I walked over to my car – the three-toned, ten-year-old Camaro with 150,000 miles and only slight rust parked in my neighbor's garage. I pushed up the garage door, activating the overhead light.

'What happened to you?' cried Jane, who was bouncing around me like a superball on speed. 'You look horrible. Your hair, it's so . . . messed up, and you got dark mascara circles under your eyes. Is that a bruise on your forehead? You get in an accident or something?'

This from the girl who underlines her eyes with something akin to black Magic Marker.

Tonight, Jane was wearing a black sleeveless shirt and khaki shorts. I determined that her hair color had changed since breakfast – from cotton candy pink to lemon lime. I was grateful that there were no new holes with metal objects in her freckled face. Every day I cross my fingers that there will be no more piercings.

I opened my purse and searched for my keys. I filled Jane in on my terrifying day. First I told her about the attempted suicide.

Jane: 'Mr. Dudko's the worst teacher; he should kill himself.'

Then the accident.

'Dead body. Ewww. Barf.'

And, finally, Stiletto.

'He must be hot. You've been twirling your hair.'

Haltingly, I fingered two strands hanging down by my ears. They were twisted tighter than nautical rope.

'What are you talking about?' I said calmly, putting the key in the door of the Camaro and thinking, Oh great, even my teenage daughter realizes that I'd practically kill for a hot and sweaty roll in the hay.

Jane let out a little snort. 'Oh, cut the act, Mom. Whenever you get, you know, sexually frustrated you twirl your hair. It's not like you've been beating away men with a stick lately. You gotta be hard up.'

Liar that I am, I cocked my head as though this was news to me! Then I changed the subject. I explained about the newspaper, how I had to get over there and write up the accident story.

'That's probably what that call was about,' Jane said as I got in the car.

'What call?'

'Gracie took it.' Gracie was Jane's best and most punctured friend. 'She said some guy called and said if you weren't at the newspaper in an hour, they were gonna give something to Lawless. Who's Lawless? He sounds cool.'

'He's not,' I said sharply, adrenaline shooting into my system at his name. I imagined fat Lawless stuffed in front of a computer screen, happily typing in the story of how a silly hairdresser who earlier in the day had nearly killed a man she was trying to save ended up mowing another one down that night. Page one all the way. He must be thanking his lucky stars for the existence of Bubbles Yablonsky.

There was no way he was claiming my Merry Metzger story, too.

Jane pulled a strip of gum from her mouth and began biting it rapidly, like a ticker tape.

'How long ago did that call come in?' I asked. 'And don't chew your gum that way. It's gross.'

Jane slurped in the last of the gum and glanced at her Rugrats watch. 'About an hour ago.'

'Geez, Jane. Why didn't you say so? I gotta rush.' I slammed the door shut and put the key in the ignition.

'Aren't you gonna put on new clothes and do your hair?' Jane asked. 'At least do your makeup.'

'Don't have time.'

'Wow. You really take this newspaper gig seriously.' Jane popped a bubble.

'Wanna come with me?' I asked through the open window. 'It's a newspaper on deadline. It might be fun.'

Jane scrunched up her face. 'To a newspaper? On a Friday night? That's fun? Where have you been for the last ten years?'

I blew my daughter a kiss and made her promise to call me at the *News-Times* once she heard from Grandma. Then I threw the Camaro in reverse, backed out of the driveway and burned rubber up West Goepp Street.

'There goes my wild mother the reporter,' Jane yelled behind me.

As a matter of fact, I was feeling a little wild. Wild with rage. In the past few hours, I'd faced death as I hung from the Philip J. Fahy Bridge with a physics teacher clutched to me, only to find I might be put in jail for saving his life. Then I had been abandoned in a dark, deserted park with a mutilated corpse.

For what? Just so I could get the big break that would get me noticed by *News-Times* Editor-in-Chief Dix Notch. Except, if I didn't get to the *News-Times* immediately, Lawless, who by all accounts had the ambition of Bill Gates and the work ethic of Homer Simpson, was going to reap the rewards of my hard work, instead.

And if that happened, let me tell you, those four-hundred-dollar scissors were coming out of my drawer down at the House of Beauty, and lips were gonna fly.

Jane's Hair Dye

It's always a shock to me when Jane shows up at breakfast with different colored hair. I wouldn't mind if she were blonde one day and auburn the next. But lime green, lemon yellow, raspberry red and bubble-gum pink? Oh well, apparently her flaming colors are a big hit with her friends, who can often be found in our bathroom dunking their hair in bowls of fluorescent drink mixes. Even some of my clients ask how my daughter *does* that. So I asked Jane and she gave me the recipe, along with a couple of caveats. The color lasts two weeks, so schedule college interviews accordingly. Also, be careful to use unsweetened Kool-Aid. One of Jane's friends spaced out on that little detail and ended up soaking her hair in what amounted to sugar syrup. It was such a mess the next morning that she shaved her head.

1 packet *unsweetened* Kool-Aid
6 cups water
Paper towels
Plastic wrap

Mix one packet of Kool-Aid with the water in a pot. Heat until boiling, stirring continuously. Remove from heat and cool to a temperature that is evenly warm, but not so hot that it will burn. Dip as much hair as possible into the mixture. Then, with your head over the pot, ladle the remaining Kool-Aid through hair. Do this for 15 minutes and immediately wring and pat hair with a paper towel. Do not wrap in a terrycloth towel because it might absorb too much color. You also may encase hair in plastic wrap and sleep on it overnight. After it dries, rinse repeatedly, shampoo and condition.

Note: Excess hair dye might stain ears, neck and forehead. To avoid this, place a band of plastic wrap around your hairline or smear petroleum jelly on exposed skin. Even if some staining occurs, dye can be scrubbed off.

Chapter 6

'YOU BLEW IT,' MR. Salvo informed me gruffly. 'The story's in and it's already been Quarked. You missed the deadline.'

Mr. Salvo was sitting in front of his cluttered computer under the bright, fluorescent lights of the *News-Times* newsroom, his white shirtsleeves rolled up to his elbows and a black grease pencil behind his ear. Around him were scattered white layout papers with stories blocked on them. He punched a button on the keyboard and walked over to the printer.

He was none too happy to see me when I arrived, breathless and sweaty, ten minutes after eleven o'clock. As night editor, Mr. Salvo was in charge of putting out the paper. His job was to assign and edit stories, then lay them out on the page. It was an overwhelming and lonely responsibility, and now I understood why editors like him ended the night as my former customers at the Tally Ho across the street. They'd order shots of rotgut gin and Jim Beam. A liver has a sorry future if its misfortune is to filter a newspaper editor's bloodstream.

'Well,' Mr. Salvo said, throwing me the printout, 'what did you expect? I couldn't wait all night. Lawless was here, and so I had him do it. Next time, remember you work for a *daily*, not a *weekly*.'

I quickly read the story. It only vaguely resembled the accident scene in the park. First, it was brief and mentioned merely that an apparent hit-and-run victim had been found, a man in his sixties, and that police were looking for the driver of a Jeep placed at the scene. Stiletto's Jeep? Score a cheap shot for the cops.

The story made no reference to Merry Metzger or her Range Rover or the blood in the tires. It was a total sham. Mickey might say the police department had changed in its treatment of steel executives, but to me it seemed like business as usual.

'Where'd Lawless get this information?' I wanted to know, holding up the printout.

Mr. Salvo was back at his desk. 'Press release. Cops faxed it over at ten-thirty.'

'But this is—'

'It's all we had to go on, Yablonsky,' Mr. Salvo said, scribbling on the white layout pages. 'You were nowhere to be found.' He tapped a button on his keyboard and yelled something unintelligible over to the copydesk, where two old men in T-shirts and green visors sat slumped over their keyboards.

Mr. Salvo visibly relaxed in his chair, put his hands behind his head and looked up at me. 'We're going to press right now,' he said. 'I just laid out the last page.'

I stared at the story in my hand and then at him. 'Mr. Salvo, this story isn't just incomplete. It's wrong. Stiletto didn't hit him with his Jeep . . .'

Mr. Salvo sat up with a start. 'Don't tell me that was Stiletto's Jeep?'

'Yes, but he didn't hit him . . .'

'Shit.' Mr. Salvo got up and thrust his hands in his pockets. 'Stiletto wasn't on the *News-Times* clock when he hit him, was he? Please say no.'

'No. He was driving me to meet my mother. And, besides, Stiletto didn't hit him,' I stressed again. 'Anyway, what does it matter if he was working for us?'

'It matters to our insurance company. Damn right it does. Whew, you had me going there.'

He sat back down and wiped his forehead with a hankie. I plunked myself on his desk. 'Mr. Salvo. Merry Metzger – *the* Merry Metzger – was the hit-and-run driver . . .'

This information took a while to sink in. After a few minutes of staring across the newsroom, Mr. Salvo said slowly, 'Merry Metzger. You mean Henry Metzger's wife?'

Realizing that I was wearing nothing but a pink halter top, I crossed my arms in an attempt to increase my credibility. 'It's true. Stiletto and I found her Range Rover parked just a few feet from the body with Merry Metzger herself in it, holding a vodka bottle and smashed out of her mind. Also, we discovered bloody tissue in the tires. Stiletto got photos. Didn't you get my message?'

'That message you left on my voice mail was so garbled. All I made out was accident and park and story. What were you calling from, a cheap cell phone?'

'Yeah, Stiletto's.'

Mr. Salvo held out his hand. 'Okay, let me look at the film.'

I shifted attention to my sandals. 'That's kind of an odd story. I was running to meet the cops and fell. When I came to, the roll of film Stiletto shot of the accident scene was gone, and so were Merry Metzger and her Range Rover.'

'Christ!' Mr. Salvo threw up his hands. 'In other words, you lost the film?'

I nodded sheepishly.

'Then you blew it again, Yablonsky. We've got nothing to go on, just your word, and I'm sorry, but that's not enough when it comes to the Metzgers. I grew up with that family. My father was a landscaper on Henry Metzger's estate for twenty-three years. Henry Metzger is a very respected man in this town, Yablonsky. You got to have your ducks in a row before you accuse his wife of that kind of crime.'

'What if the police make that accusation?'

'The cops' press release doesn't mention her or her Range Rover.'

'But I have a cop saying Merry Metzger is under investigation,' I said, delicately touching the bump on my head, which was starting to hurt again. 'Detective Mickey Sinkler told me so.'

Mr. Salvo sat up. 'Really?'

'Really. We had a long discussion about it in the cruiser. He said, specifically, that the police were investigating Merry Metzger's role in the accident.'

Mr. Salvo picked up the phone and punched in three numbers. 'You sure you got police confirmation, Yablonsky?'

I crossed my chest. 'I swear on my dead father's grave.'

'Because if you're right, this is one helluva story. Especially if we got an exclusive.' He leaned into the phone. 'Hey, Ralph. Stop the run. I got a last minute A-1 lead story. Six inches. I'll send up a new layout.'

My heart started thumping. I'd heard of 'stop the presses,' but I figured that was only in the movies. Now they were stopping the presses for me!

Mr. Salvo slammed down the receiver. 'The general rule of thumb is that for every ten minutes we print after deadline, we lose five thousand dollars. You got ten minutes, Yablonsky. This is a five-thousand-dollar story.'

Mr. Salvo let me use his own computer. I never wrote so fast in my life.

There was just one more phone call to make. I looked up the number and dialed from Mr. Salvo's phone. It rang twice and a man sharply answered. I sucked in a stress-busting breath.

'Sorry to bother you so late at night, sir,' I began efficiently, 'but I am trying to reach Merry Metzger.'

'She's not here,' the man said, and then added slowly, 'this is her husband. Who is this?'

I tried to remove from my mind all the prejudices Mama had instilled in me about Henry Metzger. His arrogance. His money. His disregard for the working class. Henry Metzger was a legend in Lehigh, not only for his vast wealth, which included a beachfront house in Avalon, New Jersey, and another in Hilton Head, South Carolina, but also for his ruthlessness.

In the days when unions were tough, Henry Metzger was tougher. Those steelworkers with enough courage to stand up to him were often the sudden victims of unfortunate accidents. Severed hands. Burned faces. Occasionally, deadly mishaps at the plant. No one was ever arrested or charged for these crimes, which were passed off as work-related injuries. But it was understood that Henry Metzger's thugs were the culprits. Even as a child, after my father was burned alive at the ingot mold, teachers forbade me to speak ill of Mr. Metzger at school. That's how deep and pervasive their fear of him was.

'My name is Bubbles Yablonsky. I freelance for the *News-Times*, and I'm writing a story, on deadline, about an accident your wife was in tonight at the Saw Mill Park.'

There was a pause, and I heard some shuffling of papers in the background. 'Who told you that?'

I gulped. Mr. Salvo was rotating his hand, motioning for me to speed it along.

'No one told me,' I said, trying to steady my voice. 'I saw your wife in the car myself. A Range Rover. We have police confirmation that she is the subject of an investigation regarding this matter. Do you have any comment?'

Again a pause and scratching. A pen on paper? 'Please spell your name.'

I complied.

After a moment, Henry Metzger said, 'Listen to me, Bubbles Yablonsky, and listen good.'

I listened as good as I could.

'You print what you just relayed to me tonight, and rest assured your life will be a living hell by tomorrow.'

He hung up.

'Did he deny it?' Mr. Salvo asked eagerly as I replaced the handset.

I decided it was best not to fill in Mr. Salvo about Henry Metzger's threat. Seeing as how he respected Metzger, Mr. Salvo would hold the story for sure.

'No. He didn't deny it.'

Mr. Salvo pumped his fist in the air. 'Yes! You got it, Yablonsky.'

I added Henry Metzger's incredibly insightful 'no comment' to the story and shipped it off to Mr. Salvo. He had it edited and Quarked with thirty seconds to spare.

'At the risk of sounding like a complete grammatical moron, you done good, Yablonsky,' Mr. Salvo said, plunking himself on the corner of my desk. 'I'm gonna give my apartment another call and see if Steve's back yet. Knowing him, he won't come home until some dame kicks him out of her place.'

We waited in silence while Mr. Salvo called his apartment. The newsroom was deserted now, except for us. The two old copy men had put on their coats and gone home. Empty desks were littered with notebooks, old newspapers and yellow telephone directories. The only sound came from Mr. Salvo's desk, where a black police scanner squawked an endless report of domestic assaults, fender benders, possible DUIs and diabetic seizures. If I had to work in this environment, I'd drink, too.

'Not in,' Mr. Salvo said, hanging up at last.

'Uh, about Stiletto,' I said cautiously.

Mr. Salvo eyed me warily. 'Yessss, Yablonsky.'

'Detective Frye down at the police department mentioned something about him having a criminal record. Is that true? Because he seems like an okay guy.'

Mr. Salvo shook his head. 'Shit, Yablonsky. What did I tell you about Stiletto? Keep your eyes off him. Ignore him. Better yet, run away.'

'No, it's not like that, it's—'

'It's always like that. I've known Steve since junior high school, and even then the girls were mad for him. They'd bake him cookies, offer to wash his gym uniform, it was disgusting. I tried to figure out what he had that I didn't have, and I gave up.'

I didn't have the heart to tell Mr. Salvo that what

Stiletto had that he didn't have was a great body; beautiful, strong hands; a warm and winning smile; an exciting life and hair.

'But I do know one thing, Yablonsky,' Mr. Salvo continued. 'I know that all those girls who killed themselves for Steve went away frustrated. That guy had such a fucked-up upbringing, he couldn't commit to a date for a movie. He'll bring you nothing but heartbreak, Bubbles, I assure you.'

I waited to make sure he was done. 'All I wanted to know, Mr. Salvo, was whether Stiletto has a criminal record.'

'Criminal record?' Mr. Salvo thought about it. 'Nope. Not in this country.'

Jane was curled up in a fetal position, fast asleep on the couch when I got home. Gracie was opposite her, stretched out on the BarcaLounger, a dribble of drool running out her mouth. The TV was on full blast, playing some MTV thing that raised my concerns about the girls' overall deafness.

I picked up the remote control and pressed POWER/OFF. I nearly jumped out of my shorts when the screen went all gray and whined like a dentist's drill at full volume. Gracie grumbled something, and I frantically searched around and under the coffee table for the *other* remote. How many times had Jane taught me to turn off the TV with the VCR remote? How many times did I forget?

Finally, I just punched the TV off manually.

I covered each with a blanket. I sat down next to Jane and pushed back her lemon-lime hair. From this angle – which happened to be the unpierced side of her face – Jane reminded me of when she was eight and believed in imaginary fairies who drank from her tiny china teacups. There were still traces of baby fat on her cheeks and a slight smile at the corner of her lips.

I bent down and kissed her forehead. Jane made a kind of gurgling sound and went back to sleep.

Starved as I was, I tiptoed into the kitchen to fix a sandwich. I flicked on the overhead light and stifled a shriek as my most detested bug – a hairy gray centipede – scurried down the kitchen wall and onto the floor. I hopped onto the counter until it was safely under the sink – where I had no intention of tracking its whereabouts.

Suddenly, I was overwhelmed with a feeling of depression. Perhaps it was the letdown of a day filled with emotion. Fear of falling. Falling in lust with Stiletto. Anger at Lawless. Worry about my mother. Horror of the dead body. Striving to write a hot story on deadline. Fear of a centipede. Of Henry Metzger. Loneliness.

You're tired, Bubbles, I told myself as I spread a thick layer of mayonnaise across a slice of rye bread. I laid on a piece of ham and a slice of Swiss. This is what comes of reaching for a dream that's way beyond you. Pure exhaustion.

It wasn't just that, though. It was seeing Jane asleep on the couch. I'd never done right by her. After years of working six days a week down at the House of Beauty, not to mention all that community college, I had still never managed to lift her out of the same neighborhood I grew up in. I didn't want Jane to fall into the same traps I had – getting pregnant in high school by some selfish lout who would dump her once he got himself established.

I grabbed a Diet Pepsi, quietly opened the screen door and pulled up a chair. I sat on the back porch and ate my sandwich, drinking in the simple pleasure of a starry summer night. I heard two passersby discussing something in low tones as they strolled down the sidewalk. A slight breeze blew the leaves on the trees and brought with it the perfume of my neighbor's honeysuckle, fragrant after the rain, from the other end of my postage stamp of a backyard.

In the distance I heard a familiar *chug, chug, chug*. Steel's coke plant closing down for the night.

A few nights from now, Stiletto would be lying on a Mexican beach, I imagined, listening to the rolling surf, maybe gazing at the same stars. Or perhaps he would be sitting at a lively sidewalk café, sipping sangria and chatting up some dark-haired beauty.

My mind began to race. I replayed Henry Metzger's threat. My life would be hell by tomorrow.

'This story's gonna change your life. You'll see,' Mr. Salvo had said when I left the newspaper tonight.

I closed my eyes and hung on to those words.

Mr. Salvo had no idea at the time how very right he was.

Chapter 7

IT SEEMED AS THOUGH I'd been asleep for five minutes when the portable phone next to my bed rang with the fury of a school bell. I knocked it off the hook and dragged the receiver to my ear.

'Whah?' I grunted.

'Hi, honey. Whatcha doing?'

My eyes popped open. 'Mama!' I screamed. 'Where have you been? I've been worried sick.'

It was my sixty-four-year-old mother, back from being on the lam. She clucked her tongue. 'This from the daughter who never calls, never visits. I indulge myself for once, and suddenly it's "Mama, where have you been? How could you?"'

I squinted at the digital alarm clock. It said 6:35.

'THIS CALL IS FROM A PRISON PHONE.'

'Mama?' I asked. 'What was that?'

'What was what?'

'IF YOU WISH TO ACCEPT THIS CALL, PLEASE PRESS ONE.'

'That,' I said.

'That?' she said. 'That was the TV.'

'IF YOU DO NOT WISH TO ACCEPT THIS CALL, PLEASE PRESS TWO.'

I pressed one, just in case. 'Mama. Is there something you want to tell me?'

'As a matter of fact,' she said, 'I want to tell you I need an attorney . . . and maybe some money to post bail.'

I sat up in a shot. 'This is about the senior center shuttle, say?'

'Mmmm. Actually, it's nothing more than a tiny disagreement with those silly salesgirls down at Hess's Department Store.'

'THIS PHONE CALL WILL TERMINATE IN THREE MINUTES.'

Hess's Department Store is Lehigh's ritziest retail outlet, kind of like Macy's, except, since it's located in the Westgate Mall, only one floor high and one-sixteenth the size. I dreaded to think what trouble Mama had gotten herself into there.

'What do you mean by *tiny disagreement*?'

'Well, I went outside to hold a dress up to the light.'

'And . . .'

'And the salesgirls made a big fuss because they said I went too far.'

'How far?'

'To Easton Avenue.'

Easton Avenue was five blocks away from the Westgate Mall.

'Then they had the nerve to accuse me of stealing simply because I was wearing the dress when they found me. For Pete's sake, I had to see how it fit!'

'THIS PHONE CALL WILL TERMINATE IN TWO MINUTES.'

With one hand, I opened the curtains behind my bed. Another warm, sunny day. A Saturday and, this being wedding season, my presence was requested at the House of Beauty bright and early.

'So, how bad can it be?' I asked, imagining a fifty-dollar Lane Bryant special.

'A felony. The dress was over three thousand dollars.'

The phone dropped out of my hand. When I picked it up, I heard Mama say something about Vera Wang.

'Shit, Mama. You're in hot water,' I said, getting out of bed and grabbing a pencil from the night table.

'Watch your potty mouth, Bubbles. After I hang up, call Dan.'

My inner safety catch released. 'Not Dan.'

'Yes, Dan,' said Mama. 'Tell him to meet me at Judge Puffenfoose's at Thirty-five May Street behind the Lehigh Shopping Center at nine a.m. for an arraignment. Afterward . . .'

There was a beep on the other line.

'Hold on, Mama.' I took the other call.

A voice exploded. 'Jesus H. Christ. Bubbles Yablonsky, I should come over to your house and strangle you right now!'

'Hold on, Mickey,' I said.

I got back to Mama. 'Gotta go, Mama. Mickey Sinkler's on the other line.' I quickly told her about the Merry Metzger accident and interviewing Henry Metzger.

'Holy mackerel!' she exclaimed. 'Henry Metzger's going to kill you. Literally. I gotta get out of here fast and get you some protection. Genevieve will know what to do.'

I was going to plead with her not to bring in Genevieve, but the line went dead. I pressed the appropriate button and got back to Mickey.

'What seems to be the problem, Mickey?'

I held the phone away from my ear while a torrent of expletives burst from Mickey's end.

'Don't yell at me, Mickey,' I said, calmly. 'I do not appreciate being yelled at.'

Mickey tried to gain control. He did the deep breathing thing. In. Out. In. Out. 'Bubbles,' he said finally, 'did you see your story in the paper today?'

I got up and walked down the stairs to the kitchen. 'Which one? The bridge story or the accident story?'

'The story in which you quote me – Detective Mickey Sinkler – as speaking for the entire Lehigh police force. Merry Metzger a suspect in a hit and run? Where'd you come up with that?'

Mickey was beginning to sound upset again.

'Watch it, Mickey. Temper. Temper.' I tiptoed past the girls, still asleep in the living room.

'Why shouldn't I be angry? I'm going to lose my job because of you.'

'Don't exaggerate, Mickey.'

'I'm not kidding.' His voice had resumed its fevered pitch. 'You had no right to quote me. I was talking to Bubbles Yablonsky the hairdresser last night, not Bubbles Yablonsky the—'

I opened the freezer and took out a bag of ground coffee. 'Listen, Mickey, if you can't discuss this in a rational tone of voice, perhaps we shouldn't talk at all. Call me when you simmer down.'

I hung up the phone. This I've learned from my experience with Dan: Don't ever let a man yell at you. Not your boss. Not your husband. Not some stupid cop who used to snort green Jell-O up his nose.

Jane came into the kitchen, her lemon-lime hair standing up on one side of her head.

'What was that about?' she asked with a yawn and a stretch.

'Nothing,' I said, turning on the coffeepot. 'But good news. Grandma called.'

'No way. Where is she?'

Gracie plodded into the kitchen and promptly rested her head on the counter.

'Of all places, jail.'

Jane gasped.

'She's going to get arraigned at nine. Daddy's gonna represent her. I've got to go to work. You want to go to her arraignment in my place?'

'I do,' volunteered Gracie. 'Boy, I wish my granny was in jail. That'd be cool.'

* * *

Gracie was ticked off that her parents wouldn't let her go to court because they needed her to baby-sit. Jane was bummed that she couldn't change her hair color to Felonious Black in time for the hearing, and Dan was pissed that I had called for his services on a Saturday morning.

'I got a golf date.'

'You can deal with it,' I said. 'I'll drop Jane off at eight-thirty.'

I grabbed a cup of coffee and marched upstairs to the shower. It wasn't yet seven, and this day already had the makings of being more dramatic than the previous one. Add to that the prospect of driving over to Dan's, and I was jonesing for cigarettes that four years ago I swore I'd never touch again.

I reminded myself that in ultimately stressful situations like this, it would be dangerous to smoke. Smoking would drive my heartbeat to 110 beats a minute and cause me to run around the living room like a toddler high on birthday cake. What I decided to do instead was my nails.

I walked over to the nail side of my medicine chest and popped it open. There, organized with the efficiency of Martha Stewart's spice rack, was my nail-polish collection. From Clear Consciousness to Rabid Red. I chose Peaceful Petunia. It sounded soothing.

After two cups of coffee, my new pink petunia nail color was dry, and I was feeling peaceful already.

Then I saw my reflection in the mirror. Ugh. Raccoon eyes. A big, ugly purple bruise on the upper right-hand side of my forehead. And that hair! I must have been twisting it in my sleep. Damn Stiletto.

I took a long hot shower finished by a shot of ice-cold spray. Dried off with a clean towel and treated myself to a Bubbles Deluxe. Afterward, I loaded my hair with gel and blew it dry so that it nearly stood on end. Then I teased it out, wrapped it into a six-inch-high French twist and sprayed it stiff. A blond beehive with bangs combed down to cover the bump.

I chose my lucky dress: a winter-white minidress that I was wearing when I won a hundred-dollar scratch Pennsylvania Lotto ticket. Underneath it I wore a strapless Wonderbra, which made my yaboos stick out like rockets, and supersheer stockings. I stepped into a pair of high-heeled white pumps. Plugged in oversize faux pearl earrings. Spritzed my body down with Chloé and assessed myself in the mirror.

'Eat your heart out, Dan the Man,' I taunted.

Downstairs, Jane was heavy with the black lipstick.

'Who'd guess you have a one-forty-five IQ?' I teased her as we walked to the Camaro.

'And who'd have guessed your ass was hanging off the Fahy yesterday?' Jane returned.

God, do I love this kid.

We turned from my familiar neighborhood of brick double row homes and took a left at the gray fortress of

Liberty High School onto Linden Street. We passed Roly's Rollicking Licking Ice Cream Shop where Jane works Saturday through Thursday nights, Schoenen's Grocery Store, St. Anne's Church and were soon in the tidy Spring Garden community of brick bungalows and Sears swing sets.

Going to Dan's was like climbing up the economic ladder.

I took a left on Macada and entered Hanover Township. Dan lived in the exclusive new Wedgewood community, over the tracks and across the creek from the rest of us. It wasn't gated, but that's only because it didn't have to be.

When I was growing up, Hanover Township was one big cornfield. No one lived in Hanover Township except Pennsylvania Dutch and cows. Now, with the new and improved Route 78, Hanover Township had been transformed into a haven for commuters from New York and Philadelphia, each sixty miles away. And not just your average haven, either.

Here onto half-acre parcels were squeezed mini-mansions with all the bells and whistles. Mansard roofs, oversize garages, professional landscaping – including mandatory weeping cherry trees – swimming pools, cathedral ceilings and master-bedroom suites the square footage of my entire house. Jacuzzis, Corian counters, Sub-Zero refrigerators and Jenn-Air ranges. And, of course, the tiny blue HOME SECURITY signs stuck right by the front doors.

These weren't homes. These were small countries. Each one guarded by the private military of Home Security, a collection of anonymous overseers equipped with hidden cameras, spying on them all twenty-four hours a day.

The only amenity missing was a mature tree over six feet.

Dan was in a navy blue blazer, white button-down Oxford shirt, khakis and a green-and-navy-striped tie. He was standing under the bright blue sky and rubbing off some invisible blemish from his shiny black BMW.

He winced as the Camaro coughed and sputtered onto his newly blacktopped driveway. If Dan had a service entrance, he'd make me use it.

'Geesh,' he said, taking in my lucky outfit. 'You going to work today on your feet or on your back?'

'Daaad,' piped up Jane. 'That's not nice.'

'You're one to talk,' Dan said, delicately shaking out a chamois cloth. 'Where we're going might be the basement of some magistrate's home, but it's still a court of law, you know. You gotta spiff up better than that.'

Jane studied her black shorts. 'What's wrong with how I look?'

'You look like Sid Vicious. Upstairs I know for a fact there's a dress you left in the spare bedroom closet. Put that on if you want to go with me.'

Jane threw me a plaintive look, but I sided with her father on this one. 'Think of Grandma, Jane. She'll need you there.'

She was about to protest further when a horrible barking and howling ensued. Out from the back of the house bounded a gangly black Labrador with a bright green collar. It jumped on Jane and then tried to jump on me until I gave it a little kick with my knee.

'What's that?' I asked as Jane knelt down and let the dog lick her face.

'That's Dudley,' Dan said dryly. 'I'm taking him duck hunting this fall.'

I bit my lip. I knew for a fact that Dan's one experience with hunting was with his Uncle Egbert up by Stroudsburg. And it didn't involve black Labs named Dudley. The only thing black at those hunting camps was Black Label beer, of which so much was consumed that leaving the camp to shoot at deer was a highly improbable event.

'So, I see from the front page of this morning's newspaper that you finally got your big break,' Dan said as Jane escaped around the back of the house with Dudley. 'Quite a story, huh?'

'You're telling me,' I said. Frankly, yesterday seemed like a dream now. I couldn't believe I stood on a ledge of the Fahy to save an old physics teacher from committing suicide. 'I took a real risk. I can't even believe it myself.'

'I don't like you taking such risks,' Dan said.

Dan's sudden concern surprised me. It must be the lucky dress working its magic. 'Thanks, Dan, but I got a new philosophy in life—'

'It's Chip now, not Dan,' he interrupted. 'Make a mental note, Bubbles.'

'Sorry, Chip. Anyway, like I was saying, I'm not going to let those sensational opportunities pass me by. I'm going to make the most of them. I saw an opportunity to make a front-page smash yesterday and I grabbed it – even if it meant jeopardizing my own life.'

Only, that front-page smash ended up being written by Lawless, instead of me. Downright unfair. 'The risk wasn't worth it, though. To tell you the truth, deep down, I was pretty pissed,' I added.

Dan smacked his head. 'What you're telling me, Bubbles, is so libelous it makes me want to shake you. Negligence. Malice. Sensationalism. You are one walking summary judgment, lady.'

I find it annoying when Dan slips into legal mumbo jumbo, so I invented an excuse to leave. I needed to check on Jane, anyway.

Wendy was in the kitchen, talking intently on the portable phone, dressed ready for tennis when I entered through the back door. She was wearing a white pleated skirt. Navy blue top. Adidas on her feet and a white headband around her bobbed brown hair.

What I'd like to know is when I am gonna get a life like this. Here it is a Saturday morning and I'm trudging off to the shop. Meanwhile other women, wealthy women, spend their days playing tennis, picking over crab salads and getting their hair done.

I softly walked up the back stairs and found Jane

slowly dressing in the guest suite she occupied when she stayed with Dan. The guest suite was painted in muted lavender with bay windows, a private bath, an antique four-poster bed and private TV, VCR, stereo and computer.

'Tell me again – why do you live in our shoe box?' I asked, fingering the handmade duvet decorated with violets and ivy.

Jane gave me a kiss. 'Because I can't stand the idea of leaving my wacky mom.'

I pushed her away. 'Yeah, right. If you moved here, your father would make you dress like that all the time. That's why you don't want to live here.'

Jane covered her eyes. She was wearing a yellow sleeveless sundress with a white tie in the back. I directed her out the door and down to Dan.

'At least your footwear hasn't changed,' I said, pointing to her black Doc Marten boots, which were galumphing down the stairs. 'You look like Sandra Dee in SoHo.'

Wendy blocked our exit through the garage door. 'May I have a word with you, Bubbles?' she chirped. 'Jane. Your father's anxious to go. He's in the car.'

Jane hesitated and then, with one last look of sympathy, stepped into the garage.

Wendy's lips were pressed into a thin line across her high-cheekboned face, and she held the portable tightly in her hand. She squinted at the bump under my bangs and shuddered.

'Chip has just informed me,' she said, rapidly blinking, 'that you slandered Merry in today's paper because – to put it in your words – you were pissed.'

What? I put up my hands. 'Whoa, there, Wendy. Dan – I mean Chip – is confused. No, I was referring to a story about a potential suicide up at the Fahy—'

'I'm not talking about *that* story,' she said, shifting sneakered feet. 'I'm talking about that collection of lies you compiled about my dear friend Merry Metzger. In one thoughtless, insignificant article you destroyed her good reputation with your sloppy reporting. I'd like to know what she ever did to you to deserve such cruel treatment.'

Little red welts were breaking out on Wendy's neck. She narrowed her eyes at me. 'You don't even know who Merry Metzger is, do you?'

I stared back noncommittally.

'You have no idea that she heads the Pace Foundation, which funds drug and alcohol rehabilitation centers around the valley. You don't know that Merry visits all the schools each year, urging kids to Just Say No to alcohol and drugs. You don't know that she is, in essence, Lehigh's Queen Mother Against Drunk Driving. Do you?'

Wendy paused. 'Now do you understand what you've done? Now do you understand what damage you've caused?'

I was as stunned as a deer in headlights. That this woman, smashed out of her mind and reeking of vodka, was supposed to be some anti-alcohol crusader was news to me. I started to explain that I'd never heard the name Merry Metzger before last night, but Wendy cut me off.

'I'm not the only one who's livid. Other people – important people – are equally incensed,' she continued with a twitch of her nose. 'Henry Metzger, for one, is furious. He's considering some very serious action against the *News-Times*.'

I smiled. Mr. Salvo had warned us in the department store community college course to expect such threats.

'Just remember,' Mr. Salvo had told us, 'the First Amendment's behind you.'

'The First Amendment's behind me, Wendy,' I said righteously.

'The First Amendment won't help you, Bubbles Yablonsky,' Wendy hissed. 'If you had been a half-decent reporter and done a little checking, you would have found that Merry Metzger wasn't even in town last night. She flew to Honduras to help hurricane survivors with her Moravian Mission group the day before yesterday.'

I put my hand on my hip. That was impossible. I saw her myself. And besides, Henry Metzger didn't mention that when I called him. 'You're full of it, Wendy.'

'What I'm full of are facts, Bubbles. I put her on the plane myself, you dimwit.'

Ten Steps to a Bubbles Deluxe

Usually clients ask me to do a makeup makeover – what I prefer to call a Bubbles Deluxe – when they are going to a wedding, a prom or some other special occasion. Frequently, though, women come into the House of Beauty merely looking for a change. Maybe it's their birthday and they want to spruce up, or their boyfriend dumped them and they want a new face. Whatever. There is no quicker and easier way to dramatically alter your appearance than through make-up. A little cover-up here, a new shade of eyeliner there, and voilà – a new you. Of course, my natural inclination is to favor teal eyeshadow, midnight eyeliner and ruby-red lips, but that's not what my clients want. They prefer a more sophisticated, together look, which is achieved by following the steps below. Oh well. Taste is subjective. Can I help it if thick black eyeliner is passé?

Step 1: Pin back hair. Apply a light astringent toner over face. Pat dry with a tissue.

Step 2: Choose a cover-up one shade lighter than your skin tone. Apply in dots under eyes, around nose or over acne. Blend with fingertips.

Step 3: Apply a foundation that complements your skin tone. If your skin has a yellowish cast, choose a foundation with more rose. If it's reddish, choose a beige. Apply lightly and sweep upward. Blend at edges of face.

Step 4: Use a neutral, light eyeshadow to cover entire eyelid up to the brow. Match to skin tone and hair color. For wider eyes apply a darker eyeshadow to the outer edges of the lid. For deep eyes apply a darker shadow to the top of the lid.

Step 5: Line eyes in pencil. Stick to soft tones. Soft gray for blue eyes. Bark for brown. Eye pencils will last longer if you keep them in the refrigerator and out of the glove compartment in your Camaro on hot days.

Step 6: Fill in eyebrows. An eyebrow should not extend beyond an eyeliner pencil held vertically against the bridge of your nose. If it does, bring out the tweezers and numb eyebrow with ice before plucking.

Step 7: Apply mascara. Once again, avoid black and match to eye color. Use mahogany for brown eyes, soft gray for blue.

Step 8: Blush should be applied by brush only on the outside of the 'apples' of your cheeks. Sweep toward hairline.

Step 9: Line lips with lip pencil if your lips are thin. Otherwise, lipstick alone is okay. Choose colors that go well with skin tones. However, this is one time when color can match clothes and should not clash. No red lips with purple dresses. Bright blondes, like me, can get away with wearing flashier colors.

Step 10: Finally, set entire face with a loose translucent powder applied lightly.

Chapter 8

'OKAY, SO LET ME get this straight,' Sandy began. 'First, you trespass and cross police lines just so you can get close to some poor man who's contemplating suicide. Then you shove him—'

'Not really a shove,' I corrected, 'more like a gentle push.'

'You *gently* push him off a bridge and he grabs you and you both dangle there, seconds from death. Is that right?'

I sipped coffee from a Styrofoam cup. 'That's right.'

'And then, after all that, you don't get to write the story anyway, but you might be charged with aiding an attempted suicide. So, you're on your way home when you run over some poor old man standing in the park in your excitement to find your loonybin mother who's stolen a shuttle owned by the senior center. Am I getting it?'

'You're skipping parts.'

Sandy put a hand on her hip. 'Which part?'

'The part about Stiletto.'

'Hm-hmm.' Sandy bent into the dryer and removed a pile of green towels. 'I should have figured as much.'

Sandy and I were going over my recent troubles in her office, aka the supply room of Sandy's House of Beauty. I was sitting on a cardboard box of Clorox sipping coffee, eating doughnuts and filling her in on the events of the last twelve hours.

Sandy, meanwhile, had been patiently folding towels and refilling shampoo bottles. She looked particularly efficient today, even for Sandy, dressed in a neat pink polyester uniform with matching shoes and stockings. Her miniature white poodle, Oscar, the salon mascot, was going to town on a chew toy shaped like a cookie.

As for Wendy's assertion that Merry Metzger wasn't in town last night, Sandy had a simple answer: 'She's lying. You know how those women down at the country club are, they stick together to protect their own.'

Sandy couldn't give a tinker's damn about Merry Metzger's reputation, either. She was far more interested in Stiletto.

'I'm going to ask you the sixty-four-thousand-dollar question, Bubbles,' Sandy said firmly. 'Did you sleep with him?'

I opened my eyes in surprise. 'No! I barely know him.'

'Oh, like you should be shocked I asked that. Twenty minutes after Ken the Radio Shack clerk installed those woofers in your Camaro, you two were in the backseat going to boogie wonderland. You ain't exactly Sister Teresa, Bubbles.'

My cheeks felt hot as I reminded Sandy of the solemn vow I took after Ken. No sex until Mr. Right came along and even then I might hold out until marriage – although that was, admittedly, a long shot. I made that promise six weeks, four days, twenty-two hours and eleven minutes ago, and I was sticking to it.

Sandy knelt down and petted Oscar. 'The only reason I believe you, Bubbles, is because of your hair.'

'Oh?'

'Yeah, it's all twisted. You used to do that in high school, too, remember? Every study hall with that guy with the black curls and bright blue eyes, Jeffrey Zimba. Back when you were a virgin. Gosh, it seems so long ago.'

I gulped the last of my coffee and tossed the cup in the trash. 'We can't all be happily married to a man who brings us coffee in bed and lets us sleep in on Sundays, Sandy.'

Sandy and her dream husband, Martin, had been sweethearts since fourth grade. Martin was a baker who owned a bread shop on the bottom floor of their double. Every day since their honeymoon, Martin had arisen at 3:00 A.M. to mix dough. At 7:00 A.M. on the dot, he walked up a plate of fresh rolls and a hot pot of coffee for his wife. No wonder they don't have kids. Who would be stupid enough to mess with a great arrangement like that?

I was about to fill in Sandy about Mama's Vera Wang mischief when the front doorbell tinkled. Sandy left to see who it was.

Oscar got up from his bed and jumped on my lap. I petted him and drank in the smells of the salon. Hair spray. The acrid, burning odor of hair dye. Of color being burned into hair and hair being burned into waves. Smoking curling irons. Hot hair dryers. Sweet shampoo. Caustic permanents. The perfume of the House of Beauty, once owned by Sandy's great aunt, was deeply embedded here.

For forty years unknown women, many now dead, sat in these chairs while hairdressers, now long retired, transformed them into bright blondes, sultry brunettes or arresting redheads. They'd talk and laugh, gossip and cry and – for once – let someone else take care of them. No dishes to do, no kids to cater to, no bosses to serve.

After my father died and my mother took on two jobs, she still never missed a Saturday morning appointment at the hair salon. I used to accompany her as a child down to Ileine's, located at the corner of West Goepp. It was a small salon, much like the House of Beauty, with only two sinks. I'd sit on a tiny rocking chair Ileine put out just for me and watch with fascination as she turned my mother's tired locks into golden curls, how she'd draw up hair through the comb so that it was perfectly straight and then tease it into fullness. It was magic to me, and I knew, even as young as six, that this was what I wanted to be when I grew up.

So why was I mucking it up with this newspaper work?

Sandy opened the supply room door. 'Don't freak. Tiffany's here.'

I made a face and pushed Oscar off my lap. 'Why?' I asked, getting up.

'Because I've got two wedding parties today and I need an extra hand. Now be nice.'

I pasted a smile on my face, but I was not exactly thrilled to see Tiffany. While I liked her as a person, I dreaded her as a co-worker. We had absolutely nothing in common, for one thing. Tiffany was a former anthropology student from Lehigh University who told me once that she became a hairdresser because she found hair 'culturally fascinating.'

However, I found her fashion sense to be one natural fiber short of hideous. Drab green cotton dresses that were shapeless and ended at the ankles. Clunky Birkenstocks and, in the winter, thick brown tights. I had it on good information that she shaved neither her armpits nor legs.

Plus, I don't mean to sound nasty, but she was one lousy hairdresser. I'd never worked with Tiffany when she hadn't caused some incident. Wrong hair color. Frizzy perm. Leg wax that stuck like cement.

Today she was wearing a flowing maroon dress and her hair in dirty blond dreadlocks. There was enough patchouli to stink up a commune.

'Wow! What an outfit, Bubbles. It's, like, so Marilyn Monroe. You should accessorize with a real-live Kennedy.'

I glanced down at my white dress. So? What's wrong with looking like Marilyn Monroe? I should be so lucky.

The bell tinkled again and in rushed the wedding party of six plus Mrs. Illick. With only two sinks, two styling chairs and two bonnet hair dryers, the House of Beauty was going to be packed today.

'Oh, hooray!' cheered Mrs. Illick. 'Tiffany's on the job today. I hope you brought some of that rosewater mask, Tiffany. I drop ten years from my face after one of your rosewater masks.'

Sensing that Tiffany's mask might be a ticket to the fountain of youth, the bride then put in her bid.

Tiffany started playing eenie, meenie, minie, moe.

'Oh, for heaven's sake,' I groaned.

'You might take a page out of Tiffany's book,' Sandy said. 'It could improve your outlook.'

For the rest of the morning I was too busy to think about Tiffany, Merry Metzger, the missing film or, more important, what was happening at Mama's arraignment. I washed, cut, teased and combed like a madwoman. The hours flew.

After treating both Mrs. Illick and the bride to her Miracle Mask, Tiffany was put in charge of highlights. That was considered a relatively safe job since all she had to do was paint strands of hair pulled out of a cap with holes. A child could master that. She started with the maid of honor and moved on to Mrs. Illick.

It was decided that I would handle the styling after

coloration. Sandy was in charge of the bride, who got special attention since this was her special day.

'Hey, Bubbles, was that you who wrote the story about Merry Metzger today? Can't imagine that there'd be another Bubbles Yablonsky in town,' said the bride, whose damp hair Sandy was carefully trimming. 'Looks like those community college classes are finally paying off, say?'

The bride was a woman named Sheila who worked in a travel agency a few blocks away on Second Street. This was Sheila's third marriage and this time she was going to Tahiti for her honeymoon. The last time it was Maui and before that St. Thomas. I think Sheila gets married so she can be the center of attention and take expensive vacations.

I finished towel-drying the maid of honor, a pinch-faced dour woman named Cheryl, who was new to the shop.

'Yeah, I wrote the story,' I said. 'What do you think?'

Before Sheila could answer, Sandy added proudly, 'Henry Metzger threatened to kill her last night if she printed it.'

'No!' said Sheila. 'Though I don't know why I should be surprised. It's not the first time his wife has killed someone, of course, and he's probably on the defensive.'

The scissors nearly fell out of my hands.

'Whoops,' said the maid of honor as I readjusted them. I tried to make eye contact with Sandy, but she was focusing on Sheila's hair. Or pretending to.

'Merry Metzger killed somebody before?' Sandy asked casually, combing up her bangs and giving them a little feathering. 'When?'

Sheila, who was never one to shy away from the limelight, launched into it. 'Ten years ago when she was a senior at Freedom, when her name was Merry Miller. Cheryl and I went to school with the girl who got killed. Didn't we, Cheryl?'

Cheryl nodded.

A prickly feeling crept up my spine as I recalled the sweetfaced girl in a Freedom High cheerleading sweater who visited the House of Beauty ten years ago. Could Sheila be talking about Laura Buchman?

Sheila continued merrily. 'It was never proved that Merry did it, but everyone in school kind of suspected her. Merry was in a bad crowd back then. Lots of hard drugs and parties. Those rich kids in that crowd had so much money they thought nothing of blowing five hundred dollars a night on cocaine or pot. Pretty funny to think that she now goes around town telling teenagers to "Just Say No." '

My head was beginning to swim. Suddenly Cheryl was gone from my chair. In her place was Laura Buchman, pale and ghostly, staring at my reflection in the mirror. I closed my eyes and opened them. Cheryl was back, glancing at me inquisitively.

'Are you okay?' she asked.

'Sure,' I lied. I got down to trimming her ends.

'Who was the girl who got killed?' asked Tiffany, who

had finished highlighting Mrs. Illick's hair and was now putting her under the bonnet hair dryer.

'Her name was Laura Buchman,' Sheila said.

Even though I expected the answer, my heart did a double beat at the sound of Laura's name.

'A real sweetheart,' Sheila went on. 'She never touched a beer or joint or any drug for that matter. The only reason Merry befriended her was because Laura had this cool place on Myrtle Lane out by Camelhump and a pool and her dad was never home. Her mom left the family a few years before that or died or I forget.'

My ears were tilted toward Sheila, catching every word. I suspected Sandy was taking her sweet time on those bangs in order to keep Sheila talking.

'Merry had it out for Laura after Laura fell for Merry's boyfriend, one of those spoiled brats with an attitude that the world owed *him*. He had this band called—'

'Riders on the Storm,' I interrupted.

Sheila looked at me in shock. 'How'd you know?'

I filled Sheila in on Laura Buchman's House of Beauty visit, ending with my frustration that I felt as though everyone but me thought her death was suicide.

'I remember that!' shouted Mrs. Illick from under the bonnet hair dryer. Mrs. Illick had been going to beauty salons for so many years, her ears had evolved to the point where she could hear in a wind tunnel if she had to. 'That was an awful death. So tragic. You've had your suspicions about that for years, say, Bubbles?'

'It definitely wasn't suicide,' Sheila said. 'That was a ruse put out by the cops right after Laura's body was found. The cops figured that by saying her death was suicide, the reputations of the kids under investigation would be protected. But we knew that Laura overdosed on morphine and barbiturates and that Merry and her boyfriend were into heavy drugs. If anyone gave Laura those chemicals, it was them.'

'You sure know a lot about that murder,' Tiffany observed. 'What'd you do, read a book on it?'

'Are you kidding? It was the main topic of dinner table conversation at our house for years. The principal at Freedom used to give updates on the investigation every morning over the intercom. He was all concerned that if kids in school thought it was suicide, there'd be copy cats. You know how teenagers are. So he made a big point of implying to us that it was murder.'

Sandy brought up a blow-dryer. 'Why didn't they charge this boyfriend? How come her death was ruled a suicide?'

Sheila shrugged. 'His dad was a pushy lawyer and superinfluential. The word around Freedom was that his father put up a big stink and got his whole law firm involved. The Lehigh police were so overwhelmed, the investigation went nowhere. In the end, they stuck with the suicide theory. Gave everybody closure.'

Sandy flicked on the blow-dryer and began fluffing up Sheila's hair. 'Sounds to me as though this is a typical situation of parental neglect and pampered children.

As I always say, if you have to become a parent, then you have to put yourself last. Sacrifice. Sacrifice.'

Personally, I want to slap Sandy when she gets on this good-parenting horse of hers. What did she know about parenting? Try raising a teenager for one day, I feel like telling her sometimes, and then we can talk.

'But you still haven't answered my question,' Tiffany pressed. 'Where does Merry Metzger come in? Why, exactly, do you think *she* was the murderer and not her obnoxious boyfriend?'

Tiffany might dress like a bag lady, but she's no one's fool. And she raised a valid point. Murder is an extreme human response, and I couldn't see any extreme reason for Merry to kill Laura. Jealousy over the boyfriend? Perhaps, but it seemed slim.

In order to answer Tiffany's question, Sheila had to shout over the hair dryer. 'Because she was the last person to see Laura alive and the first one to see her dead. Merry found the body. Anyway, there was another reason, too. There was a rumor that after Laura died, Merry was seen—'

'What's that awful stink?' yelled Cheryl.

Sandy lifted her nose in the air. It smelled slightly of fire. And ammonia.

Suddenly Mrs. Illick screamed, 'My hair! I think my hair's on fire!' Her fingers were grasping at the bonnet hair dryer. Smoke was now filling the room and it was emanating right from the top of Mrs. Illick's head.

'The highlights!' Tiffany screamed. 'I forgot to set the timer.'

What I wanted to shout was, Forget the highlights. What was Merry seen doing after Laura's death? Gosh, do I hate when this happens. Gossipus Interruptus.

Sandy walked over efficiently in her beautician's uniform to snap off the bonnet hair dryer and inspect the damage.

'Don't worry!' Tiffany yelled. 'I've got an avocado and mayonnaise treatment that will fix the damage. Mrs. Illick's hair will be silky in an hour.'

Sandy didn't appear convinced as she threw a towel over Mrs. Illick's head – in an effort to put out the last flicker of flames.

'I think I'd like to give my hair another rinse,' said Cheryl, who'd managed to survive Tiffany's highlights handiwork intact, but wasn't about to take any chances.

'Don't blame you,' I said with resignation. No chance of getting the scoop now.

I had just lowered Cheryl's head into the sink when the phone rang. Since both Sandy and Tiffany were in the hair-care crisis of the century, I took it.

'Hey, momma skins, what's up?'

Sandy had deployed the fire extinguisher and was now blanketing Mrs. Illick's head in white foam. Oscar was running around the salon, barking at the top of his tiny lungs.

'Uh, this is kind of a bad time, Jane.'

'Don't you want to know how the arraignment went?'

Boom. I heard a loud shotgun blast in the background.

'What was that, Jane?'

'That? That was nothing.' This girl was the cookie-cutter image of her grandmother.

'That was a musket, wasn't it?'

'Might've been.'

'Genevieve's over, isn't she?'

'Bingo.'

I absently reached for a nonexistent cigarette in a nonexistent pocket. Genevieve was my mother's seventy-year-old, musket-toting, conspiracy-nut friend and partner in crime. She stood six feet tall and weighed close to 250 pounds with shoulders like a linebacker. One night with Genevieve, and Mama is checking the storage shed for Commies and refusing to brush her teeth with Crest.

'Genevieve gave us a ride home for security purposes.'

I looked over at the maid of honor, who had grabbed the hose and was now rinsing herself.

Jane went on. 'She's still here. Fortifying the house. Genevieve and Grandma are convinced that after that article you printed today, Henry Metzger's gonna send one of his hit men to rub you out for sure. Isn't that intense? It's like you're the fugitive.'

Thankfully the other line beeped. I couldn't take the other call fast enough.

'Sandy's House of Beauty,' I answered as brightly as I could manage.

'I'm looking for a Bubbles Yablonsky,' said a crisp male voice.

'You got her.'

'Miss Yablonsky, my name is Dix Notch. I'm the editor-in-chief of the *News-Times*.'

Oh. My. God. Dix Notch. *The* Dix Notch. Maybe he read my story and was blown over by my talent. Maybe he thought I was staff material. Maybe this was my big break!

'Yes?' I said hesitantly.

'Miss Yablonsky, it seems there are quite a few errors in today's accident story.'

'What?'

'Serious errors. For one thing, the paper has been notified that Merry Metzger was out of the country last night and, in fact, has been out of the country since Thursday. In addition, the police are denying they ever talked to a reporter from the *News-Times*.'

I kept my silence, hoping for the best.

'You need to come down to the *News-Times* to talk to our lawyers. Now.'

That was not the best. That was, in fact, the worst. Discovering that the meter maid had finally located my Camaro would be better. Anything would be better than this.

'Things are a little hectic this morning, Mr. Notch,' I replied shakily. For one thing, I had to get out of here and look for that film in the park.

'That's a shame,' Notch said. 'Things are a little hectic

here, too. We've been faxed a letter from Henry and Merry Metzger's counsel. Because of its, uhm, sensitive nature, not to mention its dire consequences for you, I hesitate to read it over the phone. Do you understand now, Miss Yablonsky?'

'Yes, sir,' I whispered.

'Oh, and Miss Yablonsky?'

'Yes, sir?'

'Bring your notes. They'll be crucial to our initial response.'

I hung up, completely forgetting about Jane on the other line.

All I could think of was Dix Notch's parting request and the nagging questions it raised.

Notes? What notes?

Tiffany's Beauty Treatments

To this day I can't figure out how or why Tiffany ended up in the commercial beauty biz. I mean, she dresses like a hippie, she believes cosmetics are the ultimate tools of male oppression, and she disdains all chemicals. Maybe she just appreciates the 'good Karma,' as she would say, of a cozy salon like the House of Beauty. Anyway, these all-natural beauty treatments of hers really work. I tossed my expensive antiwrinkle cream after one application of Tiffany's miraculous egg white and rosewater face-lift. And clients rave about her avocado and mayonnaise therapy, which leaves hair shiny and full. Not Mrs. Illick, though. She won't let Tiffany so much as shampoo her head after the burning highlights fiasco. Too bad. A few mashed avocados might have been the perfect cure for her frizzled locks.

Tiffany's Rosewater Mask

1 egg white
1 teaspoon rosewater (can be found at health food or cooperative grocery stores)

Beat the egg white and rosewater together in a cup. Wash face thoroughly with warm water and pat dry. Apply egg white and rosewater mixture over face with a cotton ball. Let dry – about 20 minutes. Wash off. Face will feel tight and clean for hours.

Tiffany's Avocado and Mayonnaise Hair Repair

1 very ripe avocado
3 tablespoons whole-egg mayonnaise
1 tablespoon honey

Mash the avocado with the mayonnaise. Stir in honey. Rub mix into *dry* hair. Pile hair on top of head and let sit 20 minutes. Stay away from dogs, who find the mixture irresistible. Shampoo twice and condition as usual. Conditions and thickens.

Chapter 9

A LTHOUGH THE NEWSPAPER WAS only a few blocks away, I decided to take my car because it was too hot to walk and I was in a rush to read Metzger's letter. Also, it was a Saturday and meter maids were off duty. I never miss an opportunity to motorize.

I pulled up to the three-story red building that is the *News-Times* and parked right out front on Third Street. To me the *News-Times* resembled Superman's *Daily Planet*, with its red brick and green-edged windows. It was a nuts-and-bolts kind of newspaper, delivering up a consistent recitation of local meetings, high school sports, obituaries and weddings. No flowery prose on its pages. Just good hard facts you could count on when throwing a vote or throwing out a politician.

A janitor let me in the front door, and I bounded up the stairs to the newsroom, feeling a mixture of antici-pation and dread. It was a familiar kind of dread. Like going to the dentist before the days of automatic novocaine.

'Well, well, well,' singsonged a thin, twenty-something black woman sitting at the receptionist's desk. 'You've got to be Bubbles Yablonsky.'

A brass plaque read DORIS DAYE TELECOMMUNICATIONS ENGINEER.

Doris appeared none too happy sitting behind the plaque. She was wearing red-rimmed glasses, a T-shirt that said ONE HUNDRED SEVENTY-SIX THOUSAND MILES PER SECOND ISN'T JUST A GOOD IDEA, IT'S THE LAW and had several intimidating mathlike textbooks open at the receptionist's desk. Correction, the telecommunication engineer's desk.

'You a summer student at the university?' I asked.

'Usually. I'm part time here, Monday through Friday,' she said. 'Today I'm on weekend overtime. Notch called me in to handle the onslaught of phone calls we've been getting from outraged readers. Which reminds me, I have a present for you.' She leaned over to the telephone console and grabbed a shoe box.

'Here. Happy reading. And, by the way, thanks for killing my four-point-oh in biomedical physics. I got a final Monday.'

Inside the shoe box were dozens of 'While You Were Out' pink message slips, each with a message more complimentary than the last.

'Bubbles. You stink,' read one of the more succinct.

'Mrs. Metzger is a saint,' read another. 'She raised four hundred thousand dollars for the Lehigh Valley Animal Shelter last winter. Bubbles Yablonsky should be run out of town.'

But the one that really got me was this: 'Mrs. Metzger spoke to my ten-year-old daughter's class last month and told them to Just Say No to drugs. My daughter came home and told me she wanted to grow up and be just like Mrs. Metzger, she was so pretty and nice. Then this morning my daughter read that Mrs. Metzger got drunk and killed a man. She's been crying all day. I feel Bubbles Yablonsky should apologize to all of us and especially to Mrs. Metzger on the front page.'

'That's my favorite,' said Doris, who was reading over my shoulder. 'That woman made me promise to write down every word. She said something about a petition drive, too.'

I sat down in a heap. All my life I'd lived the quiet existence of a hairdresser. I had friends at the shop, friends in the neighborhood, at the grocery store, in church. Friends all around me. I may not be wealthy. I may not be educated. But one thing is true – everyone likes me.

'What did I do to deserve this?' I asked out loud to no one in particular.

Doris raised her eyebrows. 'What did you do? You wrote that the Nancy Reagan of Lehigh was a Ted Kennedy of Chappaquidick in disguise, that's what you did. Oh, and some police detective called to complain that you quoted cops without identifying yourself as a reporter first. I patched him in directly to Notch.'

Goddamn Mickey, I thought.

'Are you ready?'

'Yeah.'

'Good, I've been wanting to do this all day.' Doris pressed a button on the console. 'Mr. Notch, a Miss Yablonsky is here to see you.'

I heard an expletive and Doris quickly jerked the handset away from her ear.

'He said he'll be right out,' she said. 'I hope you brought cotton for your ears.'

I hadn't brought anything, including notes.

After a few minutes, a violently tanned man in madras shorts and a pale green golf shirt emerged from a side door. He took one look at me in my winter-white, halter-top minidress and gave a little jump. 'Bubbles Yablonsky, I presume,' he said.

'In the flesh.'

'Pretty much. Follow me.'

I hopped up and *clickety-clicked* after him across the linoleum newsroom floor. He opened a door and motioned me into an office.

'Doris?' Notch called over his shoulder. 'Put on the message machine. I need you to come in here and take notes.'

The office was painted a banker's green and looked like it hadn't been redecorated since the Eisenhower Administration. On two wing-back chairs sat two somber men in suits. Lawyers. Doris brushed past me, threw herself onto a red leather couch and began immediately scratching her ankles.

'Miss Yablonsky has arrived,' Notch announced,

walking behind his desk. 'Let the fun begin.'

The two lawyers opened their eyes wide and looked at each other. I guessed they weren't used to a full-figured woman like myself. Most likely they were accustomed to the flat-chested, gray-suited stockbroker types out of the Brooks Brothers catalog.

'Sit,' Notch said, directing me to a wooden chair in the middle of the room. Notch himself sat down at a mahogany desk piled high with files and papers. A fish bowl of candy was perched next to a marble paperweight on which was engraved in dark red, GARNET CORP. Garnet was the largest newspaper publisher in the nation. It owned the *News-Times*.

I sat down on the chair and slowly crossed my legs.

'Please let me see your notes,' Notch said, stretching out his hand.

I took a deep breath. 'Actually, I haven't any.'

Doris brought her pen to a steno pad and started scribbling away.

'None at all?' asked Notch, incredulously.

'Zippo.'

Notch slapped his forehead. 'Miss Yablonsky, the Metzgers are threatening to sue us – and you personally – for three-point-five million dollars on the claim that you negligently and maliciously reported that Merry Metzger went on a bender and killed a man. At the very least, I assumed you would have some notes.'

I shrugged. 'Sorry.'

He turned to the lawyers. 'Well, fellas, what are we gonna do now?'

'To begin with,' the tall lawyer said, 'I'd be curious to hear what Miss Yablonsky has to say.'

'This is Albert Van Kuren,' Notch said. 'A Garnet lawyer who drove up from Philadelphia to help us with this . . . problem.'

I told it as straight as I could, doing my level best to ignore Doris, who was writing down every word. When I was done, my mouth was so dry I could barely whisper.

'Any ideas?' Notch asked.

Van Kuren rubbed his chin. After a while he said, 'The best way to proceed in cases like this might be to admit a degree of negligence right off. In Cooper versus *The Santa Monica Bugle-Register*, the newspaper prevailed because the subject of the article was a public figure and the reporter had been merely negligent, not malicious. The newspaper admitted its mistake the next day in a front-page, above-the-fold correction which, apparently, was enough to satisfy the California Court of Appeals.'

'Yeah, but is Merry Metzger a public figure?' Notch asked.

'She might be and she might not be –' the short lawyer cut in.

'This is Todd Urdis,' Notch interrupted. 'Also a lawyer. He's local.'

'As I was saying,' Urdis continued, 'Mrs. Metzger hasn't held public office, nor has she sought celebrity status. On the other hand, she is the head of a couple of foundations and director of the Lehigh Valley Republican Women's Committee. So there is an argument to be made that, at least in a local arena, she's public.'

'So, that settles it,' said Notch, appearing relieved to a degree. 'Front page correction and we tell Metzger to lump it.'

'Not quite,' Van Kuren, the tall lawyer, said slowly, retrieving a set of white pages stapled together. 'Attached to the Metzgers' letter are notarized affidavits signed by friends of theirs, a Chip and Winifred H. Ritter. My understanding is that identical affidavits have been filed with the police.'

I pinched myself. My ex-husband, Dan, and his evil wife Wendy. Those creeps.

'Winifred Ritter states in her affidavit that she drove Merry Metzger to the airport Thursday night to take an eight-fifteen p.m. flight to JFK Airport. We discussed this statement before Miss Yablonsky's arrival. Do you want me to explain that, Bubbles?'

'No,' I said. 'I've heard about this already.'

'Good,' Van Kuren continued. 'Chip Ritter's affidavit mentions an issue we have yet to discuss regarding a certain statement that Miss Yablonsky apparently uttered to him this morning.'

All three men picked up their copies of the affidavit. As they hadn't been courteous enough to provide me with a copy, I pondered my nails.

Already Peaceful Petunia was chipped. Scientists can create paint on space shuttles that can withstand reentry into the Earth's atmosphere, but they still haven't been able to come up with a decent nail polish that doesn't chip the first day. Where are their priorities?

'It says here,' Van Kuren read out loud, 'that when Chip Ritter, an attorney with the law firm of Ritter and Shemp in Allentown, asked Miss Yablonsky why she wrote the false allegations about Mrs. Metzger, Miss Yablonsky responded: "I was pissed." Miss Yablonsky also said in the same conversation, "I took a risk" regarding her authorship of the said article.'

Van Kuren shook his head. 'That's negligence *and* malice right there. That's quite a hurdle for us to leap.'

Notch looked as though his brain were boiling. I imagined steam blowing out of his ears.

'Okay, Miss Yablonsky,' he said through gritted teeth, 'you got an explanation for that one?'

The bump on my forehead began to throb, and I felt a headache spreading over my entire cranium. 'May I see that?' I asked, pointing to the white papers Van Kuren was holding. He handed them over. I glanced through Dan and Wendy's affidavits and then the letter, which was signed by Max Factor, senior counsel, Lehigh Steel Corp.

'Hey!' I said. 'Max Factor. Like the makeup. Do you think—?'

'Can it,' said Notch sternly. 'Let's hear your response.'

'Okay,' I continued. 'Dan Ritter is my ex-husband—'

'Who's Dan?' Notch interrupted. 'I thought his name was Chip.'

'That's a new nickname he gave himself for society purposes.'

Notch tapped his pencil on the desk. 'If you say so. Go on.'

'Anyway, this morning when I went to his house to drop off my daughter, he asked me about the article.'

The lawyers leaned forward in their chairs. 'But, you see, I misunderstood. I thought he was talking about the picture that appeared today where I'm kind of hanging off the Philip J. Fahy Bridge with Mr. D, my old—'

Notch put up his hands. 'Hold on. Hold on. That was your picture on the front page this morning?'

I nodded.

Doris leaned over and handed him a copy of the paper. Notch spread the paper on his desk. The lawyers got up and read over his shoulder.

'I'll be a monkey's uncle,' he whistled. 'That is you, isn't it?'

'Doesn't the caption mention my name?' Lazy, selfish Lawless, I was thinking.

Notch shook his head. 'Nope. The article doesn't either. You're listed as an unidentified woman.'

I clenched my jaw. What kind of a reporter is so greedy that he won't even give a person credit for saving the life of another human being?

Notch continued to stare at Lawless's article. 'So, in response to the Metzgers' accusation, you're saying it

131

was a misunderstanding, right? That you never had a
gripe against this dame to begin with.'

'Not only didn't I have a gripe against Merry Metzger,
I didn't even know her.'

Notch jerked his head up. 'You didn't?'

'Wouldn't know her to spit on her.'

'Well, then why in the world did you have any reason
to believe it was Merry Metzger in that car?'

I shrugged. 'That's what Stiletto told me.'

'That bum?' Notch turned to the lawyers. 'Stiletto's
the one who left the scene. Which gives you an idea
how responsible AP photographers are.'

Van Kuren and Urdis nodded somberly as though
they knew only too well how irresponsible AP photographers were.

'But Stiletto shot all these pictures of Merry Metzger
in the Range Rover. That might help your case,' I
pointed out.

'Salvo mentioned something about a role of film.
What happened to it?'

I traced my kneecap with a Peaceful Petunia nail.
'Uhmm. I lost it.'

Notch stared at me in disbelief. 'The bimbo's gonna
cost us a million dollars,' he finally declared to the
lawyers.

Van Kuren came to my rescue. 'C'mon, Dix. This
isn't entirely her fault. Keep that in mind.'

'No. That's right,' Notch said. 'It's the fault of my
good-for-nothing night editor Salvo. He had a perfectly

good accident story, written by a veteran reporter, and he scrapped it for three-point-five million of *News-Times* insurance money.'

It suddenly occurred to me that Mr. Salvo wasn't at our meeting. 'Excuse me,' I said, 'but where is Mr. Salvo?'

'St. Luke's Hospital,' Notch snapped. 'Being checked out for chest pains. And it's a good thing, too. Otherwise I'd fire his ass like that.'

Super. How much damage could one Bubbles Yablonsky do in one night?

'You might be interested to know, Mr. Notch,' I said, in a last minute attempt to further my dwindling career hopes, 'that a source divulged to me this morning that Merry Metzer has killed before, in high school. The victim's name was Laura Buchman. I met the girl myself the day of or day before her murder. I think it might make an interesting follow-up story.'

Notch turned a bright red. 'What are you, a crackpot?'

He pointed to the door. 'Out of my office. There aren't going to be any follow-ups! Just corrections. And apologies. And years of embarrassment for this newspaper.'

I got up and walked out the door. 'I'm announcing a new policy,' Notch yelled. 'From here on in, all the crime stuff goes to Lawless. He's the only reporter in this newspaper worth his weight.'

❖   ❖   ❖

To keep from crying, I stood at the second-floor window of the *News-Times* and watched the afternoon sun cast shadows from the spiral-topped blast furnaces over the Lehigh River. I tried to imagine what that riverbank must have looked like before steel came, before the river was lined with smoke-spouting factories and railroad tracks and storage sheds.

The door to Notch's office opened and Doris quietly emerged. I could tell from her sympathetic grin that I had won at least one ally in there. She joined me at the window.

'You give a white man a high horse and a weak woman to drag along the ground and he will ride until she's dog meat,' Doris said. 'Don't let the Dix Notches of the world get you down, Bubbles Yablonsky. You don't look smart, but' – she tapped her temple – 'inside you got brains.'

I felt a tear at the corner of my eye. I was not going to cry. I was not going to cry.

'Thank you, Doris,' I said, taking a tissue from the box she handed me.

'I've been waiting for Dix Notch to get his comeuppance since I started this job. He treats me like I don't know nothing about birthing babies. Doesn't matter that I compute logarithms in my sleep. Someone should take a photo of him picking his nose, which he does *all the time*, and blow it—'

Doris clapped her steno pad on a desk. 'Why didn't those lawyers think of that?'

'What?' I said, balling up the tissue and tossing it into the wastepaper basket.

'To look in the morgue.' Doris turned and began running across the newsroom.

'The morgue?'

'The photo morgue,' she called over her shoulder. 'I'm going to pull a photo of Merry Metzger and have you check it out. Put all this hoo-ha to rest once and for all.'

I didn't stick around for Doris to retrieve the photos. What I did was pick up my purse and scram. I exited the side door of the *News-Times* and made a beeline for the Camaro. Turning the corner, I stopped dead in my tracks. A bright orange steel boot was fastened to my right front tire. On the windshield of my car, above yet another yellow parking ticket, was a big note tucked under the wiper. On it was written one word: Gotcha!

'Damn!' I said, throwing my purse on the ground so that a brush and my makeup mirror fell out.

A short, pudgy babushka with a kerchief on her head trod past me. She took one look at me and then the Camaro with its ugly boot and scolded me in Pennsylvania Dutch.

'Oi,' she said, shaking her head. 'That's no good for you.'

As I gathered up my purse I mumbled some obscenities about what she could do with her blintzes and headed up Third Street. With any luck, Sandy could

135

lend me a couple hundred dollars until Monday for the parking authority. The parking authority insisted on being paid in cash and, of course, this being a Saturday at 4:30 P.M., banks were closed. I'd cut up my ATM card months ago on the advice of an article I read in *Woman's Day* on how to save money.

However, I'm not your average woman, and this was not the average woman's day. It was a golden late summer afternoon. The air was hot, but a cooling breeze blew off the Lehigh. The South Side was alive with music and laughter and smoky barbecue as I marched down the street, seething with anger.

Kids zoomed by on skateboards. Housewives sat on stoops to take a before-dinner break and cool off. Church bells pealed as a bride and groom skipped down the front steps of St. Peter and Paul's Roman Catholic Church.

And I plotted revenge. There was nothing I could do about the Lehigh Parking Authority. Bombing municipal buildings might cause the deaths of innocents. Too bizarre.

Dix Notch was another matter. Yes, I decided, he would have to pay for calling me a bimbo in front of perfect strangers. Dan, too, would have to pay for his raw deception. Lawless would have to be taken down a peg. No, several pegs.

Most of all, the real Merry Metzger would have to be exposed. Her boyfriend's father might have used his influence ten years ago to prevent his son – and perhaps his son's girlfriend – from being charged with murdering Laura Buchman, but it made me physically ill to realize she would pull that same stunt again. This time she was hiding behind the power of her elderly, well-connected husband. Was I going to stand by and let Henry Metzger pull the strings of Lehigh's puppet police department for his own purposes?

In a pig's eye.

Speaking of pigs, how about that Henry Metzger? What a controlling thug, say? Now that he was retired from running Lehigh Steel, I suppose he had nothing better to do than terrorize hardworking hairdressers who were simply trying to improve their lot. So, this was what he meant when he promised to make my life a living hell. Congratulations, Henry, you did it. With one simple letter of lies to Dix Notch, you nixed my career plans and a better future for me and Jane. Bravo!

I was so consumed by my anger that I almost failed to notice a man in a cowboy hat getting out of a red Ford Escort. Or the motorcyclist cruising by my side, a black ski-mask on his face . . .

'Excuse me,' said the motorcyclist. 'Could you tell me—?'

I heard someone shout, 'Watch out!' From behind me came the sounds of footsteps and then – *whoosh!* – I was knocked onto the grass lawn of the Wysocki and Sons Funeral Home as a round of firecrackers exploded over my head and the motorcycle roared off.

All I remember was wondering out loud, 'A ski mask in August? That'd be kind of hot, wouldn't it?'

And hearing Stiletto's voice telling me to be quiet.

Chapter 10

'WHEN I SAY GO, you get up and run,' Stiletto said. 'One, two, three, go!'

I felt a weight lifted off me and then was jerked up to standing. On the sidewalk were glass and bloodstains. I wanted to kneel down and get a closer look, but Stiletto grabbed my hand and practically dragged me across the lawn of Wysocki and Sons until we reached a driveway and a ramp. It was the handicapped access to a side door of the funeral parlor.

A group of people had emerged on the wraparound porch and were now running down to the sidewalk. Someone was shouting, 'Call the police!' Others were asking loudly, 'What happened?'

'In here!' Stiletto ordered, pulling me into a breezeway, down a red carpeted hall and into a tiny room that was overpowered by the perfume of flowers. He slammed the door and locked it. Rose-and-yellow light streamed in from two small stained-glass windows and illuminated rows of uncomfortable-looking oak chairs. Between the windows was a small pulpit, next to which were several potted white lilies and a wreath of white carnations. A sash strung across the flowers said, IN MEMORY OF JACK.

Right behind the wreath was a large mahogany coffin. I was guessing, Jack.

Stiletto sat down on one of the brown wooden chairs and began inspecting the back of his leg. He was wearing a denim shirt and jeans. I noticed that his right calf was dark red.

'Oh my God!' I exclaimed, collapsing on one of the chairs.

'Shhh.' Stiletto crossed his arms over his head and, in one movement, pulled off his shirt. I quickly sneaked a peek at his chest before feigning more interest in his leg. Tan, good. Hair, not much. Washboard, yes, sir.

'Can't believe that bastard nicked me,' he said, ripping off one of the shirt arms and then tearing that in two. He tied a tourniquet around his knee, bandaged his wound, grabbed a chair and elevated his injured leg. Then, I am sad to report, he put on what remained of his shirt. He looked me over and smiled with approval.

'You don't look half bad, for a girl who's just been shot at.'

Until he said that, it hadn't occurred to me that *that* is what had happened. I had been *shot* at. Me. Bubbles Yablonsky. 'Why would anyone shoot at me?'

Stiletto checked out the back of his leg. 'Didn't I warn you about Henry Metzger? If you grew up in

Lehigh, certainly you heard the stories. Those rumors weren't invented out of thin air.'

I told Stiletto about my father and how Metzger's stinginess had caused him to be burned alive. Stiletto nodded slowly as I spoke about the last time I saw Daddy, waving to me as he went to work. About never again riding on his shoulders or hearing him sing at Christmas or smelling his aftershave. And the hardship his death put on my mother who worked from dawn until dark . . . it was too much to explain.

As a sign that he understood, Stiletto leaned over and gave my hand one quick grip. 'Looks like someone really cracked you on the noggin,' he said, lifting my bangs and inspecting my head. 'When did that happen?'

'It happened when you left me alone last night, mister.' I filled in Stiletto about being spooked in the park and then being interrogated by the police. I laid on the guilt thicker than the mayo in Mama's potato salad, and I didn't stop until I saw a glimmer of remorse.

'I'm really sorry about that, Bubbles,' he said, taking both my hands in his. 'I felt bad about leaving you, too. But I had my reasons, and they were good ones and look, you survived, didn't you?'

This was the first time I'd seen Stiletto when it wasn't pitch black or he wasn't wearing sunglasses. The corners of his eyes were creased with tiny crow's-feet. I'm a sucker for crow's-feet. Plus, his irises were a mesmerizing bright blue. Need I say it? *Just like Mel's.*

I tried to keep my mind on what we were talking about. 'Yeah, but you gotta call the police, Stiletto. You're in a heap of trouble.'

'I'll call them when I get around to it,' he said, dropping my hands and leaning back in his chair. 'Anyway, what do I have to worry about? I shot all those photos of the Range Rover with . . .'

I was shaking my head negatively.

He sat forward. 'I don't have all those photos?'

'You don't have all those photos,' I replied. 'After I fell in the park I couldn't find the film. I must have been unconscious for a moment because when I came to, my purse was there but the film wasn't.'

Stiletto thought about this. 'You didn't fall, you were hit, Bubbles. And the person who hit you did so to get the film.'

That sounded outlandish to me. 'No way! I tripped. There was a root or something and I was in these sandals . . .'

'You mean you fell last night just like minutes ago you got in the way of a bullet?' Stiletto touched my knee. 'I'm telling you, Bubbles, you've got to protect yourself. You've got enemies now.'

Bubbles Yablonsky does not have enemies. I tripped and fell, and that was that. Later I was going to go back to that spot in the park and find that film.

'Hey!' I said, hoping to change the subject. 'What're you doing in town, anyway? I thought you were supposed to be back in New York.'

'See, it's like this,' he began. 'I was on I-78 headed to Manhattan last night, and it dawned on me that I'd left you with my unlimited access cell phone. And I said to myself, "Steve. You are one big fool. You leave an unlimited access phone with a woman, do you know what kind of bill she's going to ring up?" So I decided to drop by today and get my phone before you bankrupt me. So, where's my phone?'

I bit a nail. 'Remember what happened to the film? Ditto for the cell phone.'

Stiletto threw up his hands. 'Great. I'm going to have to close that account as soon as I get out of here. God only knows who's got that phone now. I'm glad I came back.'

Gee, and here I had been under the delusion that he was back for me, instead of some fifty-dollar piece of hardware.

'I can understand why you came back to get your phone,' I said, calling his bluff, 'but I don't understand what you were doing in the South Side right when I happened to get shot.'

Stiletto stared at me with those piercing blue eyes again. 'That was pure coincidence. I was minding my own business on a nice summer afternoon, when I saw one of Metzger's goons on a motorcycle heading one way and you the other. I decided to stick around and see what might come of it.'

'How'd you know it was one of Metzger's goons?' I asked.

He started to answer when there was the sound of shuffling feet in the hallway outside the door.

'Listen, Bubbles,' Stiletto whispered, 'I don't want people making a big deal over my leg, so would you mind opening the door? Try to clear out the hallway so I can get out of here without being seen.'

'Then what am I going to do?' I did not like the idea of heading into target practice.

'You'll be safe. The shooter is in Catasauqua by now. He's not going to stick around and get pulled over by the cops.'

The doorknob jiggled. 'Hello!' a man shouted from the other side. 'Is someone in there?'

Stiletto nodded his head toward the door. We both stood up, Stiletto stiffly. He leaned down and kissed me on the forehead. The forehead? I frowned. Stiletto smiled.

Now someone was pounding. 'You in there, open up! This is a private place of business.'

'Coming,' I called out pathetically.

Stiletto grabbed me by the shoulders. He looked deep into my eyes and there passed between us an instant of profound understanding. He didn't have to say it, but instinctively I felt it. Stiletto and I had some common bond. I didn't know what it was, but I knew it was there.

He leaned down and kissed me softly on the lips. The kiss was so gentle and his grip on my shoulders so firm that I wanted to melt into his chest right there.

Here. You take all the responsibility, I wanted to say.

But all Stiletto said was, 'You'll be okay, Bubbles. Keep your chin up. This will be over soon.'

I was about to ask him if he was going for good, but decided that would make me look too needy. So I closed my eyes, backed away from him and unlocked the door. When I opened it a crack, two elderly men, one thin, one fat, in black suits were staring at me in alarm.

'What's going on in there?' asked the thin one as he tried to peer through the opening. 'We have calling hours. This room is reserved.'

I stepped out quickly and closed the door behind me, keeping my hand firmly on the knob.

'I'm sorry,' I said, wiping away a fairy tear with one hand. 'I had to have a minute alone with Jack. Is his wife here yet?'

'Wife?' said the fat one. 'I don't know . . .'

'It was a secret,' I whispered, puffing out my chest enough for distraction. 'Five years and no one knew.'

'Do you mean Mr. Willner and you –?' the thin man asked in a hushed tone. 'But he was a hundred two years old.'

I bit my lower lip. 'Yes. And what a lover. All that experience.' I could have sworn I heard Stiletto laughing on the other side of the door.

The two men glanced at each other awkwardly. The fat man stepped forward and whispered into my ear, 'You weren't there when . . . when he passed on?'

I nodded quickly.

145

'Oh, my,' he said, taking me by the elbow. 'Would you like a glass of water, dear?'

'Yes, please.' I turned to the thin one. 'Would you mind calling me a taxi? I don't think I'm able to drive.'

'Of course.'

Ten minutes later I was in the yellow cab trying to explain, in the best Armenian I could manage, why I needed to be driven only two blocks, from a funeral parlor to a beauty salon.

When I arrived at the House of Beauty, Doris was sitting in my chair sipping a Diet Coke and Sandy was perched on the vanity smoking a cigarette. No brides. No fire. No Tiffany.

'What're you doing here, Doris?' I asked, throwing my purse by the cash register.

'I think the more important question is what the hell happened to you?' Doris replied, taking me in from head to toe.

'No, wait,' Sandy said, hopping off the vanity. 'Let me guess. I'm pretty good at this by now.'

I walked behind the cash register and opened the minifridge. I pulled out a Diet A-Treat Root Beer and popped off the top while Sandy surveyed me.

'Grass stains on the front of her dress, but not the back. Tangled hair. Smudged lipstick. I'd say you got booted, finally, by the Lehigh Parking Authority so you had to walk back when Stiletto drove by and offered you a ride. You guys pulled to the side of the road, made out in a grassy field, experimenting with some unconventional sexual positions, but didn't go all the way because your hair is too twisted. Did I get it right?'

I took a sip of A-Treat. 'How did you know I ran into Stiletto?'

'Because he stopped by the shop all worried while you were gone.'

'He say anything about a cell phone?'

'Nope. Well, was I right?'

'Partly. I got shot at.'

'What!' Sandy and Doris screamed in unison. I told them about the motorcycle and Stiletto's heroism, about hanging out at Wysocki's. Sandy made a comment about Stiletto's arrival at the shop and then at the shooting not being a coincidence.

'So that's what all the commotion was about,' Doris said. 'When I walked down from the newspaper there were cops all over the place. You talk to them?'

I picked out a bottle of clear nail polish and sat down in one of Sandy's wicker chairs. 'No, and I'm not going to. I've had enough of cops, after that bridge fiasco and the Metzger accident.'

'But you've got to,' Sandy said.

'Nuh-uh,' said Doris. 'Bubbles is right. If she starts showing up all of a sudden in cop shops, those guys are so weird they'll start thinking that something's up with her. She doesn't need that kind of headache.'

'Anyway, I'm on the cops' shit list,' I said, applying some clear nail polish over a hole in my stocking.

'They're mad as hell about the accident story. I don't want to go near them.'

'For all you know,' Doris offered, 'it was a cop who shot at you today. That's what I'd be thinking.'

Personally, I thought that was a tad paranoid of Doris to say, but I politely kept my opinion to myself.

Sandy sat down in the wicker chair next to me. 'So, what do you think it means?'

I screwed the top back on the nail polish. 'Maybe the gunman is working for Dix Notch. He definitely wanted to kill me at one point today.'

I told Sandy about the meeting at the *News-Times*. Sandy said she'd been informed already by Doris, who came to the shop looking for me.

Doris opined, 'Dix Notch is a pencil prick.'

'Sounds it,' said Sandy. 'Too bad you lost that film, Bubbles.'

'Stiletto thinks someone hit me over the head to get it last night.'

'That's an exciting theory,' Sandy said. 'Stiletto been watching a lot of James Bond lately?'

'That reminds me,' said Doris. She reached in her back pocket and pulled out a folded paper. 'This is what I ran down here to show you. It might be a little fuzzy because I copied it on the bad copier, but you should be able to recognize Merry Metzger.'

Doris spread out the folded picture on the vanity. It was of a dumpy dark-haired woman with one eyebrow.

I shook my head. 'Doesn't look a thing like her,' I said sadly.

'Good,' said Doris, pulling the picture off the vanity. ''Cause that's Donna Shalala, Secretary of Health and Human Services. That was just a test. This is Merry Metzger.' She put down another picture.

Blonde. Permed. Stylishly dressed. Impeccably made up and loaded to the hilt with diamonds.

'This is her?' I asked. 'This is really her?'

'That's she,' said Doris.

'Is that the woman you saw in the car?' asked Sandy.

'Yes,' I shouted. 'Yes, yes, yes.' Sandy and I high-fived each other.

'Thank you, Doris,' I said, grabbing her by the shoulders and giving her a big hug. 'You just saved my skin.'

Sandy got up and started pacing around the room. 'You know what this means, don't you, Bubbles?'

I took my hands off Doris, who looked grateful for that. 'What?'

Sandy stopped pacing. 'Why would the Metzgers be so worried about this story that they'd sue a newspaper knowing they were in the wrong?'

'Beats me,' I said.

'Think about it,' Sandy said, lighting another cigarette. 'At the very least, the Metzgers could have said nothing. Let it blow over. And if the cops do find some dirt – which, knowing Lehigh's finest, is a long shot – Merry comes forward, admits to being drunk and gets put in rehab. What would she get at the most?'

'Reduced to a charge of manslaughter,' Doris answered quickly. 'Probably all jail time suspended, especially if it's her first offense.'

Sandy blew out a plume of smoke. 'Aha.'

I smiled. Now I knew what she was after.

'See, Doris,' I explained, 'this might not be Merry's first offense. Merry's first offense might be another murder. That might be the Metzgers' *real* concern.'

Doris snapped her fingers. 'What you were talking about in the meeting with Notch, when he called you a crackpot. Have to say, I agreed with him on that one.'

Sandy relayed to Doris the Laura Buchman murder saga. By the end, Doris's brain was cooking, too.

'But Merry Metzger was never charged with that murder, right?' Doris asked. 'So how could this be her second offense?'

'For argument's sake, let's assume that the investigation into Laura Buchman's murder was shut down by the father of Merry Metzger's boyfriend, even though the boyfriend, and maybe even Merry or her other friends, had a hand in Laura's death,' I explained. 'But that doesn't mean that investigation is over. A murder investigation is never over. I learned that in Forensics for Fun and Profit at the Two Guys community college.'

'Yeah, go on,' said Doris, who appeared skeptical. Those mathematical types need it all spelled out.

'So, now, ten years later, Merry Metzger is involved in the death of another person. And, again, she relies on the influence of Lehigh's elite to get her out of hot water. Her husband brings out the lawyers and in turn, the newspaper and the police department cave. But look what's already happened. Already people like Sheila, who knew Merry way back when, are saying, "Oh, yeah. This isn't the first time Merry Metzger's killed." '

'You think people will start talking, is that it, Bubbles?' Sandy asked. 'The old gossip will resurface?'

'The old gossip will resurface. And you better believe that the Metzgers want to shut down that gossip pipeline as fast as possible. The more newspaper stories, the more people will read them and talk. That's why the Metzgers reacted as quickly as they did today, to nix the gossip.'

'Can't shut down gossip,' Doris said. 'Gossip is gospel. Just ask my Aunt Edith.'

'So what we've got to do is take advantage of the open pipeline and find those people from Merry's past who are talking right now,' I said. I downed the A-Treat and threw the can in the trash.

'Like who?' asked Sandy. 'We can't go back to Sheila – she's on her way to Tahiti – and Cheryl wasn't eager to talk.'

'Like Merry Metzger's old boyfriend,' I said. 'You think Riders on the Storm exists anymore?'

'Sure,' said Doris. 'They play every Saturday at the Marquis Motel out by the airport. They're a cult hit with the undergrads. There's one frat on campus that books them every Friday.'

'Really?' asked Sandy.

'I don't get it, myself. But my roommate's into them big time. They're a Doors review band. You wouldn't believe the lead singer. Guy thinks he's the reincarnation of Jim Morrison.'

'What's his name?' Sandy asked.

'Jim Morrison. I'm telling you, the guy's a definite nutcase.'

'They're at the Marquis tonight?' I asked.

'Probably,' said Doris.

'You gotta go there tonight,' advised Sandy. 'But I still have a question. You interview Morrison and whomever else. You gather all this information. Then what are you going to do with it? It sounds like Dix Notch isn't interested.'

'First I might use it to help get me out of this lawsuit,' I said. 'But what I really hope to do is write an article that will show how Merry Metzger relied on her powerful connections to get her out of two crimes – Laura Buchman's death and this latest accident.'

'Whoa!' exclaimed Doris, giving her chair a twirl.

'You think the *Allentown Call* will print that?' asked Sandy.

'Fuck the *Call*,' said Doris, getting up. 'A story like that deserves *The Philadelphia Inquirer* or *The New York Times*.'

I blushed. 'Get real, Doris.'

'Get real, Doris, nothing. I feel like shouting: Watch out world! Bubbles Yablonsky's on her way. She's a one-woman Woodward and Bernstein with three-inch nails and foot-high hair. Stand back or else!'

'Boy, Doris,' Sandy observed. 'You really have a way with words.'

'Yeah? You should see me with a sine curve.'

Chapter 11

SANDY WITHDREW TWO HUNDRED dollars from her savings account and, after much lecturing, got me back in the good graces of the Lehigh Parking Authority. I wrote her a check and asked her not to cash it until Wednesday. Like a trouper, she agreed, on the condition that I take her with me to the Marquis Motel to meet Jim Morrison. I told her I'd pick her up at nine.

For the first time in months, I was able to park worry free on the street outside my house, instead of in my neighbor's garage. I gave the Camaro a kiss on its roof, turned to walk up the steps of my house and immediately noticed a gigantic red-and-yellow hex sign over my front door. A contribution, no doubt, from Mama's friend Genevieve in our now-united war against Henry Metzger's criminal organization.

The second thing I noticed was that all the locks had been changed. I tried ringing the bell, banging on the door. No luck. Shouting was useless.

'*Wheel . . . of . . . Fortune . . .*' blared from the living-room window, where my mother, or someone, had installed a set of steel bars. And then there was the wrought-iron gate to the garden of my neighbor, Mrs. Hamel. Its tips had been filed to sharp points and topped off by a roll of razor wire.

The Northampton County Prison had nothing on my home at 16½ West Goepp Street. Clearly, Genevieve and my mother had missed their calling in the corrections industry.

I was walking past the side of my house toward the back door when a musket muzzle emerged from between the bars across my kitchen window.

'Don't just stand there dawdling,' my mother screeched. 'It's all over the neighborhood how you got shot at down by Wysocki's. Get in here before you get hit by sniper fire again.'

If the outside of the house looked like it could withstand World War II, the inside looked like it should be the set for Pee Wee's Funhouse. Sandbags had been stuck up against the windows. Buckets containing a mysterious mass that looked like white Play-Doh were poised over the door frames, à la Three Stooges. Dried peas had been layered across the linoleum kitchen floor. I noted them in case I wanted to keep my balance while retrieving a late-night snack. And various implements of torture – most of them garden tools – were posted for the ready. Shears. A spade. A shovel. Two trowels. A weed claw and a bag of fertilizer.

Mama, her head barely higher than the kitchen counter, stood in a knee-length camouflage dress, support hose, daisy earrings and bright pink lipstick, a musket shaking in her wrinkled little hands. She looked like a plump, white-haired G.I. Joe fresh from a canasta party.

'What's going on here?' I asked. 'Where's Jane?'

'Genevieve decided she needed an armed escort to work and gave her a ride down to Roly's,' said Mama, leaning the musket against the kitchen counter. 'When was the last time you ate? You want a pierogi?'

The kitchen smelled wonderful. Mama must have baked her famous cinnamon hearts. I picked up a freshly made potato pastry from a white plate on the counter and sat down at the kitchen table. Mama poured a glass of milk and examined the bump on my forehead.

'I got a cucumber poultice that will have that down by morning. Does it hurt?' she asked.

'Only when editors yell at me,' I said, after swallowing the pierogi. I told Mama about the meeting with Notch and the Metzgers' lawsuit. I didn't have to tell her about the shooting at Wysocki's. She probably knew more about that than I did.

'Well, what on earth were you thinking when you wrote that story anyway?' Mama said, placing the milk in front of me. 'Didn't you know who you were messing with?'

'Listen, Mama,' I said, biting into my second pierogi, 'the story's true. I'm not lying.'

'I've no doubt it's true. That's not the point. What I want to know is how could you forget the lesson of

Brother Joe Padukis?' She grabbed my half-eaten pierogi. 'Let me heat that up for you in the microwave. You'll get worms eating that cold.'

Oh, super, I thought as Mama stuck the pierogi in the microwave. Here comes another one of my father's union folktales. Union members used to refer to each other as *brother* down at steel, and I'd been hearing about 'brother this' and 'brother that' since childhood.

'Brother Joe Padukis was a gung ho union leader, used to work with your father down at the ingot mold in the early sixties,' Mama began. 'When the ingot mold went out on strike, all the other steel families contributed to the families of the guys on the line. You know, they made us casseroles and bought us groceries. Kept us fed, basically.'

The microwave beeped, and Mama brought out the steaming pierogi. In Mama's universe, anything not heated to five hundred degrees causes disease. 'One night, after a long day on the picket line, Brother Joe comes home to find his freezer filled with steak. Thinks: great. Cooks one up. Just as he's down to the gristle, the telephone rings.'

' "How was Buster?" the voice says. Brother Joe throws up right there.'

I held the half-eaten pierogi in my hand. 'Let me guess,' I said. 'Buster was his dog.'

'Try his uncle. That's how evil Henry Metzger is.'

I dropped the pierogi onto the plate.

'Buster Padukis. Worked thirty-four years in the warehouse. The night before Brother Joe got the call, Buster went down to the store for a quart of milk and was never seen again. That is, before he popped up in his nephew's freezer.'

I pushed the plate away from me. 'Didn't Brother Joe call the cops?'

'Sure.' Mama began wiping the counter. 'He called up and said, "Don't laugh, but I think I just had my Uncle Buster for dinner."'

'And?'

'And they hung up on him.'

'What about Buster's disappearance? Didn't the cops investigate that?'

'Oh, they asked a few questions. Once they got word that Henry Metzger was involved, though, they shut the case. The cops claimed Buster was seen driving to Atlantic City. Just another man escaping the wife and taking his chances at the craps table. Bunch of malarkey, if you ask me.'

'And what happened to Brother Joe?'

'Quit his job the next day. Last I knew, he was selling bait outside Scranton.'

'Times have changed,' I said halfheartedly. 'Henry Metzger's not even chairman of the board anymore, and Mickey Sinkler said the cops aren't intimidated by steel now. He says they're more professional.'

Mama took the half-eaten pierogi and wrapped it up. Waste not, want not. 'Don't you believe it. Henry

Metzger will always run this town as long as he's alive. Mickey's a nice guy, but I've known his mother for years. We're not talking a family of geniuses, if you get my drift.' She held up a finger. 'However, that doesn't mean you should write him off as a husband. Some of the best husbands are stupid.'

'I'm not interested in Mickey,' I said, drinking my milk.

'Yeah, you're interested in sex. I know you. You got the hots for that Stiletto fellow.'

I nearly choked. 'What? How do you know about him?'

Mama took my cup over to the sink and began washing it. She's so short she had to stand on her tippy toes to turn on the water. 'As soon as I heard the words *a dead ringer for Mel Gibson*, I thought, uh-oh, my Bubbles is cooked.'

'You've been talking to Mrs. Sinkler.'

Mama put the cup in the rack. 'Let's just say, I got my sources. And stop doing that with your hair. It makes you look so *cheap* when you twirl it like that.'

I untangled my hair and walked over to the refrigerator, mindful of the peas, to get an apple. 'Anyway, Stiletto and I aren't going anywhere. He flies all over the world. He's flying to Mexico City on Monday.'

'You *shtup* yet?'

I crunched into the apple. 'Pardon me?'

'You know. Scrump. Poke. *Shtup*. What are you, deaf?'

160

'That's a pretty personal question, don't you think?' I asked, narrowing my eyes.

'Excuse me, Miss High and Mighty,' Mama sniffed, looking up at me. 'I was *about* to give you some very valuable sexual advice. But I guess your sex life is so roaring you don't need it.'

I swallowed a bite of the apple. '*You*? You are going to give me sex advice?' I imagined Mama's sexual advice centered on the magic of meat loaf, mashed potatoes and ironed underwear.

'How do you think I got Carl Johnson panting after me like a dog?' Mama pulled out a file from the pocket of her camouflage dress and began shaping a nail.

'Aha, so it is Carl Johnson. Mrs. Sinkler was right.'

'Mrs. Sinkler can eat her heart out. Try adding Roger Nisbet, Mat LaBounty and Alfredo Caggiano to that list. Not to mention Harry Hamel next door. I caught him giving me the eye.'

I shifted to one foot. 'What are you on these days? Heavy dose estrogen? What's gotten into you?'

'New attitude on life. I wasn't landing any husbands cruising funerals, so I visited a farmer's wife out in Pennsylvania Dutch country. A little witchcraft does wonders for a woman.'

I finished my apple and threw it in the garbage. 'You saying I need to see a witch?'

'Bah,' Mama scoffed. 'I remember everything she told me, and I'll tell it to you for free.'

'Yeah. Like give me an example.'

161

Mama held up a finger. 'Every night dip your feet into a peppermint bath. Relieves tired feet and if you add a drop of cinnamon oil men go crazy.'

'They do?'

'Sure. The witch said cinnamon's a natural aphrodisiac. Ever know a man to turn down a hot cinnamon roll?'

She had me there. 'Go on,' I said. 'You got my attention.'

'Number two: Take chances during the week of a full moon.'

'Hijacking a senior shuttle. Would that count?'

'In the witch's book it would.'

'I can't wait to hear the next one.'

'Number three: When he's not looking, stick a raw carrot in his shorts.'

'How could he not notice a raw carrot in his shorts?'

Mama ignored me. 'And, finally, this is the important one, Bubbles, bleach your mustache once a week.'

I slapped my head. 'That's the stupidest love advice—'

'Here's a bonus one the witch threw in for five extra bucks,' Mama said, pulling me down to her level.

'Keep your legs together until he proposes marriage,' she whispered in my ear.

I thought about this, about Mama's change in behavior, the bikini, the food fight, the hijacked senior shuttle and the stolen dress. Then I was struck by a disturbing image.

'Are you saying, LuLu Yablonsky, that before the witch gave you this advice, you didn't keep your legs together?'

'I'm the mother of Bubbles Yablonsky, ain't I? The apple don't fall that far from the tree.'

Mama's Peppermint Pep-Me-Up

At Mama's age how you feel is almost as, if not more, important than how you look. Which is why she's been a big fan of Epsom salts for a long time. I can remember Mama coming home from a grueling day of cleaning houses – vacuuming, scrubbing, running around picking up other people's trash – and pulling out the milk carton of salts. What she didn't know then is that peppermint is a wonderful stimulus for tired feet. Combined with Epsom salts and warm water, this peppermint foot soak of hers is both relaxing and exhilarating. Now all you need to do is flip out the footrest on the BarcaLounger and turn on *Wheel of Fortune*.

2 cups Epsom salts
1 gallon warm water
2 peppermint tea bags
1 cup boiling water
1 or 2 drops cinnamon oil (depending on your mood)

Brew two peppermint tea bags in one cup of boiling water. Let sit 10 minutes and remove bags. Meanwhile, dissolve Epsom salts in warm water in a tub large enough for both your feet. Mix tea with the Epsom-salt bath and stir. Add cinnamon oil. If water is too hot, add a little cold water. Soak for 15 minutes. Feet will feel exhilarated and tingly. Great for removing foot odor.

Chapter 12

MAMA WAS REQUIRED TO check in frequently with the Lehigh Police Department now as one of the conditions of her release on charges of shoplifting (a felony because the dress was three thousand dollars) and assault (misdemeanor, for allegedly kicking a salesgirl in the shins).

By all accounts, her court case was pretty unspectacular. The judge had released Mama on five thousand dollars' bond, of which she had to pay ten percent. He instructed her to stay out of trouble and mind her p's and q's until a Northampton County Grand Jury heard her case in about forty days. In the meantime, Mama was to report to the police station three times a week. Since this was her first offense, Mama was hoping the grand jury would be lenient and not charge her at all.

Normally, I wouldn't mind driving Mama over to the police, but I wasn't too keen on running into Mickey Sinkler again. The last time we spoke he wanted to strangle me. Mama consoled me that Mickey's anger was merely to mask his growing lust. When I pointed out that I didn't want to deal with Mickey's growing lust, either, Mama noted that keeping several men on the line at once was also part of the witch's game plan.

'Keep your options open,' Mama said. 'You never know. Mickey might turn out to be the one for you.'

That I highly doubted.

Fortunately, there was no sight of Mickey when we pulled up to the station, and it was a good thing, too. With my fire-engine-red, spaghetti-strap cocktail dress, red sequined high-heeled pumps and cubic zirconia dangle earrings ($19.95 Home Shopping Club), Mickey would have driven himself crazy trying to decide whether to kill me or kiss me.

I was hotter than a chili pepper steeped in Tabasco.

'You stay in the car,' Mama instructed as she got out of the Camaro. 'I don't want you getting anywhere near the cops.'

'How come?'

'You'll get busted for streetwalking in that getup, that's how come.' Mama slammed the door and trotted off. I had convinced her to leave the musket at home, but she insisted on wearing the camouflage. She said she wasn't taking any chances with Metzger's marksmen.

Thanks to Metzger's supposed marksmen, Mama had decided to temporarily move in with me. She said it was the only reasonable thing to do, for safety's sake. When I protested, Mama assured me that Genevieve would also be at the house to provide backup.

'She belongs to that militia group out in Nazareth, you know,' Mama said. 'Genevieve's got military connections. Plus free scrapple.'

When she said this, I realized right then that for the next few days, weeks or however long it took for this Metzger matter to be finished, my life would be directed by Mama and Genevieve. No longer would my house be my own. There would be DentuCreme and Epsom salts in the bathroom. Full-volume *Price Is Right* in the living room and scrapple in the refrigerator. I loathed scrapple. It was supposed to be a type of sausage, but to me it tasted like a dirty sponge.

I sat behind the wheel and watched in the rearview mirror as Mama headed over to the police department. And I asked myself: Do you trust this woman, Bubbles? Do you trust this woman who, on the drive over, asked, 'They're not gonna strip-search me, are they?'

Sure enough, in the rearview mirror I saw Mama take an abrupt right into the Lehigh Public Library, conveniently avoiding the stairs to police headquarters.

I scrambled out and caught her just as she was turning into the children's section. I escorted her into the PD and didn't let go until a scrub-faced female police officer took Mama down the hall to be frisked. While I waited, I flipped through a magazine about police equipment and glanced around the cement-walled lobby.

Mama emerged ten minutes later with Mickey Sinkler at her side. 'Look who I found!' she exclaimed.

I tried to hide my face behind the latest issue of *Law Enforcement Supply*.

'Bubbles Yablonsky, why I . . . Holy mackerel!' Mickey whistled as his eyes roamed over every one of my curves. 'You look terrific . . . even if I do want to swirl your head in the toilet.'

'Didn't I tell you?' Mama gave him a nudge.

'Where are you going tonight, Bubbles? Maybe we can meet up when I get off duty?' Sinkler was at my side now, breathing sour milk breath all over my new outfit.

'Shrimp night at the HoJo's,' I replied cheerfully. 'All you can eat.'

Sinkler gave me the thumbs-up. 'Be there or be square,' he said.

'Why did you lie to him?' Mama asked as we got back in the Camaro.

'Because he's a nerd with five kids.'

'Yeah, but he's an employee of the Lehigh Police Department with full benefits.'

'One of which,' I pointed out, 'is that he's not married to me.'

The Marquis Fly-By-Night Lounge was a karaoke bar located off the lobby of the Airport Marquis Motel on Catasauqua Road. Reflective disco balls hung from the ceiling, which was illuminated by pink and blue lights. I recalled that the place had once been a Chi-Chi's, which might explain the stucco walls behind the bar and the pervasive odor of melted Velveeta.

Sandy and I immediately loved the Marquis Fly-By-Night because we got carded at the door.

'That made me feel sixteen,' Sandy exclaimed, belly-ing up to the bar and ordering a Mudslide. Sandy looked sixteen, too. A 1978 sixteen, straight from the dance floor of *Saturday Night Fever*. Right down to the blue chiffon dress that transformed into a blue parachute when she twirled.

'We gotta take you shopping,' I said. 'Didn't you wear that to the prom?'

'Maybe,' she said defensively. 'What's it to you? How many times do I go to a place like this?'

That was true. Martin and Sandy *never* leave their house. Sandy says it's because Martin has to get up so early to mix the dough and make the doughnuts. Usually they're in bed by 7:30 P.M.

'Anyway,' Sandy told me, 'Martin and I don't need to go out. As Martin says, if you can't find happiness with a pumice stone, where can you find it?'

'A pumice stone?'

'Absolutely. One of the many ways Martin spoils me is by pumicing my heels.' Sandy sipped her drink. 'It's our Friday-night ritual.'

Being single was looking better and better.

The bartender handed me a Diet A-Treat Cola with lime. My usual. Sandy asked him for a light, and with the straightest face I could manage, I asked him if he knew how I might connect with Jim Morrison.

'Write him a note,' the bartender instructed, sliding over a white pad and a pen. 'All the chicks want to meet Jim, but Jim don't want to meet all the chicks. You might be an exclusion to the rule.'

Gee. I was flattered.

I wrote a brief note to Mr. Big Shot explaining that I was a reporter who wanted to discuss Merry Metzger as part of a profile. The bartender gave the note to a waitress who slipped it in her cleavage.

Sandy opened her purse and pulled out a package. 'This is for your new investigative journalism career.'

The package was wrapped up in 'graduation' paper and had a white bow. It turned out to be a bright yellow Radio Shack tape recorder, already equipped with batteries and tapes.

'Thanks,' I said, giving Sandy a kiss on the cheek. 'You shouldn't have.' I had remembered to bring a thin reporter's notebook, having learned from the Dix Notch experience this afternoon that in journalism, apparently, notes are good.

'I figure with everyone doubting your credibility lately, this might come in handy,' Sandy said, downing her Mudslide like it was Ovaltine.

I switched it on but it didn't start, even though the recording light was red.

Sandy pointed to a button on the side. 'You've got it on pause. I knew this was a risk, seeing how you are with electronics. This was the easiest model they have. It's for kids.'

Indeed, all the buttons were in bright colors. Red. Green. Blue. Purple.

Suddenly, the lights dimmed and a bass drumbeat filled the room. Sandy and I swung on our stools and turned our attention to the stage where a group of women my age gathered around a mahogany coffin. Not often you see a mahogany coffin in a hotel lounge.

The *thud, thud, thud* from the bass drum grew louder. A Grim Reaper type in a black robe appeared at the microphone and someone shut the doors. The room was nearly pitch black now except for a spotlight on the Reaper and the coffin.

'In 1971,' the Reaper's monotone voice boomed over the microphone, 'James Douglas Morrison, leader of the Doors, the most awesome rock-and-roll band ever assembled, died in his bathtub in Paris . . . Or so they say.'

The bartender tapped my shoulder. 'That's your guy,' he said, pointing to the coffin.

No duh, I thought.

Smoke emanated from beneath the coffin, and the women at the foot of the stage began to scream and raise their Bud Lights. The bass got louder. *THUD. THUD. THUD.*

'The day was July third. The time was five a.m. And the cause of death . . . has never been determined.'

More screams, more thudding.

The coffin lid began to rise, the smoke so thick that the women were now invisible.

'Tonight, ladies and gentlemen,' the Reaper's voice lifted, 'tonight, Jim Morrison lives. And he's not in Paris. He's not in heaven. He's not in hell. He's live! At the lovely Marquis Fly-By-Night Lounge conveniently located next to the Allentown-Lehigh-Easton Airport, eastern Pennsylvania's fastest-growing airport and hub to Allegheny Airlines.'

Sandy smacked her forehead and took a gulp of her second Mudslide.

'C'mon, c'mon, c'mon, c'mon now touch me, babe,' boomed a voice from the coffin.

The resurrected Jim Morrison leaped from the coffin, as best as a living human being can leap from a coffin, grabbed the microphone and finished the rest of 'Touch Me.' One woman collapsed in excitement, right there on the stage.

Now, I like the Doors. But, to tell you the truth, I'm more of a Rolling Stones type of gal. In my opinion, Mick Jagger is heads and tails sexier than Jim Morrison ever was.

Still, there are women who feel otherwise, and most of them were here at the Airport Marquis Fly-By-Night Lounge. I tried to fathom the attraction. Like the real and dead Jim Morrison, this one was willowy trim. His wavy hair fell to his shoulders. His pants were hip-hugging leather jeans and, of course, there was no shirt. Just a slightly oiled hairless chest. Such attire would not be acceptable at a place like, say, Wysocki's, where most stiffs are decked out in formal attire.

For a recently resurrected guy, Jim showed boundless energy through the first half of the show. Jumping on and off the coffin during 'L.A. Woman.' Howling into the microphone at the end of 'Riders on the Storm.' Sweat poured down his body in buckets.

At intermission, Sandy and I found a table. The waitress handed Jim the note and pointed in our direction. Jim took one look at me in my fire-engine-red, spaghetti-strap number and sauntered over. He collapsed in a chair, ordered a bottle of spring water and stared blatantly at my breasts.

Sandy and I identified ourselves as freelance journalists doing a puff piece on Merry Metzger. Yes, it was a lie. But people were shooting at me. Now was not the time to debate ethical fine points.

'Is Jim Morrison your real name, or did you make it up?' Sandy wanted to know.

'It's my real name,' he replied seriously. 'I got it changed legally four years ago. What's that got to do with Merry Metzger?'

'Just curious,' Sandy said primly.

'Yeah,' Jim replied, a tad hostilely I thought. 'I'm curious, too. Why the sudden interest in Merry? This have anything to do with that bullshit story in the paper today?'

Whoops! Time to go.

'As a matter of fact it does,' piped up Sandy. 'You're looking at its author right there.' Sandy pointed at me.

Thanks a lot, pal, I thought.

'Bubbles feels so bad about what she wrote that she'd like to write something nice, to make up. Say, Bubbles?'

I swallowed hard and began rambling about how, to correct its grievous error, the *News-Times* was planning a front-page feature on how wonderful Merry Metzger was, how she had dedicated her life to eradicating drugs and alcohol from the schools. I apologized up and down for being *so* mistaken at the accident scene in the Saw Mill Park. Mere inexperience, I said. Stupid dumb-blonde me!

As I spoke, Jim Morrison scrutinized my outfit, taking a deep drink from his bottled water. I, in turn, took in his whole shtick, from the slim metal cross around his neck to the tiny one in his ear. This was more than fashionable religious jewelry; this guy was paying penance to God.

When he put the bottle down, he said, 'You don't look like a reporter, you look more like a—'

'Don't say it,' Sandy warned. 'Bubbles gets pretty touchy about those kinds of comments.'

'Hey, I'm not complaining,' he explained. 'I think every woman oughta show off her best features. Men dig it.'

I was about to deliver my standard line, that I don't dress this way to entertain men, but Jim was now pointing a finger at Sandy, who sat primly in her blue chiffon. 'Like you, for instance. That's no way for a woman to dress. Show some leg. If you got leg, that is.'

Jim peeked under the table to check if Sandy had leg.

Sandy turned so red her blue dress went purple. 'Mr. Morrison,' she said officiously, 'this is not a social visit.'

Jim popped his head up. 'I gathered as much.' He turned back to me. 'So, what do you want to know?'

'Let's start from the beginning,' I said, pulling out the yellow tape recorder. 'I understand that you knew Merry from as far back as high school.'

'That's correct. What is that?'

'It's a tape recorder.'

'I think my nephew's got one like that. He's in kindergarten. Is the green button Play?'

'Anyway, Mr. Morrison, back to the interview. You and Merry dated?'

'For a while. Then she met Henry when she worked the summer before our senior year in high school operating the elevators at steel. Once she hooked up with him, I was out of the picture. Henry was love at first sight, she told me.'

I calculated the age difference in my head. 'He must have been forty years older than her.'

Jim laughed. 'Still is. Although I think the age difference is more than that. I think it's fifty years. Merry had a thing for older men. Much older men.'

At that moment a woman who appeared to be a lifetime subscriber to *Hooter's Waitress Monthly* passed by. She was dressed – if you can call it dressed – in a supertight, low-cut white T-shirt and electric-blue Lycra hot pants. I would have killed for those shorts. I would have killed for her hair. It was the biggest hair I'd ever seen.

'Hi, Jim,' she gurgled with a wave of her fingertips.

He whipped his arm around her waist. 'Where you going, babe?'

She eagerly plopped down on his lap and threw her arms around his neck.

'This is Cindy,' he said. 'Say hi, Cindy.'

'Hi, Cindy,' she said with a giggle.

Jim ran his lips over her neck. 'She's adorable, isn't she?'

I pushed the tape recorder to the couple. 'How'd you do your hair? You use mega control?'

'Nuh-uh,' said Cindy as Jim nibbled her earlobe. 'It's called hair cement. You have to order it by mail. I got it from the same place I got this shirt.' She stuck out her chest.

'Oh, baby,' Jim said.

'You got the address for that mail-order place?' I had to get me some of that attire, not to mention that hair cement. How many years had I been searching for a product like that?

Sandy kicked me under the table. 'Let's not forget why we're here, Bubbles.'

'Oh, yeah, right.'

Cindy got the message and hopped off Jim. 'It's been fun. See ya!' She gave us another fingertip wave.

'See ya,' we said in unison.

'So, besides having a grandfather complex,' I said after Cindy left, 'what was Merry Metzger like as a teenager?'

I pretended to take copious notes as Jim Morrison delivered me a long line of hooey. To hear him tell it, Merry Metzger was some Pollyanna way back when. Always helping others. Always concerned about the alcohol and drugs her peers consumed but that she, of course, never touched. Even then she was an antidrug activist, at times risking her own popularity for The Cause.

'I never did drugs myself, personally,' Jim bragged, pointing to his hairless chest.

'No?'

'I don't know why,' he said, with the piety of a Quaker. 'Maybe it's because I've always viewed my body as a temple.'

To which women were expected to offer themselves in sacrifice, no doubt. 'How about Merry? How come she became so virulently opposed to drugs?'

He bowed his head and began peeling the label off the water bottle. 'There was a horrible drug-related death when were in high school. It changed Merry forever.'

I flipped over the tape. 'Go on.'

'There was this girl, Laura Buchman. I knew her *vaguely*. She got so screwed up on acid or whatever it was she was taking, she killed herself during some bad trip.'

Blah, blah, blah, blah, blah, I thought, scribbling on the notebook.

'Oh, that's an awful story!' Sandy feigned shock. Go Sandy!

'I think that was the defining moment for Merry. That's when she made up her mind to spend her life crusading for zero tolerance in the schools.'

'You don't say,' I said. 'And Merry knew this girl?'

'Oh, yes. In fact, sadly, Laura was her closest friend.' Jim ran a hand over his eye. 'It was Merry who found the body. Stopped by to pick up Laura for cheerleading practice and, well, there she was. Dead.'

I shut my notebook. 'That's an incredible tale. It tells me,' I paused thoughtfully, 'so much about what motivates Merry to sacrifice herself tirelessly.'

Jim looked up and smiled. 'It does, doesn't it?'

'I think it is such a moving saga that I'd like to talk with other women in town who might have been close friends with Merry and Laura at the time. Know anyone?'

He drummed his fingers on the table as though this were a tough, tough question.

'Well, most have moved away, of course.' Now he was tapping his chin. 'There is this one girl, I mean, woman. Her name is Athena . . . Adler. Yes, that's it. I couldn't remember her married name there for a minute. Athena Adler. Lives out in Saucon Valley now. She might be able to add something.'

'And you and Merry are still friends, of course,' I said, fishing.

Jim shook his head. 'Gosh, I haven't seen her in years. Not that we had a falling out or anything, but with her schedule and my schedule . . . We're both so busy.'

'Hmmm,' Sandy said. 'Such a shame how rushed everyone is these days.'

'Isn't it?' Jim said.

What was this? A murder investigation or a garden party?

'Also, you might . . .' Jim glanced over my shoulder, and in a flash, his face went pale. Even in these dark surroundings Jim was as white as a ghost.

He leaned toward me. 'Tell me now,' he whispered. 'Are you working for Henry Metzger?'

I made a face. 'What?'

'Shhh,' he said, a trickle of perspiration running down his cheek. 'Don't turn around. When I stand up, you stand up. Then I'm going to kiss you. Then get your ass out of here as fast as possible.'

My heart started beating like a hummingbird's.

'What is it?' Sandy hissed.

'Just do what I tell you, okay?'

'Okay,' I said.

Jim stood up. I stood up. He pretended to look shy. 'I don't usually do autographs,' he said loudly. 'You got something to write on?'

I was going to hand him my reporter's notebook, but thought better of it. Instead, I pulled out a House of Beauty business card. I crossed out STYLIST and wrote over it *Reporter*, right under the purple profile of the pug-nosed woman with the mass of curls. The House of Beauty logo.

'You're a hairdresser?'

'More like a hairdresser slash reporter,' I corrected.

'That explains the getup.' He put the card on the table and signed it.

When he handed it to me, I said in a low voice, 'Keep it.'

He looked at me and shrugged. He stuck the card in the back pocket of his leather jeans, put his hand behind my head and kissed me. Long and hard. I threw my arms around him as though this were my raison d'être.

'Hey!' Sandy shouted. 'What gives?'

'Wow!' I exclaimed. 'Thanks a lot!'

'Anytime, babe,' he said with a wink, before turning and heading back to the stage.

I sat down and turned my eyes sideways toward the bar. On the exact stool where I had been perched was a large man facing us with both arms spread behind him across the bar. He was wearing a black jacket and white shirt, open at the throat. His head reminded me of a block of cement, and he was staring directly at me.

Our eyes met, and a smirk spread slowly across his face.

'What is going on?' Sandy wanted to know.

'We gotta go,' I said, shoving the tape recorder and notebook into my purse. 'Don't look now, but one of Metzger's thugs is at the bar.'

'What?' Sandy's eyes fluttered.

'I think it might have been the guy who took a shot at me this afternoon at Wysocki's. Though it's hard to tell. He had a ski mask on.'

'Oh, no!' Sandy said. 'What're we going to do?'

'I have no idea.'

'Look,' Sandy shouted, pointing to exactly where I told her *not* to look.

'Jesus, Sandy . . .' Then I turned and saw what had caught her attention. Stiletto, hands in pants pocket, chatting up the goon on the stool as friendly as pie.

Martin's Friday Night Pedicure

I was completely clueless when Sandy mentioned Martin's love of the pumice stone. What was she talking about? Well, I asked Martin, and he scribbled down his no-fail system for a perfect pedicure. I followed his instructions and became an immediate convert. I don't know which step I relish the most, the warm soak, the refreshing salt scrub or the soothing lotion massage. Put them all together and Martin's Friday Night Pedicure is heavenly. Feet feel and look beautiful. Plus there is something enticing about having someone of the opposite sex running their fingers through your tootsies. Now, if only I could get Mel Gibson to give me one.

Liquid soap or shower gel, preferably one with mint

Tub for soaking feet
Two towels
Toenail clipper
Manicure stick
Pumice stone
Sea salt rub (can be found in 'foot section' of drug store, along with pumice stone)
Nail file
Buffer
Lotion
Nail polish (red is classic)

First, mix a dollop of soap in with a gallon of warm water. Soak feet for 15 minutes. Remove and dry. Clip toenails and push back cuticles. File nails so that they are square. While one foot soaks, rub the other with a sea salt rub to remove excess skin. Rinse foot. Wet pumice stone and rub on heels and balls of feet, anywhere there are callouses. Rinse again. Dry and massage in nice-smelling lotion, rubbing from the calf down. Pay special attention to the tops of feet and toes. Wrap foot in hot towel. Repeat on other foot. Buff nails and apply polish.

Chapter 13

I DIDN'T HAVE TIME TO digest the scene of Stiletto mixing with the thug, although a million questions ran through my brain. Was Stiletto in on it? Was that how he knew I was going to be shot at down by Wysocki's? Is that why he didn't want to stick around Merry Metzger's accident?

'C'mon, Bubbles,' Sandy said, getting up. 'Now's our chance. The guy's not even looking at us.'

Sandy was right. I got up and followed her along the wall toward the door.

'Move it!' Sandy yanked me into the lobby. 'I don't want to get shot at like you. Let's hoof it.'

Unfortunately, Sandy and I were both in three-inch spiked high heels. So hoofing, really, was not a viable option. Mincing was the best we could manage. Mincing across the tile floor of the Airport Marquis.

We pushed through the revolving door of the air-conditioned main entrance and exited onto the Marquis's circular driveway. A warm breeze was blowing from the airport, and there was the roar of a jet taking off right above our heads. Two men in dark blue suits stood with their briefcases, chatting. Their coats flapped as the plane passed.

'Now what?' asked Sandy, glancing back at the lobby.

'Now this,' I said as the free airport shuttle arrived. I grabbed Sandy and pushed her in line with the businessmen.

'You're nuts,' Sandy said as we plopped down on the shuttle seats. 'That guy on the stool was nothing more than a salesman on a business trip. I think you're getting paranoid.'

I watched from the window as the shuttle pulled away and headed for Airport Road. I might be paranoid, but paranoid was a sight better than being dead.

'Yeah?' I said. 'Then what was Stiletto doing talking to him?'

Sandy shifted in her seat. 'I don't know. I don't have all the answers. I got my mind on other things.'

'Like what?'

'Like going to the bathroom. I've had to go for the past half hour.'

I walked shakily to the back of the shuttle and looked out the rear window. The Marquis driveway was empty. Whew. We had made it. For now.

'No standing,' the bus driver boomed.

The shuttle took forever to get to the airport, largely because of the construction on Airport Road. Orange cones glowed in the darkness. I was glad I didn't have to make a plane in five minutes.

Finally, the shuttle let us off at the first door of the main airport. US Airways and Delta. Once inside, Sandy started reading the overhead signs out loud like the hick she truly is.

'Restaurant. Newspapers. Telephone. Bar. Luggage. Where's the sign for the ladies' room? I don't see a sign for the ladies' room.' She was shouting in panic and jiggling her knees. A woman passing by in a black pantsuit curled her lip in disgust.

I wasn't reading the signs. I was searching for gun barrels.

At 11:00 P.M. on a Saturday night, the A-L-E Airport was surprisingly deserted. The only counter open was US Airways, which had a long line for the Boston shuttle. I studied each face in the line and checked the automatic doors. With everyone else dressed in street clothes, Sandy and I stood out like hookers at an Osmond Family Reunion. We might as well have been naked.

'Women's Bathroom. I see it!' Sandy yelled, pointing to the universal sign of a woman. She grasped my hand. 'Let's go or I'm going to wee right here.'

I followed Sandy until we turned a corner. 'Here it is,' Sandy said and jerked me into the ladies' room, nearly knocking over a yellow DO NOT ENTER sign and a cleaning woman along the way.

I closed the door and turned the metal lock crosswise to keep out any snipers who might have followed us. The cleaning woman yelled, 'Hey, you. This is closed.

I'm cleaning in there.' Keys rattled. A key slipped in the lock.

There must have been a hundred metal stalls. Sandy took the first one, slipping slightly on the newly washed floor.

'God, that was close,' Sandy said from her stall. 'I thought I was going to burst.'

The cleaning woman continued to try various keys. I began to sweat and ran some cold water over my wrists to cool off.

'So how'd you like that bogus story Jim Morrison told about Merry Metzger being the town's gift to sobriety?' Sandy asked.

It wasn't Morrison's proclamation of Merry Metzger's virtues that struck my attention as much as what he said about his relationship with her in high school. If Merry Metzger and Jim Morrison broke up the summer before her senior year, then why would she be compelled to go so far as to murder Laura for making the moves on Jim months later? By that time, according to Jim, Merry and Henry were already an item.

'Merry Metzger didn't kill Laura Buchman,' I said, assessing myself in the mirror. 'Someone else did. Maybe Jim, for some unknown reason, and maybe Merry helped him cover up the evidence.'

'Oh my God,' Sandy said. 'Bubbles, make up your mind.'

If my reflection under the bright lights of the A-L-E Airport bathroom was any indication, I was a wreck. My best makeup job couldn't hide the wrinkles or the dark circles under my eyes. This reporter stuff was taking its toll.

'Yipes, this girdle is giving me a rash,' Sandy complained. 'Yes, I know, a girdle. So middle-aged. But they don't call them girdles these days. They're called wonder huggers or something . . .'

There was a rustling from the closed, unoccupied stall behind me.

'Bubbles!' Sandy shouted from the stall. 'Bubbles Yablonsky. Are you listening to me?'

But I wasn't listening. I was staring in the mirror at the reflection of the woman who had stepped out of the stall and was now standing behind me.

Her hair was white, her face wrinkled and her body dumpy. She wore tan polyester slacks and a white sweatshirt on which was imprinted a deer and the word, in flowery capital letters, ALASKA. In one hand was a white plastic purse. In the other was an itsy-bitsy gun, pointed directly at me.

I was speechless.

She kept the gun aimed at my gut as she walked, backward, toward the door.

'Bye-bye, Bubbles,' she said with a smile, before opening the door and slipping out.

I'd heard that voice in Saw Mill Park. Merry Metzger. And I'd be damned if she slipped away again.

'Did someone say your name?' Sandy asked.

I didn't answer. Instead I flung open the bathroom

door and ran after Merry. The hallway was clear on either side. Not even the cleaning woman. Overhead the intercom blared that the charter to Anchorage was now boarding at Gate 8B.

Shit! I ran to the end of the corridor and read the signs. Gates 6 through 10 were to the left. I took a left and ran past a pretzel stand, an oversize-cookie stand and a Starbucks. All closed. In fact, all the stores were gated, including the newsstand and the bar. There could be only one place she was headed – a charter cruise to ooh and ahhh over icebergs, whales and groaning buffet tables.

I took another left and ran smack into a large group of elderly men and women filing up to go through the metal detector. Merry Metzger was next in line to put her purse on the conveyor belt. There were about seven people between us.

I started to march toward her when a tiny woman wearing a green visor stuck her hand out.

'Hey!' the woman shouted. 'She's cutting.'

The others turned and glared at me. 'No cutting!' they shouted.

'But I—?'

'Is she on this flight?' one of the old men asked. 'Whoopde-do!'

'Keep your pants on, Harold.'

'Get back in line, toots!'

I got to the back of the line and folded my arms. Well, it would be interesting what old Merry Metzger's purse would show when it went through the conveyor belt. I craned my neck as Merry put her purse down and limped through the metal detector. Oh, she had a walker. Nice touch! Boy she went all out.

Beeeep. The metal detector said.

'That's because she's got a gun!' I shouted.

'What?' Someone yelled.

A rent-a-cop was at my side in a flash. 'Would you mind stepping aside, ma'am?' he said, pulling me out of line.

'That woman,' I said, pointing at Merry Metzger, 'has a gun. I saw it.'

The rent-a-cop was a thin, muscular black man with serious eyes. He didn't flinch. 'You have any alcoholic beverages to drink tonight, ma'am?'

'Lookit, you'll see.'

The other security guard at the gate took away the walker and extended his hand. Merry leaned on it as she made it, slow step after slow step, through the gate.

'That's it, darlin',' the woman in the green visor urged encouragingly. 'You take your time. The plane will wait.'

There was no beep. And the purse passed with flying colors, too. On the other side of the metal detector the security guard handed Merry her walker, and she marched ahead.

'I believe it was the walker that had activated the metal detector,' my guard said. 'May I see your ticket?'

'I don't have a ticket.'

'You don't have a ticket? Then what is your business here?'

'That woman's got a gun. Maybe it's tucked inside her walker.'

'A gun tucked inside a walker, huh? Interesting. Impossible, but interesting. I'm afraid I'm going to ask you to leave.'

'But . . .'

'Immediately.' He pulled out a walkie-talkie from his pants and ordered backup or some such nonsense. All I know is that in five minutes I was placed in one of those airport golf carts and was being whisked to the front door.

Sandy was outside waiting for me, shaking her head.

'Don't tell me,' she said, holding up her hands. 'Whatever you're about to say could never match my sweet little imagination.'

'You know what, Sandy?' I said, getting on the airport shuttle to the Marquis. 'This time I think your sweet little imagination couldn't do it justice.'

I dreamed that Stiletto was lying next to me, naked, on a private beach, massaging my thigh. When I awoke, I discovered that my hair was twisted into impossible knots and that the masseuse was Mama, who happened to be poking me with her oversize floral umbrella.

'You can't sleep all morning just because you were out all night,' she nagged. 'I gotta make eight a.m. Mass. You gotta take me.'

I cocked open one eye. Mama was wearing a white dress with pink polka dots, along with a matching white hat and pink ribbon. She was drenched in Lily of the Valley perfume. It was quite a change from her guerrilla fatigues from the day before.

The alarm clock said 6:09. That was too early to be bothered on a Sunday. I closed my eye and drifted back to sleep.

'Go at ten,' I murmured. 'I'll take you at ten.'

'Ten! With all the yuppies and the kids and the minivans? No way!'

I put a pillow over my head and pretended she was a bad dream. That way she might disappear when I woke up.

'Yoo-hoo!' she shouted, nearly knocking me out of bed. 'Don't go back to sleep. The paper came and your name's in it. Again.' I felt a thud as she threw a Sunday newspaper on my sleeping body.

My name in it again? I sat up and unfolded the front page. Stripped across the top, right under the *News-Times* masthead, was the largest correction I'd ever seen. It was more than your basic correction. It was a correction exposé. A story devoted to how I, stupid, dim-witted hairdresser Bubbles Yablonsky, had been wrong, wrong, wrong.

I quickly scanned it. 'Inexperienced, amateur reporter Bubbles Yablonsky erroneously wrote ... Possibly hacked into *News-Times* computer system ... Police have confirmed Mrs. Metzger was not at the scene ... In Central America with Moravian missionaries ... Deepest apologies to Metzger family ... Matter under internal investigation at the *News-Times* ... We regret the error.'

I threw down the paper. 'This is a bunch of—'

Mama put her hands over her ears. 'Not on the Lord's day!'

'Shit!' I finished. 'Hacked into the computer system? I don't even own a computer. I barely know how to turn one on.'

'You need to go to church,' Mama said, standing on a step stool and rifling through my closet. 'We gotta find you something decent to wear. Maybe, if we're lucky, we can talk the priest into exorcising you at the door.'

The hell with church. What I needed to do was find that film in the grass at Saw Mill Park, gather my notes together from last night and start working on my story. I wondered what Dix Notch would say if he knew that Merry Metzger stood a foot away from me in the airport bathroom. He'd have to give *me* a public apology.

Mama pulled out some cotton high-necked pink number I dimly remembered wearing at a wedding once.

'Put this on!' she ordered. 'And hurry up. We're taking Genevieve.'

I fell back in bed. 'You and Genevieve can go alone. Genevieve has a car. I'm staying right here.'

'No can do,' argued Mama, pulling back my covers. 'The judge at my arraignment goes to eight a.m. Mass, and I want him to see that I'm on the straight and narrow now.'

The judge. Shoot. The biggest crisis of my life, and I gotta baby-sit Mama. Why is life always that way?

'All right, all right,' I said, swinging my legs over the side of the bed.

'Good,' Mama said. She handed me a cup of coffee and a muffin. It tasted rather odd.

'What kind of muffin is this?' I asked, spitting it out into a tissue.

'Potato. Genevieve's recipe. By the way, Mickey Sinkler called three times for you from the HoJo's lobby last night,' she said, shaking out the pink dress. 'I hadn't the heart to say you'd pulled a scam on him. He's such a nice hardworking fellow.'

I walked down the hall to the shower. I observed that Mama had placed what I assumed was bulletproof Plexiglas over the hall window, lending a cozy insane-asylum atmosphere to the place.

'I didn't pull a scam on Mickey,' I corrected, closing the bathroom door. 'Mickey owes me for bawling me out the other day.'

I looked in the mirror. There was a big green blob on my head. Mama must have tiptoed into my room in the middle of the night and plastered cucumber poultice on my bump. I scraped it off. Well, I'll be a monkey's uncle. It had worked. The bump was nothing more than a purple patch. The swelling had subsided.

'Hurry up!' Mama banged on the bathroom door. 'Genevieve's in the car, waiting.'

As though I were a kid on my way to Sunday School, Mama had laid out on my bed the pink dress, underwear, a slip and a brand-new, double-support Playtex bra that looked more like a piece of military equipment than an item of lingerie. Oh, yes, and support hose.

'I know what you're thinking, Bubbles Yablonsky,' Mama hollered from the other side of my bedroom door. 'But you're getting to that age when a woman needs some support. If you don't watch out, you'll wake up one morning, and your whole body will be nothing more than a bag of runny pudding in Glad Wrap.'

Runny pudding in Glad Wrap? I gagged. Yuk.

The doorbell rang. Genevieve, no doubt, eager to get going.

'And no Dolly Parton with the hair,' Mama added, making her way down the stairs. 'A simple ponytail will do just fine. Ditto on the eye stuff. Humor me and be modest for once. The Lord loves modesty.'

I examined myself in the mirror. Ponytail. No legs. I was a goddamn nun is what I was. I grabbed my purse, my coffee and headed down the stairs. If Mama thought I was going to sit through an hour of church, she had another think coming.

As soon as she and Genevieve passed through those

big oak doors, I planned on heading to Saw Mill Park to look for Stiletto's cell phone and the lost film.

'Guess who stopped by for breakfast?' Mama announced proudly.

Mickey Sinkler was standing by the door in full uniform examining one of Mama's mashed potato traps.

'Where were you last night, Bubbles?' Mickey asked sharply, still studying the trap.

So, that's why he was here. To check up on me, the snoop. 'None of your beeswax,' I replied.

'Bubbles!' Mama said, hands on hip. 'Manners.'

I stuck my tongue out at her. 'I don't have to report to him about my social life, even if he is a cop.'

'I dispute that,' said Mickey, turning his attention away from the bucket of potatoes and glaring at me. 'If you were at the Fly-By-Night Lounge partying with Jim Morrison, that sure is my beeswax.'

My brain did a double flip. 'Mickey Sinkler, you spy! You were following me.'

'Wish I had, Bubbles. Wish I had.' He took a few crackling leather steps in my direction until we were face-to-face. I stood at the bottom of the stairs with my arms crossed.

'Jim Morrison was abducted at three a.m. outside the Marquis this morning. Hasn't been seen since,' he said. 'Know anything about that?'

I blinked at him. 'What do you mean – abducted?'

Mickey smiled wryly. 'Well, I'd like to tell you, but

I'm a little worried my name's going to appear in the newspaper tomorrow.'

'Forget it,' Mama yelled from her place on the couch. 'Bubbles got fired. They won't even let her through the front door of that rag.'

'That's true, Mickey. I'm off the paper. I couldn't quote you if I wanted to.' After all, I wasn't *officially* writing this story for the *Inquirer*. Not yet.

Mickey sat on the stairs and motioned for me to join him.

'According to sworn statements, Morrison and a friend named Cindy were standing behind the Airport Marquis sharing a cigarette after his show early this morning when a Lincoln Continental pulled up. Two men exited the vehicle and proceeded to assault Morrison several times. Morrison was then pushed into the vehicle, which sped off.'

'Jeezum,' cried Mama. 'Like *Miami Vice*.'

It took a while for the meaning of what Mickey was saying to sink in. I recalled how nervous Jim became at the end of our conversation, how he asked me if I was working for Metzger and told me to scram.

'How come you're asking me about this?' I said.

Mickey leaned over and reached into his pocket. He held up a House of Beauty business card. The one where I had crossed out STYLIST and written *Reporter*. The one I gave to Jim Morrison.

'This was found in the parking lot where Morrison was assaulted. And this Cindy chick said Morrison spent his break talking to some stacked blonde in a bright red dress. It didn't take much detective work to put the pieces together.'

I stared at the business card.

'Want another tip?' he asked. 'Deep background only?'

I looked up from the business card. 'Sure.'

'We got a warrant to search his apartment this morning, and I found something odd.'

'Yes?' Drugs, I was thinking. Cocaine. Pot. Amphetamines.

'A datebook with an interesting entry for Friday evening. Looks like Morrison was supposed to meet a "Merry" around eight p.m. that night, no location given.'

My eyes opened wide. 'You're kidding. He told me he hadn't seen her in years.'

Mickey smiled. 'Seems like you and me should have a talk.'

'I'll talk,' I said, 'as long as you'll agree to a little deal.'

Chapter 14

MICKEY STEPPED OVER THE dried peas and sat down at the kitchen table. Mama placed before him a pot of coffee and a stack of pancakes topped with blueberry syrup. I called Sandy and gave her the news.

'No way!' Sandy exclaimed. 'What do you think?'

'I think Jim Morrison lied to save his ass, and I think Metzger roughed him up despite that.'

Sandy considered this. 'Maybe it was drug related. Aren't drug dealers always doing that, punching out people and throwing them in Lincoln Continentals?'

'You and Mama watch too much *Miami Vice*,' I said.

Mickey was positioned at the table with a pen and paper, ready to do an official inquiry.

'I'm going to look up Athena Adler's number. We better get to her before Metzger does. Call you later,' Sandy said, and hung up.

I sat down and detailed for Mickey the past forty-eight hours, including the various Laura Buchman murder theories and Merry Metzger's bathroom appearance. I even gave him the tape of our conversation with

Morrison, even though Mr. Salvo would have killed me for that. Journalists are never supposed to share their sources with cops, he told us at the Two Guys community college class. I made Mickey promise to save Cindy's mail-order info.

After I was done, Mickey wiped his mouth and leaned back. 'You've flipped,' he said. 'You're beautiful, but you've flipped.'

I tossed a muffin at his head.

'Oww!' Mickey yelled, rubbing his forehead. 'Stop it. Those things are as hard as rock.'

'Ahemm!' coughed Mama, nodding toward their creator, Genevieve.

Genevieve had gotten tired of waiting in the car. Now she was sitting on a chair against the kitchen window, so large that she was blocking all the light. She was wearing a black-and-white-striped dress she probably thought was thinning, but that I thought made her look like a referee, especially since she kept commenting on my conversation with Mickey every five minutes.

'That question's out of bounds, Butch,' she'd say. (Genevieve called all boys Butch, and all girls Sally.) There was also the occasional, 'That's foul,' which she said with a huff. All she needed was a whistle around her neck, and she'd have a career with the '76ers.

'I'm going to lay it on the line, Bubbles,' Mickey explained. 'Ever since you wrote that Merry Metzger story, I've been persona non grata down at the department. I think administration is fixing to transfer me to Hellertown.'

I grabbed Mickey's hand. 'That's awful. Oh, I'm so sorry.'

Mickey let the hand stay. 'Don't be. Here's the thing. I believe you.'

Mama dropped a pot. 'Well, that's a first. A man believing Bubbles Yablonsky. Break out the champagne.'

'Thanks, Mickey.' I had to question his motives, though. Wasn't this his way of getting into my lace underpants, perhaps?

'I know what you're thinking, Bubbles,' Mickey said, removing my hand and picking up his plate. 'I didn't come to this conclusion out of sentiment. I came to it from studying the facts.'

He carried the plate over and dumped it in the sink.

'See that?' Mama shouted. 'He buses, too. Get the cinnamon sugar, Bubbles, fast!'

'You swear we're off the record now?' Mickey leaned against the sink. 'Because if this gets in the paper, I'll not only be out of a job, I'll be out of police work forever.'

I stood up. 'May Mama stuff me full of her sauerkraut succotash if I quote you.'

Mickey let out a deep sigh. 'The department's covering this up. On Monday, the coroner's going to issue a ruling that the victim died of a heart attack hours before he was struck and that the driver – whoever it was – could have easily thought he or she was driving over roadkill. No charges are going to be filed. The case is closed.'

Mama slapped her hands. 'Didn't I tell you? Didn't I tell you Henry Metzger ruled this town?'

I slumped into the chair. 'We can't let this happen, Mickey. This is so . . . not right.'

Mickey gave his head a quick nod. 'I've thought about it long and hard. If I didn't have five kids to feed, I'd resign out of protest.'

'You're a good man, Mickey Sinkler,' Mama said, patting him on the back.

'Who's the victim, anyway?' I asked.

'A nobody named Chester Zug. Used to walk five miles every day to feed the ducks in the park.' Mickey folded up his notebook. 'A former garbage worker with no ties that I could see to the Metzgers.'

'Don't know him,' said Mama, who prides herself on being familiar with most of Lehigh's seniors. 'Where'd he live?'

'Public Housing for the Elderly. Down by Pembroke Village.'

'We're almost out of time,' barked Genevieve. 'We'll be late if we don't leave for church now. Father Paul hates it when you open the doors. It lets out the incense.'

Mickey strolled across the living room and stopped. 'By the way, Bubbles. What was that deal you wanted to talk about?'

I pulled at my high-necked pink collar. 'Don't worry

about it, Mickey. With all the hot water you're in down at the department, you better not do it.'

'Try me.'

'Get me the police file on Laura Buchman's death. The complete one, not the one they made public ten years ago. A House of Beauty client told us her classmates suspected Merry Metzger murdered Laura, but I have a hunch they were wrong. I highly doubt Merry would have done that. That's not to say she didn't know who the murderer was. I bet an internal police report from back then will point me in the right direction.'

Mickey nodded. 'You've learned a lot in the past forty-eight hours, Bubbles. You might not make such a bad reporter after all.'

Chapter 15

I DROPPED MAMA AND Genevieve on the steps of St. Anne's so I could search for parking. As soon as they were safely through the front doors and in Father Paul's care, I took a right on Washington Avenue and headed for Pembroke Village.

Before Mickey showed up, I had planned to spend the morning looking for the film in Saw Mill Park. But considering recent developments, it was more important that I find out something about Chester Zug first. Mickey said there was no connection between Chester Zug and Henry Metzger. Mickey also believed the Lehigh Police Department was more professional and less intimidated by Lehigh Steel these days.

Mickey believed a lot of fairy stories for a guy who wore a deadly weapon on his hip.

Lehigh's Public Housing for the Elderly was an eight-story firetrap of brick and rusted fire escapes. It was a far cry from the tidy high-rise where Mama and Genevieve lived. Here plastic coffee cups, candy wrappers and old newspapers were caught between the fence and the concrete sidewalk. Some optimistic soul had overturned a corner of the garbage-strewn lawn in an effort to build a garden. But the gardener must have lost either his interest or seeds, because all that remained was dirt.

I parked the Camaro and checked my reflection in the mirror. It was appalling. Without makeup my skin was white and splotchy, my eyelashes thin and cheekbones nonexistent. Plus, I was wearing a high-necked pink dress and loafers.

If the super of this place was a man, I didn't stand a chance.

I entered the gate and smiled at a woman crocheting a white blanket.

'Lovely day,' she said. 'Beautiful weather.'

'Yes,' I replied, even though the breeze from the Freemansburg paint mill a half mile away smelled like rotten eggs. 'You don't happen to know where a Mr. Zug lives, do you?'

The woman dropped her crochet hook into her lap. 'Oh, my, that was sad, wasn't it?' she whispered. 'The whole building's been talking about it all weekend. Are you a relative?'

I bit my lip. Darn. This was like one of those simulated 'ethical' questions Mr. Salvo used to put to us in his journalism class.

'Not exactly,' I said.

She eyed my dress and loafers. 'Then you must be from the church collecting for the rummage.'

Not entirely untrue. I had just come from a church. 'More like it,' I said.

The old woman shook her head. 'He doesn't have much, of course. None of us do. But I'm sure the super will be glad to show you in.'

'Oh, I don't want to bother him, I just—'

'Sorry,' she said, picking up her crocheting again. 'Can't be too cautious. You better check with the super first.'

I smiled sweetly. This old dame wasn't going to tell me where Zug lived after all.

The sound of a football game blared from the other side of the wooden door on the first-floor apartment marked SUPERINTENDENT. I knocked several times, but got no answer. Eventually, I banged so hard I thought I'd pound through the door.

It opened abruptly. 'Yeah,' growled a fat man in a flannel shirt with rolled up sleeves. He smelled of bacon, fried eggs and all varieties of grease in general. 'Whaddya want?'

'I'm here from the church to go over Mr. Zug's things,' I lied.

He eyed me suspiciously. 'You ain't supposed to be here until after church,' he said, glancing at his watch. 'Not until noon.'

'Really?' I asked with a bat of my scrawny eyelashes. 'Martha said to be here bright and early. Actually, I was worried that I was late.'

The super shook his head, stepped out into the

hallway and closed his door. 'This always happens,' he said. 'How come you church ladies can't keep your times straight?'

I smiled stupidly and followed him dutifully.

'I don't know what you're gonna find,' he said, leading me past apartment after apartment of blaring TVs. 'He don't got much. I was in there when the cops were there yesterday and the place was bare.'

The super stopped and punched the elevator button. So. The cops were there, I thought. Sweeping evidence under the rug, no doubt.

'You know him?' the super asked as we entered the elevator. He hit the button for the third floor.

'I met him once.' At least that wasn't a lie.

'Odd guy.' The super folded his arms as we rose past floors. 'Never could get a handle on him.'

'Oh. Why's that?' I tried to inquire in an innocent, churchlady kind of way. Christian concern.

The elevator door opened and we stepped out. 'You met him. You must have noticed the way he was. Squirrelly like. Twice I caught him spying on a lady's apartment on the first floor. The way I heard it, he lost his job at the Department of Sanitation for being a Peeping Tom.'

We stopped at a scratched plywood door with the number 39 on it. It was the only one without a blaring television or the smell of cabbage. The super slipped in the key and turned the knob.

'He didn't make friends in this building, I'll tell you

that much. The old folks don't look kindly on Peeping Toms. They like their privacy.'

A puff of old-man air *wuff*ed out when the door opened. The shades were drawn, and through the slits in the venetian blinds, the light illuminated rays of dust. The super was right. This place was spare. And stuffy and hot.

'Mind if I open a window?' I asked as I pulled open a blind. It looked out into the parking lot, where the Camaro was parked. Beyond that was the steel-gray view of the paint mill and its spewing smokestacks. I heard the moan of a train going by.

It was a small apartment with a kitchen and living room all in one and stained, grayish-orange carpeting on the floor. A door off the kitchen opened to what I assumed was a bathroom. Through a door leading out of the living room I saw an unmade bed.

There was one brown, beaten couch on which all the sitting must have been done. One TV. A stand-up glass ashtray packed with cigarettes and a circular, wood kitchen table and two metal chairs. That was it for the furniture. There wasn't even a coffee-maker in the kitchen. Just a teakettle. A bottle of Ajax and a rusted SOS pad in the sink.

'Rent's only two hundred fifty dollars,' explained the super, who must have read my mind. 'It ain't much, but it keeps 'em off the streets. Or out of their kids' houses.'

My conscience pricked me. I thought of Mama. The high-rise where she lived was much nicer and only affordable for her because the union insisted that Lehigh Steel still pay her what would have been my father's pension. Other than that, she had received no money from the ingot mold accident. It wasn't much. Without it, though, she would have been living like Chester.

'So I guess you can handle this yourself,' he said, backing toward the door. 'You know where to reach me if you need a hand.' The door slammed. He didn't enjoy being in this apartment any more than I did. Probably was even a little spooked.

Through the walls of the next door apartment I could hear muffled voices rising and falling.

I picked up the phone and dialed *69, in the hope of catching the last telephone number Chester dialed. But it had already been disconnected.

It felt almost rude to enter his bedroom, especially since I had never met the man alive. Think of it this way, Bubbles, I told myself. The cops have already scoured this place. Not like you're going to find any surprises.

The bedroom was similar to the living room in sparseness. There was a double bed unmade with dingy sheets that hadn't been washed in months. An odor of sweat and dirt hung over them. There was a bedside table on which sat a lamp, a glass with dried milk at the bottom and a Bible.

What a life.

I walked back into the kitchen and out of pure

nosiness started opening cabinet doors. Oatmeal. Cream of Wheat. Cremora. Folger's Crystals and two cans of double-noodle chicken noodle soup. There were four bowls. Four plates and three glasses. The fourth must have been in the bedroom.

The silverware drawer wasn't much of an improvement. Four forks. Four knives, plus one steak knife. Four spoons. Well, at least he was neat. I'll give him that much.

The corner of a piece of paper stuck out from underneath the blue plastic silverware divider. I lifted it up and was surprised to see that the bottom of the drawer was practically lined with business cards.

I picked one up. It was for Duitille's Jewelers on Fourth Street. Another, a silver-colored one, read J. DIAMOND AND SONS. FOR OVER 100 YEARS.

There were twelve cards in the drawer altogether. They belonged to jewelers in Allentown, Easton, even three from Philadelphia. Some of the names I recognized. Others I'd never heard of. I never knew there were so many jewelry stores in the Lehigh Valley.

Wouldn't be common practice for a former garbage worker to collect business cards unless there was a good reason. So I stacked them all together and shoved them in the inner side pocket of my purse. There. Stealing evidence from a crime scene. Felony number four. Good for me.

I shoved the silverware divider back and slammed the drawer shut. Maybe Chester was one of those poverty-stricken millionaires you read about. You know, they work as janitors until they drop and it turns out they've got five million dollars in stock options shoved under their mattress.

Maybe there were diamonds, sapphires or rubies hidden away in Chester's undie drawer.

Unfortunately, the drawers of his dresser were mostly empty, too, except for some underwear and flannel pj's. The digital clock on the dresser said 8:30 A.M. I could spare only about twenty minutes more before I'd have to wrap this up and get back to Mama.

The pink-tiled bathroom was also a big disappointment. Toothbrush. Toothpaste. Bottle of Scope. Bag of disposable Bic razors. Half-empty box of Depends. Poor Chester.

If the sheets hadn't been cleaned in months, the toilet hadn't been scrubbed since Chester moved in here. It was rusted brown and the toilet seat was up, exposing tiny hairs and flecks of dirt on the rim. Appetizing.

Still, tiled bathrooms have an inspiring effect on me, especially after drinking half a pot of coffee. So I put down the lid, laid down a barrier of toilet paper and used the facilities as quickly as possible, trying to keep my mind off the various germs that might be hopping up to introduce themselves.

I flushed the toilet and washed my hands. Brown, rusted water spurted out of the tap and I ran my fingers quickly under it. That wasn't the worst of it, though.

The worst of it was that the toilet was not stopping. The water was rising up and up the sides of the toilet bowl.

It was going to overflow. Right into the apartment below. And then what would the super say? Nice going, church lady.

I quickly lifted off the lid and plunked my hand in the tank. One advantage of the Plumbing Pointers class I took at the Two Guys community college was to learn a bit about ceramic engineering. I pulled up the ball and stopped the water.

Something caught my eye while I was standing there, waiting for the water to rise slowly in the tank. A small metal object lay at the bottom. It didn't look like a piece of plumbing. So, as much as it churned my stomach to do so, I dipped my hand in the water and grabbed it.

It turned out to be one of those odd, old-fashioned skeleton keys. On its handle was inscribed the word OLD, in capital letters. I'll say it's old, I thought. At least fifty years old.

Then a happy idea popped into my brain. What if this key went to a box? A box that held all those diamonds and sapphires and rubies that Chester had been storing away for years? But where was the box?

'Everything all right in here?'

I clutched the key and looked up. The superintendent darkened the doorway.

'Don't think I can spare the toilet,' he said, peering down at my hand. I put my hands on the toilet tank top.

'Thank you so much for letting me get a head start

on his apartment,' I said, replacing the top. 'To tell you the truth, I'm just finishing up the inventory. Had to use the little girl's room.'

The super folded his arms. He was a big man. Burly in addition to being fat.

'I called your church,' he said flatly. 'They was surprised to hear that someone was already here.'

I smiled and blinked. 'Must be some mix-up?'

'What'd you say your name was again? I didn't catch it.'

My mind raced for a name. 'Sally,' I said. 'Sally Hansen.' I was gambling that the super hadn't repaired many broken nails lately.

'Okay, Mrs. Hansen,' he said, turning to go. 'They said they'd call back in five minutes. Now I can tell them who you are.' Again he left abruptly. I tucked the key in my cleavage.

I waited until I heard the elevator *ding* and then quickly exited Chester Zug's apartment. I knocked on the door from which the next-door sounds had come, keeping my eyes fixed on the elevator should the big, mean super return.

The television muted and an elderly woman holding a cat opened the door on a chain lock. 'Yes?' she asked quietly.

My intuition told me to play it straight. I informed her that I was a reporter looking into Mr. Zug's death. As soon as I mentioned my name, Bubbles Yablonsky, the woman slammed the door in my face.

I heard the quiet hum of the elevator starting up again. Damn. He was going to get me and I was going to be in big trouble.

Then the door opened. This time widely and without the chain.

'Come in, come in!' the woman offered eagerly. 'I bet you're LuLu's daughter, aren't you? You're the spitting image. There aren't that many Yablonskys in town, you know.' She closed the door and triple locked it just as the elevator opened.

The woman was small and dressed completely in light purple. Purple shoes. Purple shawl. Even, almost, purple hair. A typical Mama friend.

The layout of her apartment was the same as Chester Zug's. However, whereas Chester's was nearly bare, this woman's was stuffed to the ceiling with knickknacks. China bells and crocheted lamp shades. Stuffed animals on overstuffed couches. Dolls. Metal trays advertising Coca-Cola. It was a living yard sale.

'How do you know my mother?' I asked, sitting down at a pink enameled kitchen table on which sat a porcelain dachshund with a chipped foot.

'From around,' the old lady said, pulling out the other chair. 'Of course, that food fight she organized at the senior center Friday night is the stuff of legends. I can't remember when I've had so much fun. I'll never forget that image of the senior center rec director scolding us all, his head covered in tapioca.'

The woman leaned back and slapped her thigh. Then

she added seriously, 'Of course, we were all disheartened to hear about that misunderstanding with the dress at Hess's. She didn't stay in jail long, did she?'

'No. After that she came to live with me.'

Tears welled in her eyes. 'Aren't you wonderful! I wish my daughter was half as nice. Do you know I haven't seen her since Christmas?'

I shook my head in commiseration.

'I read your article,' she said, getting up and turning on the heat under the teakettle. 'I found it very interesting. That was you who wrote the article about Chester's death, wasn't it?'

I nodded. 'Did you see today's paper?' I asked.

'No. I don't get Sunday. Too expensive.'

Whew. If she'd read that front-page correction, she might not be so trusting.

She put out two cups. 'My name's Marian, by the way. Do you like sugar?'

I informed Marian that I did and asked her why the super suggested that Mr. Zug did not get along with his neighbors.

'Because Bart didn't like him, for one thing,' she said, pouring hot water into the cup. 'Bart's the super, and he's not very nice. He's always after me for my cats.'

As soon as she said that, a fat orange tabby rubbed up against my leg. My nose itched. I happen to be deadly allergic to cats. Just my luck.

'Chester was always bringing up problems to Bart.

The water's rusty. There are roaches. Look! . . .' From under the sink she pulled out a large mayonnaise jar inside which was a bug the size of a small mouse. 'He was right. But Bart didn't want to hear none of it. He didn't want to be bothered.'

It was too hot for tea, I thought. I didn't want to offend Marian, so I sipped it. It tasted of peppermint with a slight hint of Palmolive.

'Bart mentioned something about Mr. Zug being a Peeping Tom.' I brought my finger to my nose to stifle a sneeze.

'Pooh. A rumor. A vicious rumor started by Apartment Thirteen. Those gossips. Chester was always a sweetheart to me. Wait a minute. Stay right there.'

She got up and toddled off to the bedroom. In seconds she returned with a bent silver picture frame. Inside was a picture of herself holding a cat.

'Isn't this frame lovely?' she asked.

'Very,' I fibbed.

'Chester gave it to me,' she said, polishing a corner of it with her shawl. 'He got it on the job.'

A string of sneezes made my nose explode. My chest began to tighten. A few more minutes without fresh air, and I would be unable to breathe.

'On the job?' I gasped.

'Why, yes. It's amazing what Chester picked up all those years as a garbage man. We live in such a disposable society these days people think nothing of throwing away treasures. See that china bell over there?'

She pointed to a bookshelf on which was displayed a cracked white china bell.

'A minor flaw in it, but otherwise perfect condition. Chester got that for me, too.'

My eyes were now streaming tears.

'And that tape player?' She directed me to a battered eight-track tape recorder. 'He got that out of a Dumpster at the university. If you hold on, I've got a shoe box under my bed of all the other trinkets Chester's given to me.'

As much as I would have loved to pore over bent knitting needles, unpaired earrings and empty toilet-paper rolls, I decided that I would have to breathe instead.

'You don't look well, dear,' she said.

'Window,' was all I could manage. 'Open window.'

Marian moved past a coffee table, television, sewing machine and bookshelf to open a window. I basically pushed her aside and stuck my head out, taking in several lungfuls of air. After a few minutes, oxygen returned to my brain.

I opened my eyes and sighed in relief. Marian had the same view as Chester. The paint mill. The railroad track. The parking lot. My Camaro. A pair of legs in jeans sticking out from under my Camaro.

A pair of legs in jeans sticking out from under my Camaro?

I pulled my head back in. 'Hate to appear rude, but I've got to go, Marian.'

'No,' she objected. 'You've got to see what Chester left me.' She ran into the bedroom.

My chest began to tighten again. 'I'm sorry,' I said as she emerged from the bedroom holding a pink-and-white shoe box. 'It's the cats. I'm allergic to them.'

'What a shame. Perhaps we can look at the box some other time.'

'Thank you,' I whispered. I turned to go and then stopped. The key. Marian might know about the key. I pulled it out of my cleavage and showed it to her.

'Does this look familiar?' I asked, wheezing again. 'I found it at the bottom of Chester's toilet tank.'

Marian took it from my hand and held the key up to the light. 'Never seen it before. How odd. From his toilet tank, huh? I'll rack my brain.'

'You ever know Chester to have a stash of precious jewels someplace?' I asked hopefully. 'A safe-deposit box maybe?'

Marian shook her head. 'Afraid not. He was barely getting by as it was.'

I wrote my telephone number on the back of a House of Beauty card and asked Marian to call me if she remembered anything important about Chester.

I let out a huge sneeze. I replaced the key in my cleavage and opened the door right as Bart stepped off the elevator, accompanied by a young man in a short-sleeved shirt and a tie. I turned and quickstepped to the red EXIT sign.

'Hey!' Bart shouted. 'You! Sally Hansen. Wait up.'

I slammed the metal door and raced down the steps of the emergency exit, two at a time. Bart followed.

'Hold on there, Mrs. Hansen. I've got to talk to you!' He was shouting. But Bart the super was fat and he couldn't just skip down the stairs as I was doing. He took them sideways, grasping the railing as he went.

In no time I made it to the first floor. These loafers weren't so bad, after all. I could never have made that kind of time in heels.

I slipped through the lobby and out the front door into the fresh air and sunshine. I waved 'bye to the crocheting lady in the wheelchair and ran around the block to the parking lot.

The pair of legs under my car had disappeared.

I gasped. What if those legs belonged to Metzger's goon and he had planted some type of explosive device?

I was about to bend down and check under the car – although, for what I hadn't a clue – when the rear door of the elderly housing opened and Bart burst into the parking lot, red-faced and madder than a wet hen.

I fumbled for the keys in my purse, but couldn't find them. Panicked, I yanked open the door of the Camaro. It was already unlocked, even though I had locked it earlier. This was not a good sign.

Bart started hollering. 'I'm going to arrest you for trespassing. I called the cops, Mrs. Hansen.' He stood a few parked cars away – panting, out of breath and, in my nonmedical opinion, on the brink of a major cardiac event.

I emptied out my purse on the passenger seat, found my keys, started up the Camaro. No boom, although I didn't know if explosive devices could be set to go off after a few miles or a few minutes. Well, I suppose I'll find out, I thought.

I backed the car out, put it into forward and nearly ran smack into Bart, who was the only barrier between me and the exit. And he wasn't budging.

Tiny gray heads popped out from the apartments above to see what all the hoo-ha was about.

'You're not from the church,' Bart yelled, banging on the Camaro. 'What were you doing up there?'

'Let her alone,' screamed one elderly man from the second floor. 'She's cute.'

'That's LuLu Yablonsky's daughter, Bubbles,' Marian called down to her neighbor below. 'LuLu lives with her now.'

'LuLu's living with her daughter?' called up the neighbor one floor below. 'Lucky stiff.'

'That's LuLu's kid?' someone else inquired. 'We gotta help her.'

'Stand aside, Bart,' commanded a gray head from a first-floor window.

'Nothing doing,' Bart yelled back to them. 'This ain't your business. Get back inside.'

The man in the first-floor window brought up to his lips what appeared to be a white plastic straw.

Ploink!

Bart smacked his hand across his eye. 'Ouch,' he said.

Ploink! Ploink!

Everyone had straws now, and they were using them as peashooters to hit Bart.

Ploink! Ploink! Ploink!

Bart covered his head with his arms. 'Stop it!'

Ploink!

He tucked his butt in. Whatever these seniors were shooting at him, he was dancing and skipping around like a Mexican jumping bean.

'Good luck, honey!' one of them yelled as I carefully steered around the hopping Bart. As I squeezed by, one of the pellets sailed through my driver's-side window and onto the passenger's seat. I picked it up.

Geritol. Pill form.

Chapter 16

T HE PHONE WAS RINGING off the hook when Mama, Genevieve and I returned from church-slash-snooping.

'I'll get it!' screamed LuLu, making a mad dash.

'What's with her?' I asked Genevieve, who had now assumed the role of Mama's personal bodyguard.

'We're working on a project,' Genevieve replied, removing her mirrored sunglasses and looking down at me.

'It's for you,' Mama yelled, handing the phone to me. 'It's that horse's ass, Notch.'

'I heard that,' Notch said when I got on. 'I guess I must be the bogeyman of the Yablonsky household.'

'Not quite. We got other bogeymen.'

Notch was all sugar and sweetness this morning. First he apologized for 'the tone of yesterday's meeting.' Then he spent a good five minutes explaining the severity of the correction. Bottom line? The lawyers made him do it.

'But the real reason I called,' Notch said, clearing his

throat, 'was to ask for a favor. Henry Metzger has requested that you meet him at his home today. Alone.'

I put the phone to my chest. 'Mama? Could you please go up to the medicine chest and pull down a bottle of the purple moisturizing nail polish remover and a bottle of polish? Ebony Enamel will do.'

'Uh-oh,' Mama whispered to Genevieve, who was checking the mashed potato trap above the front door. 'Bad news.'

I got back on. 'I don't think that's possible, Mr. Notch. I was planning on being alive tomorrow morning.'

'That's hardly amusing,' Notch said, stiffening his tone a bit. 'Meet with Metzger, the lawsuit's dropped. Don't meet with Metzger, and he proceeds. Which means, considering the facts, you will lose thousands, and the *News-Times* will lose millions of dollars.'

Mama arrived, polish remover and Ebony Enamel in her hands. I began wiping off Peaceful Petunia.

'Why does Henry Metzger want to meet me anyway?'

There was a pause. 'His exact words were, because he's heard so much about you.'

I could tell from the monotone Notch used that those were probably not Metzger's exact words.

'There's really no choice in the matter,' Notch continued. 'You are to meet Henry Metzger at his Saucon Valley home precisely at three. Oh, and, Bubbles, please dress accordingly.' Notch provided directions and hung up.

Mama crossed her arms. 'What was that about?'

I told her.

'No way, José,' said Mama, shaking her head. 'You'll never come back. You'll end up chops in the freezer just like Buster Padukis. You're grounded.'

I wanted to tell Mama that if she tried to ground me, I'd step on her.

'She's got to go.' It was Genevieve. 'If she doesn't, he'll come for the whole family.' Genevieve tiptoed over the peas, opened the broom closet, pulled out the musket and sighted it over the toaster.

'Good point,' nodded Mama, whose head, I noticed, came up to about Genevieve's hip.

'Don't worry,' Genevieve added. 'I'll go undercover and provide backup.'

I made a face. Undercover? Backup? Genevieve couldn't hide behind a Boeing 747 wide-body, much less one of Henry Metzger's azalea bushes.

'Roger,' responded Sgt. LuLu Yablonsky. 'And I'll be Bubbles's escort. We'll call it Operation Blowhard.'

The two old ladies high-fived each other, although Genevieve had to lean down way low and Mama had to reach up way high to accomplish that.

Before I had a chance to explain that Henry Metzger wished my presence alone, Jane sauntered around the corner and collapsed into a chair at the kitchen table. Her hair was now fluorescent tangerine, which nicely set off her bright blue lipstick.

'Was that jerk Notch on the phone?' she asked, rubbing sleep out of her eyes. 'He woke me up at nine-thirty. He's been calling every fifteen minutes. He left all these messages on the machine.'

I walked into the living room and placed one wet ebony nail on the PLAYBACK button of my answering machine. All I heard was a series of clicks.

'It's broken,' I said.

'It's not broken, Mom,' Jane yelled from the kitchen. 'You think every machine is broken. First you have to press Rewind.'

I pressed REWIND. Then I pressed PLAYBACK. *Click. Click. Click.*

'I got one like that,' Genevieve said, rounding the corner of the living room. 'Press Stop. Then Rewind. Then Stop again. Then Playback.'

I followed Genevieve's instructions to the letter. But when I pressed PLAYBACK there was only silence on the tape. We waited, listening, while I applied the last streak of ebony.

Jane strolled over, hands in pockets. 'Now what're you doing? Jesus. You're recording!'

Indeed, there was the little green recording light flickering at us. I pressed STOP.

'Doesn't matter,' Jane said. 'The first message was from Sandy.'

According to Jane, Sandy called to say that she might head down to Athena Adler's house and see if she could get an interview. Sandy would call me later with the results.

Then Doris Daye called. She said Mr. Salvo had been

fired and rumor around the newsroom was that he had been holed up in his Fountain Hill apartment on a bender ever since he left the hospital for what turned out to be psychosomatic chest pains.

I flapped my newly polished nails in the air. 'I was afraid of that. I knew I'd get Mr. Salvo fired.'

'I'll send him over some halupies,' Mama concluded. 'Nothing sobers up a drunk faster than halupies.'

Jane fooled around with the answering machine and resurrected the last message.

It was from Dan the Man, aka Chip. He'd gotten wind of how I'd been shot at down by Wysocki's, and he was furious.

'For Jane's sake, you better drop this journalism stuff. Now!' Dan growled. 'If you don't, I'll be in court tomorrow morning arguing that your reckless behavior is putting our child in danger. Any judge will give me an emergency restraining order so fast you won't have time to kiss Jane good-bye.'

I leaned against the wall and fought to keep my head clear. Dan always did know what buttons to push with me.

'No matter what,' he concluded. 'For her own safety, I want Jane at my house, today.'

Plus, he added, I owed him seven hundred dollars for Mama's court bill and legal costs.

Drop the story? Hand over Jane to that Son-of-a-Bum Dan? Restraining order?

In a pig's eye.

Genevieve paused momentarily in cleaning her musket. 'He's got a point. Sally here should be in a secure environment.'

'Oh, no,' whined Jane. 'I'll, like, have to have normal hair color and eat three squares with Wendy and Dan. Mommm! Can't you do something?'

'Shh, Jane,' I said, massaging my temples. 'I'm still trying to think how I can come up with seven hundred dollars.'

I helped Jane put together her stuff while Mama wrapped up the noodle kugel she had removed from our now perpetually stocked freezer. Meanwhile, I changed out of the high-necked pink number into a perfectly sensible jeans miniskirt and sleeveless white cotton blouse. I wrapped my hair in a bun because of the heat and made up my face as God intended.

The only reason I was looking so respectable was desperation. I hadn't done laundry in a week, and I was down to my least favorite clothes. Next thing you'd know I'd be wearing a jumper and a headband.

When Jane and I pulled up to their house, Wendy's Eddie Bauer SUV was missing, and there was no sign of Dan being on the premises either. However, Dudley the duck-hunting Labrador zipped around the corner as soon as we stepped out of the car.

'Yipes!' I screamed, hopping onto the hood of the Camaro.

Dudley stopped at the edge of the driveway, barking up a storm.

'Electric fence,' said Jane. 'That's what the flags are for.'

This was my lucky day!

'Well, I suppose this is it,' Jane said morosely, slinging her knapsack over her shoulder. 'The next time you see me I'll be playing soccer and wearing a pageboy.'

'Buck up,' I said, hopping off the Camaro and walking her to the garage door. 'It'll only be a couple of days. After I get this story done, Dan won't have a leg to stand on. Besides, this way you can experience teenage rebellion. How could I deny you that?'

'You mean don't trust anyone over thirty? You're barely thirty-four.' Jane opened the door into the back hallway and went up to the guest room to dump her stuff.

I proceeded to the kitchen to write Dan a note begging for an extension on the seven hundred dollars. Of course, I didn't have a pen. So I borrowed one of his from a desk in the kitchen where Wendy and Dan kept their calendars and bills and a basket of crucial papers.

Which is my long-winded explanation for how I started nosing around.

Like a squirrel rooting for nuts, instinct led me on. Somewhere in this basket of papers on the kitchen desk was a piece of information that I needed to read. I knew it in my bones.

I hit gold halfway through the pile. It was a letter written on Lehigh Steel stationery welcoming Dan to his new job. It opened with a chatty paragraph mentioning how enjoyable lunch was on Saturday. I looked up and checked the calendar. The Saturday to which the letter referred was yesterday. I resumed reading.

Employment would begin officially in one month. In the meantime, Dan should check with the department of personnel regarding health, dental and life insurance. There would be a physical, of course. And an orientation at the country club. (Membership is automatic. The fifty-thousand-dollar annual fee is picked up by Lehigh Steel.)

Welcome aboard! it concluded. Signed, Max Factor.

Max Factor didn't have to identify himself. I recognized his name from Henry Metzger's letter threatening to sue me for $3.5 million. I never forget a makeup brand.

Now, I don't have very much experience with corporate jobs. I've only worked as a hairdresser and a waitress. But I was willing to bet that most employees in Lehigh Steel's legal department did not receive their job offers by letter, on a Sunday, one day after having lunch with the senior counsel.

No, let me correct that. One day after getting their wives to sign a false affidavit that would benefit the former chairman of Steel immeasurably.

Dan, you scum-sucking, cheating, two-faced, needle-nosed creep, I thought. So damn ambitious, so desperate to get in that league that you and Wendy would falsify legal documents so Henry Metzger would owe you a job in Steel's legal department.

I thought about replacing the letter in the middle of the pile – where Dan had obviously hidden it to keep it out of sight – but I decided to hold on to it instead. For evidence.

Dudley started yipping again. A car door slammed. Either Dan or Wendy was home. Showtime.

I peeked out the kitchen window. Both of them, damn it. Dan was smiling ear-to-ear, a *New York Times* under his arm, patting Dudley. He was wearing a tan golf shirt with a navy blue cotton sweater tied around his neck.

Oh, would someone *please* take him off the L.L. Bean mailing list.

I accosted Dan as he entered the kitchen. 'So,' I said, holding up the letter. 'New job at Steel, eh? How *convenient.*'

Dan slammed *The New York Times* on the Corian.

'You've sunk to a new low, Bubbles. Rifling through my stuff. I ought to have you arrested.'

I walked around and faced him. 'Rifling through an ex-husband's personal papers might be tacky, Dan, but it's hardly illegal. Pressuring your wife to falsify an affidavit to provide an alibi for a murderer is.'

Dan stared at me. He was assessing how much I knew.

'Listen, Dan,' I pressed. 'You're worried about Jane's safety because I was shot at. Who do you think shot at me? It wasn't an angry House of Beauty client, I can tell you that much. That hit was on order of your new best buddy, Henry Metzger.'

'Point one. It's Chip, not Dan. Chip. Chip. Chip. Do I have to tattoo it on my forehead?' Dan opened a coffee canister on the counter and busily scooped beans into a Krups coffee grinder. 'Point two. Henry's retired, Bubbles. He's got an office at Steel as chairman emeritus. That's it.' He turned on the Krups. 'He's a little old man.'

Dan couldn't look at me. That fact alone spoke volumes.

'You wouldn't take that job with Steel if you knew what I know about Henry Metzger,' I said.

Dan stopped the grinder.

'Don't believe her, Chip.' It was Wendy. She walked into the kitchen dressed in a blinding green wrap skirt and a white cotton blouse, holding a trowel and a pair of gardening gloves. 'She's untrustworthy. That's her problem.'

'That's not my problem, Wendy. My problem is that you lied when you swore that you drove Merry Metzger to the airport last week. My problem is that your husband ratted out the mother of his only child because he wanted to get in Henry Metzger's good graces. That's my problem.'

Wendy threw up her arms and went out the kitchen door, giving it a good hissy slam.

After she left, I turned to Dan. 'By the way, I need an extension on the seven-hundred-dollar court bill.' I waved the Lehigh Steel letter and dropped it in my purse. 'I think you'll give it to me.'

'You can't do that!' Dan yelled. 'That's theft of personal property.'

I strolled to the door. 'Really, *Chippy*. Why don't we discuss it with the police? And when we do, let's talk about those affidavits as well. I'm sure by now the police have had a chance to check the airplane logs and have discovered that no Merry Metzger was on a plane Thursday night.'

'Good luck, Bubbles. The case is closed. Detective Frye told me so this morning. And there won't be any charges.'

I blinked and tried to keep my temper. 'Is Frye your buddy, too?'

Dan smiled. 'Not really. But I happen to know that his father is three months from retirement down at Steel's paint division.'

We glared at each other, two people who once engaged in the act of lovemaking, who now wanted more than the world to rip off each other's heads. We were spiders.

'There's a place in hell for all your Steel execs,' I said. 'And I'm praying it's made of bright, hot molten ore.'

I stood for five minutes holding a plate of halupies and knocking on the door to Mr. Salvo's apartment. I was about to leave when I saw his eye in the peephole. When he opened the door, a wave of eau de Schlitz wafted out.

'Christ,' Mr. Salvo said, peering nervously over my shoulder. 'What do you want?'

Mr. Salvo was in bare feet, wearing black pants and a white T-shirt stained liberally with beer, Nacho Cheese Doritos and ketchup.

'I want to say I'm sorry for all that's happened and I want to give you this. My mother made it.' I thrust out the kugel.

Mr. Salvo reluctantly took the casserole and let me in.

'Sorry the place is a mess. I'm packing,' he said, walking into the kitchen and placing the halupies in the refrigerator.

I glanced around the living room. Packing was one term for it. General slobbery was another.

White boxer shorts lay on the floor along with dirty black socks, a pair of grimy jeans, two flannel shirts and a stack of foil TV-dinner plates. Empty beer bottles were positioned randomly along bookshelves, window-sills and coffee tables in an almost artistic fashion.

There was no sign of Stiletto.

'Stiletto still here?' I asked, carefully pinching a fetid T-shirt from the couch and placing it on the floor. Mr. Salvo returned from the kitchen with a fresh beer.

'Is that why you stopped by?' he asked, taking a swig. 'No. Golden Boy's not here. I haven't seen him since before leaving for work on Friday. He split town right after that accident in Saw Mill Park, is my guess.'

I had an alternative theory, but I kept my mouth shut. Best to change the subject.

'What are you packing for?'

'I'm off to my camp in the Poconos,' he said, picking up a shirt from the floor. 'To fish.'

'I can't believe you got fired, Mr. Salvo. I feel really bad.'

He shrugged and shoved the shirt into an army green duffel bag. 'Things like this happen at newspapers, Bubbles. I'll find another job eventually. How about you?'

I detailed for him my conversation with Notch and how I was banned from the newspaper.

'I'm not giving up on journalism, though,' I announced proudly. I told him about my hope to sell a story to *The Philadelphia Inquirer* that would show how Merry Metzger relied on her connections to absolve her of two possible murders.

'Since seeing Merry Metzger last night, I'm even more convinced that she's covering up her involvement in the Saw Mill Park accident at least.'

Mr. Salvo stopped packing and turned to me. 'What?'

'In the bathroom of the A-L-E Airport on Saturday night. She was disguised as an old woman on her way to Alaska and she had a little gun.'

He reached for his beer. 'You tell anyone?'

Hmm. That wouldn't have been my first question.

'I didn't tell anyone,' I lied, thinking of Mickey's concern for his job. 'I was alone.'

'Good. Keep it to yourself. You know how the Metzgers are.'

Actually, I hadn't a clue as to how the Metzgers were.

'What are the Metzgers like, Mr. Salvo?'

Mr. Salvo collapsed onto a blue chair covered with old newspapers and mail. 'Henry Metzger started as a chipper at Steel, only nineteen at the time. Worked his way up to be chairman of the board. A lot of people in Lehigh resent his success and would like to see him ruined. Henry needs a rumor that his wife was in town last night like he needs a hole in the head.'

Mama would be up for that.

'Sounds to me, Mr. Salvo, like you're regretting the story we ran.'

'I've been talking to Henry this weekend. He called me several times, as an old friend of the family, out of concern for me, the son of his former gardener,' he said, bowing his head. 'After discussing it with him, I think it might have been prudent to wait a day. I think we rushed the story when we didn't have to.'

I absorbed the idea of Mr. Salvo and Henry Metzger being so chummy. If I'd had an inkling that they were such close buddies, I never would have told him about seeing Merry Metzger, much less about my plans to write an investigative piece on her.

'You tell Dix Notch you talked to Metzger?' I couldn't imagine the *News-Times* lawyers approving *that*.

'To hell with Notch,' he said, emptying the bottle. 'What has Notch done for me? At least Henry Metzger put food on my family's table, gave us a nice caretaker's cottage to live in when I was a kid. Notch canned me as soon as he got the chance.'

There was a tapping sound and I looked down. The beer bottle was clicking against one of Mr. Salvo's rings. He was shaking. And it wasn't from drink. Mr. Salvo wasn't drunk; he was frightened.

'Is there something wrong?' I asked, picking up a paper plate. Perhaps I could pitch in and clean this place up a bit.

'You mean, besides getting fired from a job you've had for nearly twenty years?' There was a sharp bitterness to his voice.

'Sorry,' I said. I dropped a plastic fork and leaned over to get it. When I did, the key from Chester Zug's toilet fell out of my cleavage and onto the floor. Mr. Salvo picked it up and examined it.

'Where'd you find this?' he asked. 'I haven't seen an Odd Lots Drinkers Club key in years.'

I stood still and waited for the next lie to surface. 'Found it sweeping up at the shop,' I said, removing the key from his hand and slipping it back in my cleavage. 'What is an Odd Lots Drinkers Club?'

Mr. Salvo glanced up at the ceiling. 'Like all the private drinking clubs around town, it's members only. Which is to say that a bunch of middle-class white men gather to drink on Sundays or after hours, times when the state's blue laws used to prohibit the sale of alcohol.'

He walked to the kitchen, pulled out the halupies from the refrigerator and began eating out of the pan. 'Odd Lots is a famous one. You've probably walked past it a million times and never known it was there.'

He told me it was behind St. Anne's in a hole-in-the-wall. I filed that away, in case I got around to returning the key.

'You want a beer?' Mr. Salvo asked, apparently rejuvenated by Mama's food.

I glanced at my watch and suddenly remembered my meeting with Metzger. I apologized for leaving so soon. Mr. Salvo walked me to the door.

'Bubbles,' he said, haltingly, 'you need to know that . . . that . . .'

There were tears in his eyes.

'That you're a good reporter. Don't give up journalism because of what's happened.' He put his hand on my shoulder. 'Swear to me.'

I didn't know what to say. It was kind of embarrassing, really, to see your former teacher so emotional. 'I won't, Mr. Salvo.'

'I got a feeling,' he said, 'that your big break is right around the corner. You've got a computer, of course.'

I shook my head.

'Here.' He yanked a key chain from his pocket and took off a key. 'This goes to my apartment. Come here and use my computer anytime. I'll leave a set of operating instructions out for you.'

Mr. Salvo's computer was covered with magazines and beer bottles and dust. It looked as though it had never been used.

'Thanks,' I said, taking the key. 'But aren't you gonna need it?'

He frowned. 'Where I'm going, I won't need a computer.'

I didn't exactly like the sound of that. 'You mean fishing?'

'That's right, Bubbles. Fishing.'

Chapter 17

MAMA WAS PERCHED ON the couch wearing a bright floral dress, coral lipstick and a white plastic purse when I walked through the door. Genevieve was dressed head to toe in camouflage, those mirrored sunglasses, army boots and a canvas hat topped off with sprigs of rhododendron.

'Time's a-wasting. I just put a chicken in the oven,' Mama said. 'Let's hop to.'

My watch said five past two. 'We got an hour almost.'

'Yeah, but Genevieve's got to get into position. Don't you, Genevieve?'

Genevieve headed for the door, carrying her musket. 'Surveillance takes preparation.' She ducked her head and stepped outside. I could only imagine what the neighbors were thinking.

Minutes later we were all squeezed into the Camaro, Genevieve taking up the entire backseat with her rhododendron leaves blocking my rearview. I hadn't had time to 'dress appropriately,' as Notch suggested, and that was fine by me. It was ninety degrees last I checked. Too hot for anything below the knee.

'How about some inspirational music to pump us up?' suggested Mama, flipping through my tapes.

'Like what, the Mormon Tabernacle Choir?'

Mama popped in a tape and soon David Lee Roth was screaming in my ear.

'Van Halen?' I asked, turning it down a bit. 'Since when did you get into heavy metal?'

Mama was playing imaginary drums on my dashboard. 'Since lockup. And it's not heavy metal, it's electric rock. Metallica, now that's heavy metal.'

Genevieve stuck her fingers in her ears.

'Speaking of jail, Mama,' I said, heading up Wyandotte Hill through the South Side, 'I've been mulling over your escapades recently, and I've wondered if you're acting on more than some wacky advice from a witch. I mean, you've changed, Mama. Like that whole dress incident. Why'd you walk five blocks from Hess's wearing a three-thousand-dollar dress you hadn't paid for?'

Mama stopped playing air guitar. 'Well, let me ask you a question, Bubbles. How come you wrote up that story on Merry Metzger? How come you risked your life for a physics teacher?'

I shook my head. 'I'm not following you.'

'After your father died on the job, bronzed alive for Almighty Steel, leaving us without a penny in savings, I had to go to work to support the family. What did I know? Nothing. So I cleaned houses. Who did I clean houses for? Wives of steel executives, that's who.'

The landscape was more rural now. Farmland. The South Side row homes far behind us.

'Now I'm going on sixty-five. And I've come to accept that I will never live in the big house or take the Caribbean vacations or wear the fancy clothes those steel wives did. So I—'

'Took a chance,' I suggested, finally understanding where Mama was coming from with the questions about Metzger and the bridge.

'That's right.' Mama nodded her head. 'When I saw that Vera Wang wedding dress hanging up at Hess's—'

'It was a wedding dress?' I asked, amazed.

'I never had one when I married your father down at the J.P.'s. I wanted to know what it felt like to wear such a beautiful thing.'

We were now a half mile from Metzger's house, on a private lane bordered by stone walls and overhanging oaks on either side. Beyond the walls was a deep green forest. I figured we were already at his estate.

'If you ask me,' Genevieve said, 'you two sound like angry dames in serious denial.'

Mama and I threw each other quick guilty looks.

'Let me off,' Genevieve said, when we arrived at what appeared to be a metal farm gate on the side of the road. 'I can hike in from here.'

I pulled over, and we all got out of the Camaro so Genevieve could exit.

'Okay, Bubbles,' Genevieve said, sighting the musket

243

on the roof of my car. 'Remember what I told you. Leave the keys in the Camaro. Keep yourself outside and visible to me at all times and if you start feeling nervous, here . . .'

She reached into her top right-hand pocket and pulled out a pack of Lucky Strikes. 'Light up one of these. I know you quit, but it won't kill you to have one. The Nazareth militia trained me to smell cigarette smoke from as far as five hundred feet away. When I pick up your signal, I'll start up the car and be there to retrieve you in a flash. And, LuLu, you be ready to go, too, if you hear me beeping.'

'Roger, Bratwurst Babe,' responded Mama with a salute.

'Back at ya, Waffle Woman,' said Genevieve.

'Code names,' Mama explained to me. 'Yours is Hairdo Honey, in case you're interested.'

Mama and I sat in the car and watched as Genevieve's broad, camouflaged backside became one with the underbrush.

Operation Blowhard was officially under way.

In twenty minutes, we started up the Camaro and drove along the long driveway to Henry Metzger's estate. It was, as I expected, large. A massive stone house decorated with white shutters and black wrought-iron railings, surrounded by a bright green lawn, a huge garden that included hosta and rhododendron.

The bright blue of an in-ground swimming pool peeked from behind the house.

An older man in a white coat came down the steps to greet us. He took one look at Mama and frowned. The butler, I assumed.

I introduced ourselves and explained that my frail and elderly mother could not be left home alone.

'Not an imposition,' said the butler. 'Please follow me.'

Once inside, he immediately directed us to a large room that was surprisingly not stuffy. Floor-to-ceiling windows framed by cheerful drapes patterned with red cardinals. A large leather couch and, best of all, a surround-sound TV.

The butler handed Mama a remote control. Mama parked herself in a La-Z-Boy and flipped out the footrest.

'How do you get *Price Is Right*?' Mama asked, punching the buttons on the remote.

He explained that, with this TV, it was possible to watch *Price Is Right, Wheel of Fortune* and Home Shopping Club all at the same time.

'Oh,' Mama gasped. 'It's a miracle.'

So much for my escort.

After setting her up with a tall glass of lemonade, an entire tin of Danish cookies and a *TV Guide*, we left Mama and walked through the large French doors to the backyard.

'Mr. Metzger is down in the orchard,' the butler explained as we stood on the stone terrace. 'Past the pool, past the tennis courts and after the hedge maze.

We've had a bit of an emergency with the bees.'

I took a deep breath. Not bees. I was allergic to bees, along with cats and certain eye cosmetics. Not deadly allergic, just allergic enough to blow up like a blimp and get sick to my stomach if I was stung.

Don't use that as an excuse, Bubbles, I told myself as I passed the inviting cool pool. Keep your head. A half hour with the jerk, and you've fulfilled your duty. Metzger will drop the suit. And maybe, if you're lucky, call off his hit men.

The orchard was down the hill in the back. I saw no sign of Metzger, although his Macintosh apples seemed to be coming along nicely. I strolled past the high green hedges. The sky was bright blue and the air so fragrant with the flowers from his garden that their perfume made me dizzy. If I didn't have to meet *him*, my heart would have been as light as air.

Near a stand of apple trees was a bench in front of five large boxes connected by clear plastic pipes. Bees. I sat down and watched them fly in and fly out. Still no sign of Metzger.

One of those apples looked ready to pick. I took a wide berth around the bees, reached up into the tree and plucked it.

'I'd watch that if I were you,' said a voice. 'What if someone plucked something off of you? How would you like it?'

I turned. Henry Metzger stood behind me holding a large bucket and a rake. His face was covered by a heavy white veil so that I couldn't make out any of his features. His body was trim, dressed in neat white slacks.

'The Wizard of Oz,' he said, walking slowly toward me. 'Unfortunately, I never had any children of my own, but that hasn't stopped me from adding that movie to my private collection. I think my favorite scene is Dorothy and the Scarecrow in the apple orchard, fighting with the trees as the Wicked Witch of the West looks on.'

I dropped the apple. My head buzzed. It was freaky what Metzger had said. As though he had read my mind, my emotions. Of course, I felt exactly like Dorothy. And this manicured estate was the wonderful Land of Oz.

'In all seriousness,' he said, standing by my side, 'the swarm is right above you. You'll need to move if I'm to hive them.'

A cluster of bees the size of a football was suspended directly above my head. So that's what the buzzing was.

'Yowzy!' I exclaimed, backing up. 'I'm allergic to bees.'

'Nothing to fear, my dear,' said Metzger. His voice was calming, refined. Not at all what one would expect in a thug. 'They're sated with honey. They couldn't sting you if they wanted to. Still, this might take a while, so please, have a seat on the bench.'

I sat down and brought my knees up to my chest, hugging them.

'By the way,' he said, lifting the rake into the tree so that several apples fell off, accidentally, 'I assume you are the lovely Bubbles Yablonsky.'

'I am.'

'And I am the awful, ruthless Henry Metzger. I bet you've been told horror stories about me since childhood.'

I had to stop myself from smiling. I almost liked the guy. Was Mr. Salvo right? Was Henry Metzger's reputation the fabrication of his enemies?

'You see,' he explained, 'bees usually swarm when the queen is laying, in late spring. But this year, partly due to my own neglect of the hive, they decided to swarm in late summer. And when they do, I've got only a few hours to bring them to a new hive. If I don't, the scout bees will find other places to live and take them there. And I'll lose them forever to a crab apple tree in the forest.'

Metzger was lifting off rakefuls of bees, gently dropping them into the bucket.

'Have you ever been stung?' I asked.

'Certainly, but only through mishap and misstep. I am human, you know. I, too, make mistakes.'

Most of the bees were in the bucket now, and Metzger was delicately removing the remainder with a paint stirrer. Out of the corner of my eye, I spotted a moving sprig of rhododendron behind some blueberry bushes. Genevieve.

'There.' Metzger covered the bucket with a cloth.

'I'll let them rest awhile and move them this evening. Would you care for an iced tea?'

'Love one,' I said cheerfully, inhaling a big breath of fresh air. 'With the sky so blue, I hope we can drink it outside.'

'I wouldn't have it any other way.' Metzger walked ahead of me, still wearing the veil. What was underneath it, a scar? Beady little eyes?

'Why do you keep bees?' I asked as we passed the empty clay tennis courts.

'Part of being a good steward of the environment. If it weren't for apiaries, all the honeybees would be extinct now because of widespread viruses and pollutants. I'm doing my part to see that doesn't happen.'

My mind was reeling with confusion. Order the uncle of a union worker chopped into steaks; save honeybees for generations to come. It didn't make sense.

At the house, Metzger led me up a flight of steps to a balcony above the stone patio. From here we could see the entire estate, past the orchards and woods and hills for miles.

'It's spectacular,' I exclaimed.

'Yes,' he said. 'It is rather pleasant.'

He excused himself and disappeared inside. He returned moments later, his veil removed.

I was stunned. Henry Metzger was a strikingly handsome man, even though he must have been close to seventy. His white hair was wavy and neat. And his tanned face, while wrinkled, was angular and attractive.

His teeth were pearly white, and his eyes were a brilliant green, made more so by the lime polo shirt he was wearing.

'Please, sit,' he said, pulling out a white iron chair. The butler came in and set two iced teas on the glass table.

I stirred the iced tea nervously.

'I know this can't be easy for you, Miss Yablonsky,' Metzger began, sitting back. 'But, frankly, if I'm about to drop a three-point-five-million-dollar lawsuit that my lawyers have indicated I am certain of winning on summary judgment, I'm not about to lose my opportunity to give you a lecture.'

Great. A lecture. What was it about me that men never hesitate to give me a lecture?

As though he understood my dread, Henry Metzger flashed a smile. It was disarming. I sipped my tea.

'Perhaps it might surprise you to know that I am quite familiar with your situation, Miss Yablonsky. For example, I am aware that, through tragic error, your father was incinerated in the ingot mold during my tenure as chairman of the board. And some part of you blames me for his death.'

I nearly spat out my tea. How did he know that?

'Sadly, lawyers, being lawyers, would have made hay in court of what a jury might easily construe as your long-abiding hatred toward me stemming back to that fatal accident. My lawyers would have argued that you intentionally wrote a false story alleging that my wife became intoxicated and killed a man with a vehicle simply out of retribution. That's called malice, Miss Yablonsky, and juries have delivered huge verdicts in favor of plaintiffs when they determine journalists have been guilty of malice.'

This would have been the perfect opportunity to tell Metzger to hold on, buddy. That what I saw in the Saw Mill Park or what I wrote in the *News-Times* had nothing to do with my father. What I wrote were the facts.

I kept my peace, though, because I'm Bubbles Yablonsky. To Henry Metzger, I'm a nobody. A hairdresser. Daughter of a worker. Granddaughter of a worker. Great-granddaughter of a worker. Who was I to contradict him?

But I did summon enough gumption to ask him one question.

'If you are so sure of being right,' I began, wringing my hands under the table, 'then why are you dropping the suit?'

'Moral obligation,' he answered, getting up and walking over to the balcony. 'When you called the night of the accident in which you thought you saw my wife, I should have answered you civilly. I should have explained that my wife was in Central America.'

Aha, I thought. But she wasn't.

'Instead, I stooped to crudeness. I was tired. I had been woken out of my sleep by police at my door minutes before you called, and I was angry. What I said, about making your life a living hell, was out of line. And for that, I apologize.'

Imagine that. Henry Metzger apologizing to me. His words injected me with courage. The apology reminded me that Henry Metzger, not just Bubbles Yablonsky, made mistakes. Henry himself acknowledged that while he was attending to the bees.

'Pardon me, Mr. Metzger,' I piped up, 'but what you said about malice and my father, that's plain wrong. I mean, I wrote what I saw. And I still stand by what I wrote.'

Henry Metzger turned toward me, and I could tell he was taken aback. I think he assumed that this surprise lecture would go uninterrupted, and I would docilely sit and take it like a naughty puppy.

'You know what I consider to be my greatest accomplishment as chairman of the board, Miss Yablonsky? It was that I was able, through keen business skill and management, to provide thousands of jobs to unskilled, uneducated, innately untalented people like your father for a whopping twenty-one dollars an hour, full benefits and six weeks vacation.'

I got up. Watch it, Bubbles, my conscience cautioned. Watch what you say and do.

'I think you should apologize again, Mr. Metzger. My father was not unskilled. He was not untalented.'

'I have nothing to be sorry for,' he said, leaning over the balcony. 'What I said is a fact, not an opinion. What I expect is a little gratitude from my workers' families.'

I reached in my purse for a Lucky. Get me the hell out of here, Genevieve.

'I'll never be grateful to you for killing my father,' I said, now searching for a match. 'Full benefits, twenty-one dollars an hour or not.'

Metzger looked at me disgustedly as I lit up. I tried to stifle a cough and keep my brain from flying off my neck.

'Andre,' he ordered. 'Ashtray, please.'

The butler hurried in, placing an ashtray in front of me. I carried it over to the balcony and blew out a plume of smoke. Come on, Genevieve, where are you?

I didn't feel like chatting with Henry Metzger any-more. Instead I studied the silver ashtray, which had an ornate EMB engraved at the bottom.

'Who's EMB?' I asked, in an attempt to return the conversation to a civil tone.

'Those are the initials of my first wife, Eva,' said Metzger. 'That ashtray's a fitting keepsake since she died of lung cancer ten years ago. That's the French for you, passionate but undisciplined.'

I looked up and stared into his green eyes. 'And a Pole? Or do you refer to us as Pollacks?'

'Great workers,' he said wryly, 'except when they are stupid enough to fall into an ingot mold.'

A plume of smoke escaped from between my lips. Mama had been right all along. Henry Metzger was pure evil.

If Genevieve hadn't started beeping the car horn, I would have pushed him over the edge right then and there. But she did, and I didn't. Instead, I headed for the stairs.

'Where are you going?' Metzger was blocking my way. 'It isn't time for you to leave.'

'Sorry, Mr. Metzger. That's my ride.'

Beep. Beep.

'We've much more to discuss. I won't drop the lawsuit until you've heard me out.' He stood at the top of the stairs, obstructing my exit.

I started to panic. There was no way out.

I headed toward the French doors at the house. Freaky Andre locked them in front of me. I ran to the other side of the balcony and looked down. Genevieve was out of the car now, hopping up and down, her rhododendron sprigs bouncing like springs.

'You can do it, Bubbles!' she shouted. 'Jump and roll. Jump and roll.'

'What in tarnation is *that*?' Metzger said, gaping at Genevieve. 'It's a Sherman tank with breasts.'

In a second Mama was at her side. 'Do it, Bubbles!' she screamed up at me. 'We'll catch you. Wait. Don't jump yet. I gotta place a price on that refrigerator.' She ran back inside.

'You *know* these people?' Metzger asked, still blocking my way to the stairs.

I put my knee up on the ledge of the balcony and, without much mental debate, rolled over the side.

It was a terrifying, albeit quick, fall. I landed right in the prickly azalea bushes with a crash. Owww.

Genevieve was there, hands on hips. 'I told you to jump and roll, not roll and jump. Oh, well. Let's go!'

She grabbed my hand and pulled me out of the bushes. We dashed toward the car. I didn't stop to see if Metzger was peering over the balcony or bounding after me. We ran around the side of the house. Genevieve had the Camaro door waiting open. I got in the back. At the last minute, Mama hopped into the passenger's seat.

'And we're out of here,' Genevieve yelled, the Camaro screeching down Metzger's driveway. 'Operation Blowhard is a wrap.'

Chapter 18

I HAD TO MAP out a new strategy now that I'd queered Metzger's deal with the *News-Times*. There was no other option. I must concretely prove his wife was the driver of the car that killed Chester Zug. When I jumped off Metzger's balcony, I insulted and infuriated a powerful, violent man who was used to having his way.

It was just a matter of hours before he retaliated.

My legs and arms were bloody and covered with scratches from the fall. I went upstairs to take a shower after dropping off Genevieve. Mama made a beeline for the kitchen to baste her roasting chicken. It could be 110 degrees inside, but if it was Sunday, Mama would make chicken. It's like a law.

As I got undressed, the Odd Lots key fell out of my bra. I threw on my bathrobe and called Sandy. I related my visit to Henry Metzger's awful world of Oz. Sandy agreed that I had done the right thing by telling him off and then running away like a chicken. I sighed and changed the subject.

'Want to go to a private drinking club with me?' I asked, explaining about the key I found in Chester Zug's toilet tank.

'You forget, Sunday night's our clogging night.'

'What?'

'Martin can't miss it, either. He just finished sewing a new pair of lederhosen, and he's bringing his toe tappers.'

Some married couples are into kinky sex, others play tournament bridge or tennis doubles. I could never quite grasp what Sandy and Martin were into. It all seemed innocent enough, but somehow it smacked of the bizarre.

I decided it was a good policy not to probe. 'You find anything out from Athena Adler?'

'Only how it feels to have a door slammed in my face. When she answered the door she was real pleasant, but as soon as I asked some questions about Merry, she went ballistic.'

Shoot. What did I expect? If a total stranger came to my front stoop and started asking questions about Sandy, would I be nice?

'I was so upset that when I came home I found four gray hairs on my head,' Sandy whined.

'No! What did you do?'

'Well, I'm not about to start covering gray, that's for sure. I spritzed on a coffee and vinegar rinse. At least it will make my hair shiny. Maybe I won't notice the gray.'

Sandy suggested I call Doris to go to Odd Lots.

258

'What!' is how Doris answered the phone.

I laid out my offer.

'Are you kidding? I got a final tomorrow. I can't go out drinking.'

'You don't have to drink. Besides, how many times do you get to crash an all-white, all-male private drinking club?'

It was a no-brainer. 'Pick me up at eight outside the *News-Times*. I'll be the one dressed to the nines in silver.'

I had no intention of letting Doris outdo me. After a nice, long shower and a thorough application of anti-septic, I carefully pulled on a pair of supersheer black stockings, to hide the scratches. Then I poured myself into a black Lycra minidress dotted here and there with tiny glass beads.

I did a Bubbles Deluxe to my hair, letting it hang loose this time. And put in those cubic zirconia earrings.

'All this for chicken?' Mama asked, dishing out drumsticks, green beans and salad. There was a lot to be said for this Mama-living-with-us stuff. She was doing all the shopping, the cooking and cleaning. Now if I could just get her to do laundry.

It was lonely without Jane at the table, though. After dinner I wrapped up a plate of leftovers.

'I think I'll go up to Roly's Rollicking Licking Ice Cream Shop and give this to Jane,' I announced.

'I think I'll call Genevieve and ask her to come over,' said Mama. 'I don't want to be by myself.'

The line was one block long out the door of the ice cream shop when I arrived. Considering that it was still eighty-five degrees and a Sunday, that came as no surprise. I went around the counter and placed the plate of leftovers in the ice cream shop refrigerator.

I ran into Roly, as rotund and jolly as ever, a tiny pink-and-white-striped paper hat perched on his large red head. Roly was a few years ahead of me in school and, even then, was obsessed with ice cream. During study hall he'd come up with creative flavors – mouthwash mint chip – and as a teenager could talk your head off about the advantages of guar gum.

But what always struck me as pathetic about Roly is his last name. Poly. And what's worse, he is Roly Poly III. The original Roly, his grandfather, was the founder of Roly's Rollicking Licking Ice Cream Shop.

'Why, my, my, it's Bubbles Yablonsky,' he boomed, sticking a spoon of black ice cream in my face. 'It's licorice leather, wanna try it? The kids love it.'

'No, thanks,' I said, gently pushing the spoon aside. Roly plunked it in his mouth.

'Jane's out front,' he said. 'Getting swamped. Hard worker, that one.'

'Maybe I'll give her a hand,' I said, swallowing a temptation to suggest that perhaps the boss might pitch in, too.

When I walked out to the counter, Jane was scooping out the bottom of a tub of peppermint twist. A fan in the window was blowing right on her back. Unhealthy.

'I'm up to my neck in work, Mom, literally,' she said. 'My help's been in the bathroom for the past half hour.' I kissed her on the cheek and was shocked to discover that under her pink striped hat, her hair had been dyed to its natural brown. I wisely hid my shock.

'How are things going at Dad's?' I asked. Like I couldn't tell.

'Sucks.' She pounded the peppermint into a sugar cone, rang it up and took the next order. A double banana split with hot fudge. Plus one child's-size vanilla.

'Ugh,' groaned Jane. 'A line a half mile long and he orders a double banana split.'

'I'll make it,' I offered, grabbing the bunch of bananas.

'Thanks.' Jane proceeded to scoop out a child's-size vanilla.

'What's with the hair?' I sliced the bananas the long way into a cardboard boat.

'Wendy made me do it. She blamed you for letting me get away with murder.'

Hah. That was ironic, I thought, as I placed scoops of vanilla, chocolate and strawberry ice cream on top of the bananas.

'Which reminds me.' Jane poured chocolate syrup into soda water. 'I found out about the Range Rover.'

I held the ladle of chocolate sauce in midair. '*The* Range Rover? How?'

'It belongs to a friend of Wendy's. It was reported stolen Friday night. Dad and Wendy were talking about the whole thing in the kitchen this morning when they thought I was asleep. But I listened in on the intercom.'

That's my girl. I did the whipped cream, sprinkled nuts and handed it to the guy – $5.50 and 1,600 calories of pure heaven.

'Hey,' he said when I gave him the change. 'How come all the soda jerks don't dress like you?'

I mustered up a wink.

'So, what else?' I asked, when Jane's help returned from the bathroom. 'They know who owns it?'

'Not Merry Metzger. Some other woman who's a friend of hers. They said Merry took it without asking and that this friend is all upset, but that she won't go to the police because Merry's her best friend.'

'You catch the name of this friend?'

'Nope. They never said her name. They kept calling her the Goddess in this sarcastic way. Like "The *Goddess* had a fit" and "The *Goddess* wants her Range Rover." You know anyone with a name out of a myth, Mom?'

That one was over my head. The only myths I learned in school were that you couldn't get pregnant if the boy had a cold and that, if you did get pregnant, the man would marry you and take care of you for the rest of your life.

'Name some goddesses, Latin major,' I ordered Jane, who'd been studying the language since sixth grade.

Jane stirred the soda. 'Diana. Hera. Venus. Vesta. But I only know the Roman ones.'

'What other kind are there?'

'Greek. Norwegian, I think. Druid. A lot of common names come from gods and goddesses. Mine even.'

'Jane?'

'From Janus, a Roman god.'

Wow, I never knew that. And I named her.

'How about Bubbles?'

Jane handed a customer the soda. 'Right. Bubbles. The goddess of soap operas and hair spray.'

Just what you need in the middle of a murder investigation. A wise-guy teenager in a pink paper hat.

What bugs me about Mama is that she's so Lehigh. Kugel. Van Halen. Sunday dinner at 4:30 P.M. sharp. Which meant that by the time Jane kicked me out of the ice cream store, I had over an hour to kill before meeting Doris at the *News-Times* at eight.

I decided to spend the time productively, stopping by Laura Buchman's old neighborhood on Myrtle Lane.

I'd been out that way once in my life, on a field trip to hike Camelhump in sixth grade. It was wooded and remote. Upper class.

I drove down Center Street and took a right just before the interstate to Bierys Bridge Road. I had to check a map in my glove compartment to figure out where I was going.

Occasionally the burning charcoal and lighter fluid smell of evening summer cookouts wafted into the Camaro as I headed into the forest. Houses were spaced farther apart now, hidden from one another by tall trees and lush foliage.

Myrtle Lane turned out to be an extremely private dead-end road. There were three large houses on it. The one on the left was a traditional clapboard colonial, beige with blue shutters. Pink and yellow petunias cascaded from flower boxes at each window. Hedges were neatly trimmed and mallards flew on the mailbox.

The one on the right was a sizable Cape, painted red, with a matching red mailbox that said CROWLEY.

The house at the end had a FOR SALE sign stuck in the lawn, and I sensed immediately that it had been Laura Buchman's. I recognized its angular, modern architecture from TV reports of her suicide ten years ago. The cedar siding needed to be restained. Grass and weeds crept up between the white stones around the foundation. Cream-colored curtains inside were drawn, and the redwood deck showed signs of rot. It screamed neglect.

A horror movie couldn't have set a better scene for the murder of a teenage girl.

I parked the Camaro and walked up that property's gravel driveway. A high picket fence delineated a backyard and was locked. The rear of the property extended down a hill to the Monocacy Creek and a set of railroad tracks.

Those high school kids must have felt like they won the lottery when they found this place. Pool. Deck. Privacy. Woods. No parents.

Inside the fence was a shaggy lawn and an in-ground swimming pool covered with a dark green cloth and leaves. That backyard must have been where Merry Metzger found her friend's cold corpse in the rain: Poor Laura Buchman.

'Help ya?'

I nearly jumped out of my skin. 'You surprised me,' I said, bringing my hand to my throat. 'Caught me snooping, you did.'

The spitting image of an elderly Henry Fonda in a golf hat was standing behind me wearing a red-and-white-checked apron and holding a metal spatula.

'Hah!' he laughed. 'Didn't think you were a house hunter in that getup.'

I absently ran my hand over the beaded dress. But this is the way I always look, I wanted to say.

'I'm on my way to a party.' I held out my hand and introduced myself as Bubbles Yablonsky, freelance reporter, doing a retrospective on Laura Buchman's suicide.

The man, who identified himself as John Crowley, removed his cap and scratched a mosquito bite. 'Laura Buchman. Now that's a name I haven't heard in a long time. How come you're writing about her now?'

I kept it vague. 'Seems new information has surfaced about her death. This is her house, right?'

'Was. Her father moved out shortly after her death, and it's stood empty all that time. When Mr. Buchman died of a heart attack three years ago, the estate's executors put it on the market. It didn't sell. Now they got it listed at rock bottom price. Gonna devastate the value of my property, that's for sure.'

'Catch, Grandpa!'

Without hesitating, John swung on his heels and caught a football, tossing it back to two young boys who tried to check me out without being obvious. He handed the oldest one his spatula.

'Flip the burgers,' he ordered. 'I'm going to be a while talking to this lady. Don't let them burn.'

Reluctantly the two boys ran back to their grandfather's home, whispering to each other along the way.

'Did you know her family?' I asked, picking up a white stone.

'Sure.' He put his hands in his pockets and looked around. 'I'm probably the only one left in the neighborhood who did, except for Mrs. Arbogast across the street.' He pointed to the beige colonial. 'People move around so much nowadays. Used to be you held a house for thirty years. Now folks buy and sell them like trading cards.'

I turned my attention back to the Buchmans' house. 'Yes, but to hear you speak, no one's bought or sold this one.'

'That's true. In this real estate market why buy a house where there's been a murder when you can purchase a brand-spanking-new one for the same price?'

I opened my eyes wide. 'So you don't believe it was suicide, either?'

John shook his head and strolled to the rear of the property. I tiptoed after him. 'No, I don't. Never have. My wife made a big stink about that investigation being closed and Laura's death being ruled a suicide.'

'Where's your wife now?' I asked. She and I might have a lot to discuss.

'Died four years ago of cancer.' He shuffled a foot on the ground, overturning a rock.

'I'm sorry.'

'So'm I.'

I picked up a twig and began bending it, nervously. 'So why don't you think it was suicide?'

'My wife looked after the girl – casually, you know, out of concern. No one else seemed to care for her, what with her own mother gone and her father being a traveling salesman. If my wife were here today, she'd tell you that Laura had never been happier. No depression as far as we could see.'

The twig broke in two. 'But you didn't happen to notice a car that day or any activity at the Buchman house the day she died.'

'Nothing out of the ordinary,' said John. 'My wife was home all day the day Laura died, which I remember as a Friday, and we were both home the night before. No unusual cars. No voices. You might try Mrs. Arbogast. Boy, what a snoop. I bet she knows what brand of corn flakes I eat for breakfast.'

We both chuckled.

Birds filled the trees, trilling an evening song.

'How lovely,' I commented, shading my eyes to see them better.

'Warblers,' John said, shading his eyes, too. 'This part of the creek is famous for them. They flock here every September to fly south and bird-watchers come from miles to watch them with binoculars and take counts. It's a big event.'

At that moment a flock rose into the air, across the setting sun.

'September was when Laura died,' I said.

John folded his arms. 'That's true. I remember clearly there being a bird-watcher positioned right on that part of the track.' He pointed straight ahead. 'She was documenting bird counts the week of Laura's death.'

'Who was she?'

'Never caught her name.' John shrugged. 'My wife chatted with her a few times, just remarked that the woman was extremely knowledgeable about birds. Warblers especially. When Laura died, my wife told the police about the bird-watcher, suggested they ask her if she saw anything.' He scratched the ground again with his sneaker. 'Slipshod investigation,' he grumbled. 'Keystone cops.'

'I guess that's what you get living in Pennsylvania,' I said with a lilt in my voice. 'This being the Keystone State and all.'

John frowned. That joke wasn't funny. I got the impression that when it came to Laura Buchman's death, nothing was funny. About this he was dead serious.

I thanked John and let him return to his grand-children. After he left, I strolled across the street to Mrs. Arbogast's. The blue garage door was closed, the lights were off and the house seemed empty. But John assured me she kept it dark inside, in order to better spy on the neighbors.

Mrs. Arbogast owned one of those unnecessarily long door chimes. *Ding. Ding. Dong. Dong. Ding. Ding. Dong. Dong.*

A hand parted the sheer curtains in a nearby window. The door swung open and a woman in blue hair, blue sparkly pointed glasses and a plaid sundress stood in front of me. The funny thing about women with blue hair, which is achieved through a weekly wash, is that they don't know they have blue hair. They look in the mirror and see silver and they love it. Only the rest of us see blue.

Mrs. Arbogast squinted her eyes at my beaded dress. 'You sure don't look like a Jehovah's Witness,' she said. 'What're you selling? Avon?'

I explained my purpose, stressing that I was apparently trustworthy enough for John Crowley to speak to.

'Crowley,' she muttered. 'Liberal granola freak. Okay, come on in. The air-conditioning's on.'

I stepped into the air-conditioned house, and Mrs. Arbogast slammed the door. She wasn't about to let me enter beyond the foyer, which was carpeted with a thick, red oriental rug. A large walnut grand-father clock stood in the corner, its brass pendulum swinging somberly. *Tick. Tick. Tick. Tick.*

'A bit late to be checking into that Laura Buchman's death, don't you think?' she asked, pushing up her glasses. 'I don't know how many nights I called the police before she died. Maybe fifty times. I'd say, "You got to stop this racket. It's three a.m. These kids are in school." The cops would come. The kids would go home, and the next night there'd be another party. I always figured something sad would come of it.'

I opened my purse and removed a notebook. 'You don't mind if I take a few notes, do you?'

She waved her hand. 'Little good it will do you. That was ten years ago.'

I wrote down all she had told me. At a time like this, I'm really thankful for snoops.

'You see anything else, perhaps the day of her death?'

Mrs. Arbogast crossed her arms. 'Nothing the day of. That was the odd thing. The day after. The week after,' she smacked her forehead, 'it was like before. All these kids hanging around, dropping off flowers, hugging, crying, kissing, smoking cigarettes, playing their car stereos loud. That poor girl's suicide turned into just another excuse to party. There was even a Peeping Tom.'

My pen scribbled fast. 'Really? At your house?'

'If he'd been at my house I'd have shot him between the eyes with the .22. No one's getting a glimpse of me in my nightie. No, at the Buchmans' house. I got him fired for it, too.'

'Fired?'

'Yup. He was a professional. He should have known better than that.'

I lifted my pen. 'What kind of professional?'

'Garbage man. Bad enough they can root through all our trash without having them spy into our living rooms, too.'

Sandy's Coffee, Rosemary and Vinegar Rinse (for brunettes only)

You'd expect someone who runs a beauty salon to experiment with radical hair color or the latest fashionable haircuts. Not Sandy. She is perhaps the most conservative, down-to-earth person on the face of this earth. Her clothes are either practical polyester uniforms or simple cotton dresses. Her hair has been the same since we were in high school – short and curly. She has worn the same shade of lipstick – Mostly Mauve – for fifteen years. So when it comes to touching up a few of her gray hairs, Sandy doesn't take any chances. She sticks to coffee. Specifically, coffee mixed with vinegar in a spray bottle. She swears that it works, is a wonder on brunette hair and, best of all, eventually washes out. I have to admit that her hair does look spectacular after one of these rinses, rich and shiny. I wonder if there is an equivalent for bottle-bright blondes.

½ cup boiling water
1 teaspoon rosemary leaves
1 cup very strong coffee cooled to lukewarm
¼ cup vinegar
2 vitamin E capsules
1 plastic misting bottle

Steep rosemary leaves in boiling water and let cool to lukewarm, about a half hour. Mix the rosemary solution with lukewarm coffee and vinegar in a spray bottle, the kind you might use to mist plants. Break open the vitamin E capsules and squeeze their contents into the bottle. Close cap and shake. Wrap a towel around your neck and spray rinse completely over hair, making sure the mix penetrates down to the roots. Let sit for a half hour. Rinse. Shampoo and condition.

Chapter 19

'WHAT IS THIS, A competition for who can be most 'ho?" Doris Daye stepped into the Camaro, barely recognizable from the bookish four-eyes I'd met yesterday. Underneath that T-shirt and jeans was a killer body. And tonight the killer body was wrapped in a form-fitting silver lamé dress and matching pumps. Glasses were replaced with contacts.

'Wow, Doris,' I said. 'You look so . . . wow.'

'Don't I?' she agreed, leaning over to check herself in the rearview mirror. She turned on the tape player and Van Halen blared out.

'Valley music . . . yuk,' she said, grabbing the tape and throwing it back in the box. 'Don't you have good stuff?'

'Like Earth, Wind and Fire?' I asked, crossing the Philip J. Fahy Bridge where two days ago I'd been a hero.

'No. Just because I'm African American doesn't mean I only listen to black guys. Maybe I listen to Mozart? Or salsa. Jazz. Japanese drum music. You ever think of that?'

'Sorry, Doris.'

'Relax,' she said, punching me on the arm. 'Let's hear Maurice do his stuff.' She slipped in EWF and I filled her in about Jim Morrison, Chester Zug and what Mrs. Arbogast had told me minutes before about the Peeping Tom.

'You think that was old Chester?'

'Worth checking out, say?'

'Yeah. Say.'

We stopped talking to listen as Maurice hit the high note on the live version of 'Reasons.' The air was warm, stars were coming out and I was single. Boy, I wished I owned a convertible.

That thought reminded me of Jeeps, which reminded me of Stiletto. Which was a dangerous idea considering the way I was dressed, the hot summer night and EWF's powerful bass beat.

I parked the Camaro in front of St. Anne's and tried to recall Mr. Salvo's directions. Doris and I thought we followed them exactly, but found only a small house where the club was supposed to be. Gray. Unspectacular. Shades drawn.

'This is it,' Doris said confidently.

'It's a house,' I protested as she marched up the front walk.

'It's a club.'

On Doris's urging, I put in the key. The lock clicked open.

'See,' she said. 'You gotta go out more.'

We opened the door to a small dark hallway with brown carpeting. A pay phone was attached to the fake wood paneling next to a string of coat hooks. There were approximately ten hooks, none of which had coats on them.

'Nice decor,' said Doris, running her hand over the paneling. 'I guess when you want to get drunk, you don't give a hooey about atmosphere, huh?'

Doris and I tiptoed toward a door at the opposite end, from which came the mumbling of voices and the smell of cigarette smoke.

We entered a large room lined at one end by a mirrored bar. There was a billiards table in one corner, a jukebox in another corner and several low wooden tables in the center. There were no windows.

The place was empty except for a slim man in a ponytail shooting pool and two porky men in their mid-sixties with thinning gray hair and beefy faces, sitting at a table. They were dressed in what Mama referred to as the Official Polka Uniform – black pants, white shirts, white socks and black shoes.

Even from across the room I could tell their arteries were clogged with grease after decades of sausage, Schlitz and multi-channel cable. One man wore glasses. Other than that, they were identical.

My experienced eye pegged them as boombas players on their way home from a gig at Dorney Park. How did I know? The boombases on the chairs next to them were dead giveaways, as were their shirts, on which the word BOOMBASTICS was embroidered in red. Add to that the Dorney Park baseball caps.

Most people outside the Lehigh Valley have never seen a boombas. A boombas is, essentially, a pogo stick with wood blocks, cymbals, cow bells, beer taps and assorted odds and ends attached to it. There's a large faction in town who swears this is a musical instrument. I have yet to be convinced.

Supposedly no two boombases are alike and often they run to themes. I've seen auto parts boombases adorned with spark plugs and hubcaps. Irish boombases decorated with leprechauns. Of course, kitchen boombases are always popular and versatile. Mama's is adorned with odds and ends she pilfered from the senior center.

Just so you know, the word *boombas* translated means bang clang. Enough said.

Doris spied the two boombases and groaned. 'The first sound I heard getting off the bus at Lehigh was "I Don't Want Her, You Can Have Her, She's Too Fat for Me" some old ladies were playing on the boombas. I was tempted to climb back on the bus and go home.'

'Yeah,' I said, leading her over to the two men. 'Folks feel pretty strongly about the boombas, one way or the other.

'Excuse me,' I said, tapping one of the Boombastics, 'but I'm trying to locate the person who runs this place.'

Both men took a long time sizing me up, their eyes pausing at each one of my major physical attractions for a closer analysis. I was considering charging admission when the guy I tapped said, 'No women.' Turning to Doris, he added, 'No blacks neither.'

Doris raised an eyebrow. 'Guess that makes me two for two. Damn.'

'I'm here to return a key,' I explained. 'A key that belongs to Chester Zug.'

'You say something about Chester?' The young man who had been playing pool laid down his cue stick and sauntered over. 'You have Chester's key?' He had a pleasant smile and welcoming brown eyes. Not to sound cliché, but what was he doing in a place like this?

I held up the key, and he plucked it from my fingers, taking it over to the bar.

'That's Jason. He's the bartender,' said the man with glasses, who seemed the most civil of the two. 'By the way, I'm Paul and this' – he pointed to his partner – 'is Ralph. Say hello, Ralph.'

Ralph frowned and slurped his beer.

Doris gave Ralph a flirtatious finger wave. 'Nice to see you, Ralphie.'

Ralph glanced sideways at Doris, who pursed her lips and blew him a kiss. I couldn't figure out what was going on between the two of them. It was like being back in grade school when all the girls used to whisper in each other's ear, making sure to leave one girl out.

There was a loud *thunk* as Jason the bartender slapped a gray metal box onto the bar. He opened it, dropped in the key and replaced the box under the bar.

'May I get you women anything?' he called out.

'How about a nice tall Coke?' Doris said, sashaying over to the bar and plunking herself down on a stool.

'No way!' called out Ralph, shaking his head. 'You know the club rules, Jason. These girls have got to go.'

'Anyone who returns an Odd Lots key gets a complimentary beverage, Ralph,' Jason said calmly. 'Don't you give me a hard time, now.'

Ralph grunted. I joined Doris at the bar and ordered an A-Treat Root Beer.

'How do you know Ralph?' I whispered to her.

Doris put one long silver-nailed finger to her lips and said, 'Shhh.' Then she pinched my behind so hard I nearly fell off the chair.

Jason placed our drinks in front of us. He slid mine over to me slowly and with deliberate eye contact. 'You related to Chester?'

'Actually it's me who's the connection,' Doris answered quickly. 'Used to be a client of mine. Quite a trip he was.'

I coughed several times into my napkin. Jason only said, 'Oh,' and proceeded to busily wash a glass.

'Awful thing that happened to him, say?' he said, placing the glass in a rack. 'I read in the newspaper that it was Merry Metzger who ran him over. But I didn't read nothing about her getting charged. Figures.'

Doris pinched my butt again. Hard. I kicked her with my left foot. We were going to have some nasty bruises in the morning if this kept up.

I planned on keeping mum and letting Jason do all the talking but Doris couldn't resist noting that steel executives in this town are so privileged they could get away with murder.

'Don't I know it,' Jason agreed. 'Merry Metzger's as bad as her husband. Thinks she's the queen of Lehigh or something, at least to hear her talk.'

Doris kicked my ankle. I kicked her back.

'Owww,' she moaned. 'Knock it off.'

'You started it.'

On the other side of the room Ralph cleared his throat and tapped his watch.

'You two need another?' Jason asked in fearless defiance of Ralph's imminent wrath.

'No thanks,' I said, downing the rest of my A-Treat. 'I'm just a little surprised that you even know who Merry Metzger is. I mean, the Odd Lots is nice and all but it's not exactly Merry's kind of hangout, if you get my drift.'

'I don't know about that.' Jason pulled out a wooden tooth-pick from a jar on the bar and picked at a back molar. 'She showed up here a few nights ago, throwing a tantrum and threatening to—'

'Hey, hey, hey.' Ralph was up from the table, waving his hands. 'Don't you be telling these girls Odd Lots secrets. Ain't none of their business.'

That's where Ralph was mistaken. Merry Metzger at the Odd Lots was very much my business.

Ralph approached us, swaying slightly. His eyes were

red and watery. There was a big, ugly mustard stain on the front of his Boombastics shirt, right over the belly, and he reeked of stale beer. 'You girls drink your drinks and then skedaddle,' he ordered. 'You've been here long enough.'

Paul attempted to calm him down. 'C'mon, Ralph,' he said, getting up and patting his friend's back. 'Let them stay awhile. They ain't doing no harm.'

Ralph brought a fist down on the bar. Doris and I concentrated on our drinks. Jason filled up a jar with more swizzle sticks.

'It's not right,' Ralph shouted. 'This club's been here since Prohibition, and the only times blacks and skirts have been allowed in was to wash the floors. Now they're taking up the bar like they live here.'

Doris twisted a napkin in her lap. A paper substitute for Ralph's neck. She abruptly swung around on her stool.

'What's gotten into you, Ralphie?' she purred. 'You sure were happy to see me last time. Now you act like we're strangers.' She slid off the stool and slipped an arm across his shoulders.

'Last time?' Paul inquired.

'There wasn't no last time. She's fibbing.' Ralph tried to pry Doris's arm off him, without much success. 'Get off me.'

Doris took her arm off Ralph and placed her hands on her hips. 'Excuse me? Need I remind you of the beer tent at last summer's Musikfest? North corner behind the speakers. I believe the band was playing "Roll Out the Barrel," if memory serves me.'

Ralph's jaw dropped.

She pointed one of those long nails at Paul. 'And weren't you there, too? I remember because Ralphie here kept ragging on your boombas. Said trash can lids sounded better than what you used for a cymbal.'

A look of pain swept over Paul's face. 'You don't like my ham can, Ralph?'

Doris nodded. 'That was it. The ham can. Ralph said it was all flat. No style.'

'It's not true,' Ralph protested. 'I like your ham can. I do.'

Paul strolled over to Ralph so they were nose to nose. 'Don't lie to me, Ralph Mutter. Admit it. You hate my boombas.'

A bead of sweat rolled down Ralph's chin. 'I love your boombas. Okay. There was that one time with the toilet seat. Other than that you got a great boombas. Who else has fishing bobbers for castanets?'

Paul didn't seem to be buying it, though. His eyes flickered, and he removed his glasses, placing them on a nearby table. Both men had forgotten about Doris, who returned to her stool to get a better view of the action.

'My grandfather made that toilet seat from one piece of oak,' Paul growled. 'It had a sound all its own, and you made me get rid of it.'

'Yeah?' Ralph rolled his shirtsleeves right up to his pasty white shoulders. 'It was that toilet seat that cost us the Allentown Fair 1993 Best in Polka Boombas award. That toilet seat got us disqualified from the Mummers Parade. Your grandfather was about as musical as you are, Paul. And that ain't saying much.'

The grandfather dig did it. Paul brought back a fist and slammed it into Ralph's stomach. Ralph went, 'Ooooff.'

When he had recovered Ralph stood up and immediately slugged Paul across the jaw. Jason, who had been strangely silent behind the bar, decided now was the time to step in, especially when Paul grabbed his boombas and prepared to bring it crashing down on Ralph's head.

'That's enough,' Jason said, pulling the boombas out of Paul's hand. 'You two take it outside.' He escorted both men to the door.

Doris trotted after them. 'I better stand watch.' She stepped into the hallway. Jason and I were alone.

'You're not a hooker, are you?' he asked, sitting on Doris's stool.

'No. I'm a reporter. I wrote the story on the hit-skip that killed Chester. Doris is a university student. She's helping me out.'

Jason absorbed this. 'You going to quote me? 'Cause I could lose my job if my name appears in the newspaper over this.'

I twirled my straw. 'I don't have to quote you. Anyway, this isn't much of a job to lose.'

He shrugged. 'A few nights ago Merry Metzger

crashed the Odd Lots. She burst in armed with pamphlets and said she was from some organization—'

'The Pace Foundation?'

'Sounds about right.' There was a *bang, boom, ugh* from the hallway.

'She threatened to close down the bar. Said she planned on ridding Lehigh of all the private drinking clubs. Wait.'

He leaned over the bar and retrieved a pamphlet. It was basically a sheet of white paper folded sideways. On it were lots of statistics about deaths caused by alcohol and other drugs. At the top was a toll-free number one could dial for help or to make a donation.

Inside the pamphlet was a statement signed by Merry Metzger. It explained how the death of a friend in high school, Laura Buchman, directed her to the Just Say No path.

'May I keep this?' I asked.

'Sure. She left about a dozen.'

The fighting in the hallway took a hiatus. Jason and I held our breaths. When it resumed, he said, 'She had a baseball bat. She was about to smash all the bottles.'

'What stopped her?'

'I told her the mayor wouldn't be too happy about that. He's a member.'

'Ahh.' I made a mental note to write a story on the mayor's being a member of an all-white, all-male drinking club.

At that moment Doris entered the room, shutting

the door behind her. 'That's that. Paul put Ralph in his car and is driving him home to sleep it off. I gotta get the boombases.'

She picked up the two boombases and left. When she returned, I handed her a pamphlet and told her what Jason just told me about Merry Metzger's visit.

Doris read it over. 'Did Chester Zug see this?'

Damn. Why hadn't I thought to ask that?

'Probably,' Jason said. 'He was here that night, and he kept staring at her like he was trying to figure out where he'd seen her before. I thought of that when I read the story about his death.'

Doris and I exchanged knowing looks.

'I got one question,' I said as Doris and I left the Odd Lots. 'How did you know that Ralph was at the beer tent during Musikfest?'

'Oh, c'mon. You got a white bigot in black pants and white socks who plays the boombas. Where else was he?'

'At the Handel recital?'

'Yeah, right. The boombas plays *Messiah*. I don't think so.'

Chapter 20

I T WAS A HOT and sticky morning when I woke up to
the sound of Mama's vacuuming downstairs. Normally, Mondays are my day off, and I would have spent
this one lying on my couch in the direct line of a fan,
sipping iced tea and catching up on *All My Children,
One Life to Live* and *General Hospital*.

Instead, I planned to spend the day linking a
dead garbage worker to the wife of a former steel
executive and the murder of a teenage girl ten years
ago. Luke and Laura would have to take a rain
check.

I took a shower, put my hair in a ponytail and slipped
into a pair of jeans shorts and a yellow tank top, no bra.
My sandals were moderately low-heeled (one inch) and
my makeup was minimal (only three layers). Mama's
cucumber poultice was a wonder. The bump had completely disappeared.

When I arrived downstairs I found Mama facedown
on the living room floor, arms stretched in front of the
couch.

'Bob Barker finally retires and you can't go on with life?' I asked.

'Hush, such blasphemy,' she said, getting up onto her knees. Mama was wearing a white apron, and that meant business. Even worse, a tape measure was stretched between her hands.

'Look what I'm doing for you and you don't even notice.'

'What are you doing?'

'I'm *re*doing the furniture.'

Please no. Redoing the furniture might sound like an extremely ambitious undertaking, but if Mama was redoing the furniture, it could mean only one thing: plastic.

'Go look in the kitchen,' she ordered, writing down the measurements of the couch arm on a pink tablet.

I peeked into the kitchen. Good news. The peas were gone. Sucked up by the Hoover this morning.

Bad news. Plastic covered the table, the four chairs and even the overhead lamp.

Mama called from the living room. 'Don't it look nice?'

'It don't look nice,' I said, sitting down on one of the chairs. Immediately the plastic became one with the delicate underside of my thighs.

'You'll thank me later,' she screamed from the other room. 'The next time you spill a glass of purple grape juice, you'll thank God for plastic.'

I surveyed the room. It was bad enough that the troughs of mashed potatoes were still over the door, not to mention the sandbags against the windows. Now everything was coated in plastic. In eighty-five-degree heat and tropical humidity, too. Egads.

Ding. Dong.

Mama ran to the door like a schoolgirl and peeked out the eyehole. 'Oh, goody,' she said, unlocking a set of Genevieve's booby traps, 'it's Mickey.'

And me here without my bra.

Mickey stepped in wearing plainclothes. That was a relief. I was beginning to think he slept in that uniform. The plastic on the chair made a ripping sound as I got up to greet him.

'Here, LuLu, this is for you.' He handed Mama a white Entenmann's box.

'Ooooh. Blueberry coffee cake,' she squealed. 'Come on in and sit awhile, Mickey.'

Mama rushed to the kitchen to make a pot of coffee. Mickey and I stared at each other, him using every ounce of law-enforcement discipline to fight the temptation to check out whether I was or was not wearing a bra. Me trying to appear pleased as punch to see him.

'You look tired, Bubbles,' he said, closing the door.

I advised him to sit on the only unlaminated piece of furniture remaining, the couch. One of his last chances to come in contact with upholstery before Mama attacked it. I sat next to him and explained what I'd been up to, carefully omitting snooping around Chester Zug's apartment.

'You get the police reports on Laura Buchman's death?' I asked.

'Nope, not yet. Saw a copy of the coroner's report, though. Looks like she did herself in with liquid morphine and barbiturates. Standard suicide ingredients, Bubbles.'

'She didn't kill herself, Mickey.'

'I think you might be wrong, Bubbles.'

Mama brought out the coffee cake sliced up and frowned. 'Gee. I wish you two would move to the kitchen. The couch hasn't been plasticized yet. What if you squish a berry?'

'I'll deal, Mama. The couch is fifteen years old.'

'In Poland we'd be proud to have a couch fifteen years old. It would be like new.'

'You've never even been to Poland.'

'I've seen pictures.'

'May I have some coffee, LuLu?' Mickey asked sweetly.

Mama made a dash for the kitchen. Anything for her beloved Mickey.

'Anyway, Bubbles, the real reason I came over was to tell you that we found the Range Rover.'

I took a bite of coffee cake. 'No. Where was it?'

'Ricker's Quarry, out in Whitehall,' he said, wiping his hands on a napkin. 'Some kids went swimming there yesterday and spotted it. Totally stripped, of course. Except for the serial number. Other than that, no tires, no upholstery even. No radio, of course. Typical car theft job.'

'Who'd it belong to?'

Mickey smiled. 'What's your reporter's status these days?'

'Nonexistent,' I lied. Why tell Mickey I hoped to get this into *The Philadelphia Inquirer* when that would only complicate matters?

'Off the record,' he said, 'it is registered to a woman named Athena Adler out in Saucon Valley.'

I swallowed hard. Athena Adler was the name of the woman Jim Morrison said was a good friend of Merry Metzger's, the same woman who shut the door on Sandy.

'Is Athena the name of a goddess, Mickey?'

Mickey shrugged.

Mama entered the room with a tray of coffee. 'What's the name of a goddess?' she asked, setting down a cup in front of each of us.

'Athena.'

'Goddess of wisdom,' Mama said. 'Sprung from Zeus's head.'

Mickey took a sip of coffee. 'Does this have cinnamon in it?'

'It does,' Mama said, giving me a sly wink. 'Do you like it?'

'It's delightful.'

'How'd you know about Athena?' I asked.

'*Jeopardy*,' Mama said. 'Everything I know I learned from *Jeopardy*. If you watched educational TV like I do, Bubbles, you'd be a lot smarter.'

The cinnamon must have gone to work on Mickey because as he walked out the door he asked me if I'd be interested in sharing a picnic lunch with him down at the park. That reminded me that I had to find some time to go over there and hunt in the grass for the cell phone and film. I could not do that with Mickey looking over my shoulder, though. Besides, I didn't want to lead him astray, romantically, so I demurred.

'Maybe after you're done working on this story that you claim you're not working on, then?' he asked.

'Sure, Mickey. But really, I'm not working on a story.'

'And I'm not searching high and low for confidential police reports.'

'Good. We're agreed.'

After he left, Mama said, 'I would clean your house every day for a week if you would give me a son-in-law like Mickey. I would scrub your toilets.'

Once again I was saved by the phone. It was Jane, ostensibly calling to ask for some more clothes, but really calling to complain about Wendy.

'Gracie came over and we were outside, not inside, and Gracie lit up a cigarette on the deck and Wendy came out of the house, yelling, "Put it out! Put it out! I will not have punks in my house!"'

I listened patiently, holding my tongue like the true diplomatic single mother that I rarely am.

To change the subject before I, too, started railing about Wendy, I clued Jane in about Athena Adler. I griped about the difficulty of getting an interview with her, which I felt was crucial to the story.

'I don't see why you don't pretend to be someone

else and pump the Goddess for information,' Jane said. 'Sandy didn't have any luck playing it straight with her. You won't, either. Why can't you call up and say you are an old friend of Merry Metzger's or something?'

The thought had occurred to me, too, but I had decided against it. Instead, I used this as an 'educational opportunity' – to borrow Doris's words – to teach Jane about the ethics of journalism.

'Finally, Jane,' I concluded, parroting one of Mr. Salvo's lectures, 'journalists are only as trustworthy as their ethics. A journalist who lies, cheats, steals, trespasses or misrepresents himself in order to gather facts for a story loses all credibility and breaks the law.'

Jane was silent for a minute. 'You said *himself* not *herself*.'

'So?'

'So, you're a woman. You're not a himself. I bet that code of ethics doesn't even mention herselfs.'

I thought about this. It was a total stretch, but I'm a very flexible gal.

'You sold me,' I said. We developed a strategy for interviewing Athena.

'Think Valley girl,' Jane said. 'And I don't mean Lehigh Valley girl.'

I hung up and got the phone book. I looked up Athena Adler's number in Saucon Valley, went upstairs to my bedroom and dialed. The last thing I needed was Mama shouting in the background about her plastic coverings.

Athena Adler answered on the second ring.

'Hi!' I said in my perkiest, most upbeat imitation of a cheerleader on Prozac. 'This is Carol Mrgshm? I'm in town doing some consulting for the Pace Foundation on their upcoming fundraiser, and since Merry's out of the country, she left me a note suggesting I might call you for lunch? She said you have some interesting ideas on this year's theme?'

Every sentence, Jane instructed, should end like a question. I crossed my fingers as Athena Adler, aka the Goddess, absorbed it all. I heard the sound of pages flipping on the other end. A date book?

'How nice of Merry to think of me,' she said. 'My husband returned from a four-day business trip this morning, and I'm still unpacking him so today's out. Hmmm. How about Tuesday?'

I giggled. 'Gee willikers, I'm in New York Tuesday. I know it's *awfully* last minute, but is there any way we can meet this afternoon?'

Beep. Boop. Beep. Beep. Boop. Boop. Boop

Mama was on the other phone, dialing away. I got up and ran with the portable downstairs to stop her.

'What's that?' Athena inquired.

'Whoops! There's my other line,' I said. 'Gosh. I so wanted to speak with you, especially since Merry mentioned that you might be chairing the fundraiser this year?'

'Really?' That caught Athena's attention.

Beep. Boop. Boop.

'I suppose I can rearrange a few things. How about noon? It just so happens I've got a tennis date at the club then. I'm sure you can play tennis . . .'

Tennis! Yipes. I don't play tennis. 'Oh, boo-hoo. I slightly injured my wrist . . .'

'Great. Then tennis at noon it is,' Athena said cheerfully, ignoring my bogus injury excuse. 'We'll meet at the summer bar in the Greenbriar—'

'Hello?' Mama was shouting into the receiver. 'Hello?'

'Is there someone else on the line?' Athena inquired.

I ran into the kitchen and unplugged the telephone line. 'Not anymore.'

'Good. See you then.' *Click*.

I stood stunned, the portable in my hand.

'If this is gonna be my house, I can use the phone, too,' Mama complained, pouting.

I let Mama call Genevieve and then I woke up Sandy. Since the House of Beauty was closed on Monday, Martin let Sandy sleep in as long as she wanted.

'Meet me at the House of Beauty in fifteen minutes,' I said. 'I need an emergency soccer mom by noon.'

'An emergency soccer mom?' Sandy sounded alarmed. 'Don't tell me. In order to get an interview with Athena Adler, you're going to pretend to be Merry Metzger's friend.'

'More like co-worker.'

'You know what I think? I think you've been inhaling too much nail glue. That's what I think.'

* * *

Sandy, Tiffany and I stared in the vanity mirror in shock. Even the shop mascot, Oscar the miniature poodle, was repelled. He sniffed my leg, ran to the corner and started shivering.

'You look so . . . old,' said Tiffany.

'Not old, exactly,' said Sandy. 'So respectable.'

I was dressed in tennis whites, right down to a pair of Nikes and Peds. My hair, once long, bright blonde and feathered, had been cut to a reverse bob, died dark ash blonde and foiled. The process took three hours.

Sandy redid the makeup. Muted tones. No eyeliner. Brown lipstick. Gone was my bright pink lipgloss and midnight-blue eyeliner, not to mention the rose blush and my beloved Maybelline Great Lash Mascara in the pink-and-green tube.

I began to cry. 'I hate it,' I sobbed. 'It's so brown and boring and . . .'

'Matronly,' offered Tiffany.

'I'm so middle-aged!'

Sandy rushed up with a tissue. 'You're going to smear your mascara. Stop it.'

'What mascara?' I shouted. 'That's not mascara!'

'Okay, mineral oil then.'

The phone rang. Tiffany got it. 'It's some suit, Bubbles,' she called out, not bothering to cover the receiver. 'I think it's that jerky editor.'

I yanked it out of her hand. No doubt Notch was

calling to ream me out for my behavior around Metzger yesterday.

'Where's Salvo?' he yelled.

'Mr. Notch . . .'

'The neighbors said the last time they saw him was yesterday afternoon with some bimbo, and I said to myself, goddamn Bubbles Yablonsky. So, where is he?'

'He told me he was going to his fishing camp in the Poconos.'

'Tried him there. Even sent a reporter up to his cabin. Salvo never showed.'

Mr. Salvo's odd demeanor – the shaking, the nervousness – came back to me. Deep down inside I feared something like this might happen. Morrison. Now Salvo.

'Sorry, Mr. Notch. I left him at two yesterday and then I went to Henry Metzger's like you told me to.'

'Oh, yeah, right,' he said, shifting gears. 'How'd it go?'

'You didn't hear?' Sandy and Tiffany were openly eavesdropping on the other phone.

'I guess it went okay, then,' Notch said, 'because I haven't heard a word.'

'I'm sure you'll hear from Henry Metzger. Trust me,' I said, eager to get off the phone. 'I'll let you know if I hear from Mr. Salvo.'

'Wait, Bubbles, what did—?'

I hung up. What did I have to lose? Dix Notch had no power over me now.

'Too bad about Mr. Salvo,' Tiffany said. 'You'd think with a name like Salvo he'd be safe. Get it?'

Sandy and I stared at her, clueless about what she was saying, as usual.

'You know, like in Italian? How *salvo* means safe?'

'The only Italian I know,' said Sandy, 'is spaghetti.'

'You'd be surprised,' Tiffany said sincerely. 'There are a lot more Italian words than that.'

The one time I was beaten up was in the girls' room of Northeast Junior High School in eighth grade. The bully was a 180-pound juvenile delinquent named Ginger Soto – named after the movie-star character in *Gilligan's Island* – who distinguished herself by selling pot and wearing a bright green plastic pick in her hair.

It was that pick that got me in trouble with Ginger when I innocently bumped her and knocked it off in the hall between sixth and seventh periods.

'You're gonna pay,' Ginger growled, shoving the pick back in her bushy hair. 'Basement girls' room next period, you and me, one on one, or else.'

Technically, we were supposed to tell the principal when things like this happened. But practically all the kids at Northeast Junior High School knew that if the threat wasn't dealt with that day, a bully like Ginger would track her targets later and then she would be accompanied by her gang.

Better to get it over with. One on one.

I remember that as I smoked a cigarette alone in the

basement girls' bathroom that day waiting for Ginger to show, an awful feeling of dread descended on me. Seconds later the bathroom door opened and Ginger appeared, along with five of the toughest girls in school. My head had to be slammed only once against the metal stall for me to pass out.

As I lay on the dirty, cracked pink tile, amidst the odd bits of toilet paper and tampon wrappers, I thought, Why? Why do I get myself in situations like this?

I was mentally back in the pink-tiled girls' room of Northeast Junior High School when I found myself stirring a soda and lime at the white oak bar of the Greenbriar Country Club waiting to meet Athena Adler. Once again, I had the premonition that something really bad was going to happen to me. If I had had any sense at all, I would have fled right then.

So far, the only obstacle to getting into the club had been my three-toned Camaro, which I ended up parking in the employees' lot two miles away. My new hairdo and tennis togs got me through the front door of the country club with no problem.

Thankfully, Doris had a complete tennis outfit, right down to the frilly underpants. I picked it up before heading to the House of Beauty. I found her collapsed in her dorm room, exhausted after a three-hour final. She handed me the racket and told me how to use it.

Following her instructions, I bent my knees and kept my feet moving. But when Doris tossed an eraser right at 'the sweet spot,' I didn't swing until it had already bounced off the racket and was lying on the floor.

'Maybe you can beg myopia,' she said. 'Or do you want me to really break your ankle right now?'

I told Doris I would take my chances.

The Greenbriar Country Club summer bar reminded me of the Miller High Life grandstand up at the Pocono Speedway. One side of it was open and looked out to the tennis courts below. It was fenced by a white trellis covered by bright green ivy. Only this ivy was real, not green plastic like the kind at the Pocono Speedway.

Against the trellis were small tables and white Adirondack chairs so that club-goers could sip drinks and watch the court action.

On two chairs sat boys as young as nine, without an ounce of fat on them, wearing colorful T-shirts and boxy swim trunks. Their feet were propped up on the trellis and they were gleefully sucking on cherry licorice. They hadn't a clue that the privilege of doing that cost their parents three times my annual salary.

The actual bar was against the walled end of the room, and that's where I was sitting, ruffled white panties and all, when Athena Adler walked in.

Athena Adler looked like the type of woman who had Tiffany's on speed dial. Elegant diamond-and-sapphire earrings, diamond tennis bracelet and a beautiful platinum-and-sapphire watch.

She was extremely tall, almost six feet, with pale skin and shiny black hair pulled into a severe ponytail. Her black eyebrows were plucked to perfection and – there's no need to say this because I'm sure you've already assumed as much – she was very, very thin. Even in a white silk pantsuit she was thin.

'You must be Carol!' she exclaimed, arms wide open. 'How wonderful.'

She quickly kissed me on the cheek.

'Hope I didn't keep you. Gosh, I wish we could chat now,' she glanced at the watch on her wrist, 'but already I'm late for doubles. C'mon. We'll talk while I change.'

I hopped up and followed her to a dressing room decorated in white wicker. It was larger than the square footage of my entire house and more comfortable, too. Couches with bright lime cushions. Large vanities. Fresh flowers. Stacks of warm towels and makeup and bottles of hair spray everywhere, left like no one was going to stick them in their purses.

Two other women were at the mirrors, one brushing her hair, the other tying a sneaker.

'Brett. Markie.'

'Hi, Athena,' they responded blandly.

Athena made no attempt to introduce me. Instead, she carried her tennis bag into a small changing room and closed a louvered door. Brett and Markie left.

'How long have you known Merry?' I yelled over the door to her. After all, this is why I was taking this risk, to get a story, right? I didn't ruin my hair just to twiddle my thumbs in the locker room of the Greenbriar Country Club.

'Eons. From as far back as summer camp. And you?'

Whoops. I hadn't quite counted on that question. 'Not long. Since I started doing some work for Pace.'

'Ahh.' Zippp.

'I thought Merry mentioned that you two went to high school together,' I said, recalling the tip from Jim Morrison.

Athena emerged, dressed ready for tennis, a thin smile on her face. 'We did.'

This interview was the pits. I'd get more out of quizzing a federal undercover agent.

'I'm curious,' I strived on. 'How'd she meet Henry?'

Athena plunked herself down in front of the makeup mirror, unzipped a plastic bag and began vigorously powdering her face. 'Merry was an intern at Steel, worked in the elevator the summer after her freshman year in college. Henry's wife had died the year before after a long, long illness. He was completely depressed. Anyway, one night somewhere between the tenth and first floor, Henry and Merry met and fell in love. Instantaneously.'

Athena spun around, her purple eyes flashing. 'Isn't that romantic?'

Isn't that a lie, I thought. Who was it who told me that Merry met Henry when she was in high school? Was it Jim Morrison? The now missing Jim Morrison?

A toilet flushed and a blonde woman emerged from the bathroom. She began conversing with Athena. 'Clark dropped out and we're one short. Poopers.'

Athena turned to me. 'Carol's going to fill in. Right?'

Uh-oh. I knew this was going to happen if I was dressed for tennis. I'd told Doris maybe I should go in my street clothes. Doris said what if Athena only had time to talk over tennis. Bring a racket, Doris said. Put on some tennis togs. Play the part.

And where was Doris? Passed out from studying all night. Little good she was doing me now.

'I don't think so,' I said weakly. 'I hurt my wrist the other day.' I wriggled my wrist to somehow show that it hurt. Athena smirked.

'Oh, come on,' said the other woman. 'We'd love to have you. By the way, I'm Susie.' She held out her hand, and I shook it.

'Sure,' pressed Athena. 'Hit a few balls with us for warm-up at least.'

At that moment Susie gasped and grabbed a tube of Athena's eyeliner.

'Is this Sancôn?' she asked. 'I hear it's fantastic, but so expensive.'

'Only a hundred fifty dollars,' replied Athena. 'But the color's so true and lasting. I think because it's French.'

I gulped. Expensive French eyeliner. I'd heard of such wonders, but I had never been lucky enough to see them in reality. My eyes began to water at the thought of actually trying it on.

'Here,' offered Athena, handing the tube to me. 'I'll let you try it, Carol, if you promise to warm up with us.'

'I promise,' I whispered, practically snatching the tube out of her hand. I carefully applied it in a fine, black line. It drew smoothly and flawlessly across my bottom lid. I stood back. My eyes were positively brilliant.

'Amazing,' said Susie. 'Your eyes sparkle.'

'Let's go,' said Athena, putting the tube back in her purse.

I blinked. The eyeliner didn't run. I blinked again. Something was wrong.

'It stings,' I complained, following Athena out to the tennis court.

'It does?' she asked. 'You must be used to cheaper makeup. It never stings me.'

Not only was she the Goddess, she was also the Bitch.

The tennis courts were set under large willow trees, clipped so that the long branches on one side did not hang into the court and so that the other side of the tree could usher in a constant breeze. A rail-thin woman in a white hat and sunglasses was already waiting for us. She was Athena's partner. Once again, Athena didn't bother to introduce me.

I shaded my eyes. Since it was lunchtime, a substantial crowd had gathered and was watching us from the summer bar above. Oh, great. Mortification with an audience.

Susie and I walked to the other side of the court.

'You want to play forehand or backhand?' Susie asked.

'Which is easier?'

She slapped me on the back. 'That's funny.'

Susie positioned herself right by the net. I stood next to her.

'Just do what they do,' Doris had said.

'Aren't you going to move back?' Susie asked.

Athena was bouncing a ball with her racket behind the baseline while her partner was at the net, so I moved back, too.

In fact, I was so far back that I could hardly see Athena, even though I'm hardly nearsighted.

So why couldn't I see the ball?

'How about a warm-up?' Athena yelled. She brought the racket over her head and behind her, meanwhile tossing up a tennis ball. *Pop*. The ball whizzed by me.

'Sorry, Carol. I didn't know you weren't ready,' Athena said.

This time I tried to be alert. I bent my knees and kept my feet moving, as Doris had showed me. I rubbed my eyes. They were itching uncontrollably. Damn French eyeliner. Boy, I hoped it didn't have toluene-propyl-glycol in it. I was so allergic to toluene-propyl-glycol, my eyes would swell up and shut in minutes.

Pop, whizz.

'Nice service, Athena,' Susie called. 'How about taking it a little easier on Carol?'

Pop, whizz, thud.

That one went off the corner of my racket. A few people at the bar above chuckled.

Pop, whizz. I didn't even see it. Now there was outright laughter. Dimly I made out shapes on the balcony. People were gathering, drinks in hand, to watch the scene below.

I rubbed my eyes again. They were not only itching, they were burning. As though needles were being inserted into my eyeballs.

Pop, whizz, oof.

Pain shot through my gut. I bent over. Athena Adler had slammed the ball into my stomach. I clutched my middle in agony, dropping to the clay court. The breeze from the willow trees did nothing to soothe me.

'Are you okay?' asked Susie, kneeling by my side, her voice full of genuine concern.

'It's my eyes,' I whimpered. 'I can't see.'

'We've got to call a doctor,' Susie said. 'Something's wrong with her eyes.'

'It's one of her many allergies. Certain things are too rich for your blood, aren't they, Bubbles?'

I coughed. At that moment, the truth hit me. Wendy was the tennis player Athena hadn't introduced me to – on purpose. Athena and Wendy had set me up for one mean round of double embarrassment here on the ritzy tennis courts. Their turf. I absently wondered if Wendy was aware of my allergy to toluene-propyl-glycol, too.

'You mean,' Athena queried with false alarm, 'this is not Carol Mrgshm?'

The two women howled with laughter.

'What's this about?' Susie asked.

'Bubbles Yablonsky, did you seriously think that you could pull this off?' Athena asked. 'First you have your fellow hairdresser bother me at home on a Sunday. Then this, pretending to be someone else, trying to sniff out dirt on a good, good friend of mine like the cheap tabloid reporter you are. Why don't you give it up?'

'Enough, Athena,' Susie said. 'She's hurting.'

'I disagree,' said Wendy. 'It's Bubbles Yablonsky who's causing *Athena* pain.'

I may have missed the ball, but I didn't miss the point. My investigation was causing trouble for Athena.

I knew then that Laura Buchman's murderer was within my grasp.

Chapter 21

'THE LAST TIME I saw you was at Nana Yablonsky's funeral, and you were commenting on her makeup job. Now it looks like makeup's done a job on you.'

The voice belonged to my second cousin once removed, Donna Transue, a nurse in the emergency room of St. Luke's Hospital up on Fountain Hill. Donna was a large woman with bright blond hair and three kids and a husband who drove trucks. I'd never known Donna to have a bad day even though she had spent most of her life tending to victims of heart attacks, near drownings, car accidents and, occasionally, shootings. If you have to be in an emergency room, Donna's the nurse you want.

I had requested her specifically, although for reasons way beyond Donna's warm bedside manner.

Donna gave me firm instructions as she taped two pieces of gauze over my eyes. Wear the patches at least until morning. No bright lights. My eyes would probably hurt tonight.

'Here are some painkillers,' she said, handing me a

bottle. I'd already been shot with antihistamines and smeared with eye cream. 'Street price two hundred dollars.'

'Mind if I ask you a question, Donna?' I carefully sat up, trying to get used to the concept of being without sight.

'Is this about sex? Because I don't think I'm certified to answer any Bubbles Yablonsky sex questions. That Stiletto would require a continuing education credit alone.'

'You've been talking to Mama?'

'Actually, I believe it was my mother talked to her sister-in-law who heard about Stiletto from LuLu's friend Alice.'

Ah, yes. Mama's overgrown grapevine. 'Don't worry. My question's not about sex. It's about drugs.'

'By the way,' Donna sounded like she was throwing papers in one of those trash cans with the pedal, 'don't take those painkillers with alcohol. That'll knock you out.'

'It's about morphine.'

'No way. You're not sick enough for that.'

I told Donna about Laura Buchman's death, about the coroner's report and Mickey Sinkler's assertion that morphine and barbiturates were standard suicide fare.

'He's right,' she said, lowering her voice. 'We don't like to talk about death in hospitals. We have a way of pretending, for sanity's sake, that it doesn't exist, especially suicide. But a lot of old people or terminal patients, you'll find they'll save up morphine and do themselves in that way. Barbiturates kind of seal the deal.'

I sighed. 'So, in other words, Laura did commit suicide?'

'Who knows? I couldn't tell that simply from knowing what meds she took. But if I were you, I'd try to figure out where she got the morphine, if you can. That stuff's not sold in the high school hallways.'

'No? It was liquid.'

'Liquid morphine? Wow,' Donna said, grabbing hold of my elbow and lifting me off the gurney. 'Now that is unusual. We administer liquid morphine in only very rare cases, usually when patients can't swallow pills.'

'Like what kind of patients?'

'Like cancer patients, mostly, unless they're in the hospital. Then we put them on a drip.'

'I must look very attractive,' I said to Mickey when I got into his cruiser at St. Luke's Hospital. 'Most men go for women with white cotton eye patches, say?'

'A lot of men have never even seen your eyes,' Mickey said, closing the door for me. 'You got too much else that's pleasant to look at.'

After Donna telephoned Sandy for me, she called Mickey, who offered to pick me up even though he had to arrange a baby-sitter to do so. Sandy and Martin retrieved my car from the Saucon Valley Country Club employees' lot and were bringing it to my house.

Mickey didn't even pry as to why I was pestering Athena Adler. We were developing a good working relationship and let me stress the word *working*.

'I got good news and bad news for you, Bubbles,' Mickey said, not offering me a preference. 'The bad news is the chief of police issued a statement today that closes the case on the Chester Zug accident forever. Zug had a heart attack and Stiletto – or whoever – ran over his body after he was dead. No charges, except we're still investigating Stiletto for leaving the scene.'

'Super. What's the good news?'

'They're not going to charge you in the Fahy attempted suicide case. Dudko raved to his psychiatrist about you, said you saved his life, and disputed eyewitness accounts that you pushed him. He said he was so taken aback by the kiss he gave you that he was—'

'Taken aback. Literally,' I guessed.

Mickey laughed. 'Right.' He stopped the cruiser. 'We're at your house now.'

Mickey opened my door and helped me out, retrieving Doris's tennis racket from the back. 'Also, I got a surprise for you inside,' he said, leading me by the arm up the walkway.

'Is it a Jacuzzi?'

'Don't you wish.'

I lay down on the couch and Mickey got me a Diet A-Treat Cola. It was weird, not being able to see, having to rely on voices for soda and help up the stairs.

'You're being awfully nice, Mickey. How should I return the favor?'

I heard Mickey fiddling with the change in his pocket. 'It's like this, Bubbles. Remember first grade when I used to snort Jell-O?'

'Who could forget?'

'Well, there was only one girl I wanted to impress, and that was you.'

My cheeks felt flushed. I sipped my A-Treat.

'I mean, even if you had patches on your eyes for the rest of your life, I'd still . . . be nice to you.'

He stopped. I slurped. The chair creaked as he sat down.

Mickey was trying to tell me he loved me and there was no way I could return the sentiment. It wasn't only his satellite-dish ears and his five kids – although those weren't check marks in his favor, either. He simply wasn't a Stiletto. Stiletto made my hair twist and my toes curl. Mickey made my hair flat and my toes sweat.

Still, if Mama were here, she'd point out that it was Mickey who had picked me up at the hospital. Mickey who was sitting by my side, helping me up the stairs. Mickey fetching me sodas.

And where is Mr. Stiletto? Mama would ask. No doubt left on the plane to Mexico City this morning. Ah, if only I had taken Mama's advice and bleached my mustache.

Then again, where was Mama?

Mickey found a note. Mama, Genevieve and Jane

had gone to the park. They would be back this after-noon.

'So,' I said, 'where's my surprise?'

From Mickey's side of the room came a rustling of papers. 'The police reports on Laura Buchman's un-timely death.'

I sat up. 'Police *reports*.'

'You were right, Bubbles. There was an official and *unofficial* report. Both conclude suicide, but what's really interesting is what the second report says that the first one doesn't.'

'How'd you get it?'

'Janice, the clerk in records. She's in love with me.'

'Get out of here!'

'Don't sound so shocked, Bubbles. Anyway, the second report is an addendum filed two months after the first. The officer who wrote it is long gone, but he had enough intelligence to note in the record that the police suspected the scene at Laura Buchman's house had been tampered with before they arrived.'

'Merry Metzger?'

'Don't jump to conclusions.' I could hear him get up and pace the room. 'Apparently there were tons of kids in and out of that house hours after her death.'

That made sense. I relayed Mrs. Arbogast's account.

'What else does the second report note?' I asked.

'A car was seen parked on Myrtle Lane the morning of the day of Laura's suicide, which the police put at Friday evening. It was a light blue Lincoln Town Car. A

neighbor named Mrs. Crowley, however, made a statement that the car belonged to a bird-watcher who had
been tracking warbler migrations. She said it had been
parked there every day for a week.'

I told Mickey that Mrs. Crowley had died of cancer
four years ago.

'I see you've been doing quite a bit of research for a
story you're not even writing, Bubbles.'

I ignored the insinuation. 'So, that Town Car means
nothing?'

'Maybe,' Mickey said, 'maybe not. I went all out for
you, Bubbles. I stuck my neck out on this one.'

Mickey sat down next to me on the couch and took
my hand. My heart broke. If I could love Mickey Sinkler,
I would. Why was I this way? Why was he this way?
Why couldn't he and the records clerk get together and
make each other happy?

'The file contains a DMV check on the vehicle. It
was registered to Henry Metzger.'

I gasped. 'So the police knew all along?'

'I don't know, Bubbles. I don't know what it all
means. I do know that the day her death was ruled a
suicide came one day after the police received the DMV
report on Metzger's car.'

A *chug, chug, chug* in the driveway announced the
arrival of Genevieve and her Rambler. A few minutes
later, there was a lot of moaning and shrieking and
crying when I explained to the three women what had
happened. Mickey quietly slipped out somewhere

between the third 'Oh, that's awful,' and the fifth 'They should pay.'

'You need a eucalyptus branch waved over your eyes,' asserted Genevieve, who, I noticed, put out a remarkably strong perfume of garlic. 'It'll speed the healing.'

'No,' Mama countered. 'Not eucalyptus. Bee balm.'

'Bee balm? Are you nuts? Bee balm's for sore throats.'

Mama snickered. 'You're mixing that up with lemon verbena. Say, are you rusty. You should take some milk thistle for your brain.'

Genevieve was ticked now. 'Milk thistle? That's for your liver, you stupid Pollack.'

'Okay, you two,' interrupted Jane. 'Mom, don't you want to know what we found in the park?'

'First, what color's your hair today?' I asked.

'Ugh. Same old boring brown. I can't wait to come home. When can I come home?'

'Don't whine, Jane. Tell me what you found in the park. Did you find Stiletto's cell phone?'

'Nope. But Mama picked a lot of dandelions,' Jane said. 'She's going to make wine!'

'Oh, great.' I lay back.

'Of course, we also found the film,' Jane added under her breath.

'Yahoo!' I shouted, nearly rolling off the couch.

'Now we don't know if it's *the* film,' Mama stressed. 'It's *a* film. It's getting developed over at Q-Mart. We can pick up the pictures at noon tomorrow.'

It was comforting to know that the most important photos of my life were being handled by an insolent high school junior making minimum wage in a job he despised.

The phone rang. Mama answered it. 'It's for you, Bubbles,' she said, bringing it over to me.

'Hi, Bubbles, this is Susie from the club. Don't hang up.'

If she hadn't said that, I would have.

'First, how are you feeling? Better?'

'Yep.' If Susie was calling to satisfy her conscience, I didn't plan on obliging.

'Okay, uhmm, good, I guess. Uhmm. My lawyer didn't want me to call.'

Lawyer? These women make it a habit of calling their lawyers before they apologize?

'But I was feeling so . . . guilty that I had to. I'm not a bad person. I'm not. I want you to know that.'

'Uh-huh.'

'It's Athena who sometimes goes a little crazy. I'm so furious at her, I could . . .' Susie took a deep breath. 'I have to tell you how this came about. Athena called me this morning and said some tabloid reporters had been snooping around for dirt on Merry. She said a reporter was going to go undercover and try to get information from her at the club—'

'That undercover reporter was me?' I took a sip of A-Treat.

'Yes. Anyway, she said all I had to do was get you to

315

play tennis with us. What was the harm in that? So, I said sure.'

'How'd Athena know I was a reporter?'

'That's easy. From Wendy. Wendy overheard you and your daughter talking on the telephone this morning about how you were going to trick Athena into an interview.'

That made me simultaneously angry and embarrassed. I was angry that Wendy was spying on Jane and embarrassed that she had caught us cooking up such a deceitful scheme.

'But I didn't call to talk about Athena.'

I crossed my legs. 'Oh?'

'I called to apologize and also to let you know that we all know you're prying into Laura Buchman's death.'

'Who's we?'

'All of Laura's old friends. Anyway, I don't think there's anything wrong with that. In fact, I wish someone would find out who killed her. It's disturbed me for years. I was a close friend of Laura's, along with Merry and Athena, back in high school.'

Jane started to say something, and I shut her up with a gesture of my hands.

'Laura's death was so horrific that I tried not to think about Merry's involvement in it,' Susie went on. 'But then, when this accident in the park made the papers, well, like I said to my husband, she's going to get away with it again.'

The gossip pipeline opened. 'Can you hold on a

minute, Susie. I have to adjust my eye patches.'

'Oh, sure. Oh, gee. Eye patches.'

I placed my hand over the receiver and told Jane to get a pen, a tablet and turn on the portable. She was going to take notes for me while listening in on the other phone. Mama and Genevieve rushed around trying to find a pen and tablet. When everyone was set, I got back on.

'It occurred to me while I was on hold,' Susie said. 'You're not taking notes or anything, are you?'

'Me?' I asked in shock. 'How could I take notes when you guys blinded me today?'

'Oh, right.'

'So, you actually think Merry had some involvement in Laura's death?' I asked chattily, as though we were discussing the advantages of hair extensions.

'I never knew how much involvement. But I know, for example, that Merry was over at her house all the time, using Laura.'

'Using? In what way?'

'Using her house. When I was in the bathroom at the country club today I overheard what Athena told you about Merry meeting Henry when she was in college. That was a lie. They started having sex the summer before Merry's senior year.'

No duh, I thought, although all I said was, 'A seventeen-year-old girl and a sixty-year-old man. Yuk.'

'He didn't look sixty, if that's what you're thinking,' Susie said. 'He was very debonair – we all had crushes on him. And he bought Merry these beautiful clothes and jewelry. Once he flew her by private plane to New York and took her shopping on Fifth Avenue for a pearl necklace.'

'What did her parents think?'

'Are you kidding? Henry promoted Merry's father to vice president of operations. Her parents thought it was pretty great. But still, they never imagined Henry was sleeping with their daughter, especially since he was still married at the time. I think they assumed he was merely her mentor.'

Ah, denial. A powerful parental tool. 'So,' I said, knowing now where this conversation was going, 'where did they have sex?'

'At Laura's house. Look, they couldn't go to a hotel. If they had, everyone in town would have known what was going on behind the first Mrs. Metzger's back.'

I thought of the blue Town Car that Mrs. Crowley no doubt wrongly assumed was the bird-watcher's. It didn't belong to a bird-watcher. It belonged to Henry Metzger, who was stopping by for some afternoon delight.

'There's one piece in this puzzle I can't figure out,' I told Susie. 'What is Athena's involvement? Why would she care so much that I was snooping into Laura Buchman's death that she would try to set me up for the Wimbledon of humiliation at the country club?'

'Oh, that? That's a no-brainer,' Susie said. 'You know how Laura died, right?'

'Yes. Some drug-laced milkshake.'

'It was Slim Fast. Athena's Slim Fast. Back then, Athena lived on nothing else. You can understand why she doesn't want that to get out.'

After I hung up, Jane and I high-fived each other, which is not easy to do when you can't see the other hand.

'You got the police reports, you got the interviews, and soon you'll have the photos,' Jane said. 'Mom, you've dug up one great story.'

I considered what I did have. 'I know that Merry and Henry were using Laura's house for sex, but that doesn't mean they killed her. I need to ask some more questions.'

Jane threw her arms around my neck. 'Go ask more questions, then. I'm so proud of you I could burst. I can't wait to tell Gracie and everybody what you've done so far.'

'So, you don't think I'm down on my luck?'

'Down on your luck?' Jane looked confused. 'Whoever said that?'

Chapter 22

MARTIN DROPPED OFF SANDY and the Camaro along with a vase of roses from their backyard. The flowers filled the room with a wonderful summer fragrance, and Mama invited everyone to a cold Monday-night dinner. Martin couldn't stay, though. He had to rush home and tend to his yeast collection.

'He's growing Japanese yeast, Russian yeast and even Tanzanian yeast so he can bake authentic breads from around the world,' Sandy exclaimed. 'Isn't it exciting?'

'About as exciting as winning the world clogging championship,' I said.

'Stop,' Sandy said. 'You're teasing.'

Sandy and I spent the entire dinner hour readjusting our butts on the plastic-covered chairs and dissecting the implications of Susie's phone call. Sandy was of the opinion that Henry Metzger must have had something to do with Laura Buchman's death. I wasn't so sure.

'Picture this,' Sandy said, stabbing her salad. 'Metzger's trysts are a secret until Laura comes home early from school one day and discovers Henry and

Merry in her parents' bed. Henry Metzger's got a wife, a prominent position in town. Doesn't want to risk it all, so he has Laura murdered.'

I pondered her theory, feeling around for a piece of ham, which Mama had cut up for me like I was four. 'Henry Metzger might be evil, but he's not stupid. Kill the friend of the girl you're fooling around with? I mean, would you keep sleeping with a guy who did that?'

'I wouldn't sleep with a guy fifty years older than me to begin with.'

After dinner, Sandy drove Jane to work at the ice cream shop in my Camaro. I sat at the kitchen table by the window enjoying the breeze on my neck while Mama cleaned up and Genevieve spread a fresh layer of dried peas on the kitchen floor.

A stiff wind was picking up, wafting the sulfur smell from the steel plant across town. Genevieve said we were in for quite a storm, what with the intense heat and the way the leaves on the trees were blowing inside out now.

'I wouldn't be surprised if I lose power out my way,' she said. 'We always do in that kind of weather, don't we, LuLu?'

'We do,' Mama agreed. 'The power lines to that high-rise are made out of dental floss, they're so flimsy.'

'Mind if I bunk here?' Genevieve asked.

That power excuse was convenient, but Genevieve wasn't fooling me. Here she was, a card-carrying, lifelong conspiracy nut, and for the first time in her seventy years she had a real, live conspiracy to work with. Murder. Shootings. Missing editors. Missing dead rock star impersonators. Dangerous eyeliner.

Genevieve was in hog heaven.

Plus, Mama was happy to have her around.

My eyes began to hurt, as Donna had forewarned, right after nightfall. Genevieve brewed me a eucalyptus potion. I drank it and popped a few painkillers from the hospital, sat back in the BarcaLounger and felt my brain spin as I listened to *Wheel of Fortune*.

'Uhm, Genevieve,' I mumbled sleepily, 'there wasn't any alcohol in that drink, was there?'

'Nah,' she said. 'A tablespoon of Vladisk, for medicinal purposes.'

I groaned. Vladisk is a Slovakian brandy that could clean rust from pots. One tablespoon of Vladisk on a full stomach without painkillers would be enough to plaster an elephant.

At one point, I heard Mama say to Genevieve, 'Help me get her upstairs,' and the next thing I knew two old ladies were ripping Doris's tennis outfit off me, pulling a nightgown over my head and brushing my teeth.

Then they were gone. I lay in bed, the breeze from the approaching storm blowing over my body. I didn't know if it was eight o'clock or midnight. Light or dark. I faintly heard the mumbling of the TV downstairs and then Genevieve and Mama talking quietly. Car horns beeped outside.

When I woke up again it was to the sound of a loud

thunder clap. Rain was pouring down in buckets outside my half-open window. The TV was off. Mama and Genevieve were asleep.

But I was not alone in my room.

The breathing was controlled, deep and ultimately frightening. In. Out. In. Out. As though the person had been through great exertion, run a race, climbed a mountain.

Whoever he was, he was almost motionless. Waiting to see if I was asleep. A gust of wind blew in the bedroom, toppling a picture frame. It came from the east window by my bureau.

It crossed my mind to call out, 'Mama' or 'Genevieve.' If this was a Metzger thug, though, he'd take down all three of us, and that was one risk I wasn't willing to take.

The phone by my bed was useless. It wasn't like the intruder would tap his fingers while I called the police.

The urge to survive bubbled up with intensity. I could kick. I could scratch. I could fight.

What I couldn't do was see. Or could I? Maybe if I just rolled over and lifted my fingers to my patches . . .

When it happened, it was so quick my mind couldn't comprehend it. A pillow over my face. Boom. The intruder didn't say a word. No speech. No explanation.

In a flash, he was on top of me. Knees on each arm. Entire body weight on my chest. Kicking did no good. His strong body was concentrated on my life center, on cutting off my breath, stifling my cries, even pushing old air out of my lungs, eliminating my reserves. The pain in my chest was unbearable.

I felt a thumb on each carotid artery, and my mind raced to Jane. It was not my life that was flashing before me; it was my daughter's. Here she was being born. Her red fists flailing and cries hearty. As a baby, rolling naked and chubby on our bed. A toddler chasing seagulls on the beach, laughing as though the sea and air and sand and birds existed just for her. Her reaching out to me. Her little legs running to catch up to me.

'Mommy,' she was crying. 'Mommy!'

The lack of oxygen was causing me to hallucinate. Things were going black. The pain was subsiding.

Whack! I felt a tremendous blow, as though someone had kicked the side of me.

He's beating me up, I thought vaguely. It's not enough that he's killing me.

Then there was another whack and the weight was gone. I pushed the pillow off my face and took in several deep breaths. Relief swept over me. I heard struggling and punching, but no voices. Could it be Genevieve? Someone scrambled out the window. Suddenly it was silent.

My face felt damp. I ripped off my eye patches. The light was on. I blinked, squinted and looked up.

Stiletto was leaning over me dripping wet. Water and sweat were pouring off his face onto my face, and there was a large cut on his forehead. A rivulet of blood was running down his ear and onto his gray T-shirt. It appeared as though he hadn't shaved in days.

I never noticed before how the wrinkles in the corners of his eyes projected the illusion of constant amusement and wisdom. He examined my neck.

'If you hadn't –' I began.

'Are you okay?' He was intent, focused.

'Yes, but—'

'I gotta go,' he interrupted. 'That was Wilson Brouse, and if I don't find him, he'll come back for you.'

I was shaking. 'No, you can't leave me. I don't care if he gets away, don't leave me.'

There was a glass of water by my bed. Stiletto gave me a drink and sat down next to me. My room was a mess. All the perfume bottles on my bureau had been knocked to the floor, along with Betsy, my porcelain doll I'd had since I was eight. The window where the intruder had come in was wide open, and a picture frame on the floor was broken. How had Mama and Genevieve slept through it all?

'Who's Wilson Brouse?' I asked, putting the water glass back on the nightstand with one hand, maintaining my grip on Stiletto with the other.

Stiletto smoothed my hair back from my forehead, leaned down and kissed my right temple.

'I thought I was too late,' he whispered. 'When I got in through the window and saw him over you, I thought you were dead.'

'I almost was dead.'

'I didn't want you to be dead.' He kissed my cheeks and then my lips, softly.

'No?' I said, watching Stiletto's finger run the length of my arm. My toes began to tingle.

'Of course not, I really—'

I smiled. 'You really admire me.'

Stiletto smiled. 'Yes. I really admire you.'

He lay down next to me and began running his fingers through my newly cropped hair.

'You admire me so much you hang around in the middle of the night outside my window.'

There was a loud clap of thunder, and I nearly jumped three feet off the bed. Stiletto wrapped one of his big arms around my shoulders and held me close.

'Actually,' he whispered, slipping the strap of my nightgown off my shoulder, 'I was following Brouse. Brouse is the man who shot at you down at Wysocki's. He's also the one who was about to slash your throat as soon as you stepped outside the Marquis Saturday night.'

'Until you showed up?'

'Right.' Stiletto kissed my bare shoulder. 'Until I showed up. Fortunately, I caught him before he could attach the bomb.'

Bomb? 'What bomb?'

'Down at the public housing parking lot. Brouse followed you and I followed him. As soon as you went into the building, he was under your car like a shot.'

'So those were Brouse's legs I saw under my Camaro?'

'Probably they were mine. I spooked him and then checked out your undercarriage, speaking of which . . .' Stiletto ran his hand down my arm.

I was beginning to feel funny and not simply because I'm Bubbles Yablonsky and I had a Mel Gibson look-alike stroking my arm, or because, minutes ago, I had faced death. Stiletto made me feel funny for other reasons.

I put my hand under his chin and forced him to look at me. 'You're not being straight with me,' I said. 'You know Brouse. You know how to follow him. You know Henry Metzger. What is it?'

Stiletto propped himself up on one elbow and pushed back the bedcovers with one hand.

'You changed your hair, didn't you?' he asked, his glance everywhere else but on my hair.

'Temporarily.'

'Why?'

'Long story. Do you like it better?'

'It doesn't matter. You are stunning, Bubbles,' he said. 'Your body is beautiful; your skin is so soft. Your sense of humor makes me laugh. It doesn't matter about makeup and hair and clothes—'

'Yeah, no clothes,' I interrupted as Stiletto pulled down the other strap of my nightgown. He ran his hand slowly from my neck to my shoulder and down my arm.

'Shhh. What I'm trying to say is that I have been completely, totally surprised by you, Bubbles. You intrigue me.'

I swallowed a wisecrack. For the record, it had something to do with Stiletto being an international man of mystery.

His finger traced my cleavage. His other hand . . .

I scooched up on the bed. 'You're trying to make out with me, aren't you?'

Stiletto brought the roving hand to his chest. 'Who? Me?'

I pushed up my nightgown straps. 'Yes, you. Minutes ago a man was trying to kill me, almost succeeded, too, and now you're here trying to cop a feel.'

'Oh, c'mon, Bubbles.' Stiletto's eyes twinkled.

'Don't c'mon Bubbles me, and cut that out with the eyes. You men are all the same. A woman could be hit by a truck, and if she was hot you'd probably put the moves on her.'

'Not any woman. Just you, Bubbles.'

I folded my arms.

'I don't know,' he said, grinning. 'Maybe it's the thunderstorm or the way you're dressed. You're so vulnerable. So irresistible. Anyway, it's a known fact that danger is a turn-on for men.'

'Not for women. Candlelight dinners. Moonlight swims. Walks on the beach. Diamonds. Fat paychecks. Toilet seats returned to their proper positions. Those are turn-ons for women.'

'Yeah, but I'm not a woman. I'm a man. You got a problem with that?'

I opened my mouth to object and then shook myself.

What was I complaining about? This guy was gorgeous. Before Ken the Radio Shack clerk forced me into making that vow, I would have hopped Stiletto's bones in a heartbeat.

'Sorry, Bubbles,' he said, laying me back on the bed, 'I was out of line. You've survived a horrendous experience. I don't know what I was thinking. I let my body take over, I guess.'

'Listen, Stiletto,' I said slowly, 'I made this vow. No more, what should I say, casual sex – not to say I did much of that before. Anyway, I've been dealt a bad hand when it comes to men. Just once I want a full house.'

He smiled. 'Me, too.'

'You do?'

'Yeah, though I never thought I would. I think the fact that I didn't get on that plane to Mexico City says something.'

'By the way, you didn't answer my question on how you know Brouse,' I pointed out, turning my back to him.

'In a way, I think I have. I think you should sleep, Bubbles. We can call the police tomorrow.'

'Will you stay here while I do?'

'Absolutely. I'll stay until dawn, and then I've got to go. Okay?'

'Okay.'

'You know what you never told me, Bubbles?'

'What?'

'How you got your name.'

'That's easy.' I curled down into his arms. Stiletto put a pillow under my head and a protective arm over me. 'When I was born my parents didn't know what to name me. For a year I was called Baby Girl Yablonsky. Then when I was in the jumper watching my mother do dishes, I said, "Bubba." My mother thought it was so cute she named me Bubbles.'

I pulled a sheet over my shoulders and finished the story. 'Of course, my father told a different version. He said I was named after his favorite stripper, Bubbles DaSilva. Bubbles DaSilva used to cover herself with bubbles and hand out hatpins to the biggest tippers. Strange, but I think both versions are true.'

I leaned over to Stiletto. 'What do you think?'

Snore.

There he was, my knight in shining armor. Eyes closed. Mouth open. Blood crusted on his head.

I rolled back into his arms and inhaled his aroma. Sweat. Rain. Stiletto. Life.

I was pretty happy, for a nearly dead girl.

Chapter 23

STILETTO WAS GONE WHEN I woke up the next morning, a Tuesday. A gray dawn broke outside my window, bringing with it a cool and wet breeze, the first relief from heat in days. The storm from the night before was over. I turned over in bed and saw the bloodstain on the pillow where Stiletto had laid his head. What a night!

The first thing I had to do was call Mickey. The clock said 5:15 A.M. Too early, even for Mickey. The next thing . . .

There was a crash downstairs. *Boom. Bang.*

I hopped out of bed, not realizing until my feet hit the floor how much pain my entire body was in. I put a hand to the back of my neck. Boy, that Brouse. He really did a number on me.

There came a shout. A man's voice – and I was struck by a frightening thought. What if Brouse had waited for Stiletto to leave and was now returning to finish the job?

Clang. 'I got him in my sights, Genevieve, don't let him get away!' It was Mama.

333

I grabbed my white terry-cloth bathrobe and headed out the door.

Boom! A musket went off. I raced to the top of the stairs.

'You ain't going nowhere, Butch!' Genevieve was shouting. 'I got the fifth division of the Nazareth Militia on its way, and they're gonna make groundhog meat out of your brains.'

I took the stairs two at a time and arrived to find a man prone on the kitchen floor, a metal bucket of mashed potatoes over his head. I was dumbstruck.

'Geesh, Bubbles,' Mama exclaimed. She was wearing one of Jane's old white-and-pink Barbie bathrobes with bows on the sleeves. Her head was covered in turquoise curlers, and she was pointing a musket straight at the man's derriere. 'Don't stand there gaping like a schoolgirl, call the fuzz.'

'We got us one of them Metzger thugs you were talking about,' announced Genevieve, who was wearing a baby blue chenille robe and standing with one foot on top of the man, a sharp spade pointed at the small of his back. 'Caught 'im with my peas-and-potato traps.'

'He's going to suffocate in those potatoes,' I said, gripping the bucket and pulling with all my might. The potatoes created such a suction that at the moment I got the bucket off I fell backwards across the living-room floor.

It was Stiletto, covered in spuds and swearing up a blue streak.

'What is this?' he asked, peeling mashed potato off his face. 'What were you trying to do to me? I couldn't breathe.'

Genevieve removed her foot and Mama put down the musket. Stiletto stood up and I introduced him around.

'And what, exactly, were you doing at five a.m. in my house?' Mama wanted to know.

'It's my house, Mama,' I corrected, 'and Steve was here, saving my life.' I explained how Stiletto had crawled up the drain spout and into my window after Brouse, how he fought him off me and kept me from being murdered.

Mama sniffed. 'That's a new one, Bubbles.'

Stiletto pointed out the bruises around my eyes and on my neck, proof that I had nearly been strangled. When Mama realized I was telling the truth, she turned into a one-woman whirling dervish.

'We gotta call the cops . . . We gotta take Bubbles to the hospital . . . This is awful . . . How could that happen? . . . If I see that guy Brouse . . . Where was Harry Hamel? He's usually up at that hour . . .'

I explained that I would wait and call Mickey because I suspected that much of the Lehigh Police Department was in Metzger's pocket. There would be no trip to the hospital and as for Harry Hamel being up at that hour, how did Mama know?

'I got my sources,' she said.

Throughout it all, Genevieve was silent. Finally she

extended her hand to Stiletto. 'I'm sorry, Butch,' she said gruffly. 'To tell you the truth, I'm somewhat shame-faced that I hadn't secured the upstairs quarters. Every bedroom window should have a mashed potato bucket.'

'Righto!' agreed Mama. 'And maybe a layer of peas, too.'

'Of course, the peas. How could I forget the peas?' Genevieve said.

'How about a twenty-four-hour security guard?' Stiletto suggested. 'Or, at the very least, an electronic alarm system?'

Genevieve and Mama stared at him as if he had suggested Martians might make good neighbors.

'We got dried peas,' Genevieve said. 'Who needs guards when you got peas?'

Stiletto threw up his hands in exasperation.

'Don't scoff. They took you out, didn't they?' Mama said, pointing to the pea-covered kitchen floor.

To make amends, Mama and Genevieve insisted Stiletto stick around for a big breakfast of scrambled eggs, sausage, scrapple, apple butter, shoofly pie, orange juice and coffee. Stiletto ate it with gusto as I filled him in about all that had happened, including the interviews with Jim Morrison, Mrs. Arbogast and Mr. Crowley in Laura Buchman's old neighborhood. By the end, he and Genevieve were arm-wrestling at the table.

It would have been one big happy scene if not for the fact that Brouse – identified by Stiletto as Metzger's favorite thug – had tried to kill me last night and was on the loose now. When I reminded them of that, Stiletto abruptly got up from the table, thanked the old women profusely and said he had to go.

'I don't want you sleeping here tonight,' he said to me, 'even with the peas. Why don't you go to a hotel?'

'Or Mickey's,' Mama chimed in.

'Who's Mickey?' Stiletto asked.

'Forget it,' I said, pulling him aside. 'I'm going to Salvo's. He's at the Poconos taking time off and gave me the key to his apartment. Anyway, I need to use his computer. Now that I have the police reports, I want to start writing that story.'

That seemed to satisfy Stiletto, who gave me a kiss on the forehead and left. What was it with this guy? Was I lips material or not lips material? Make up your mind, I wanted to shout.

As soon as I closed the door behind him, the phone rang. It was Marian, she of the many cats, from the Public Housing for the Elderly. And she sounded upset. 'I didn't know who to call,' she said anxiously. 'I told the police, but they don't care.'

I pulled my terry-cloth robe tighter and sat down on the couch.

'Chester Zug's apartment was burglarized after midnight,' she said. 'So much throwing of chairs and knocking around. It took forever for the police to arrive. By the time they did, the burglars were gone. The police said nothing was taken, it was only ransacked.'

She began to cry. 'I showed the police officers the box Chester gave me. I thought, you know, it might be what the burglars wanted. But the police . . . they called it junk. They laughed at me, Bubbles.'

My head began to throb from all the excitement last night and all the coffee this morning. There were a million things I had to do today. I had to verify that Chester Zug had been fired because of Mrs. Arbogast's complaint that he had been peeping in Laura Buchman's windows. I had to ask Doris to look up some articles in the *News-Times* morgue. I had to start writing my story. I had to get the pictures back from Q-Mart. And, if memory served me, I had a perm to do this afternoon.

But I could not ignore poor Marian, not after the police treated her so callously.

'Could you come over and get the box right away?' she said. 'I'd feel so much better if it was out of my house.'

'I'll do you one better, Marian. I'll bring a cop with me. A good cop. He'll check everything out for you.'

When I hung up, Mama was wagging her finger. 'Mickey's not going to stand for this much longer, Bubbles,' she said. 'Sooner or later, he's going to expect a little affection in return, and I don't mean a peck on the cheek, if you get my drift.'

I winced. For once I got Mama's drift, and it was deep.

* * *

'I got other cases, you know,' Mickey explained in the cruiser. 'Someone's been dumping bottles of Tide at the ShopRite. Housewives are slipping and suing the store. And we got a syrup thief over at the I-Hop.'

'Geez, Mickey,' I said. 'Hope you're wearing a bulletproof vest.'

'Yeah, well, each one of them's more important than walking down memory lane with a little old lady and her trinkets. But, hey, what are *friends* for? I sure do like being a *friend*. Nothing more I want to be than your *friend*, Bubbles.'

'Okay, I got the message, Mickey.' I turned my attention to the scenery passing by.

'I guess if I was some in-ter-na-tion-al photographer, traveling around the world, sleeping with this woman and that woman, you'd like me, right, Bubbles? But, noooo, I hold down a job, feed, raise and clothe five kids. Who wants a responsible man like me these days?' Mickey took a sip from his 7-Eleven plastic coffee mug and sighed.

Mickey was in a bad mood this morning. For one thing, it had finally dawned on him that he wasn't going to get any action by extending himself for me. I'd made it clear yesterday afternoon, friendship was the best he could hope for. Sex was not an option.

For another, despite this bleak romantic horizon, I had the feeling Mickey was deep down angry and upset that someone had managed to climb in my room and nearly strangle me. Most men act angry when they get scared.

Mickey was no exception.

'What're you doing sleeping with an open window in the first place?' he'd shouted when Mama had showed him the bruises on my neck.

'It's summer. I always sleep with the window open.'

'Not anymore, you don't.'

Mickey had had his cop buddies comb the place over, dusting for fingerprints, examining window jambs and drainpipes. Everyone at the house had filled out a statement. The only person not to fill out a statement was Stiletto.

'Let me remind you, Bubbles,' Mickey had said when we were alone in the kitchen, 'that Steve Stiletto is wanted for leaving the scene of an accident. If he—'

'I don't have any control over Steve Stiletto,' I interrupted. 'He comes and goes as he pleases.'

'Yeah, apparently he comes and goes whenever Wilson Brouse is around.'

Ouch. I maintained a straight face, but Mickey's words pierced like darts. He had zeroed in on the very same concern that had kept me tossing and turning last night. Why was Stiletto around whenever Brouse was around? And how could he and Brouse have chatted at the Marquis bar so amiably if they, to hear Stiletto tell it, were bitter enemies?

Something didn't add up.

'Wilson Brouse is bad news, Bubbles,' said Mickey,

who was surprised to learn that Brouse was back in town. He said Brouse was last seen in Newark a few months ago, shortly after being released from Trenton State Prison on a charge of attempted murder. Prior to that, he had been incarcerated for grand theft auto, passing false checks, kidnapping and assault with a deadly weapon.

'You don't want Wilson Brouse on your bad side,' Mickey said as we left my house to drive over to Marian's. 'You don't want Wilson Brouse, period.'

Genevieve offered to drive me to Marian's, but Mickey said that if I stepped into any car besides his cruiser, he'd shoot the tires out. Both refused to let me drive myself.

In other words, because I wouldn't sleep with him, Mickey was mad that he was driving me to Marian's, but because I'd nearly been murdered, he'd be damned if someone else would take me.

And men claim women are irrational?

We passed a low white Cellular One building on Freemansburg Avenue, and I got an idea.

'Who reported that Athena Adler's Range Rover was missing?'

Mickey shifted in his seat so that his left elbow was propped on the armrest. 'A male. Identified himself as Mr. Adler.'

'How do you know?'

'Listened to the 9-1-1 tape. Like I said, I went all out for you, Bubbles.'

'Athena's husband was out of town Friday night.' I told him about my telephone conversation when I pretended to be Carol Mrgshm, inviting Athena out to lunch. Athena had tried to beg off, saying that her husband had just returned from a four-day business trip and there was so much unpacking to do.

'I'm thinking maybe she made her husband call the police, even if he was out of town. Some women are like that.'

'I'm thinking maybe it was Wilson Brouse who made the phone call,' I said.

'Should be easy enough to find out. Emergency 9-1-1 traces the call.'

'What would be great,' I said, 'is if 9-1-1 could trace Brouse.'

'There's something I need to confess,' I whispered to Mickey as we got to the door of the Housing for the Elderly.

'You changed your mind. You realize you lust after me like a hot-blooded baboon?'

'Give it up, Mickey. What I want to tell you is that the super here, he already knows me as a woman named Sally Hansen from when I kinda searched Chester Zug's apartment.'

Mickey's fist hit the wall. 'Bubbles! It's like you break laws left and right, and you're totally oblivious. You're a walking misdemeanor. Hell, a walking felony.'

'Save the lecture, Mickey. I'm only warning you about

the super in case he mentions something. Try to act cool if he does.'

Bart, the super, didn't say a word, although he did squint at me in the elevator. It must have been the new soccer mom hairdo and the fact that, unlike last time we met, I wasn't wearing a high-necked pink cotton dress and no makeup. Today I was made up to the nines, partly to cover the bruises. I was wearing a sleeveless white knit top that clung to my curves like a roller-coaster and a black spandex miniskirt.

The outfit was so good, Bart didn't waste time examining my face.

The elevator doors slid open and Bart led us to Marian's door.

'Don't say I didn't warn you,' he whispered before knocking. 'Sometimes she don't take her meds.'

Marian answered, threw Bart a dirty look and pulled us inside.

'It's all over the building what happened to you, Bubbles. LuLu says you nearly got strangled,' Marian said, sitting me at the table. 'We're so sorry.'

Mama. She must be broadcasting her own twenty-four-hour cable news channel from the basement. Senior Citizen DirecTV.

'I locked my babies in the bedroom and opened the windows, Bubbles,' Marian said, sliding me a teacup. 'I hope that helps the allergy situation.'

Except for the introduction, Mickey remained mum. He sat on the sitting-room couch with his arms crossed, like a kid being brought to Grandma's against his will.

'This is the box,' Marian said as she opened it and placed the pink lid on the table. 'It's all here. The best of Chester.'

I tried to keep a straight face.

'Mickey,' I asked as sweetly as possible, 'with your expert law enforcement background, I bet you could distinguish any valuables here.'

Mickey cleared his throat and walked over to the kitchen table. Another sucker for flattery. 'Let's see now.' He began probing through the box's contents. 'Here's a parking stub from the Allentown Fair, 1977. An old-fashioned green Coke bottle—'

'They don't make those anymore,' Marian said with a sigh.

'A Moravian star, cracked on one side. A paperweight replica of that ugly bronze sculpture on City Center Plaza. Two dog biscuits. Bet that came in handy as a garbage man, eh? Two tin cookie boxes and a memo pad with all the pages ripped out . . .'

'That must have been the diary I was thinking about,' Marian said.

Mickey continued. 'And what's this? An iron-on *L* for Liberty High School. I had one of those. A coaster from the Old Brewery Tavern and a Miller Auto key chain, without the key.'

'That's it?' I asked, disappointed.

'That's it,' said Mickey, straightening his back. 'C'mon, Bubbles, I've got to report for work.'

'So there's nothing here of value?' asked Marian. 'I thought for sure the bronze paperweight was what they were after.'

Mickey anxiously jingled change in his pocket. He acted antsy, strolling around Marian's sitting room, absently studying her trinkets. He lifted up the lid on the china teapot and rang a tiny gong as I tried to console poor Marian, who was beginning to weep.

'You know, Chester gave me this box the afternoon of the day he died,' Marian said tearfully. 'He knocked on my door and said, "Here, Marian, I want you to keep this. In case I don't come back tonight." And I remember saying, "Why, Chester, every day you walk down to the park, every day you come back. Why would today be any different?" '

Rustle. Zonk. Marian pulled out a tissue and blew her nose loudly.

'And you know what he said to me, Bubbles?'

'What?' My nose was beginning to itch from the cats again. I figured the antihistamine coursing through my body was fighting off most of the allergens.

'He said, "When you get to be our age you're lucky to live each day." And then he said the most wonderful thing. He said, "Get your best dress washed and ironed, Marian, 'cause tomorrow night I'm taking you out for steak and potatoes and a fancy cake at Widow Brown's Restaurant. On me." Those were his last words.'

She began crying noisily now. I patted her arm. Mickey was oblivious.

'My mother has one of these racks,' he observed, holding up a tiny silver spoon. 'You got the Niagara Falls, the Grand Canyon, Graceland, the White House . . .'

'What's that, Mickey?' I asked.

'My spoon collection,' Marian said. 'I've got twenty-five spoons from around the country. I ordered most of them through Timeless Collectibles from an ad I saw in *Parade* magazine.'

Mickey continued to read them off. 'The Washington Monument. Disneyland . . . How come this one's wrapped in plastic?'

'It's wrapped up in plastic so it won't get tarnished. It's too big for the rack. It's lying on the bottom of the shelf.'

Marian hobbled over to where he was.

'Sterling silver, of course, and such a detailed pattern,' she said. 'I need to hang it up, but haven't found the right spot.'

Mickey handed me the spoon to feel it. It was sealed in plastic and placed in a Ziploc bag. Even in its plastic wrapping, I could detect scalloped edges and fancy engravings.

'Chester gave it to me,' Marian said. 'Actually, it was in the box, but Chester insisted I include it in my collection. He said it would look nice there.'

So this is what the burglars were looking for. I removed it from the bag and unrolled layers of plastic wrap.

'What are you doing?' Marian gasped.

I stopped when I got to the last layer and I could clearly read the initials on the spoon, EMB, exactly as it appeared on the ashtray at Henry Metzger's house.

Yes, I thought. Yes, yes, yes!

'What is it, Bubbles?' Mickey asked, carefully taking the spoon and holding it to the light.

'It's not so much what it is,' I said, 'as what's on it. I'm guessing morphine and barbiturates.'

Chapter 24

'Henry Metzger is not the murderer,' I informed Sandy. 'But someone wanted him to appear as though he was.'

'How do you know?'

'Because a control freak like Henry Metzger doesn't leave spoons around after he's poisoned his lover's best friend. That's how I know.'

Sandy checked on Mrs. Grebnar, who was busy with a *Cosmopolitan* sex survey under the bonnet hair dryer.

Mickey had refused to drop me off at home, although I'd protested that I needed my car. As a compromise, he'd let me pick up the Camaro – after checking the brake lines first – and followed me as I drove it to the House of Beauty.

'I can't wait until all this sleuthing of yours is over and we can get back to normal here at the shop,' Sandy complained. 'You're not going to be able to do that four-thirty perm, are you?'

'Afraid not,' I said, flipping through my notebook. 'Mickey took the spoon down to the university's lab for

349

testing. He'll have the results later today or tomorrow. Meanwhile, I've got to write this story before the *Allentown Morning Call* gets wind of it. I'm sorry to leave you stranded.'

'It's not that, Bubbles. You were nearly strangled last night. You were blinded yesterday. It's not the work, it's you. I'm not sleeping. I'm not eating. Martin's been so worried he twisted all the crullers the wrong way this morning—'

'Martin's worried?'

'Are you kidding? Worried sick. Last Sunday his clogging was completely off. He and I were discussing your situation this morning. We worry that this might be the end for you, Bubbles. Consider Metzger's history of violence.'

I shoved the notebook in my purse. 'Consider how close I am to solving not just the Laura Buchman murder, but the Chester Zug murder, too. I got a responsibility, Sandy, to tie up the remaining loose ends.'

I turned off Mrs. Grebnar's dryer, lifted the bonnet and checked her rollers. Dry. 'Jim Morrison is probably missing because of me. That's one reason to go on right there.'

Sandy escorted Mrs. Grebnar over to her chair and began taking out her curlers. 'There's another reason, too. On the front page of today's *News-Times* is an article by your favorite reporter, Bob Lawless.'

'Oh, great. What'd he write?' No doubt something that didn't require him to leave his desk.

'It's about how the police closed the Chester Zug case yesterday. The chief is quoted as saying it was a big misunderstanding because of you. The story also mentions that Henry Metzger finally filed his lawsuit against you and the *News-Times*—'

'For three-point-five million dollars?'

'He's upped it to ten-point-five million dollars now.'

Mrs. Grebnar let out a low whistle.

I shrugged. 'What does it matter to me whether it's three-point-five million or ten-point-five million? I got four hundred dollars in my checking account, not like he's going to get blood out of a stone.'

'So, what loose ends do you have to tie up?' Sandy asked.

I sat down in my chair. 'For one thing, how and when did Chester Zug get that spoon? I collected a stack of jeweler's cards from his kitchen drawer, and I know there's some connection between them and the spoon.'

Sandy nodded. 'Makes sense.'

'For another, when did Eva Metzger die, and how well did she know birds?'

'Who's Eva Metzger?' asked Sandy. 'And what's this about birds?'

'You'll see.' I got up and headed to the supply room-office. 'Mind if I use the phone?'

But all Sandy said was, 'Birds?'

I telephoned the *News-Times* and prayed that Doris was in.

I got lucky.

351

'You owe me one after encouraging me to play tennis,' I told her.

'Sandy brought me up to speed yesterday,' Doris said. 'Three rich white girls beating up on a townie hairdresser at a country club. I mean, could it get any better than that?'

I gave Doris her assignment.

'You think I got time to while away my hours doing research for you in the morgue?'

'It'll take ten minutes on the computer, Doris. I was blind for one day because of you.'

'You were blind for one day because you're addicted to makeup,' Doris said.

After Doris hung up, I opened my purse, unzipped the special compartment and pulled out the jewelers' cards. There were twelve in all. I laid them out on Sandy's desk and tried to decide which one to call first. Better consult the Polish Pendulum.

I took a length of twine and tied a piece of potato to the end of it. I held the other end and dangled it over each of the cards. It circled all of them except one, A. H. Harrison Jewelers of Allentown. Since 1883. The name on the bottom said Arthur H. Harrison III. On the back, circled in black pen, was the file number 26-55. In no time I was on the phone.

'Sorry,' said the person who answered the phone. 'Art Harrison retired three years ago. Perhaps his nephew, Randolph, could help you?'

'Funny,' said Randolph. 'I've got the file handy

because we got a call on that one last week.'

'What a coincidence,' I observed brightly. 'And here I am, trying to duplicate a pattern I fell in love with at a dinner party last night.' Chester must have been checking up on his old research, to see if he was on the money.

'Hmmm,' said the great-grand nephew. 'Registered to an Eva DuBois Metzger. The design is called Ladybird Magnolia by DeGourcey. Very rare. It will take six weeks to order.'

'Thank you. You don't happen to know who else called about this pattern?' I inquired. 'I'd be crestfallen to find out that one of my friends had the same idea. You understand, don't you?'

'Of course, but, sadly, you needn't worry. The man who viewed the pattern at our shop Friday died over the weekend. His obituary appeared in the newspaper this morning.'

I clucked the appropriate sounds of sympathy and hung up. In truth, I had little sympathy for a man who hoped to cash in on evidence, instead of submitting it to the authorities to find a murderer.

My next thought was to visit the Lehigh Department of Sanitation office down at the Hellertown dump and landfill. Since Sandy had promised Mickey that she'd call him if I left the House of Beauty, I stood on her desk and climbed out through the supply-room window. It was hard enough gathering all this information without the police tailing me every step.

Twenty minutes later I was knocking at the gate of the Hellertown dump – the favorite repository for most Lehigh Valley trash. The rain from last night's storm, along with this afternoon's blazing heat, did wonders in bringing out the aroma of rotting grapefruit, milk and disposable diapers. Seagulls circled overhead. Beyond the wire fence, bulldozers shoved huge piles of trash into sand pits.

'We're closed,' a voice yelled from behind the door of a wooden shack near the gate. 'Read the hours. Open six a.m. to noon for recycling.' My watch read two-thirty.

I walked over to a dirty glass-paned window and knocked. A short man in a dirty blue uniform sat inside smoking a cigarette and reading a paper. When I knocked a second time, he looked up. I put my hands together prayerfully and made a pleading face.

'I really need to talk,' I shouted. 'It's important.'

'You can pout all you want,' he said, throwing open the door, 'but I ain't taking no motor oil. No refrigerants, either. You gotta wait for hazardous-waste day next week.' He threw his cigarette on the floor and ground it out with the heel of his shoe.

He was a dirty man. Short and squalid. Rough fat fingers cracked with grime. The name MANNY was embossed in white lettering on his shirt.

'I'm not here about hazardous waste,' I said. 'May I come in?'

He let me in with as much reluctance as if I had asked for a free tour of Buckingham Palace. And a palace this place was not. Inside, a wooden desk was piled high with paper, files, candy wrappers, an ashtray and two empty cans of Coke. Against one wall was a row of gray file cabinets on top of which was a small dusty fan and a filthy Mr. Coffee with a carafe half full of burnt, crusted black tar. In the corner was a photocopier. There was an old torn leather chair, where Manny had been sitting, next to which was a pile of *Penthouses* and *Playboys*. Snagged, no doubt, from prurient customers.

I introduced myself as Bubbles Yablonsky, freelance reporter. I didn't have to say more.

'I know you,' he said, waving a dirty finger. 'You're the one who wrote about Chester Zug's accident. The police told me not to talk to no one, especially you.'

He unfolded the paper and sat back down on the leather chair.

Police told him not to talk, eh? Since when had the police become so concerned about Chester Zug?

I grabbed his newspaper and threw it on the floor. Then I plopped myself on the desk opposite him, giving Manny a nice view of my long legs. Judging from the state of those *Playboys,* I figured my legs might hold Manny's interest.

It was a trashy move, but then again, this was a trashy place.

'Lookit, Manny,' I said, running my index finger slowly up my shinbone, 'all I want is Chester Zug's personnel record so I can find out when he was fired.

355

I'm not going to quote you. No one will know I got it from you. You can be my Deep Throat.'

Manny's eyes followed my finger until it reached the hem of my black spandex miniskirt.

'Anything,' he whispered. 'Just don't stop the finger, please.'

I held the finger where it was. 'The personnel file, Manny.'

Manny scrambled out of his chair and went over to the file cabinet, pulled a bottom drawer open, removed a manila folder and opened it.

'Ten years ago last September. September tenth. That's when he was fired.'

Depending on what Doris's research showed, that would be right around the time of Laura Buchman's death.

'Why?' My finger inched up the skirt an inch.

Manny gulped and read, 'For looking in the window of a customer on Myrtle Lane. A Mrs. Arbogast called in the complaint.'

I held out my other hand.

He handed me the file and continued to stare at my legs. I flipped through old yellow photocopies. Somewhere there was an original file. Hmmm. Could it be on the desk of Detective Frye in the Lehigh Police Department, perhaps?

This file was thin and made up mostly of time sheets, W-2 forms, vacation logs and retirement information. There was one brief letter dated September 10 from the sanitation commissioner notifying Chester of his termination for violating department policy. The last page was Chester's poorly written, grammatically incorrect, misspelled and very interesting response.

I picked out the termination letter and Chester's response. 'I need these photocopied.'

Manny took them and, looking over his shoulder, placed them on the machine. *Zip. Zip.* Two copies.

'Thanks, Manny,' I said, folding up the photocopies and plunking them into my purse. 'You won't regret it.'

'Hey!' he complained. 'What about the skirt? That's not fair.'

'Not much in life is, Manny. That's why I paid you this little visit.'

There was no way in the world that I was going home or to the shop or to any place where Metzger's thugs might find me. Even so, I had more important worries on my mind now. Like Jane. She was as much a target of Brouse's brutality as I was.

There was no answer at Dan's, so I tried Gracie's house from a pay phone at a 7-Eleven in Hellertown. I left the car running while I dialed. Thankfully, Jane was there.

'Don't go to work today, Jane,' I said firmly. 'Go to Daddy's. Stay inside, lock the doors and turn on the security system.'

Jane gave me a hard time.

'It's like a hundred degrees outside. Do you know

how much ice cream they're gonna sell? I'll get fired if I don't show,' she said. 'And you of all people. You're always lecturing me against playing hooky from work.'

'This is a matter of life or death, Jane. I have a feeling the only place where you'll be safe is at your father's. Daddy has Home Security. They won't get you there.'

'Who won't? Has something happened?'

Mama and I had agreed there was no need to frighten Jane about Brouse's midnight attack. 'I'll explain later. Just swear to me that you will get Gracie to drive you to Daddy's. I am begging you.'

Jane paused. 'Wow, Mom. You sound freaked. Okay, but where are you going to be?'

'I'm going to be at a friend's house.' Talking to Jane like this was making me very emotional. I started to cry, against my will. 'I love you, Jane. Please keep that in mind. I love you and I'll never stop loving you. You are my inspiration.'

'Get a grip, Mom,' Jane said, trying to calm me down. 'You're my hero, right? You are a kick-ass reporter, right? I love you, too. Come home.'

'I will, baby. I will.'

I hung up the phone and tried to compose myself. Just then a red Ford Escort rolled into the parking lot. It swung around the gas pump and came within inches of hitting me. I dashed to the Camaro, closed the door and stepped on the gas.

I didn't know if that was the exact same Escort that

had been parked by Wysocki's the day I got shot at on Fourth Street, but I wasn't going to stick around to find out. I had to be on guard, alert to sounds, people, things.

The way I saw it, my only chance at survival was to write this article and publish it in *The Philadelphia Inquirer* or whatever paper would print it. Henry Metzger had been able to intimidate, threaten and bully people in Lehigh for decades only because his deeds had remained secret. Sure, there had been whispers and rumors, but no one had had enough guts to come out in public and point the finger directly at him.

That's where I came in. Once I had laid out in black and white Henry Metzger's role in covering up the murder of a seventeen-year-old girl and the murder of Chester Zug, I was confident the floodgates would open. Readers would be incensed. They would recall their own Henry Metzger horror stories and recite them to others. There would be investigations and inquiries into Metzger's dealings. Politicians would condemn previous administrations for aiding in Metzger's corruption. Metzger would run for cover.

Then the last people Metzger, or his henchman Wilson Brouse, would dare come near would be me and my family. If something happened to us, certainly Metzger would be blamed. We'd be safe.

My interviews were done. I had all the documents I needed – the police reports on Laura Buchman's death plus Zug's termination letter and his response. The film

359

would have to wait. I could not waste time standing in line at Q-Mart to pick it up.

All I needed were the results of Doris's research, and I'd be set.

The question was, could I write the story in time?

The sun was beginning its afternoon descent when I arrived at Mr. Salvo's apartment on Fountain Hill. For safety's sake, I parked the Camaro in the underground lot of the hospital, gathered my purse and tape recorder and walked the six blocks to his apartment. I couldn't take the chance that the Camaro would be seen.

My hands were shaking as I put the key in the lock. Inside, Mr. Salvo's apartment smelled of old socks and stale beer. I closed and locked the door behind me, pulled the shades down and conducted a quick tour.

Off the living room was a small kitchen, with a door to a patio, and a bathroom. Both rooms, while not sparkling clean, were relatively tidy and freshly painted. On the other side of the living room was a hall that led to Mr. Salvo's bedroom, which was heaped with dirty clothes and scattered newspapers, another bedroom and a door. A quick check under the beds and in the closets turned up no dead bodies.

I was famished. I opened the refrigerator and found a couple of cans of Coke and the remains of my mother's halupies. I took the halupies and Coke to the computer and studied the directions taped to the side – which Mr. Salvo must have written with me in mind.

Step one read: Press the power button on the terminal. (The big rectangular thing on the floor by the desk.)

I saw a white box by the desk. I pressed the button marked POWER and heard a noise.

Step two: Press the button on the monitor. (That's the big screen facing you.)

I pressed the button on the lower right corner. It flicked on.

Now these were directions I could live with.

As the computer did its thing, I called Sandy at the shop.

'Where are you?' she shouted. 'Mickey Sinkler's been calling every five minutes. He's driving me nuts.'

'I got a question for you, Sandy,' I said, my mouth full of halupies. 'What do women do when they get pissed?'

'What? Are you crazy?'

'Please, Sandy, I'm about to write this story and I need to talk it through. What do women do when they get pissed?'

'Oh, brother. Okay, give me a for instance.'

'For instance, what would you do if you found Martin in bed with another woman?'

Sandy thought about this. 'Martin in bed with another woman? The only woman Martin said he'd ever leave me for is Julia Child. And in that case they wouldn't be having sex, they'd be puffing pastry.'

'Right. I forgot we were talking about Martin. Skip that. Consider Eva Metzger. What if you were she and you only had weeks to live? Body thin and ruined. Had nothing to lose and you discovered that your husband was sleeping with a young woman in the prime of her youth. Then what would you do?'

Without missing a beat, Sandy said, 'I'd shoot Henry Metzger right in the bum.'

I swallowed another mouthful of halupies. 'Wouldn't it be better, Sandy, if you could kill the young mistress and frame your husband for the murder so that he would suffer after you were dead and gone? I mean, if you were really angry, wouldn't that be the cruelest revenge?'

'Wow,' said Sandy. 'You think that's what Eva Metzger did?'

'I think that's what Eva Metzger tried to do. Unfortunately, she got the wrong girl.'

'I'm calling the police, Bubbles,' Sandy said. 'This is heavy stuff. Where are you?'

'Can't tell you, Sandy. I need total isolation to write this story. I don't mean to be rude; I'm just in the groove. The last thing I need is to waste another four hours down at the police station.'

I hung up and did step three of Mr. Salvo's computer directions. I clicked on a word-processing program, and suddenly, it was just as I remembered it down at the computer library at the Two Guys Department Store community college.

The phone rang.

'Whew, I was hoping you were in.' It was Stiletto. 'I

followed you to the 7-Eleven in Hellertown and you ran away. Why'd you do that?'

'You were driving the red Escort?'

'That was me.'

'*You* in a red *Escort*. It doesn't seem possible. I thought you only drove Jeeps, MGs, Triumphs, Jags, that kind of car.'

'Desperate times call for desperate measures. How's the story going?'

I told Stiletto all about the spoon and how I had connected it to Eva DuBois Metzger, Henry Metzger's first wife. I told him Mickey Sinkler was having it tested.

Stiletto was silent.

'Hello?' I said. 'Are you still there?'

When he spoke again Stiletto sounded terse and angry. 'Stay right there, Bubbles,' he said. 'I'm coming to get you. Do you understand?'

'Why? What'd I do?'

'You're not safe now.'

'I was safe before?'

'Don't argue with me, Bubbles,' he yelled. 'Promise me you'll wait until I arrive. I'm out in Hellertown. It'll take me twenty minutes to get to Salvo's. Don't leave!'

He hung up.

Geesh, what had gotten into him? Guy needed more sleep or something.

I telephoned Doris. 'You got the info?' My fingers were positioned over the keyboard ready to take notes.

'Yeah, but it took a lot longer than ten minutes. I want you to appreciate that.'

'Consider it appreciated. First, what day did Laura Buchman die?'

Doris flipped through some pages. 'September fifth. A Friday.'

I typed that in. 'And Eva Metzger? What day did she die?'

More flipping. 'October eleventh. Same year. She was quite a woman, by the way.'

'How do you know?'

'I'm reading her obituary. Born in Paris. Lived in Italy. Emigrated to America – gosh, let me do the math, twenty-five years ago. Spoke five languages, including Russian. Started a program at St. Luke's Hospital to fund translators for ethnic patients who couldn't speak English.'

'Sounds like the opposite of her old man.'

'Got that right. Big environmentalist, too. On some watershed committee, a committee to clean up the Monocacy Creek and even wrote a book.'

I was typing away. 'What on?'

'*Warbler Migration along the Monocacy*. Published by Foundation Press.'

'Bull's-eye,' I exclaimed. 'Mrs. Crowley's bird-watcher.'

'Pardon?' Doris asked.

'Nothing, Doris. It's all coming together, is all.'

'Whatever. I guess that's it. Except for survivors, besides old creepy Henry.'

'Yeah, who?' I took another bite.

'Only one child. A son named Steven. Says here a resident of Somalia. Can you believe that? How pretentious.'

I dropped the halupies on the floor.

'Who doesn't know Henry Metzger?' is what Stiletto had said in the park. Was he talking about his own stepfather?

It couldn't be the same Steve. My Steve. Could it? If so, why would his last name be Stiletto?

'My wife was French,' Henry Metzger had said. 'Passionate, but undisciplined.' Yes, but she *lived* in Italy. She emigrated to this country twenty-five years ago, Doris said. Stiletto would have been a mere boy, about ten. And his last name sure sounded Italian to me.

Doris confirmed it with the obituary. The anniversary of Eva DuBois Metzger's birthday was a few days ago. And if my hunch was correct, there were fresh flowers on her grave, placed there by her devoted son.

And I was the one who'd told him everything. I was the one who'd dug up the dirt that would bury his mother again. *Your mother was a murderer, Steve, and I have the proof,* is what I essentially told him minutes ago on the phone. She had mistakenly killed the wrong girl, poor Laura Buchman, when she had meant to kill her husband's mistress instead. She murdered Laura with the very drugs that were meant to ease her own final pain – liquid morphine and barbiturates.

I wrote, my fingers flying over the keyboard. I wrote to get down on paper all the poisonous human stories that had accumulated in my brain – murder, infidelity, lies, blackmail, corruption.

As I wrote Stiletto was rushing to get me.

'Promise you won't leave,' he had said. He was angry. Furious. Steaming. 'You're not safe.'

Was he coming to shut me up? To shut me up for good? We were in a race.

Did Eva Metzger even realize her mistake? Or did she only know that nearly every day her husband visited that house on Myrtle Lane and that he cavorted with some young girl there?

Standing on the railroad tracks, she watched them through binoculars, calculating. She copied the key to Laura's house from her husband's own keychain. Then, when no one was home, she let herself in. She spiked the Slim Fast. How was she to know that this cocky teenager, her husband's lover, acted as though she owned the house, but that she didn't really?

It was Laura Buchman's house and Athena Adler's Slim Fast that Eva Metzger tainted. And Laura, on a mission to drop pounds before her big debut with Jim Morrison, unfortunately drank it.

Eva was careful to scatter incriminating evidence, such as the Metzger spoon. She left the spoon, a wedding gift no doubt, in full view of police. She envisioned the cops finding it and matching it to the man whose fingerprints were everywhere throughout the house he had visited so many, many times.

Henry Metzger.

Merry somehow knew what had happened. Perhaps she saw Eva leave the house. Maybe Eva told Henry out of spite and he, in turn, instructed Merry on what to do. Or did Eva learn that she had killed the wrong girl and tearfully confess? However Merry discovered Eva's evil deed, she knew enough to clean it up. It wouldn't have surprised me to learn that a member of Henry Metzger's household staff had lent a hand.

At the House of Beauty on Saturday, Sheila the bride had laid out her reasons for assuming that Merry Metzger was Laura's murderer. 'There was a rumor that after Laura died, Merry was seen . . .' She never finished, but now I knew what she was going to say. Merry was seen coming in and out of the house before the police arrived.

The crime scene was tainted, the police report said. There was evidence that certain items were removed. Police weren't called until hours after the body was discovered.

Shame on the Lehigh police for sweeping this under the rug. Jim Morrison's father might have been a lawyer with powerful connections, but he wasn't the one to shut down this investigation. Henry Metzger was.

With his professional calm, he confidently showed the police evidence that his wife was the murderer. He explained that she was jealous of his bright, young mistress. He said she mistakenly killed the wrong girl.

And when Eva Metzger died the following month, the police closed the case. Why not? The murderer was dead. Why prolong the pain? Call it suicide and let the community's closure begin.

It was a closed circle. No one knew the truth.

Except Chester Zug when he found the spoon. Perhaps he had been looking for it, fascinated as he was by the goings-on in that house. For months he had been peeking in on Merry and Henry Metzger's afternoon trysts, which he initially noticed while going about his job.

Then, when the murder on his very route occurred in the very house he had been spying on, Chester began to probe. He rifled through garbage piles and found the spoon. His fun ended when Mrs. Arbogast spotted him and reported his peeping to police. Chester was fired on the spot.

According to his response, filed at the Hellertown dump, Chester said that he saw suspicious activity in the house the day of Laura Buchman's suicide. No one listened, though, especially when Chester described other activities that went on there, activities that involved the chairman of the board of Lehigh Steel. He was terminated and his response was buried at the Hellertown dump.

Bitter and outcast, Chester Zug had a mission. He didn't know exactly what the spoon meant, but he had a hunch. It had cost him plenty, and he wanted compensation.

Ten years ago he brought the spoon to jeweler after jeweler. When he finally found A. H. Harrison – who confirmed the spoon's pattern was registered to an Eva DuBois Metzger – Zug was both ecstatic and disappointed. There was wealth for a blackmailer, but there was also Henry Metzger. And no one would dare mess with him.

So Zug stored the spoon away. Waiting for the opportunity when his ship would come in.

That day came when Merry Metzger sauntered into the Odd Lots Drinkers Club. He saw sails on the horizon as soon as he read in her pamphlet that Merry Metzger had been good friends with Laura Buchman, that Laura's 'suicide' had changed her life. He contacted the new Mrs. Metzger and she agreed to meet him in the Saw Mill Park last Friday. He had planned to blackmail her with scandal and endless publicity.

I stopped writing the story and leaned back. I was stuck. Back at that same nagging question.

If Merry Metzger killed him, why did she do it with Athena Adler's Range Rover? Drunk, no less? Why would she allow herself to be found by the likes of Stiletto and me? It didn't make sense.

I picked up the phone and dialed Sandy. She was my sounding board. She could help me sort this out.

'Where are you, Bubbles, I need to know!' Sandy was frantic. 'Mickey is down here now. He wants to talk to you. He's found out something about Stiletto . . .'

'I know, I . . .'

A door slammed.

'I've got to go, Sandy. I'm at Salvo's, and someone's just come in.'

I heard footsteps.

'But . . .'

I hung up and grabbed a letter opener lying on the desk. The steps came up the hallway and stopped.

I glanced up. In front of me stood a ragged man wearing an old flannel shirt and a wild look in his eyes.

'Mr. Salvo!' I yelled. Relieved, I placed the letter opener back on the desk.

'Gather your notes, Bubbles,' he said. 'I'm getting you out of here before it's too late. I'm getting you out of here before Stiletto comes.'

Only then did I notice that he was carrying a gun.

Chapter 25

'IT'S ALL MY FAULT,' Mr. Salvo said as we got into his truck. 'I've known about Stiletto all along, and I didn't tell you. I thought by warning you to stay away, that would be enough.'

I threw my notes and purse on the truck floor. Mr. Salvo put his .22 on the gun rack, and we headed down Fountain Hill.

'What did you know about Stiletto?' I asked.

'I've known him since we were kids. I knew who his mother was and, you know, my father worked for his stepfather. Steve and I used to hang out together at Henry Metzger's house, playing pool, hitting golf balls. That is, when Steve was in town.'

'Why didn't you tell me who his parents were?'

'Steve asked me not to. He said it was some class thing, didn't want you shying away from him because he was Henry Metzger's stepson. I guess he was pretty impressed by how you hung off that bridge. I swore I wouldn't interfere, but now I see that it was wrong to make that promise. Steve had other motivations.'

I felt a lump in my throat as we crossed the Hill to Hill Bridge, where Stiletto and I had hid to get out of the pouring rain. There was so much hope back then. Steve Stiletto was dashing and inspiring, unlike any man I had ever met here in Lehigh. In his eyes I saw a new world of possibilities. He could take me places.

He could kill me.

Mr. Salvo glanced frequently in the rearview. Occasionally he would lift off his baseball cap and wipe away a line of sweat on his forehead.

'Where are we going, anyway?' I asked.

'Henry's got a hunting cabin out past . . .'

'Henry!' I shouted. 'Henry Metzger?'

'Like I tried to explain before, he's not a bad man, Bubbles. You met him. An asshole at times, but essentially a decent man. He called me up at my fishing camp a few days ago and updated me about your investigation. He was worried about what Steve might do if he knew his mother was a murderer. Steve and his mother were always very close.'

We got onto Route 22 and headed toward the Poconos.

'But Henry Metzger's trying to have me killed,' I said. I told him about Brouse. 'Although, I have to admit, it made me wonder the way Brouse and Stiletto were always together.'

Mr. Salvo nodded. 'Brouse and Steve know each other from way back. Hard to conceive of now, but Brouse came from a wealthy family. He and Steve were peers and usually get together whenever Steve's in town.

They probably wanted to scare you so you wouldn't write the story.'

Some scare. Brouse nearly killed me.

We left the highway and wove through Stroudsburg, past neat town houses and white porches. After Stroudsburg, Mr. Salvo took a left and headed into the hills.

'Why are you taking me to Henry's cabin, though?' I asked as Mr. Salvo handed me a soda from a cooler in the back.

'Henry asked me to bring you here so you'd be safe. In the meantime, he's going to try to track down Steve and talk some sense into him. Maybe even institutionalize him, if necessary. He told me Steve hasn't been right since his mother died. And here I always thought he was crazy from leading that wild life overseas.'

I grabbed a blanket from the seat behind me and covered my shoulders. It was getting dark and cold.

'We're almost there, Bubbles,' he said, patting my knee. 'Everything's going to be all right.'

'One thing I don't understand, Mr. Salvo, is if you and Henry got along so well why did you let that story about his wife get in the paper?'

Mr. Salvo frowned. 'I thought I taught you better than that at the Two Guys community college, Bubbles. You know that personal feelings should never get in the way of the facts. If Dix Notch's wife had hit a man, we'd have printed that, too.'

'Really?'

'Sure, that'd make a terrific story,' he said. 'I'd kill to print that story.'

Of course, you'd kill to print a story like that, Mr. Salvo, I thought. Dix Notch fired your ass. You'd strip it across the front page.

We rolled up an unpaved road, climbing over rocks and underbrush. Finally we came to the top. It was pitch black now. I could barely make out a flicker of light.

'Well, here we are!' he said, turning off the ignition. We got out. I was stiff from the drive and my neck was sore from the bruises. I grabbed my purse with its notes and tape recorder and he led me by the elbow. My heels tripped over rocks and twigs. We stepped onto the porch and Mr. Salvo tried the lock.

The woods were all around us. There was no other light nearby and the only sounds were crickets and a faraway owl.

'I don't know why it won't open,' he said, puzzled. 'Henry said it should be unlocked.'

There was a click. A light shone on the lock. Mr. Salvo and I both looked up.

Standing in front of us was Brouse with a flashlight – and a gun.

'I'll take care of this, Tony.'

'Wilson Brouse,' Mr. Salvo hissed. Brouse kept the gun pointed at us while he slipped a key in the lock.

'Did you know Mr. Salvo—?'

'Shut up!' Brouse barked, opening the door. 'Get

inside, Bubbles. Your boyfriend's waiting for you.'

I pressed my lips together and did as I was told. Mr. Salvo patted me on the back as I passed between him and Brouse. Mr. Salvo was so frightened he was shaking.

The door slammed shut and was locked. I heard Brouse tell Mr. Salvo to walk. My heart stopped while I waited for a gunshot. None came. Instead, I heard struggling and then someone fall. A truck started and tore up gravel as it sped down the hill. In a few seconds another engine started and left.

What was happening?

I turned around and surveyed the rough cabin. It amounted to little more than a tiny log room lit by a kerosene lamp on a table. Near the door was a small water closet. In the corner by the fireplace was a single bed with a quilt. On top of that quilt, facedown, was Stiletto.

My heart sank. I wanted to hug him and kill him and kiss him and beat on him all at the same time. 'You dirty, rotten, stinking bastard!' I yelled, whipping my purse at his head. 'How could you do this to me?'

I stopped. The purse had hit Stiletto, and he hadn't flinched. I hesitated. What was wrong? I walked over and grabbed his arm. Ice cold. I pushed back his hair and stifled a scream.

Not Stiletto. Jim Morrison. Shot through the temple. A victim of Brouse's cruelty.

There was no doubt in my mind. I would be next.

Chapter 26

IN THE END, JANE saved me.

Not physically. She didn't rush in the door with an Uzi and an army and rescue my sorry spandex-clad body. Although, gosh, it would have been swell if she had.

No, instead she gave me a reason to fight. She had said the very words I had longed to hear all her life. She'd reminded me of why I had been pursuing this heartless, aggravating, time-consuming profession called journalism to begin with.

'You're my hero, Mom,' had been her last words to me. I focused on that. I was her hero. I was the one she looked to. Not her teachers. Not her punctured, punked-out friends. Not Dan.

Me. Bubbles Yablonsky. Mere high-school graduate, former teen mother, hairdresser. A walking dumb-blonde joke.

I slumped against the wall, as far away as I could get from Jim Morrison's corpse, and began to breathe slowly. I would have to keep my wits about me. I would have to think on my feet. I wasn't very good at thinking on my feet. Some who know me might argue that I wasn't very good at thinking – period. But I had to push those negative thoughts down.

Stiletto. My feelings had been a bittersweet mixture of relief, guilt and sadness when I first assumed that it was his corpse lying on the bed, instead of Morrison's. Of course, I didn't wish Stiletto dead, but I desperately prayed that he was not the soulless monster Mr. Salvo had made him out to be – an ally of Brouse. Stiletto might have many faults, but as far as I had been able to tell, soullessness was not one of them. I could only hope Mr. Salvo had been wrong.

I covered Morrison's body with a blanket and tried the doorknob again, for fun. Well, what do you know, it was locked. Surprise. Surprise.

There were no windows. The light I saw when Mr. Salvo and I drove up must have come from under the door. Or perhaps the door was open. Or maybe that was Brouse's flashlight. All I knew was that there was no way of escape.

This quaint little hunting cabin with its solitary bed and fireplace was a prison. Who did it belong to? Mr. Salvo said it was Henry Metzger's. Did that mean that Henry Metzger and his stepson, Stiletto, were on the same team? Despite all of Mr. Salvo's flowery words about the chairman of the board, I wasn't ready to join the Henry Metzger fan club. If I was still here in the morning – as I doubted I would be – I would probably find the final words of many a steelworker – or other

Metzger enemy – carved in the floor.

Who had been here before me? Buster Padukis maybe. Or had Buster been killed on the spot?

Stop, Bubbles. Stop thinking about death. Think about life. I had forgotten that I still had my purse. In it was my trusty yellow tape recorder. Notepad. Pen. Hairbrush. Makeup case. Batteries.

I went to the bathroom, washed my hands in a weak trickle of brown water, brushed my hair and did up my face using the kerosene lamp to illuminate the small mirror.

My clothes still reeked faintly of garbage from the Hellertown dump. But freshening up did wonders for me. Makeup always does.

I smiled at my warped reflection in the rusted mirror. 'Bubbles Yablonsky, you are a newspaper reporter now. Act like one.'

You are my hero, Mom.

I stuck out my jaw. I could do it. If I played at being a reporter I could remain detached. I could keep calm.

There was the sound of wheels over rocks outside. I got the tape recorder, turned it on and shoved it back in my purse. I wasn't relying on it to record evidence but, psychologically, it gave me an edge.

My assassin would be the subject; I would be the interviewer. And that was how I planned to survive. A strange peace settled over me.

I stood up and waited for Brouse to arrive. Or would it be Stiletto?

There was a sliding sound outside the door and then the bolt turned. I held my breath as it opened. Brouse walked in and locked the door behind him. He was a large man, and I understood that his massive size was why I didn't have a chance against him when he tried to strangle me the night before. His head was the same old block of cement. His hair was blond and cut short. He was pretty damn ugly.

He stood there expressionless. Not a smile. Not a frown. Just there to do a job.

'Did you leave him here for me?' I asked, pointing to where Jim lay.

'You like it?' he asked, a smile forming at the corner of his lips. 'I'll get rid of him later. You ready to go?'

I picked up my purse. 'Where?'

'Down to the lake.' He glanced at his watch. 'Salvo crashed into a tree at the bottom of the mountain. I don't want to be here if he tips off the state police. If he's alive. I would've popped him, but a damn do-gooder pulled up to the accident scene. I decided not to stick around.'

'What about Morrison?' I was stalling.

'Let me worry about that,' he said, showing me his revolver. I hadn't seen many guns in my life, and this one looked ridiculously small, although it was not as small as Merry Metzger's at the A-L-E Airport.

As though he had read my mind, Brouse said, 'It's a .38 caliber snub nose. It'll do the job on you. Nice and neat.'

'If you kill me here, the cops will trace my death to Henry Metzger,' I said.

Brouse eyed me quizzically. 'How?'

'Doesn't he own this place?'

Brouse shook his head and waved the pistol. 'Hurry up or I'll do ya right here. And I don't want to because blood and brains . . . It's a real mess.'

I touched the side of my head. I liked my blood and brains.

'Hold on,' I said, leaning down to take off my shoes. 'I can't walk down to the lake in these heels.'

'Yeah, right,' he said, rocking on his feet. 'Keep them on. You practically sleep in those heels.'

'I guess you would know, right?'

Brouse opened the door. I felt the barrel of the gun in my back. 'Why don't you shut your trap and walk.'

It was blacker than black. I couldn't see my hand in front of my face.

'Move it,' he said, taking me by the elbow down the steps. 'By the way, don't worry about Jane. I won't touch her. If she needed to be dead, I'd have snapped her neck walking home from the ice cream store this weekend.'

My knees nearly buckled underneath me. That this cruel and heartless killer knew my daughter's name and where she worked nearly brought me to the brink of instant insanity. He's trying to screw with your mind. Keep your cool, Bubbles. *Play the part of reporter. Keep the interview going*.

Brouse turned on a flashlight and shined it on the ground as he escorted me down to the lake. His car, a Mercedes SUV, was parked where Salvo's pickup truck had been. What an ad for the off-road qualities of a Mercedes four-wheel drive, I thought.

I decided to court his ego.

'So, you're the hired gun, huh?' I asked, gingerly stepping over a rock. 'How much does that pay, being a hired gun?'

'Lately, not much,' Brouse said as we moved into the underbrush. 'I've been fucking up so bad, the boss is withholding pay.'

A branch snapped in my face. Owww. I stopped and pushed it over my head. 'Fucking up? How so?' I thought it best not to ask who the boss was. Not at that moment.

'For starters, you. I figured you would have been scared off long ago. Dimwit hairdresser, they told me. Yeah, dimwit hairdresser with a smart attitude is what you are.'

'Thanks.' My feet squished over moss. 'But you didn't really start with me. You started with Chester Zug.'

'No. I was supposed to start off with Jim Morrison. Zug got in the way.'

'I'm a little confused.'

'So what? So what if you're a little confused? In five minutes you're going to be a little dead.'

We pushed into some bushes. 'Hey,' he said. 'I think we're off the path.'

'I think we're off the path, too. It's dark.'

'Yeah, we got to go over here.' Brouse grabbed me by the neck with one hand and pushed me up the hill.

Once we were back on the path – or what we assumed was the path – I said to Brouse, 'My life has been pretty standard up until this past week. This is the most exciting week I've ever had. If I got a lot of questions, who's it gonna hurt if you answer them?'

Brouse thought about it. 'Okay. I'll tell you 'cause it's so basic you must be a moron if you couldn't tell what was going on.'

Let him insult me. I opened my purse so that my yellow tape recorder's microphone (which happened to be shaped like a crayon) would catch every word.

'For months, Henry's wife Merry has been cheating on him with her old boyfriend, right? She married Henry for his money, but what twenty-something woman wants to have sex with an old fart who swallows Viagra by the truckload when she can scrump with a guy like Jim Morrison?'

'I hear that,' I said. I never could understand what Merry Metzger saw in that old coot – plane rides to New York or not.

'Henry warned her and warned her. Said cut it out or else. Did Merry listen? No. After Henry came down with his final warning last week, she made plans to meet Morrison at their old haunt down by The Mill on Friday night.'

The Mill was the hippie hangout where ten years ago

Laura Buchman was supposed to sing backup with Morrison. It sat at the end of Saw Mill Park – hence the name – and was boarded up three years ago.

'Henry hit the roof. There was no question in his mind. Morrison needed to be dead. Fast. I, of course, got the assignment.'

Brouse shined the flashlight ahead of us. I could see silver dock on other side of some reeds and tall grass. There was a small shed at the edge of the lake.

'But I'd never seen Morrison before in my life. All I knew was that I had to be at the park at eight p.m. to shoot the man Merry was meeting. Ding. No complications. Boom. Gone. Go out for a slice and call it a night.'

We waded through the reeds. If this was a path, it wasn't a very well-maintained one. I let Brouse talk.

'So, I show up. Merry's there talking to this old man, and I walk up, put the gun to this old man's forehead and say, "Hi, Merry. This Morrison?" And she shouts, "No. You got the wrong guy." And I say, "You're shitting me." And she says, "No, really. This is Chester Zug. Jim and I broke up." "Chester Zug," I say. "Who the fuck is –?" And the next thing you know there's this thud, and Merry and I both look down and Zug is passed out. He looks dead.'

We found the dock. I stopped. 'Then what?' I examined my nails like I might get a manicure later.

'Merry panics. I said to her, "Zug's out. Easy target. Let me pop him right here to make sure." But she gets hysterical, runs over to the Range Rover, starts it and puts it into reverse. Here, you better give me your purse. I'll have to toss it off the Delaware Bridge later.'

I handed him my purse.

'Anyway, Merry says to me "You don't know who he is." She's so confused that she backs up . . .'

'Right over Chester Zug.'

Brouse leaned down and picked up a set of handcuffs he must have stashed at the base of the dock. 'Got it,' he said, clicking open the handcuffs.

I stuck out my hands. He snapped on the cuffs and continued his story.

'Now we got a problem. Merry stops the Range Rover, and I light into her. I mean, really light into her. I call her a stupid bitch, dumb . . . whatever. I not only got a dead body, I got the wrong dead body, tire treads to clean and evidence to mop up. Not simple like a gun. Messy. I hate messy. I holler at her, "I hate messy!" And what does she do? She pulls out a bottle of Absolut and starts downing it. Do you mind moving back a bit to the end of the dock?'

He was holding up a pair of metal ankle weights. I stepped backward and whimpered slightly as he leaned down and attached them to my ankles. I licked my dry lips, closed my eyes and prayed fervently for divine intervention.

When I opened them I saw movement by the tiny boathouse. For a second I saw a head. Or was I hallucinating?

After he was done, Brouse stood back and brought out his revolver.

'Okay, but that's not the end, is it?' I begged.

'Uhmm. Pretty much. She and I got in a fight over control of the Rover and I had the not very bright idea to hit her over the head with the bottle because I was so damned pissed at her. Then you guys showed up, and I headed for the bushes. I got a record. I can't risk sticking around to answer questions about a manslaughter. When Stiletto ran off and left you alone, I saw my opportunity. I drove off with the car. Simple. Except you turn out to be a goddamn reporter.'

'You didn't hit me over the head?'

'No. You tripped in those idiotic hooker's heels. You really ought to consider new footwear, you know. You'll have back problems by the time you're fifty.'

'I don't think so. Not at the rate we're going tonight.'

'True. True.'

'But that's still not the end.'

'Yes, it is.' He laughed. 'You remind me of my four-year-old at bedtime. "Not now, Daddy, please." Give me a break.'

He pointed the gun at me.

The bushes moved and a figure stepped out silently. My heart leaped with hope. I thought fast. 'Wait!' I said.

'They always say that.' Brouse released the safety catch.

'I have to know what Stiletto's role was in all of this.'

The figure moved closer. Since Brouse was shining the flashlight at me, I couldn't see who it was. Mr. Salvo? The state police? Genevieve?

'Stiletto?' Brouse aimed the gun at my head. 'How the fuck should –? Ugh.'

I closed my eyes. When I opened them, there was a rope around Brouse's neck held tightly in Stiletto's strong hands. Brouse's eyes bulged. He gasped and clawed at the noose, dropping his gun to the dock. I would have loved to help, except, gee, my hands and feet were tied.

'Get down!' Stiletto said. I promptly bent my knees and lay down, using my manacled feet to kick the gun into the water with a splash. Only then did I understand his concern. One step in the wrong direction, and I would have been in the water. Blonde fish bait.

Stiletto dragged Brouse backward. He was kicking and throwing a fit. In a flash, Stiletto had him tied up with the rope around his neck, hands and feet. If Brouse struggled, he'd kill himself by strangulation. It was brilliant.

'Where'd you learn that?' I asked as Stiletto snapped off the ankle weights and handcuffs.

'Which part? The sneaking out of the woods part or the hog-tying?'

'I don't care. Just keep talking.'

Stiletto freed my hands first. 'Treading silently in the woods I learned from some Indians in Maine who ran a camp I went to as a kid.'

He worked on my feet. 'And the hog-tying?'

'Montana. A half-ton calf is harder.'

I stood up and stared at his brilliant blue eyes. 'So, are you going to kill me now?'

Stiletto laughed. 'What? I just risked my neck to save that fine, fine body of yours. I'm not about to do away with you, not just yet.' He put his hands on my shoulders.

'Aren't you angry at me about your mother and Laura Buchman's murder and—'

Stiletto leaned down and kissed me hard. Brouse let out a groan as flashlights started to dot the edge of the lake and we heard tree branches snapping and men shouting. The Pennsylvania State Police had arrived.

'Just our luck,' Stiletto said. 'We get a moment alone and a goddamn posse arrives.'

Two state troopers were walking up to the dock. Stiletto left me to talk with them.

'If you'd have been here sooner, we could've shared some more quality time,' I chided when he returned. 'Not to mention, I might have been spared Brouse's hike of horror.'

'Complaints, complaints. Next time I witness a friend crashing his car into a tree, I'll keep on driving.'

I stepped back. Several troopers were shining flashlights on Brouse. One was reminding him of his Constitutional rights.

'You were the motorist Brouse said stopped to help Mr. Salvo?'

'Regular good Samaritan, ain't I? I tracked you and Tony all the way from his apartment to the foot of the mountain. I decided to hang back awhile before making my appearance. Next thing I knew, Tony was careening down the hill with Brouse on his tail.'

I shook my head. 'Well, I'll be snookered.'

'And, for the record, I also notified the troopers about you – that is, before I rushed up the mountain to do my Superman impression. And what thanks do I get?'

I reached up and pulled Stiletto's lips to mine.

'Maybe you ought to stick around Lehigh more,' I whispered.

'Maybe I will. Maybe I will.'

He took me in a bear hug, and I blubbered like a baby.

Epilogue

BROUSE SQUEALED LIKE A greased pig at the Allentown Fair. Henry Metzger had hired him to bump off Morrison and attack me. Brouse had telephone bills, personal loans, even credit card receipts tying his deeds to the former chairman of the board of Lehigh Steel. For a career felon, Brouse kept extremely good records. If he had invested his time in a Two Guys community college course on accounting instead of choosing to make license plates at Trenton State Prison, he might have had a fulfilling life. Instead, he will be fulfilling a life sentence at the Pennsylvania State Penitentiary.

Athena Adler, too, provided police with a lengthy statement after she was informed that the Northampton County Prison's tennis courts were constructed out of macadam instead of clay. In the privacy of her lawyer's office, she tearfully confided that Merry Metzger had erroneously convinced her for ten years that she was partly responsible for the death of Laura Buchman because it was Athena's Slim Fast that had been spiked.

391

For that reason, Athena did not make a fuss when Merry borrowed her Range Rover to meet Chester Zug, who promised to relate new and incriminating evidence about Laura's murder and perhaps other 'embarrassing information' concerning Laura's friends. Borrowing the Range Rover was nothing new for Merry, who apparently took it often to rendezvous with Morrison so that her husband – the ultimate control freak – would not be able to follow her.

She took it that Friday night, Athena said, because Merry wanted to hear what Zug's 'embarrassing information' was without Henry butting in. We may never know what that information was since Zug is dead, and it is unlikely Merry will be seen again – at least not in this hemisphere.

After Zug's death, Merry ran crying to Henry and, as usual, Henry promised to fix everything. He instructed Brouse to dump the Range Rover in the quarry, except for the car phone, which Brouse used to report the stolen vehicle. Henry told Athena to keep quiet about the matter, or else. He filed suit against the *News-Times* and me. He flew Merry out of the country.

This scam would have been much harder to pull off without the eager compliance of Dan and Wendy and the unwitting assistance of poor Mr. Salvo. As soon as Dan comprehended my involvement, he got on the horn to Henry Metzger, who promised a glorious future in Steel's legal department if he provided aid in the form of a few false affidavits. Dan didn't have to be asked twice.

Mr. Salvo, I am sad to report, was completely duped. For all his training as a hard-news journalist, he was a slavish puppy when it came to Henry Metzger, once his father's powerful but benevolent boss. And Henry manipulated that weakness masterfully. He did not name Mr. Salvo in the suit – I had missed that point – and used that 'kindness' to prompt Mr. Salvo to leak personal information about me and also to find out where I was heading with the story. He was able to convince Mr. Salvo that Stiletto had gone bad and might even be insane.

The cabin, by the way, is official property of Perkiomen Metal Works, a nonexistent company once vaguely associated with Lehigh Steel. No one has ever seen Henry Metzger in it or even near it.

Now for the punishments. Brouse, as I said earlier, received life in prison.

Because of her sincere cooperation, not to mention intimidating attorney, Athena Adler was never charged – although her membership at the Greenbriar Country Club was permanently revoked.

Dan and Wendy did not fare so well. Both were charged and convicted of filing false affidavits with police, although both were spared jail time. Wendy was assigned to six hundred hours of community service in the form of running the teen center for drug-addicted juvenile delinquents, most of whom smoke. Jane's friend Gracie – whom Wendy once referred to as a punk for lighting up on the deck – has found this very amusing.

However, Wendy's law-abiding father, Hans Hauckman, president of Hauckman's Cheeseballs, failed to see the humor. While supportive of his daughter during her trial, he disowned her as soon as the judge brought down the gavel and declared Wendy guilty. In doing so, Hans cut off Wendy from her multimillion-dollar trust fund and most of her social circle.

Wendy might have been able to deal with the loss of income had not Dan lost his attorney's license as well. The Professional Conduct Board will permit him to reapply in two years. In the meantime, he has been assigned to work for minimum wage at legal aid, whose clients refuse to call him Chip. The McMansion is up for sale, and the Eddie Bauer SUV is up on blocks.

As for Henry and Merry Metzger, that was the salt in the wound. While I was standing on a dock saying my prayers in the Poconos, Henry was flying his jet to visit his copper mines down in Chile, supposedly after picking up his wife in Honduras, where she was completing her 'missionary work.'

Except there was an awful mishap with the plane, which crashed on the runway. As you might have expected. Henry and Merry Metzger's untimely and unfortunate deaths were confirmed by an obscure Chilean coroner. What luck.

This is a lot of hooey, of course. I am willing to bet that somewhere on some Central American beach,

Henry and Merry Metzger are sipping fruit drinks and marveling at the excellent house help they obtained for a pittance of what they used to pay in America. The way I see it, they might have been able to escape justice, but no person can escape a guilty conscience.

The Lehigh police officially established that Eva DuBois Metzger murdered Laura Buchman. Faint traces of morphine and barbiturates were confirmed on the spoon and Mickey did a good job of tracking down the police officer who wrote the addendum to the original police report. That officer told Mickey that 'higher ups' had nixed the investigation once Henry Metzger got involved.

The current mayor – the one who is a member of Odd Lots – decried this case as an example of rampant corruption found in previous Democratic administrations. He called my home and congratulated me personally. Wait until he reads my story about his secret membership in the all-male, all-white drinking club.

Yes, my journalism career is far from dead. My story on Merry Metzger's crimes and her husband's efforts to cover them up appeared front page, double byline in *The Philadelphia Inquirer*. The *Inquirer* couldn't bear the thought of a hairdresser writing a piece like that solo, so they assigned a feature writer to help me out. I have to confess, with his skill it was a much better story.

The reporting was solid and none of the information was obtained through illegal means. I relied on Mickey's police reports, Chester Zug's statement to the Department of Sanitation and my last interview with Brouse, which was tape recorded as I walked to the dock. Stiletto's photos survived the Q-Mart's photo shop intact and provided concrete illustrations.

I must admit that the day that story was published was one of the happiest days of my life – second only to Jane's birth. Mama immediately had the newspaper clipping laminated in plastic. Sandy placed a stack of newspapers in the House of Beauty, and I couldn't help noticing that Jane folded up a copy and stuck it in her purse to show her friends.

The AM radio station called me a few days later and did a five-minute interview with me, which they played during morning rush hour. The South Side was abuzz for weeks as more and more people admitted their personal Henry Metzger stories and *The Philadelphia Inquirer* wrote a scathing editorial on his thuggery. When I am reminded that this all started with Laura Buchman's walk-in to the House of Beauty, I have to pinch myself.

My story was so good that the publisher of the *News-Times* called me into his office the day after it ran. His office is one floor above the Eisenhower green one occupied by Dix Notch, who was also summoned to the meeting. After a few careful questions, the publisher berated Notch for taking the Metzgers' word over mine when the lawsuit was filed and for not recognizing a potential Pulitzer Prize when it landed in his lap. As punishment, Notch was assigned to work the lobster shift, midnight to eight, along with Mr. Salvo for an unspecified period of time.

Notch has vowed to get even.

Let him try.

In addition, the publisher offered me a full-time job, but I declined – for now. Sandy found my one week as an investigative reporter tough enough; she said she couldn't bear it if I left for good. Martin even promised to sacrifice his Friday nights pumicing Sandy's heels in order to pumice my elbows if I agreed to stay. I told him thanks, but no thanks. I decided to stick with the House of Beauty, which has enjoyed a boom in business lately, and continue journalism as a hobby for other reasons.

I didn't want to admit to Sandy that this experience taught me that while I may have the makings of an excellent reporter, I'm not quite there yet. I need to hone my skills at gathering information, interviewing effectively and keeping notes. But someday I will break out, and then I'm going big time. *The Philadelphia Inquirer*. Maybe even *The New York Times*. Don't be surprised if one spring the Pulitzers are announced and Bubbles Yablonsky wins an award for public interest reporting.

Nor was I the only one to experience success. Jane scored a 1580 on her SATs and is a good candidate for a scholarship at an Ivy League school – if I can keep her out of trouble that long.

Mama and Genevieve have opened a gourmet pierogi shop on the other side of Sandy's House of Beauty. Occasionally they run a 'Free dozen pierogis with a wash and set' special, which is very popular with the patrons of Uncle Manny's Bar and Grille and is one reason why business at the salon has picked up.

Charges against Mama were dropped, by the way. The judge on the bench happened to be a member of Mama's generation who understood perfectly well what Mama meant when she 'held the dress up to the light.' The judge chastised the 'silly clerks' at Hess's for being so disrespectful to a senior citizen and, as a compromise, ordered Mama to write an apology for walking 'too far.' Case closed.

Doris finished summer school with a 3.9 in biomedical engineering. That seemed pretty spectacular to me, but Doris insists that if I hadn't entered the picture, she would have been 4.0. Anyway, she is now in Seattle, drinking big cups of coffee and fooling around with microchips. Already her salary is five times my annual earnings at the House of Beauty.

Lastly, Mickey Sinkler, much to everyone's happiness, has found bliss with that oh-so-helpful Janice, the records clerk at the Lehigh Police Department. His mother says to expect a wedding next year. We'll see.

As for Stiletto and me – that takes a bit of explaining.

Miraculously, he talked his way out of getting charged with leaving the scene of an accident. Stiletto claims he floored the police commissioner with his insightful, logical rhetoric. But I think it had more to do with the fact that the police commissioner is a fifty-two-year-old spinster and that Stiletto stripped to his boxers to show her the scars from bullets and cuts he received at the hands of Brouse. Why else did the judge unfasten the top buttons of her blouse and request that the air-conditioning be turned up after his 'insightful, logical,' arguments were delivered?

Once the *Inquirer* story ran, Stiletto and I saw each other nearly every day for a month. During that time, he tidied up Metzger's estate and discovered a nice fat trust fund left to him by his mother. Decent man that he is, Stiletto used it to establish a scholarship in Laura Buchman's name at Freedom High School.

You might have expected that Stiletto and I spent that month under the covers playing footsie or other physical games, but we didn't. Oddly enough, we passed the time shooting pool and drinking Rolling Rock. Often we talked in his Jeep parked at the lookout up by Lehigh University or, when it rained, at what we've come to call 'our spot' under the Hill to Hill Bridge.

One issue we did not discuss was his mother, and I assume it has become yet another item packed away with the rest of his emotional baggage. As I later learned, Stiletto has a matching set left over from childhood.

Stiletto explained to me that the French-born Eva had once lived happily with his father, a doctor, in a northern Italian village. When his father died, relatives convinced Eva to join them in Lehigh where they had found great jobs at Steel. Eva, who was apparently a multilingual knockout, landed a great job herself as Henry Metzger's private secretary. They married when Stiletto was ten.

Metzger hated the boy because he was half French, half Italian and wholly not his own. He sent him to boarding schools, camps, distant relatives, any place to get him out of his hair. He made Stiletto miserable. Stiletto grew up despising Metzger, who, in turn, insisted Eva terminate all contact with her son when he turned eighteen. Stiletto went overseas and didn't see his mother again until her wake seven years later, hence the annual guilt trip to place flowers on her grave each birthday.

It was at the somber occasion of Eva Metzger's funeral that Merry Metzger – then Merry Miller – apparently offered her condolences to Stiletto in the pool cabana of the Greenbriar Country Club. Stiletto was wise to decline. Knowing what I know now of Henry Metzger, I can only imagine how he would have reacted upon finding out that his despised stepson had made it with his wife-to-be.

Now for sex.

Let me make it clear that Stiletto tried every move known to woman – wine, music, moonlight, blatant grabbing – to get me into bed, but I was able to stiff-arm him. Before taking my chastity vow, I assumed that a man in Stiletto's situation would have passed frustration and gone hunting for new prey by now. But not him. He came to view me as some sort of challenge. He even took to running up mountains to work off the sexual frustration.

Unfortunately, I don't run, although I admire those Lycra tights. Anyway, if I did, a single mountain wouldn't do it. I'd need the whole Appalachian range to work off Stiletto. One look from those blue eyes of his, one flex of that jaw muscle, and I go all squishy inside. Once I ripped through the green felt with my pool cue when Stiletto bent over to pick up a piece of chalk. Don't even ask about the knots in my hair.

So, you might be wondering, why didn't I surrender to my sexual drive and hop his handsome bones? The short answer is that I was waiting for a commitment, which is a lot to ask from Stiletto. Growing up with Henry and Eva Metzger, he developed a dim view of domesticity. He said as much the night he left to accept an assignment shooting photos of a skirmish on the India-and-Pakistan border.

'Well, this is it, Yablinko,' he said as we sat under the Hill to Hill Bridge watching the rain. 'I'm off to war.'

'You're off to *photograph* a war,' I reminded him. 'I don't consider staying in a four-star hotel and receiving daily massages from a half-naked Indian woman as going off to war.'

'Lot you know. Those massages can be pretty rough. Speaking of half-naked, why don't we go all the way tonight, Bubbles?' He cupped my chin and kissed me softly. 'After all, who knows when we'll see each other again. I could be shot. I could die in a plane crash. This might be your last chance.'

'You'll be back.'

'Oh, and how can you be so sure? Those Indian women are pretty sexy in their flowing saris. The Kama Sutra's like the Bible to them.'

'What's the Kama Sutra?'

Stiletto stroked my hair. 'Ancient book of sexual positions.'

'I don't need a book. I got them memorized.'

He raised an eyebrow. 'Oh, really?'

'Either that or I make them up as I go along.'

'You're driving me nuts, you know that, don't you? What do I have to do, Bubbles?'

'Stay.'

'Can't.'

'How come?'

'I don't know. I'm trying to figure that out. When I do, you'll be the first to know.'

The last time I saw Stiletto he was running up Fountain Hill, sweat pouring down his back.

Mama says don't try to change a man, but I disagree. Look at my experience. Once upon a time, people in this town passed me off as another dumb blonde fascinated by sex, soap operas and gossip. And now I'm known as the hairdresser who brought down the chairman of the board.

If I can come that far, there's got to be hope for Stiletto.

Fleeced

Georgina Wroe

Dominic Peach isn't your usual sort of environmental campaigner. The only environment he cares about is one that doesn't include his girlfriend. Thus far the job at Save Our Species has suited him quite nicely, especially since he rigged the database to make sheep (surely the planet's least endangered mammal?) his only responsibility. So when he's ordered to the former Soviet Republic of Belugastan on a high-profile mission to protect the *Beluga argali argali*, a rare wild sheep, it's a bit of a shock.

Particularly as it turns out that Belugastan's head of state, ex-gangster Tim the First, has invented the *Beluga argali argali* as a lure to cash-rich game hunters, props courtesy of his friend Erik's motorbike and his mum's sheepskin coat. And when the hunters include a mad Texan millionairess and her gun-crazy sons Hubba and Bubba, Dominic discovers chasing wild sheep can be an extremely hairy business . . .

Praise for Georgina Wroe's previous novel, SLAPHEAD

'If Kathy Lette had been born in Omsk, this is the book she'd write' *Mirror*

'Compulsive . . . crammed with action and wisecracks and eminently readable' *Big Issue*

0 7472 5551 3

headline

Something for the Weekend

Pauline McLynn

When private investigator Leo Street is sent away to County Kildare to spy on the supposedly cheating wife of a loathsome client, she's delighted to be getting away from rainy Dublin and her hopeless, permanently resting actor boyfriend Barry. The one catch is that she has to masquerade as a member of a cookery course and the only piece of culinary equipment Leo can handle is a tin opener – Weekend Entertaining Part One is daunting to say the least.

As she strips away layers of marital infidelity – not to mention several other scandalous secrets – she battles with bread-making and brûlée. But where will it all end – in triumph or tragedy?

'*Something for the Weekend* introduces an amiable anti-heroine who clearly has a great deal of life in her' *The Times*

'A fabulously funny novel' *Sunday Independent*

'Packed with cheeky sarcasm and wit' *Company*

'An upbeat, chatty novel' *Daily Mail*

'A novel that demonstrates a sure ear for dialogue' *Marie Claire*

'Lively characters . . . satisfying authenticity' *Image*

0 7472 6397 3

headline

The Cat Who Smelled a Rat

Lilian Jackson Braun

As autumn draws to a close in Moose County, four hundred miles north of everywhere, Qwilleran and the rest of Pickax City are awaiting the annual snow storm which marks the official start of winter. But this year the storm is particularly significant. After months without rain, brush fires are starting with alarming regularity and it is only a matter of time before one of them gets out of control.

But it is soon evident that the fires are following a pattern that defies any force of nature and when Edd's Editions, the much-loved bookstore, is destroyed in a clear case of arson, the inhabitants of Pickax are forced to accept that they are facing a very human enemy. Luckily for them all, it's not long before Qwilleran & Co begin to sniff out the rat responsible.

Qwilleran – a prize-winning reporter with a nose for crime. Koko – a Siamese cat with extraordinary talents and a flair for mystery. Yum Yum – a loveable Siamese adored by her two male companions. The most unlikely, most unusual, most delightful team in detective fiction!

0 7472 6505 4

headline

Now you can buy any of these other bestselling
Headline books from your bookshop or
direct from the publisher.

FREE P&P AND UK DELIVERY
(Overseas and Ireland £3.50 per book)

A Place of Safety	Caroline Graham	£6.99
Running Scared	Ann Granger	£5.99
Shades of Murder	Ann Granger	£5.99
Biting the Moon	Martha Grimes	£5.99
The Lamorna Wink	Martha Grimes	£5.99
Tip Off	John Francome	£6.99
The Cat Who Robbed a Bank	Lilian Jackson Braun	£5.99
Screen Savers	Quintin Jardine	£5.99
Thursday Legends	Quintin Jardine	£5.99
A Chemical Prison	Barbara Nadel	£5.99
Stronger Than Death	Manda Scott	£5.99
Oxford Shift	Veronica Stallwood	£5.99
Fleeced	Georgina Wroe	£6.99

TO ORDER SIMPLY CALL THIS NUMBER

01235 400 414

or e-mail <u>orders@bookpoint.co.uk</u>

Prices and availability subject to change without notice.